I0667832

Ghetto Tragedies by Israel Zangwill

Israel Zangwill was born in London on 21st January 1864, to a family of Jewish immigrants from the Russian Empire.

Zangwill was initially educated in Plymouth and Bristol. At age 9 he was enrolled in the Jews' Free School in Spitalfields in east London. Zangwill excelled here. He began to teach part-time at the school and eventually full time. Whilst teaching he also studied with the University of London and by 1884 had earned his BA with triple honours in philosophy, history, and the sciences.

His writing earned him the sobriquet "the Dickens of the Ghetto" primarily based on his much lauded novel 'Children of the Ghetto: A Study of a Peculiar People' in 1892 and its glimpse of the poverty-stricken life in London's Jewish quarter.

As a writer he was keen to reflect on his political and social outlooks. His simulation of Yiddish sentence structure in English aroused great interest. His mystery work, 'The Big Bow Mystery' (1892) was the first locked room mystery novel.

Zangwill was also involved with narrowly focused Jewish issues as an assimilationist, an early Zionist, and later a territorialist. In the early 1890s he had joined the Lovers of Zion movement in England. In 1897 he joined Theodor Herzl (considered the father of modern political Zionism) in founding the World Zionist Organization.

Zangwill quit the established philosophy of Zionism when his plan for a homeland in Uganda was rejected and founded his own organisation; the Jewish Territorialist Organization. Its stated goal was to create a Jewish homeland in whatever territory in the world could be found for them.

Amongst the challenges in his life he found time to write poetry. He had translated a medieval Jewish poet in 1903 and his volume 'Blind Children' in 1908 shows his promise in this new endeavour.

'The Melting Pot' in 1909 made Zangwill's name as an admired playwright. When the play opened in Washington D.C., former President Theodore Roosevelt leaned over the edge of his box and shouted, "That's a great play, Mr. Zangwill, that's a great play."

Israel Zangwill died on 1st August 1926 in Midhurst, West Sussex.

Index of Contents

PREFACE

The "Ghetto Tragedies" collected in a little volume in 1893 have been so submerged in the present collection that I have relegated the original name to the sub-title. "Satan Mekatrig" was written in 1889, "Bethulah" this year. Anyone who should wish to measure the progress or decay of my imagination during the ten years has therefore materials to hand. "Noah's Ark" stands on the firmer Ararat of history, my invention being confined to the figure of Peloni (the Hebrew for "nobody"). The other stories have also a basis in life. But neither in pathos nor heroic stimulation can they vie with the literal tragedy with which the whole book is in a sense involved. Mrs. N.S. Joseph, the great-hearted lady to whom "Ghetto Tragedies" was inscribed, herself walked in darkness, yet was not dismayed: in the prime of life she went down into the valley of the shadow, with no word save of consideration for others. I trust the new stories would not have been disapproved by my friend, to whose memory they must now, alas! be dedicated.

I.Z.
OCTOBER, 1899.

I

"THEY THAT WALK IN DARKNESS"

I

It was not till she had fasted every Monday and Thursday for a twelvemonth, that Zillah's long yearning for a child was gratified. She gave birth—O more than fair-dealing God!—to a boy.

Jossel, who had years ago abandoned the hope of an heir to pray for his soul, was as delighted as he was astonished. His wife had kept him in ignorance of the fasts by which she was appealing to Heaven; and when of a Monday or Thursday evening on his return from his boot factory in Bethnal Green, he had sat down to his dinner in Dalston, no suspicion had crossed his mind that it was Zillah's breakfast. He himself was a prosaic person, incapable of imagining such spontaneities of religion, though he kept every fast which it behoves an orthodox Jew to endure who makes no speciality of sainthood. There was a touch of the fantastic in Zillah's character which he had only appreciated in its manifestation as girlish liveliness, and which Zillah knew would find no response from him in its religious expression.

Not that her spiritual innovations were original inventions. From some pious old crone, after whom (as she could read Hebrew) a cluster of neighbouring dames repeated what they could catch of the New Year prayers in the women's synagogue, Zillah had learnt that certain holy men were accustomed to afflict their souls on Mondays and Thursdays. From her unsuspecting husband himself she had further elicited that these days were marked out from the ordinary, even for the man of the world, by a special prayer dubbed "the long 'He being merciful.'" Surely on Mondays and Thursdays, then, He would indeed be merciful. To make sure of His good-will she continued to be unmerciful to herself long after it became certain that her prayer had been granted.

II

Both Zillah and Jossel lived in happy ignorance of most things, especially of their ignorance. The manufacture of boots and all that appertained thereto, the synagogue and religion, misunderstood reminiscences of early days in Russia, the doings and misdoings of a petty social circle, and such particular narrowness with general muddle as is produced by stumbling through a Sabbath paper and a Sunday paper: these were the main items in their intellectual inventory. Separate Zillah from her husband and she became even poorer, for she could not read at all.

Yet they prospered. The pavements of the East End resounded with their hob-nailed boots, and even in many a West End drawing-room their patent-leather shoes creaked. But they themselves had no wish to stand in such shoes; the dingy perspectives of Dalston villadom limited their ambition, already sufficiently gratified by migration from Whitechapel. The profits went to enlarge their factory and to buy houses, a favourite form of investment in their set. Zillah could cook fish to perfection, both fried and stewed, and the latter variety both sweet and sour. Nothing, in fine, had been wanting to their happiness—save a son, heir, and mourner.

When he came at last, little that religion or superstition could do for him was left undone. An amulet on the bedpost scared off Lilith, Adam's first wife, who, perhaps because she missed being the mother of the human race, hankers after babes and sucklings. The initiation into the Abrahamic covenant was graced by a pious godfather with pendent ear-locks, and in the ceremony of the Redemption of the First-Born the five silver shekels to the priest were supplemented by golden sovereigns for the poor. Nor, though Zillah spoke the passable English of her circle, did she fail to rock her Brum's cradle to the old "Yiddish" nursery-songs:—

"Sleep, my birdie, shut your eyes,
O sleep, my little one;
Too soon from cradle you'll arise
To work that must be done.

"Almonds and raisins you shall sell,
And holy scrolls shall write;
So sleep, dear child, sleep sound and well,
Your future beckons bright.

"Brum shall learn of ancient days,
And love good folk of this;
So sleep, dear babe, your mother prays,

And God will send you bliss."

Alas, that with all this, Brum should have grown up a weakling, sickly and anæmic, with a look that in the child of poorer parents would have said starvation.

III

Yet through all the vicissitudes of his infantile career, Zillah's faith in his survival never faltered. He was emphatically a child from Heaven, and Providence would surely not fly in its own face. Jossel, not being aware of this, had a burden of perpetual solicitude, which Zillah often itched to lighten. Only, not having done so at first, she found it more and more difficult to confess her negotiation with the celestial powers. She went as near as she dared.

"If the Highest One has sent us a son after so many years," she said in the "Yiddish" which was still natural to her for intimate domestic discussion, "He will not take him away again."

"As well say," Jossel replied gloomily, "that because He has sent us luck and blessing after all these years, He may not take away our prosperity."

"Hush! don't beshrew the child!" And Zillah spat out carefully. She was tremulously afraid of words of ill-omen and of the Evil Eye, against which, she felt vaguely, even Heaven's protection was not potent. Secretly she became more and more convinced that some woman, envious of all this "luck and blessing," was withering Brum with her Evil Eye. And certainly the poor child was peaking and pining away. "Marasmus," a physician had once murmured, wondering that so well dressed a child should appear so ill nourished. "Take him to the seaside often, and feed him well," was the universal cry of the doctors; and so Zillah often deserted her husband for a kosher boarding-house at Brighton or Ramsgate, where the food was voluminous, and where Brum wrote schoolboy verses to the strange, fascinating sea.

For there were compensations in the premature flowering of his intellect. Even other mothers gradually came round to admitting he was a prodigy. The black eyes seemed to burn in the white face as they looked out on the palpitating universe, or devoured every and any scrap of print! A pity they had so soon to be dulled behind spectacles. But Zillah found consolation in the thought that the glasses would go well with the high black waistcoat and white tie of the British Rabbi. He had been given to her by Heaven, and to Heaven must be returned. Besides, that might divert it from any more sinister methods of taking him back.

In his twelfth year Brum began to have more trouble with his eyes, and renewed his early acquaintance with the drab ante-rooms of eye hospitals that led, at the long-expected ting-ting of the doctor's bell, into a delectable chamber of quaint instruments. But it was not till he was on the point of Bar-Mitzvah (confirmation at thirteen) that the blow fell. Unwarned explicitly by any physician, Brum went blind.

"Oh, mother," was his first anguished cry, "I shall never be able to read again."

IV

The prepared festivities added ironic complications to the horror. After Brum should have read in the Law from the synagogue platform, there was to have been a reception at the house. Brum himself had written out the invitations with conscious grammar. "Present their compliments to Mr. and Mrs. Solomon and shall be glad to see them" (not you, as was the fashion of their set). It was after writing out so many notes in a fine schoolboy hand, that Brum began to be conscious of thickening blurs and dancing specks and colours. Now that the blind boy was crouching in hopeless misery by the glowing fire, where he had so often recklessly pored over books in the delicious dusk, there was no one handy to write out the countermands. As yet the wretched parents had kept the catastrophe secret, as though it reflected on themselves. And by every post the Confirmation presents came pouring in.

Brum refused even to feel these shining objects. He had hoped to have a majority of books, but now the preponderance of watches, rings, and penknives, left him apathetic. To his parents each present brought a fresh feeling of dishonesty.

"We must let them know," they kept saying. But the tiny difficulty of writing to so many prevented action.

"Perhaps he'll be all right by Sabbath," Zillah persisted frenziedly. She clung to the faith that this was but a cloud: for that the glory of the Confirmation of a future Rabbi could be so dimmed would argue an incomprehensible Providence. Brum's performance was to be so splendid—he was to recite not only his own portion of the Law but the entire Sabbath Sedrah (section).

"He will never be all right," said Jossel, who, in the utter breakdown of Zillah, had for the first time made the round of the doctors with Brum. "None of the physicians, not even the most expensive, hold out any hope. And the dearest of all said the case puzzled him. It was like the blindness that often breaks out in Russia after the great fasts, and specially affects delicate children."

"Yes, I remember," said Zillah; "but that was only among the Christians."

"We have so many Christian customs nowadays," said Jossel grimly; and he thought of the pestilent heretic in his own synagogue who advocated that ladies should be added to the choir.

"Then what shall we do about the people?" moaned Zillah, wringing her hands in temporary discouragement.

"You can advertise in the Jewish papers," came suddenly from the brooding Brum. He had a flash of pleasure in the thought of composing something that would be published.

"Yes, then everybody will read it on the Friday," said Jossel eagerly.

Then Brum remembered that he would not be among the readers, and despair reconquered him. But Zillah was shaking her head.

"Yes, but if we tell people not to come, and then when Brum opens his eyes on the Sabbath morning, he can see to read the Sedrah—"

"But I don't want to see to read the Sedrah," said the boy petulantly; "I know it all by heart."

"My blessed boy!" cried Zillah.

"There's nothing wonderful," said the boy; "even if you read the scroll, there are no vowels nor musical signs."

"But do you feel strong enough to do it all?" said the father anxiously.

"God will give him strength," put in the mother. "And he will make his speech, too, won't you, my Brum?"

The blind face kindled. Yes, he would give his learned address. He had saved his father the expense of hiring one, and had departed in original rhetorical ways from the conventional methods of expressing filial gratitude to the parents who had brought him to manhood. And was this eloquence to remain entombed in his own breast?

His courageous resolution lightened the gloom. His parents opened parcels they had not had the heart to touch. They brought him his new suit, they placed the high hat of manhood on his head, and told him how fine and tall he looked; they wrapped the new silk praying-shawl round his shoulders.

"Are the stripes blue or black?" he asked.

"Blue—a beautiful blue," said Jossel, striving to steady his voice.

"It feels very nice," said Brum, smoothing the silk wistfully. "Yes, I can almost feel the blue."

Later on, when his father, a little brightened, had gone off to the exigent boot factory, Brum even asked to see the presents. The blind retain these visual phrases.

Zillah described them to him one by one as he handled them. When it came to the books it dawned on her that she could not tell him the titles.

"They have such beautiful pictures," she gushed evasively.

The boy burst into tears.

"Yes, but I shall never be able to read them," he sobbed.

"Yes, you will."

"No, I won't."

"Then I'll read them to you," she cried, with sudden resolution.

"But you can't read."

"I can learn."

"But you will be so long. I ought to have taught you myself. And now it is too late!"

V

In order to insure perfection, and prevent stage fright, so to speak, it had been arranged that Brum should rehearse his reading of the Sedrah on Friday in the synagogue itself, at an hour when it was free from worshippers. This rehearsal, his mother thought, was now all the more necessary to screw up Brum's confidence, but the father argued that as all places were now alike to the blind boy, the prominence of a public platform and a large staring audience could no longer unnerve him.

"But he will feel them there!" Zillah protested.

"But since they are not there on the Friday—?"

"All the more reason. Since he cannot see that they are not there, he can fancy they are there. On Saturday he will be quite used to them."

But when Jossel, yielding, brought Brum to the synagogue appointment, the fusty old Beadle who was faithfully in attendance held up his hands in holy and secular horror at the blasphemy and the blindness respectively.

"A blind man may not read the Law to the congregation!" he explained.

"No?" said Jossel.

"Why not?" asked Brum sharply.

"Because it stands that the Law shall be read. And a blind man cannot read. He can only recite."

"But I know every word of it," protested Brum.

The Beadle shook his head. "But suppose you make a mistake! Shall the congregation hear a word or a syllable that God did not write? It would be playing into Satan's hands."

"I shall say every word as God wrote it. Give me a trial."

But the fusty Beadle's piety was invincible. He was highly sympathetic toward the human affliction, but he refused to open the Ark and produce the Scroll.

"I'll let the Chazan (cantor) know he must read to-morrow, as usual," he said conclusively.

Jossel went home, sighing, but silenced. Zillah however, was not so easily subdued. "But my Brum will read it as truly as an angel!" she cried, pressing the boy's head to her breast. "And suppose he does make a mistake! Haven't I heard the congregation correct Winkelstein scores of times?"

"Hush!" said Jossel, "you talk like an Epicurean. Satan makes us all err at times, but we must not play into his hands. The Din (judgment) is that only those who see may read the Law to the congregation."

"Brum will read it much better than that snuffling old Winkelstein."

"Sha! Enough! The Din is the Din!"

"It was never meant to stop my poor Brum from—"

"The Din is the Din. It won't let you dance on its head or chop wood on its back. Besides, the synagogue refuses, so make an end."

"I will make an end. I'll have Minyan (congregation) here, in our own house."

"What!" and the poor man stared in amaze. "Always she falls from heaven with a new idea!"

"Brum shall not be disappointed." And she gave the silent boy a passionate hug.

"But we have no Scroll of the Law," Brum said, speaking at last, and to the point.

"Ah, that's you all over, Zillah," cried Jossel, relieved—"loud drumming in front and no soldiers behind!"

"We can borrow a Scroll," said Zillah.

Jossel gasped again. "But the iniquity is just the same," he said.

"As if Brum made mistakes!"

"If you were a Rabbi, the congregation would baptize itself!" Jossel quoted.

Zillah writhed under the proverb. "It isn't as if you went to the Rabbi; you took the word of the Beadle."

"He is a learned man."

Zillah donned her bonnet and shawl.

"Where are you going?"

"To the minister."

Jossel shrugged his shoulders, but did not stop her.

The minister, one of the new school of Rabbis who preach sermons in English and dress like Christian clergymen, as befitted the dignity of Dalston villadom, was taken aback by the ritual problem, so new and so tragic. His acquaintance with the vast casuistic literature of his race was of the shallowest. "No doubt the Beadle is right," he observed profoundly.

"He cannot be right; he doesn't know my Brum."

Worn out by Zillah's persistency, the minister suggested going to the Beadle's together. Aware of the Beadle's prodigious lore, he had too much regard for his own position to risk congregational odium by flying in the face of an exhumable Din.

At the Beadle's, the Din was duly unearthed from worm-eaten folios, but Zillah remaining unappeased, further searching of these Rabbinic scriptures revealed a possible compromise.

If the portion the boy recited was read over again by a reader not blind, so that the first congregational reading did not count, it might perhaps be permitted.

It would be of course too tedious to treat the whole Sedrah thus, but if Brum were content to recite his own particular seventh thereof, he should be summoned to the Rostrum.

So Zillah returned to Jossel, sufficiently triumphant.

VI

"Abraham, the son of Jossel, shall stand."

In obedience to the Cantor's summons, the blind boy, in his high hat and silken praying-shawl with the blue stripes, rose, and guided by his father's hand ascended the platform, amid the emotion of the synagogue. His brave boyish treble, pursuing its faultless way, thrilled the listeners to tears, and inflamed Zillah's breast, as she craned down from the gallery, with the mad hope that the miracle had happened, after all.

The house-gathering afterward savoured of the grewsome conviviality of a funeral assemblage. But the praises of Brum, especially after his great speech, were sung more honestly than those of the buried; than whom the white-faced dull-eyed boy, cut off from the gaily coloured spectacle in the sunlit room, was a more tragic figure.

But Zillah, in her fineries and forced smiles, offered the most tragic image of all. Every congratulation was a rose-wreathed dagger, every eulogy of Brum's eloquence a reminder of the Rabbi God had thrown away in him.

VII

Amid the endless babble of suggestions made to her for Brum's cure, one—repeated several times by different persons—hooked itself to her distracted brain. Germany! There was a great eye-doctor in Germany, who could do anything and everything. Yes, she would go to Germany.

This resolution, at which Jossel shrugged his shoulders in despairing scepticism, was received with rapture by Brum. How he had longed to see foreign countries, to pass over that shining sea which whispered and beckoned so, at Brighton and Ramsgate! He almost forgot he would not see Germany, unless the eye-doctor were a miracle-monger indeed.

But he was doomed to a double disappointment; for instead of his going to Germany, Germany came to him, so to speak, in the shape of the specialist's annual visit to London; and the great man had nothing soothing to say, only a compassionate head to shake, with ominous warnings to make the best of a bad job and fatten up the poor boy.

Nor did Zillah's attempts to read take her out of the infant primers, despite long hours of knitted brow and puckered lips, and laborious triumphs over the childish sentences, by patient addition of syllable to syllable. She also tried to write, but got no further than her own name, imitated from the envelopes.

To occupy Brum's days, Jossel, gaining enlightenment in the ways of darkness, procured Braille books. But the boy had read most of the stock works thus printed for the blind, and his impatient brain fretted at the tardiness of finger-reading. Jossel's one consolation was that the boy would not have to earn his living. The thought, however, of how his blind heir would be cheated by agents and rent-collectors was a touch of bitter even in this solitary sweet.

VIII

It was the Sabbath Fire-Woman who, appropriately enough, kindled the next glimmer of hope in Zillah's bosom. The one maid-of-all-work, who had supplied all the help and grandeur Zillah needed in her establishment, having transferred her services to a husband, Zillah was left searching for an angel at thirteen pounds a year. In the interim the old Irishwoman who made a few pence a week by attending to the Sabbath fires of the poor Jews of the neighbourhood, became necessary on Friday nights and Saturdays, to save the household from cold or sin.

"Och, the quare little brat!" she muttered, when she first came upon the pale, gnome-like figure by the fender, tapping the big book, for all the world like the Leprechaun cobbling.

"And can't he see at all, at all?" she asked Zillah confidentially one Sabbath, when the boy was out of the room.

Zillah shook her head, unable to speak.

"Nebbich!" compassionately sighed the Fire-Woman, who had corrupted her native brogue with "Yiddish." "And wud he be borrun dark?"

"No, it came only a few months ago," faltered Zillah.

The Fire-Woman crossed herself.

"Sure, and who'll have been puttin' the Evil Oi on him?" she asked.

Zillah's face was convulsed.

"I always said so!" she cried; "I always said so!"

"The divil burrun thim all!" cried the Fire-Woman, poking the coals viciously.

"Yes, but I don't know who it is. They envied me my beautiful child, my lamb, my only one. And nothing can be done." She burst into tears.

"Nothin' is a harrd wurrd! If he was my bhoy, the darlint, I'd cure him, aisy enough, so I wud."

Zillah's sobs ceased. "How?" she asked, her eyes gleaming strangely.

"I'd take him to the Pope, av course."

"The Pope!" repeated Zillah vaguely.

"Ay, the Holy Father! The ownly man in this wurruld that can take away the Evil Oi."

Zillah gasped. "Do you mean the Pope of Rome?"

She knew the phrase somehow, but what it connoted was very shadowy and sinister: some strange, mighty chief of hostile heathendom.

"Who else wud I be manin'? The Holy Mother I'd be for prayin' to meself; but as ye're a Jewess, I dursn't tell ye to do that. But the Pope, he's a gintleman, an' so he is, an' sorra a bit he'll moind that ye don't go to mass, whin he shpies that poor, weeshy, pale shrimp o' yours. He'll just wave his hand, shpake a wurrd, an' whishtl in the twinklin' of a bedposht ye'll be praisin' the Holy Mother."

Zillah's brain was whirling. "Go to Rome!" she said.

The Fire-Woman poised the poker.

"Well, ye can't expect the Pope to come to Dalston!"

"No, no; I don't mean that," said Zillah, in hasty apology. "Only it's so far off, and I shouldn't know how to go."

"It's not so far off as Ameriky, an' it's two broths of bhoys I've got there."

"Isn't it?" asked Zillah.

"No, Lord love ye: an' sure gold carries ye anywhere nowadays, ixcept to Heaven."

"But if I got to Rome, would the Pope see the child?"

"As sartin as the child wud see him," the Fire-Woman replied emphatically.

"He can do miracles, then?" inquired Zillah.

"What else wud he be for? Not that 'tis much of a miracle to take away the Evil Oi, bad scran to the witch!"

"Then perhaps our Rabbi can do it, too?" cried Zillah, with a sudden hope.

The Fire-Woman shook her head. "Did ye ever hear he could?"

"No," admitted Zillah.

"Thrue for you, mum. Divil a wurrd wud I say aginst your Priesht—wan's as good as another, maybe, for ivery-day use; but whin it comes to throuble and heart-scaldin', I pity the poor craythurs who can't put up a candle to the blessed saints—an' so I do. Niver a bhoy o' mine has crassed the ocean without the Virgin havin' her candle."

"And did they arrive safe?"

"They did so; ivery mother's son av 'em."

IX

The more the distracted mother pondered over this sensational suggestion, the more it tugged at her. Science and Judaism had failed her: perhaps this unknown power, this heathen Pope, had indeed mastery over things diabolical. Perhaps the strange religion he professed had verily a saving efficacy denied to her own. Why should she not go to Rome?

True, the journey loomed before her as fearfully as a Polar Expedition to an ordinary mortal. Germany she had been prepared to set out for: it lay on the great route of Jewish migration westwards. But Rome? She did not even know where it was. But her new skill in reading would, she felt, help her through the perils. She would be able to make out the names of the railway stations, if the train waited long enough.

But with the cunning of the distracted she did not betray her heretical ferment.

"P—o—p—e, Pope," she spelt out of her infants' primer in Brum's hearing. "Pope? What's that, Brum?"

"Oh, haven't you ever heard of the Pope, mother?"

"No," said Zillah, crimsoning in conscious invisibility.

"He's a sort of Chief Rabbi of the Roman Catholics. He wears a tiara. Kings and emperors used to tremble before him."

"And don't they now?" she asked apprehensively.

"No; that was in the Middle Ages—hundreds of years ago. He only had power over the Dark Ages."

"Over the Dark Ages?" repeated Zillah, with a fresh, vague hope.

"When all the world was sunk in superstition and ignorance, mother. Then everybody believed in him."

Zillah felt chilled and rebuked. "Then he no longer works miracles?" she said faintly.

Brum laughed. "Oh, I daresay he works as many miracles as ever. Of course thousands of pilgrims still go to kiss his toe. I meant his temporal power is gone—that is, his earthly power. He doesn't rule over any countries; all he possesses is the Vatican, but that is full of the greatest pictures by Michael Angelo and Raphael."

Zillah gazed open-mouthed at the prodigy she had brought into the world.

"Raphael—that sounds Jewish," she murmured. She longed to ask in what country Rome was, but feared to betray herself.

Brum laughed again. "Raphael Jewish! Why—so it is! It's a Hebrew word meaning 'God's healing.'"

"God's healing!" repeated Zillah, awestruck.

Her mind was made up.

X

"Knowest thou what, Jossel?" she said in "Yiddish," as they sat by the Friday-night fireside when Brum had been put to bed. "I have heard of a new doctor, better than all the others!" After all it was the doctor, the healer, the exorcist of the Evil Eye, that she was seeking in the Pope, not the Rabbi of an alien religion.

Jossel shook his head. "You will only throw more money away."

"Better than throwing hope away."

"Well, who is it now?"

"He lives far away."

"In Germany again?"

"No, in Rome."

"In Rome? Why, that's at the end of the world—in Italy!"

"I know it's in Italy!" said Zillah, rejoiced at the information. "But what then? If organ-grinders can travel the distance, why can't I?"

"But you can't speak Italian!"

"And they can't speak English!"

"Madness! Work, but not wisdom! I could not trust you alone in such a strange country, and the season is too busy for me to leave the factory."

"I don't need you with me," she said, vastly relieved. "Brum will be with me."

He stared at her. "Brum!"

"Brum knows everything. Believe me, Jossel, in two days he will speak Italian."

"Let be! Let be! Let me rest!"

"And on the way back he will be able to see! He will show me everything, and Mr. Raphael's pictures. 'God's healing,'" she murmured to herself.

"But you'd be away for Passover! Enough!"

"No, we shall be easily back by Passover."

"O these women! The Almighty could not have rested on the seventh day if he had not left woman still uncreated."

"You don't care whether Brum lives or dies!" Zillah burst into sobs.

"It is just because I do that I ask how are you going to live on the journey? And there are no kosher hotels in Italy."

"We shall manage on eggs and fish. God will forgive us if the hotel plates are unclean."

"But you won't be properly nourished without meat."

"Nonsense; when we were poor we had to do without it." To herself she thought, "If he only knew I did without food altogether on Mondays and Thursdays!"

XI

And so Brum passed at last over the shining, wonderful sea, feeling only the wind on his forehead and the salt in his nostrils. It was a beautiful day at the dawn of spring; the far-stretching sea sparkled with molten diamonds, and Zillah felt that the highest God's blessing rested like a blue sky over this strange pilgrimage. She was dressed with great taste, and few would have divined the ignorance under her silks.

"Mother, can you see France yet?" Brum asked very soon.

"No, my lamb."

"Mother, can you see France yet?" he persisted later.

"I see white cliffs," she said at last.

"Ah! that's only the white cliffs of Old England. Look the other way."

"I am looking the other way. I see white cliffs coming to meet us."

"Has France got white cliffs, too?" cried Brum, disappointed.

On the journey to Paris he wearied her to describe France. In vain she tried: her untrained vision and poor vocabulary could give him no new elements to weave into a mental picture. There were trees and sometimes houses and churches. And again trees. What kind of trees? Green! Brum was in despair. France was, then, only like England; white cliffs without, trees and houses within. He demanded the Seine at least.

"Yes, I see a great water," his mother admitted at last.

"That's it! It rises in the Côte d'Or, flows N.N.W. then W., and N.W. into the English Channel. It is more than twice as long as the Thames. Perhaps you'll see the tributaries flowing into it—the little rivers, the Oise, the Marne, the Yonne."

"No wonder the angels envy me him!" thought Zillah proudly.

They halted at Paris, putting up for the night, by the advice of a friendly fellow-traveller, at a hotel by the Gare de Lyon, where, to Zillah's joy and amazement, everybody spoke English to her and accepted her English gold—a pleasant experience which was destined to be renewed at each stage, and which increased her hope of a happy issue.

"How loud Paris sounds!" said Brum, as they drove across it. He had to construct it from its noises, for in answer to his feverish interrogations his mother could only explain that some streets were lined with trees and some foolish unrespectable people sat out in the cold air, drinking at little tables.

"Oh, how jolly!" said Brum. "But can't you see Notre Dame?"

"What's that?"

"A splendid cathedral, mother—very old. Do look for two towers. We must go there the first thing to-morrow."

"The first thing to-morrow we take the train. The quicker we get to the doctor, the better."

"Oh, but we can't leave Paris without seeing Notre Dame, and the gargoyles, and perhaps Quasimodo, and all that Victor Hugo describes. I wonder if we shall see a devil-fish in Italy," he added irrelevantly.

"You'll see the devil if you go to such places," said Zillah, who, besides shirking the labor of description, was anxious not to provoke unnecessarily the God of Israel.

"But I've often been to St. Paul's with the boys," said Brum.

"Have you?" She was vaguely alarmed.

"Yes, it's lovely—the stained windows and the organ. Yes, and the Abbey's glorious, too; it almost makes me cry. I always liked to hear the music with my eyes shut," he added, with forced cheeriness, "and now that'll be all right."

"But your father wouldn't like it," said Zillah feebly.

"Father wouldn't like me to read the Pilgrim's Progress," retorted Brum. "He doesn't understand these things. There's no harm in our going to Notre Dame."

"No, no; it'll be much better to save all these places for the way back, when you'll be able to see for yourself."

Too late it struck her she had missed an opportunity of breaking to Brum the real object of the expedition.

"But the Seine, anyhow!" he persisted. "We can go there to-night."

"But what can you see at night?" cried Zillah, unthinkingly.

"Oh, mother! how beautiful it used to be to look over London Bridge at night when we came back from the Crystal Palace!"

In the end Zillah accepted the compromise, and after their dinner of fish and vegetables—for which Brum had scant appetite—they were confided by the hotel porter to a bulbous-nosed cabman, who had instructions to restore them to the hotel. Zillah thought wistfully of her warm parlour in Dalston, with the firelight reflected in the glass cases of the wax flowers.

The cab stopped on a quay.

"Well?" said Brum breathlessly.

"Little fool!" said Zillah good-humouredly. "There is nothing but water—the same water as in London."

"But there are lights, aren't there?"

"Yes, there are lights," she admitted cheerfully.

"Where is the moon?"

"Where she always is—in the sky."

"Doesn't she make a silver path on the water?" he said, with a sob in his voice.

"What are you crying at? The mother didn't mean to make you cry."

She strained him contritely to her bosom, and kissed away his tears.

The train for Switzerland started so early that Brum had no time to say his morning prayers; so, the carriage being to themselves, he donned his phylacteries and his praying-shawl with the blue stripes.

Zillah sat listening to the hour-long recitative with admiration of his memory.

Early in the hour she interrupted him to say: "How lucky I haven't to say all that! I should get tired."

"That's curious!" replied Brum. "I was just saying, 'Blessed art Thou, O Lord our God, who hath not made me a woman.' But a woman has to pray, too, mother. Else why is there given a special form for the women to substitute?—'Who hath made me according to His will.'"

"Ah, that's only for learned women. Only learned women pray."

"Well, you'd like to pray the Benediction that comes next, mother, I know. Say it with me—do."

She repeated the Hebrew obediently, then asked: "What does it mean?"

"'Blessed art Thou, O Lord our God, who openest the eyes of the blind.'"

"Oh, my poor Brum! Teach it me! Say the Hebrew again "

She repeated it till she could say it unprompted. And then throughout the journey her lips moved with it at odd times. It became a talisman—a compromise with the God who had failed her.

"Blessed art Thou, O Lord our God, who openest the eyes of the blind."

Mountains were the great sensation of the passage through Switzerland. Brum had never seen a mountain, and the thought of being among the highest mountains in Europe was thrilling. Even Zillah's eyes could scarcely miss the mountains. She painted them in broad strokes. But they did not at all correspond to Brum's expectations of the Alps.

"Don't you see glaciers?" he asked anxiously.

"No," replied Zillah, but kept a sharp eye on the windows of passing chalets till the boy discovered that she was looking for glaziers at work.

"Great masses of ice," he explained, "sliding down very slowly, and glittering like the bergs in the Polar regions."

"No, I see none," she said, blushing.

"Ah! wait till we come to Mont Blanc."

Mont Blanc was an obsession; his geography was not minute enough to know that the route did not pass within sight of it. He had expected it to dominate Switzerland as a cathedral spire dominates a little town.

"Mont Blanc is 15,784 feet above the sea," he said voluptuously. "Eternal snow is on its top, but you will not see that, because it is above the clouds."

"It is, then, in Heaven," said Zillah.

"God is there," replied Brum gravely, and burst out with Coleridge's lines from his school-book:—

"'God! let the torrents, like a shout of nations,
Answer! and let the ice-plains echo, God!
God! sing ye meadow-streams with gladsome voice!
Ye pine-groves, with your soft and soul-like sounds!
And they, too, have a voice, yon piles of snow,
And in their perilous fall shall thunder God!'"

"Who openest the eyes of the blind," murmured Zillah.

"There are five torrents rushing down, also," added Brum. "'And you, ye five wild torrents fiercely glad.' You'll recognize Mont Blanc by that. Don't you see them yet, mother?"

"Wait, I think I see them coming."

Presently she announced Mont Blanc definitely; described it with glaciers and torrents and its top reaching to God.

Brum's face shone.

"Poor lamb! I may as well give him Mont Blanc," she thought tenderly.

XIV

Endless other quaint dialogues passed between mother and son on that tedious and harassing journey southwards.

"There'll be no more snow when we get to Italy," Brum explained. "Italy's the land of beauty—always sunshine and blue sky. It's the country of the old Gods—Venus, the goddess of beauty; Juno, with her peacocks; Jupiter, with his thunderbolts, and lots of others."

"But I thought the Pope was a Christian," said Zillah.

"So he is. It was long ago, before people believed in Christianity."

"But then they were all Jews."

"Oh no, mother. There were Pagan gods that people used to believe in at Rome and in Greece. In Greece, though, these gods changed their names."

"So!" said Zillah scornfully; "I suppose they wanted to have a fresh chance. And what's become of them now?"

"They weren't ever there, not really."

"And yet people believed in them? Is it possible?" Zillah clucked her tongue with contemptuous surprise. Then she murmured mechanically, "'Blessed art Thou, O Lord our God, who openest the eyes of the blind.'"

"Well, and what do people believe in now? The Pope!" Brum reminded her. "And yet he's not true."

Zillah's heart sank. "But he's really there," she protested feebly.

"Oh yes, he's there, because pilgrims come from all parts of the world to get his blessing."

Her hopes revived.

"But they wouldn't come unless he really did them good."

"Well, if you argue like that, mother, you might as well say we ought to believe in Christ."

"Hush! hush!" The forbidden word jarred on Zillah. She felt chilled and silenced. She had to call up the image of the Irish Fire-Woman to restore herself to confidence. It was clear Brum must not be told; his unfaith might spoil all. No, the deception must be kept up till his eyes were opened—in more than one sense.

XV

After Mont Blanc, Brum's great interest was the leaning tower of Pisa. "It is one of the wonders of the world," he said; "there are seven altogether."

"Yes, it is a wonderful world," said Zillah; "I never thought about it before."

And in truth Italy was beginning to touch sleeping chords. The cypresses, the sunset on the mountains, the white towns dozing on the hills under the magical blue sky—all these broad manifestations of an obvious beauty, under the spur of Brum's incessant interrogatory, began to penetrate. Nature in unusual combinations spoke to her as its habitual phenomena had never done. Her replies to Brum did rough justice to Italy.

Florence recalled "Romola" to the boy. He told his mother about Savonarola. "He was burnt!"

"What!" cried Zillah. "Burn a Christian! No wonder, then, they burnt Jews. But why?"

"He wanted the people to be good. All good people suffer."

"Oh, nonsense, Brum! It is the bad who suffer."

Then she looked at his wasted, white face, grown thinner with the weariness of the long journey through perpetual night, and wonder at her own words struck her silent.

XVI

They arrived at last in the Eternal City, having taken a final run of many hours without a break. But the Pope was still to seek.

Leaving the exhausted Brum in bed, Zillah drove the first morning to the Vatican, where Brum said he lived, and asked to see him.

A glittering Swiss Guard stared blankly at her, and directed her by dumb show to follow the stream of people—the pilgrims, Zillah told herself. She was made to scrawl her name, and, thanking God that she had acquired that accomplishment, she went softly up a gorgeous flight of steps, and past awe-inspiring creatures in tufted helmets, into the Sistine Chapel, where she wondered at people staring ceilingwards through opera-glasses, or looking downwards into little mirrors. Zillah also stared up through the gloom till she had a crick in the neck, but saw no sign of the Pope. She inquired of the janitor whether he was the Pope, and realized that English was, after all, not the universal language. She returned gloomily to see after Brum, and to consider her plan of campaign.

"The great doctor was not at home," she said. "We must wait a little."

"And yet you made us hurry so through everything," grumbled Brum.

Brum remained in bed while Zillah went to get some lunch in the dining-room. A richly dressed old lady who sat near her noticed that she was eating Lenten fare, like herself, and, assuming her a fellow-Catholic, spoke to her, in foreign-sounding English, about the blind boy whose arrival she had observed.

Zillah asked her how one could get to see the Pope, and the old lady told her it was very difficult.

"Ah, those blessed old times before 1870!—ah, the splendid ceremonies in St. Peter's! Do you remember them?"

Zillah shook her head. The old lady's assumption of spiritual fellowship made her uneasy.

But St. Peter's stuck in her mind. Brum had already told her it was the Pope's house of prayer. Clearly, therefore, it was only necessary to loiter about there with Brum to chance upon him and extort his compassionate withdrawal of the spell of the Evil Eye. With a culminating inspiration she bought a photograph of the Pope, and overcoming the first shock of hereditary repulsion at the sight of the large pendent crucifix at his breast, she studied carefully the Pontiff's face and the Papal robes.

Then, when Brum declared himself strong enough to get up, they drove to St. Peter's, the instruction being given quietly to the driver so that Brum should not overhear it.

It was the first time Zillah had ever been in a cathedral; and the vastness and glory of it swept over her almost as a reassuring sense of a greater God than she had worshipped in dingy synagogues. She walked about solemnly, leading Brum by the hand, her breast swelling with suppressed sobs of hope. Her eyes roved everywhere, searching for the Pope; but at moments she well-nigh forgot her disappointment at his absence in the wonder and ghostly comfort of the great dim spaces, and the mysterious twinkle of the countless lights before the bronze canopy with its golden-flashing columns.

"Where are we, mother?" said Brum at last.

"We are waiting for the doctor."

"But where?"

"In the waiting-room."

"It seems very large, mother."

"No, I am walking round and round."

"There is a strange smell, mother—I don't know what—something religious."

"Oh, nonsense!" She laughed uneasily.

"I know what it smells like: cold marble pillars and warm coloured windows."

Her blood froze at such uncanny sensibility.

"It is the smell of the medicines," she murmured. Somehow his divination made it more difficult to confess to him.

"It feels like being in St. Paul's or the Abbey," he persisted, "when I used to shut my eyes to hear the organ better." He had scarcely ceased speaking, when a soft, slow music began to thrill with life the great stone spaces.

Brum's grasp tightened convulsively: a light leapt into the blind face. Both came to a standstill, silent. In Zillah's breast rapture made confusion more confounded; and as this pealing grandeur, swelling more passionately, uplifted her high as the mighty Dome, she forgot everything—even the need of explanation to Brum—in this wonderful sense of a Power that could heal, and her Hebrew benediction flowed out into sobbing speech:—

"'Blessed art Thou, O Lord our God, who openest the eyes of the blind.'"

But Brum had fainted, and hung heavy on her arm.

XVII

When Brum awoke, in bed again, after his long fainting-fit, he related with surprise his vivid dream of St. Paul's, and Zillah weakly acquiesced in the new deception, especially as the doctor warned her against exciting the boy. But her hopes were brighter than ever; for the old lady had beneficently appeared from behind a pillar in St. Peter's to offer eau de Cologne for the unconscious Brum, and had then, interesting herself in the couple, promised to procure for her fellow-Catholics admission to the next Papal reception. Being a very rich and fashionable old lady, she kept her word; but unfortunately, when the day came round, Brum was terribly low and forbidden to leave his bed.

Zillah was distracted. If she should miss the great chance after all! It might never recur again.

"Brum," she said at last, "this is the only day for a long time that the great eye-doctor receives patients. Do you think you could go, my lamb?"

"Why won't he come here—like the other doctors?"

"He is too great."

"Well, I daresay I can manage. It's miserable lying in bed. Fancy coming to Rome and seeing nothing!"

With infinite care Brum was dressed and wrapped up, and placed in a specially comfortable brougham; and thus at last mother and son stood waiting in one of the ante-chambers of the Vatican, amid twenty other pilgrims whispering in strange languages. Zillah was radiantly assured: the mighty Power, whatever it was, that spoke in music and in mountains, would never permit such weary journeyings and waitings to end in the old darkness; the malice of witches could not prevail against this great spirit of sunshine. For Brum, too, the long pilgrimage had enveloped the doctor with a miraculous glamour as of an eighth wonder of the world.

Drooping wearily on his mother's arm, but wrought up to joyous anticipation, Brum had an undoubting sense of the patient crowd around him waiting, as in his old hospital days, for admission to the doctor's sanctum. His ear was strung for the ting-ting of the bell summoning the sufferers one by one.

At last a wave of awe swept over the little fashionable gathering, and set Zillah's heart thumping and the room fading in mist, through which the tall, venerable, robed figure, the eagle features softened in benediction, gleamed like a god's. Then she found herself on her knees, with Brum at her side, and the wonderful figure passing between two rows of reverent pilgrims.

"Why must I kneel, mother?" murmured Brum feebly.

"Hush! hush!" she whispered. "The great doc—" she hesitated in awe of the venerable figure—"the great healer is here."

"The great healer!" breathed Brum. His face was transfigured with ecstatic forevision. "'Who openeth the eyes of the blind,'" he murmured, as he fell forward in death.

II

TRANSITIONAL

I

The day came when old Daniel Peyser could no longer withstand his wife's desire for a wider social sphere and a horizon blacker with advancing bachelors. For there were seven daughters, and not a man to the pack. Indeed, there had been only one marriage in the whole Portsmouth congregation during the last five years, and the Christian papers had had reports of the novel ceremony, with the ritual bathing of the bride and the breaking of the glass under the bridegroom's heel. To Mrs. Peyser, brought up amid the facile pairing of the Russian pale, this congestion of celibacy approached immorality.

Portsmouth with its careless soldiers and sailors might be an excellent town for pawnbroking, especially when one was not too punctiliously acceptant of the ethics of the heathen, but as a market for maidens—even with dowries and pretty faces—it was hopeless. But it was not wholly as an emporium for bachelors that London appealed. It was the natural goal of the provincial Jew, the reward of his industry. The best people had all drifted to the mighty magic city, whose fascination survived even cheap excursions to it.

Would father deny that they had now made enough to warrant the migration? No, father would not deny it. Ever since he had left Germany as a boy he had been saving money, and his surplus he had shrewdly invested in the neighbouring soil of Southsea, fast growing into a watering-place. Even allowing three thousand pounds for each daughter's dowry, he would still have a goodly estate.

Was there any social reason why they should not cut as great a dash as the Benjamins or the Rosenweilers? No, father would not deny that his girls were prettier and more polished than the daughters of these pioneers, especially when six of them crowded around the stern granite figure, arguing, imploring, cajoling, kissing.

"But I don't see why we should waste the money," he urged, with the cautious instincts of early poverty.

"Waste!" and the pretty lips made reproachful "Oh's!"

"Yes, waste!" he retorted. "In India one treads on diamonds and gold, but in London the land one treads on costs diamonds and gold."

"But are we never to have a grandson?" cried Mrs. Peyser.

The Indian item was left unquestioned, so that little Schnapsie, whose childish imagination was greatly impressed by these eventful family debates, had for years a vivid picture of picking her way with bare feet over sharp-pointed diamonds and pebbly gold. Indeed, long after she had learned to wonder at her father's naïve geography the word "India" always shone for her with barbaric splendour.

Environed by so much persistent femininity, the rugged elderly toiler was at last nagged into accepting a leisured life in London.

II

And so the family spread its wings joyfully and migrated to the wonder-town. Only its head and tail—old Daniel and little Schnapsie—felt the least sentiment for the things left behind. Old Daniel left the dingy synagogue to whose presidency he had mounted with the fattening of his purse, and in which he bought for himself, or those he delighted to honour, the choicest privileges of ark-opening or scroll-bearing; left the cronies who dropped in to play "Klabberjagd" on Sunday afternoons; left the bustling lucrative Saturday nights in the shop when the heathen housewives came to redeem their Sabbath finery.

And little Schnapsie—who was only eleven, and not keen about husbands—left the twinkling tarry harbour, with its heroic hulks and modern men-of-war amid which the half-penny steamer plied; left the great waves that smashed on the pebbly beach, and the friendly moon that threw shimmering paths across their tranquillity; left the narrow lively streets in which she had played, and the school in which she had always headed her class, and the salt wind that blew over all.

Little Schnapsie was only Schnapsie to her father. Her real name was Florence. The four younger girls all bore pagan names—Sylvia, Lily, Daisy, Florence—symbolic of the influence upon the family councils of the three elder girls, grown to years of discretion and disgust with their own Leah, Rachael, and Rebecca. Between these two strata of girls—Jewish and pagan—two boys had intervened, but their stay was brief and pitiful, so that all this plethora of progeny had not provided the father with a male mourner to say the Kaddish. But it seemed likely a grandson would not long be a-wanting, for the eldest girl was twenty-five, and all were good-looking. As if in irony, the Jewish group was blond, almost Christian, in colouring (for they took after the Teuton father), while the pagan group had characteristically Oriental traits. In little Schnapsie these Eastern charms—a whit heavy in her sisters— were repeated in a key of exquisite refinement. The thick black eyebrows and hair were soft as silk, dark dreamy eyes suffused her oval face with poetry, and her skin was like dead ivory flushing into life.

III

The first year at Highbury, that genteel suburb in the north of London, was an enchanted ecstasy for the mother and the Jewish group of girls, taken at once to the bosom of a great German clan, and admitted to a new world of dances and dinners, of "at homes" and theatres and card parties. The eldest of the pagan group, Sylvia—tyrannically kept young in the interests of her sisters—was the only one who grumbled at the change, for Lily and Daisy found sufficient gain in the prospect of replacing the elder group when it should have passed away in an odour of orange blossom. The scent of that was always in the air, and Mrs. Peyser and her three hopefuls sniffed it night and day.

"No, no; Rebecca shall have him."

"Not me! I am not going to marry a man with carroty hair. Leah's the eldest; it's her turn first."

"Thank you, my dear. Don't give away what you haven't got."

Every new young man who showed the faintest signs of liking to drop in, provoked a similar semi-facetious but also semi-serious canvassing—his person, his income, and the girl to whom he should be allotted supplying the sauce of every meal at which he—or his fellow—was not present.

Thus, whether in the flesh or the spirit, the Young Man—for so many of him appeared on the scene that he hovered in the air rather as a type than an individual—was a permanent guest at the Peyser table.

But all this new domestic excitement did not compensate little Schnapsie for her moonlit waters and the strange ships that came and went with their cargo of mystery.

And poor old Daniel found no cronies to appeal to him like the old, nothing in the roar of London to compensate for the Saturday night bustle of the pawn-shop, no dingy little synagogue desirous of his presidential pomp. He sat inconspicuously in a handsome half-empty edifice, and knew himself a superfluous atom in a vast lonely wilderness.

He was not, indeed, an imposing figure, with his ragged graying whiskers and his boyish blue eyes. In the street he had the stoop and shuffle of the Ghetto, and forgot to hide his coarse red hands with gloves; in the house he persisted in wearing a pious skull-cap. At first his more adaptable wife and his English-bred daughters tried to fit him for decent society, and to make him feel at home during their "at homes." But he was soon relegated to the background of these brilliant social tableaux; for he was either too silent or too talkative, with old-fashioned Jewish jokes which disconcerted the smart young men, and with Hebrew quotations which they could not even understand. And sometimes there thrilled through the small-talk the trumpet-note of his nose, as he blew it into a coloured handkerchief. Gradually he was eliminated from the drawing-room altogether.

But for some years longer he reigned supreme in the dining-room—when there was no company. Old habit kept the girls at table when he intoned with noisy unction the Hebrew grace after meals; they even joined in the melodious morceaux that diversified the plain-chant. But little by little their contributions dwindled to silence. And when they had smart company to dinner, the old man himself was hushed by rows of blond and bugle eyebrows; especially after he had once or twice put young men to shame by offering them the honour of reciting the grace they did not know.

Daniel's prayer on such occasions was at length reduced to a pious mumbling, which went unobserved amid the joyous clatter of dessert, even as his pious skull-cap passed as a preventive against cold.

Last stage of all, the mumbling of his company manners passed over into the domestic circle; and this humble whispering to God became symbolic of his suppression.

IV

"I don't think he means Rachael at all."

"Oh, how can you say so, Leah? It was me he took down to supper."

"Nonsense! it isn't either of you he's after; that's only his politeness to my sisters. Didn't he say the bouquet was for me?"

"Don't be silly, Rebecca. You know you can't have him. The eldest must take precedence."

This changed tone indicated their humbler attitude toward the Young Man as the years went by. For the first young man did not propose, either to the sisterhood en bloc or to a particular sister. And his example was followed by his successors. In fact, a procession of young men passed and repassed through the house, or danced with the girls at balls, without a single application for any of these many hands. And the first season passed into the second, and the second into the third, with tantalizing mirages of marriage. Balls, dances, dinners, a universe of nebulous matrimonial matter on the whirl, but never the shot-off star of an engagement! Mrs. Peyser's hair began to whiten faster. She even surreptitiously called in the Shadchan, or rather surrendered to his solicitations.

"Pooh! Not find any one suitable?" he declared, rubbing his hands. "I have hundreds of young men on my books, just your sort, real gentlemen."

At first the girls refused to consider applications from such a source. It was not done in their set, they said.

Mrs. Peyser snorted sceptically. "Oh, indeed! and pray how did those Rosenweiler girls find husbands?"

"Oh, yes, the Rosenweilers!" They shrugged their shoulders; they knew they had not that disadvantage of hideousness.

Nevertheless they lent an ear to the agent's suggestions as filtered through the mother, though under pretence of deriding them.

But the day came when even that pretence was dropped, and with broken spirit they waited eagerly for each new possibility. And with the passing of the years the Young Man aged. He grew balder, less gentlemanly, poorer.

Once indeed, he turned up as a handsome and wealthy Christian, but this time it was he that was rejected in a unanimous sisterly shudder. Five slow years wore by, then of a sudden the luck changed. A water-proof manufacturer on the sunny side of forty appeared, the long glacial epoch was broken up, and the first orange blossom ripened for the Peyser household.

It was Rebecca, the youngest of the Jewish group, who proved the pioneer to the canopy, but her marriage gave a new lease of youth even to the oldest. And miraculously, mysteriously, within a few months two other girls flew off Mrs. Peyser's shoulders—a Jewish and a pagan—though Sylvia was not yet formally "out."

And though Leah, the first born, still remained unchosen, yet Sylvia's marriage to a Bayswater household had raised the family status, and provided a better field for operations. The Shadchan was frozen off.

But he returned. For despite all these auguries and auspices another arctic winter set in. No orange blossoms, only desolate lichens of fruitless flirtation.

Gradually the pagan group pushed its way into unconcealable womanhood. The problem darkened all the horizon. The Young Man grew middle-aged again. He lost all his money; he wanted old Daniel to set him up in business. Even this seemed better than a barren fine ladyhood, and Leah might have even harked back to the parental pawn-shop had not another sudden epidemic of felicity married off all save little Schnapsie within eighteen months. Mrs. Peyser was knocked breathless by all these shocks. First a rich German banker, then a prosperous solicitor (for Leah), then a Cape financier—any one in himself catch enough to "gouge out the eyes" of the neighbours.

"I told you so," she said, her portly bosom swelling portlier with exultation as the sixth bride was whirled off in a rice shower from the Highbury villa, while the other five sat around in radiant matronhood. "I told you to come to London."

Daniel pressed her hand in gratitude for all the happiness she had given herself and the girls.

"If it were not for Florence," she went on wistfully.

"Ah, little Schnapsie!" sighed Daniel. Somehow he felt he would have preferred her hymeneal felicity to all these marvellous marriages. For there had grown up a strange sympathy between the poor lonely old man, now nearly seventy, and his little girl, now twenty-four. They never conversed except about commonplaces, but somehow he felt that her presence warmed the air. And she—she divined his solitude, albeit dimly; had an intuition of what life had been for him in the days before she was born: the long days behind the counter, the risings in the gray dawn to chant orisons and don phylacteries ere the pawn-shop opened, the lengthy prayer and the swift supper when the shutters were at last put up—all the bare rock on which this floriage of prosperity had been sown. And long after the others had dropped kissing him good-night, she would tender her lips, partly because of the necessary domestic fiction that she was still a baby, but also because she felt instinctively that the kiss counted in his life.

Through all these years of sordid squabbles and canvassings and weary waiting, all those endless scenes of hysteria engendered by the mutual friction of all that close-packed femininity, poor Schnapsie had lived, shuddering. Sometimes a sense of the pathos of it all, of the tragedy of women's lives, swept over her. She regretted every inch she grew, it seemed to shame her celibate sisters so. She clung willingly to short skirts until she was of age, wore her long raven hair in a plait with a red ribbon.

"Well, Florence," said Leah genially, when the last outsider at Daisy's wedding had departed, "it's your turn next. You'd better hurry up."

"Thank you," said Florence coldly. "I shall take my own time; fortunately there is no one behind me."

"Humph!" said Leah, playing with her diamond rings. "It don't do to be too particular. Why don't you come round and see me sometimes?"

"There are so many of you now," murmured Florence. She was not attracted by the solicitors and traders in whose society and carriages her mother lolled luxuriously, and she resented the matronly airs of her sisters. With Leah, however, she was conscious of a different and more paradoxical provocation. Leah had an incredible air of juvenility. All those unthinkable, innumerable years little Schnapsie had conceived of her eldest sister as an old maid, hopeless, senescent, despite the wonderful belt that had kept her figure dashing; but now that she was married she had become the girlish bride, kittenish, irresistible, while little Schnapsie was the old maid, the sister in peril of being passed by. And indeed she felt herself appallingly ancient, prematurely aged by her long stay at seventeen.

"Yes, you are right, Leah," she said pensively, with a touch of malice. "To-morrow I shall be twenty-four."

"What?" shrieked Leah.

"Yes," Florence said obstinately. "And oh, how glad I shall be!" She raised her arms exultingly and stretched herself, as if shooting up seven years as soon as the pressure of her sisters was removed.

"Do you hear, mother?" whispered Leah. "That fool of a Florence is going to celebrate her twenty-fourth birthday. Not the slightest consideration for us!"

"I didn't say I would celebrate it publicly," said Florence. "Besides," she suggested, smiling, "very soon people will forget that I am not the eldest."

"Then your folly will recoil on your own head," said Leah.

Little Schnapsie gave a devil-may-care shrug—a Ghetto trait that still clung to all the sisters.

"Yes," added Mrs. Peyser. "Think what it will be in ten years' time!"

"I shall be thirty-four," said Florence imperturbably. Another little smile lit up the dreamy eyes. "Then I shall be the eldest."

"Madness!" cried Mrs. Peyser, aloud, forgetting that her daughters' husbands were about. "God forbid I should live to see any girl of mine thirty-four!"

"Hush, mother!" said Florence quietly. "I hope you will; indeed, I am sure you will, for I shall never marry. So don't bother to put me on the books—I'm not on the market. Good-night."

She sought out poor Daniel, who, awed by the culture and standing of his five sons-in-law, not to speak of the guests, was hanging about the deserted supper-room, smoking cigar after cigar, much to the disgust of the caterer's men, who were waiting to spirit away the box.

Having duly kissed her father, little Schnapsie retired to bed to read Browning's love-poems. Her mother had to take a glass of champagne to restore her ruffled nerves to the appropriate ecstasy.

V

Poor portly Mrs. Peyser was not destined to enjoy her harvest of happiness for more than a few years. But these years were an overbrimming cup, with only the bitter drop of Florence's heretical indifference to the Young Man. Environed by the six households which she had begotten, Mrs. Peyser breathed that atmosphere of ebullient babyhood which was the breath of her Jewish nostrils; babies appeared almost every other month. It was a seething well-spring of healthy life. Religious ceremonies connected with these chubby new-comers, or medical recipes for their bodily salvation, absorbed her. But her exuberant grandmotherliness usually received a check in the summer, when the babies were deported to scattered sea-shores; and thus it came to pass that the summer of her death found her still lingering in London with a bad cold, with only Daniel and little Schnapsie at hand. And before the others could be called, Mrs. Peyser passed away in peace, in the old Portsmouth bed, overlooked by the old Hebrew picture exiled from the London dining-room.

It was a curious end. She did not know she was dying, but Daniel was anxious she should not be reft into silence before she had made the immemorial proclamation of the Unity. At the same time he hesitated to appall her with the grim knowledge.

He was blubbering piteously, yet striving to hide his sobs. The early days of his struggle came back, the first weeks of wedded happiness, then the long years of progressive prosperity and godly cheerfulness in Portsmouth ere she had grown fashionable and he unimportant; and a vast self-pity mingled with his pitiful sense of her excellencies—the children she had borne him in agony, the economy of her house management, the good bargains she had driven with the clod-pated soldiers and sailors, the later splendour of her social achievement.

And little Schnapsie wept with a sense of the vanity of these dual existences to which she owed her own empty life.

Suddenly Mrs. Peyser, over whose black eyes a glaze had been stealing, let the long dark eyelashes fall over them.

"Sarah!" whispered Daniel frantically. "Say the Shemang!"

"Hear, O Israel, the Lord our God, the Lord is one," said the sensuous lips obediently.

Little Schnapsie shrugged her shoulders rebelliously. The dogma seemed so irrelevant.

Mrs. Peyser opened her eyes, and a beautiful mother-light came into them as she saw the weeping girl.

"Ah, Florrie, do not fret," she said reassuringly, in her long lapsed Yiddish. "I will find thee a bridegroom."

Her eyes closed, and little Schnapsie shuddered with a weird image of a lover fetched from the shrouded dead.

VI

After his Sarah had been lowered into "The House of Life," and the excitement of the tombstone recording her virtues had subsided, Daniel would have withered away in an empty world but for little Schnapsie. The two kept house together; the same big house that had reeked with so much feminine life, and about which the odours of perfumes and powders still seemed to linger. But father and daughter only met at meals. He spent hours over the morning paper, with the old quaint delusions about India and other things he read of, and he pottered about the streets, or wandered into the Beth-Hamidrash, which a local fanatic had just instituted in North London, and in which, under the guidance of a Polish sage, Daniel strove to concentrate his aged wits on the ritual problems of Babylon. At long intervals he brushed his old-fashioned high hat carefully, and timidly rang the bell of one of his daughters' mansions, and was permitted to caress a loudly remonstrating baby; but they all lived so far from him and one another in this mighty London. From Sylvia's, where there was a boy with buttons, he had always been frightened off, and when the others began to emulate her, his visits ceased altogether. As for the sisters coming to see him, all pleaded overwhelming domestic duty, and the frigidity of Florence's reception of them. "Now if you lived alone—or with one of us!" But somehow Daniel felt the latter alternative would be as desolate as the former. And though he knew some wide vague river flowed between even his present housemate's life and his own, yet he felt far more clearly the bridge of love over which their souls passed to each other.

Figure then the septuagenarian's amaze when, one fine morning, as he was shuffling about in his carpet slippers, the servant brought him word that his six daughters demanded his instantaneous presence in the drawing-room.

The shock drove out all thoughts of toilet; his heart beat quicker with a painful premonition of he knew not what. This simultaneous visit recalled funerals, weddings. He looked out of a window and saw four carriages drawn up, and that completed his sense of something elemental. He tottered into the drawing-room—grown dingy now that it had no more daughters to dispose of—and shrank before the resplendence with which their presence reinvested it. They rustled with silks, shone with gold necklaces, and impregnated the air with its ancient aroma of powders and perfumes. He felt himself dwindling before all this pungent prosperity, like some more creative Frankenstein before a congress of his own monsters.

They did not rise as he entered. The Jewish group and the pagan group were promiscuously seated—marriage had broken down all the ancient landmarks. They all looked about the same agelessness—a standstill buxom matronhood.

Daniel stood at the door, glancing from one to another. Some coughed; others fidgeted with muffs.

"Sit down, sit down, father," said Rachael kindly, though she retained the arm-chair—and there was a general air of relief at her voice. But the old embarrassment returned as the silence reëstablished itself when Daniel had drooped into a stiff chair.

At last Leah took the word: "We have come while Florrie is at her slumming—"

"At her slumming!" repeated Sylvia, with more significance, and a meaning smile spread over the six faces.

"Yes?" Daniel murmured.

"—Because we did not want her to know of our coming."

"It concerns Schnapsie?" he murmured.

"Yes, your little Schnapsie," said Daisy viciously.

"Yes; she has no time to come and see us," cried Rebecca. "But she has plenty of time for her—slumming."

"Well, she does good," he murmured apologetically.

"A fat lot of good!" sniggered Rachael.

"To herself!" corrected Lily.

"I do not understand," he muttered uneasily.

"Well—" began Lily. "You tell him, Leah; you know more about it."

"You know as much as I do."

He looked appealingly from one to the other.

"I always said the slums were dangerous places for people of our class," said Sylvia. "She doesn't even confine herself to her own people."

The faces began to lighten—evidently they felt the ice broken.

"Dangerous!" he repeated, catching at the ominous word.

"Dreadful!" in a common shudder.

He half rose. "You have bad news?" he cried.

The faces gloomed over, the heads nodded.

"About Schnapsie?" he shrieked, jumping up.

"Sit down, sit down; she's not dead," said Leah contemptuously.

He sat down.

"Well, what is it? What has happened?"

"She's engaged!" In Leah's mouth the word sounded like a death-bell.

"Engaged!" he breathed, with a glimmering foreboding of the horror.

"To a Christian!" said Daisy brutally.

He sank back, pale and trembling. A tense silence fell on the room.

"But how? Who?" he murmured at last.

The girls recovered themselves. Now they were all speaking at once.

"Another slummer."

"He's the son of an archdeacon."

"An awful Christian crank."

"And that's your pet Schnapsie."

"If we had wanted Christians, we could have been married twenty years ago."

"It's a terrible disgrace for us."

"She doesn't consider us in the least."

"She'll be miserable, anyhow. When they quarrel, he'll always throw it up to her that she's a Jewess."

"And wouldn't join our Daughters of Mercy committee—had no time."

"Wasn't going to marry—turned up her nose at all the Jewish young men!"

"But she would have told me!" he murmured hopelessly. "I don't believe it. My little Schnapsie!"

"Don't believe it?" snorted Leah. "Why, she didn't even deny it."

"Have you spoken to her, then?"

"Have we spoken to her! Why, she says Judaism is all nonsense! She will disgrace us all."

The blind racial instinct spoke through them—the twenty-five centuries of tested separateness. But Daniel felt in super-addition the conscious religious horror.

"But is she to be married in a Christian church?" he breathed.

"Oh, she isn't going to marry—yet."

His poor heart fluttered at the reprieve.

"She doesn't care a pin for our feelings," went on Leah. "But of course she won't marry while you are alive."

Lily took up the thread. "We all told her if she'd only marry a Jew, we'd all be glad to have you—in turn. But she said it wasn't that. She could have you herself; her Alfred wouldn't mind. It's the shock to your religious feelings that keeps her back. She doesn't want to hurt you."

"God bless her, my good little Schnapsie!" he murmured. His dazed brain did not grasp all the bearings, was only conscious of a vast relief.

Disgust darkened all the faces.

He groped to understand it, putting his hand over the white hairs that straggled from his skull-cap.

"But then—then it's all right."

"Yes, all right," said Leah brutally. "But for how long?"

Her meaning seized him like an icy claw upon his heart. For the first time in his life he realized the certainty of death, and simultaneously with the certainty its imminence.

"We want you to put a stop to it now," said Sylvia. "For our sakes make her promise that even when—You're the only one who has any influence over her."

She rose, as if to wind up the painful interview, and the others rose, too, with a multiplex rustling of silken skirts. He shook the six jewelled hands as in a dream, and promised to do his best; and as he watched the little procession of carriages roll off, it seemed to him indeed a funeral, and his own.

VII

Ah God, that it should have come to this. Little Schnapsie could not be happy till he was dead. Well, why should he keep her waiting? What mattered the few odd years or months? He was already dead. There was his funeral going down the street.

To speak to Schnapsie he had never intended, even while he was promising it. Those years of silent life together had made real conversation impossible. The bridge on which his soul passed over to hers was a bridge over which hung a sacred silence. Under the weight of words, especially of angry parental words, it might break down forever. And that would be worse than death.

No; little Schnapsie had her own life, and he somehow knew he had not the right to question it, even though it seemed on the verge of deadly sin. He could not have expressed it in logical speech, was not even clearly conscious of it; but his tender relation with her had educated him to a sense of her moral rightness, which now survived and subsisted with his conviction that she was hopelessly astray. No, he had not the right to interfere with her life, with her prospect of happiness in her own way. He must give up living. Little Schnapsie must be nearly thirty; the best of her youth was gone. She should be happy with this strange man.

But if he killed himself, that would bring disgrace on the family—and little Schnapsie. Perhaps, too, Alfred would not marry her. Was there no way of slipping quietly out of existence? But then suicide was another deadly sin. If only that had really been his funeral procession!

"O God, God of Israel, tell me what to do!"

VIII

A sudden inspiration leapt to his heart. She should not have to wait for his death to be happy; he would live to see her happy. He would pretend that her marriage cost him no pang; indeed, would not truly the pang be swallowed up in the thought of her happiness? But would she be happy? Could she be happy with this alien? Ah, there was the chilling doubt! If a quarrel came, would not the man always throw it in her face that she was a Jewess? Well, that must be left to herself. She was old enough not to rush into misery. Through all these years he had taken her pensive brow as the seat of all wisdom, her tender eyes as the glow of all goodness, and he could not suddenly readjust himself to a contradictory conception. By the time she came in he had composed himself for his task.

"Ah, my dear," he said, with a beaming smile, "I have heard the good news."

The answering smile died out of her eyes. She looked frightened.

"It's all right, little Schnapsie," he said roguishly. "So now I shall have seven sons-in-law. And Alfred the Second, eh?"

"You have heard?"

"Yes," he said, pinching her ear. "Thinks she can keep anything from her old father, does she?"

"But do you know that he is a—a—"

"A Christian? Of course. What's the difference, as long as he's a good man, eh?" He laughed noisily.

Little Schnapsie looked more frightened than ever. Were her father's wits wandering at last?

"But I thought—"

"Thought I would want you to sacrifice yourself! No, no, my dear; we are not in India, where women are burnt alive to please their dead husbands."

Little Schnapsie had an irrelevant vision of herself treading on diamonds and gold. She murmured, "Who told you?"

"Leah."

"Leah! But Leah is angry about it!"

"So she is. She came to me in a tantrum, but I told her whatever little Schnapsie did was right."

"Father!" With a sudden cry of belief and affection she fell on his neck and kissed him. "But isn't the darling old Jew shocked?" she said, half smiling, half weeping.

Cunning lent him clairvoyance. "How much Judaism is there in your sisters' husbands?" he said. "And without the religion, what is the use of the race?"

"Why, father, that's what I'm always preaching!" she cried, in astonishment. "Think what our Judaism was in the dear old Portsmouth days. What is the Sabbath here? A mockery. Not one of your sons-in-law closes his business. But there, when the Sabbath came in, how beautiful! Gradually it glided, glided; you heard the angel's wings. Then its shining presence was upon you, and a holy peace settled over the house."

"Yes, yes." His eyes filled with tears. He saw the row of innocent girl faces at the white Sabbath table. What had London and prosperity brought him instead?

"And then the Atonement days, when the ram's horn thrilled us with a sense of sin and judgment, when we thought the heavenly scrolls were being signed and sealed. Who feels that here, father? Some of us don't even fast."

"True, true." He forgot his part. "Then you are a good Jewess still?"

She shook her head sadly. "We have outlived our destiny. Our isolation is a meaningless relic."

But she had kindled a new spark of hope.

"Can't you bring him over to us?"

"To what? To our empty synagogues?"

"Then you are going over to him?" He tried to keep his voice steady.

"I must; his father is an archdeacon."

"I know, I know," he said, though she might as well have said an archangel.

"But you do not believe in—in—"

"I believe in self-sacrifice; that is Christianity."

"Is it? I thought it was three Gods."

"That is not the essential."

"Thank God!" he said. Then he added hurriedly: "But will you be happy with him? Such different bringing up! You can't really feel close to him."

She laughed and blushed. "There are deeper things than one's bringing up, father."

"But if after marriage you should have a quarrel, he would always throw up to you that you are a Jewess."

"No, Alfred will never do that."

"Then make haste, little Schnapsie, or your old father won't live to see you under the canopy."

She smiled happily, believing him. "But there won't be any canopy," she said.

"Well, well, whatever it is," he laughed back, with horrid imagining that it might be a Cross.

IX

It was agreed between them that, to avoid endless family councils, the sisters should not be told, and that the ceremony should be conducted as privately as possible. The archdeacon himself was coming up to town to perform the ceremony in the church of another of his sons in Chalk Farm. After the short honeymoon, Daniel was to come and live with the couple in Whitechapel, for they were to live in the centre of their labours. Poor Daniel tried to find some comfort in the thought that Whitechapel was a more Jewish and a homelier quarter than Highbury. But the unhomely impression produced upon him by his latest son-in-law neutralized everything. All his other sons-in-law had more or less awed him, but beneath the awe ran a tunnel of brotherhood. With this Alfred, however, he was conscious of a glacial current, which not all the young man's cordiality could tepefy.

"Are you sure you will be happy with him, little Schnapsie?" he asked anxiously.

"You dear worrying old thing!"

"But if after marriage you quarrel, he will always throw it up to you that you are—"

"And I'll throw it up to him that he is a Christian, and oughtn't to quarrel."

He was silenced. But his heart thanked God that his dear old wife had been spared the coming ordeal.

"This too was for good," he murmured, in the Hebrew proverb.

And so the tragic day drew nigh.

X

One short week before, Daniel was wandering about, dazed by the near prospect. An unholy fascination drew him toward Chalk Farm, to gaze on the church in which the profane union would be perpetrated. Perhaps he ought even to go inside; to get over his first horror at being in such a building, so as not to betray himself during the actual ceremony.

As he drew near the heathen edifice he saw a striped awning, carriages, a bustle of people entering, a pressing, peeping crowd. A wedding!

Ah, good! There was no doubt now he must go in; he would see what this unknown ceremony in this unknown building was like. It would be a sort of rehearsal; it would help to steel him at the tragic moment. He was passing through the central doors with some other men, but a policeman motioned them to a side door. He shuffled timidly within.

Full as the church was, the chill stone spaces struck cold to his heart; all the vast alien life they typified froze his soul. The dread word Meshumad—apostate—seemed echoing and reëchoing from the cold pillars. He perceived his companions had bared their heads, and he hastily snatched off his rusty beaver. The unaccustomed sensation in his scalp completed his sense of unholiness.

Nothing seemed going on yet, but as he slipped into a seat in the aisle he became aware of an organ playing joyous preludes, almost jiggish. For a moment he wondered dully what there was to be gay about, and his eyes filled with bitter tears.

A craning forward in the nondescript congregation made the old man peer forward.

He saw, at the far end of the church, a sort of platform upon which four men, in strange, flowing robes, stood under a cross. He hid his eyes from the sight of the symbol that had overshadowed his ancestors' lives. When he opened his eyes again the men were kneeling. Would he have to kneel, he wondered.

Would his old joints have to assume that pagan posture? Presently four bridesmaids, shielded by great glowing bouquets, appeared on the platform, and descending, passed with measured theatric pace down the farther avenue, too remote for his clear vision. His neighbours stood up to stare at them, and he rose, too. And throughout the organ bubbled out its playful cadenzas.

A stir and a buzz swept through the church. A procession began to file in. At its head was a pale, severe young man, supported by a cheerful young man. Other young men followed; then the bridesmaids reappeared. And finally—target of every glance—there passed a glory of white veil supported by an old military looking man in a satin waistcoat.

Ah, that would be he and Schnapsie, then. Up that long avenue, beneath all these curious Christian eyes, he, Daniel Peyser, would have to walk. He tried to rehearse it mentally now, so that he might not shame her; he paced pompously and stiffly, with beautiful Schnapsie on his arm, a glory of white veil. He saw himself slowly reaching the platform, under the chilling cross; then everything swam before him, and he sank shuddering into his seat. His little Schnapsie! She was being sucked up into all this hateful heathendom, to the seductive music of satanic orchestras.

He sat in a strange daze, vaguely conscious that the organ had ceased, and that some preacher's recitative had begun instead. When he looked up again, the bridal party before the altar loomed vague, as through a mist. He passed his hand over his clouded brow. Of a sudden a sentence of the recitative pierced sharply to his brain:—

"Therefore if any man can show any just cause why they may not lawfully be joined together, let him now speak, or else hereafter forever hold his peace."

O God of Israel! Then it was the last chance! He sprang to his feet, and shouted in agony: "No, no, she must not marry him! She must not!"

All heads turned toward the shabby old man. An electric shiver ran through the church. The bride paled; a bridesmaid shrieked; the minister, taken aback, stood silent. A white-gloved usher hurried up.

"Do you forbid the banns?" called the minister.

The old man's mind awoke, and groped mistily.

"Come, what have you to say?" snapped the usher.

"I—I—nothing," he murmured in awed confusion.

"He is drunk," said the usher. "Out with you, my man." He hustled Daniel toward the side door, and let it swing behind him.

But Daniel shrank from facing the cordon of spectators outside. He hung miserably about the vestibule till the Wedding March swelled in ironic triumph, and the human outpour swept him into the street.

XI

His abstracted look, his ragged talk, troubled Schnapsie at the evening meal, but she could not elicit that anything had happened.

In the evening paper, her eye, avid of marriage items, paused on a big-headed paragraph.

"I FORBID THE BANNS!"
STRANGE SCENE AT A CHALK FARM CHURCH.

When she had finished the paragraph and read another, the first began to come back to her, shadowed with a strange suspicion. Why, this was the very church—? A Jewish-looking old man—! Great heavens! Then all this had been mere pose, self-sacrifice. And his wits were straying under the too heavy burden! Only blind craving for her own happiness could have made her believe that the mental habits of seventy years could be broken off.

"Well, father," she said brightly, "you will be losing me very soon now."

His lips quivered into a pathetic smile.

"I am very glad." He paused, struggling with himself. "If you are sure you will be happy!"

"But haven't we talked that over enough, father?"

"Yes—but you know—if a quarrel arose, he would always throw it up—that—"

"Nonsense, nonsense," she laughed. But the repetition of the old thought struck her poignantly as a sign of maundering wits.

"And you are sure you will get along together?"

"Quite sure."

"Then I am glad." He drew her to him, and kissed her.

She broke down and wept under the conviction of his lying. He became the comforter in his turn.

"Don't cry, little Schnapsie, don't cry. I didn't mean to frighten you. Alfred is a good man, and I am sure, even if you quarrel, he will never throw it—" The mumbling passed into a kiss on her wet cheek.

XII

That night, after a long passionate vigil in her bedroom, little Schnapsie wrote a letter:—

"DEAREST ALFRED—This will be as painful for you to read as for me to write. I find at the eleventh hour I cannot marry you. I owe it to you to state my reason. As you know, I did not consent to our love being crowned by union till my father had given his consent. I now find that this consent was not the free outcome of my father's soul, that it was only to promote my happiness. Try to imagine what it means for an old man of seventy odd years to wrench himself away from all his life-long prejudices, and you will realize what he has been trying to do for me. But the wrench was beyond his strength. He is breaking his heart over it, and, I fear, even wandering in his mind.

"You will say, let us again consent to wait for a contingency which I am not cold-blooded enough to set down more openly. But I do not think it is fair to you to let you risk your happiness further by keeping it entangled with mine. A new current of thought has been set going in my mind. If a religion that I thought all formalism is capable of producing such types of abnegation as my dear father, then it must, too, somewhere or other, hold in solution all those ennobling ingredients, all those stimuli to self-sacrifice, which the world calls Christian. Perhaps I have always misunderstood. We were so badly taught. Perhaps the prosaic epoch of Judaism into which I was born is only transitional, perhaps it only belongs to the middle classes, for I know I felt more of its poetry in my childhood; perhaps the future will develop (or recultivate) its diviner sides and lay more stress upon the life beautiful, and thus all this blind instinct of isolation may prove only the conservation of the race for its nobler future, when it may still become, in very truth, a witness to the Highest, a chosen people in whom all the families of the earth may be blessed. I do not know; all this is very confused and chaotic to me to-night. I only know I can hold out no certain hope of the earthly fulfilment of our love. I, too, feel in transition, and I know not to what. But, dearest Alfred, shall we not be living the Christian life—the life of abnegation—more truly if we give up the hope of personal happiness? Forgive me, darling, the pain I am causing you, and thus help me to bear my own.

"Your friend till death,
"FLORENCE."

It was an hour past midnight ere the letter was finished, and when it was sealed a sense of relief at remaining in the Jewish fold stole over her, though she would scarcely acknowledge it to herself, and impatiently analyzed it away as hereditary. And despite it, if she slept on the letter, would it ever be posted?

But the house was sunk in darkness. She was the only creature stirring. And yet she yearned to have the thing over, irrevocable. Perhaps she might venture out herself with her latch-key. There was a letter-box at the street corner. She lit a candle and stole out on the landing, casting a monstrous shadow which frightened her. In her over-wrought mood it almost seemed an uncanny creature grinning at her. Her mother's death-bed rose suddenly before her; her mother's voice cried: "Ah, Florrie, do not fret. I will find thee a bridegroom." Was this the bridegroom—was this the only one she would ever know?

"Father! father!" she shrieked, with sudden terror.

A door was thrown open; a figure shambled forth in carpet slippers—a dear, homely, reassuring figure—holding the coloured handkerchief which had helped to banish him from the drawing-room. His face was smeared; his eyelids under the pushed-up horn spectacles were red: he, too, had kept vigil.

"What is it? What is it, little Schnapsie?"

"Nothing. I—I—I only wanted to ask you if you would be good enough to post this letter—to-night."

"Good enough? Why, I shall enjoy a breath of air."

He took the letter and essayed a roguish laugh as his eye caught the superscription.

"Ho! ho!" He pinched her cheek. "So we mustn't let a day pass without writing to him, eh?"

She quivered under this unforeseen misconception.

"No," she echoed, with added firmness, "we mustn't let a day pass."

"But go to bed at once, little Schnapsie. You look quite pale. If you stay up so late writing him letters, you won't make him a beautiful bride."

"No," she repeated, "I won't make him a beautiful bride."

She heard the hall door close gently upon his cautious footsteps, and her eyes dimmed with divine tears as she thought of the joy that awaited his return.

III

NOAH'S ARK

I

On a summer's day toward the close of the first quarter of the nineteenth century after Christ, Peloni walked in "the good place" of the Frankfort Judengasse and pondered. At times he came to a standstill and appeared to study the inscriptions on the tumbled tombstones, or the carven dragons, shields, and stars, but his black eyes burnt inward and he saw less the tragedy of Jewish death than the tragedy of Jewish life.

For "the good place" was the place of death.

Here alone in Frankfort—in this shut-in bit of the shut-in Jew-street—was true peace for Israel. The rest of the Jew-street offered comparative tranquillity even for the living; yet when, ninety years before Peloni was born, the great fire had raged therein, the inhabitants had locked the Ghetto-gate against the Christians, less fearful of the ravaging flames than of their fellow-citizens. Even to-day, if he ventured outside the Judengasse, Peloni must tread delicately. The foot-path was not for him: he must plod on the dusty road, with all the other beasts. In some places the very road was too holy for him, and any passer-by might snatch off his hat in punishment for his breaking bounds. The ragged street urchin or the staggering drunkard might cry to him "'Jud,' mach mores: Jew, mind your manners."

Some ten years ago the Frankfort Ghetto had been verbally abolished by a civilized archduke, caught up in the wave of Napoleonic toleration. Peloni had shared in the exultation of the Jews at the final dissipation of the long night of mediævalism. He had written a Hebrew poem on it, brilliantly rhymed, congested with apt quotations from Bible and Talmud, the whole making an acrostic upon the name of the enlightened Karl Theodor von Dalberg. Henceforth Israel would take his place among the peoples, honour on his brow, love in his heart, manhood in his limbs. A gracious letter of acknowledgment from the archduke was displayed in the window of Peloni's little bookselling establishment, amid the door-amulets, phylacteries, praying-shawls, Purim-scrolls, and Hebrew volumes.

But now the prince had been ousted, Napoleon was dead, everywhere the Ghetto-gates were locked again, and the Poem lay stacked on the remainder shelves. In vain had the grateful Jews hastened to fight for the Fatherland, tendered it body and soul. Poor little curly-haired Peloni had been attacked in the streets as an alien that very morning. Roysterers had raised the old cry of "Hep! Hep!"—fatal, immemorial cry, ghastly heritage of the Crusades. Century after century that cry had gone echoing through Europe. Century after century the Jews thought they had lived it down, bought it down, died it down. But no! it rose again, buoyant, menacing, irresponsible. Ah, what a fool he had been to hope! There was no hope.

Rarely, indeed, since the Dark Ages had persecution flaunted itself so openly. Riots and massacres were breaking out all over Germany, and in his own Ghetto Peloni had seen sights that had turned his patriotism to gall, and crushed his trust in the Christian, his beautiful bubble-dreams of the Millennium. Rothschild himself, whose house in the Judengasse with the sign of the red shield had been the centre of the attack, was well-nigh unable to maintain his position in the town. And these local successes inflamed the Jew-haters everywhere. "Let the children of Israel be sold to the English," recommended a popular pamphlet of the period, "who could employ them in their Indian plantations instead of the blacks. The best plan would be to purge the land entirely of this vermin, either by exterminating them, or, as Pharaoh, and the people of Meiningen, Würzburg, and Frankfort did, by driving them from the country."

"Oh, God!" thought Peloni, as his mind ran over the long chain from Pharaoh to Frankfort. "Evermore to wander, stoned and derided! Thou hast set a mark on his forehead, but his punishment is greater than he can bear."

The dead lay all around him, one upon another, new red stones shouldering aside the gray stones that told to boot of the death of the centuries. And the pressure of all this struggle for death-room had raised the earth higher than the adjacent paths. He thought of how these dead had always come here; even in their lifetime, when the enemy raged outside. Here they had put the women and children and gone back to the synagogue to pray. Ah, the cowards! always oscillating betwixt cemetery and synagogue, why did they not live, why did they not fight? Yes, but they had fought—fought for Germany, and this was Germany's reply.

But could they not fight for themselves then, with money, with the sinews of war, if not with the weapons; with gold, if not with steel? could they not join financial forces all through the world? But no! There was no such solidarity as the Christians dreamed. And they were too mixed up with the European world to dream of self-concentration. Even while the Frankfort Rothschild's house was surrounded by rioters, the Paris Rothschild was giving a ball to the élite of diplomatic society.

No! the old Jews were right—there was only the synagogue and the cemetery.

But was there even the synagogue? That, too, was dead. The living faith, the vivid realization of Israel's hope, which had made the Dark Ages endurable and even luminous, were only to be found now among fanatics whose blind ignorance and fierce clinging to the dead letter and the obsolete form counterbalanced the poetry and sublimity of their persistence. In the Middle Ages, Peloni felt, his poems would have been absorbed into the liturgy. For when the liturgy and the religion were alive, they took in and gave out—like all living things. But no—the synagogue of to-day was dead.

Remained only the cemetery.

"Jude, verrek!" Jew, die like a beast.

Yes, what else was there to do? For he was not even a Rothschild, he told himself with whimsical anguish; only a poor poet, unread, unknown, unhealthy; a shadow that only found substance to suffer; a set of heart-strings across which every wind that blew made a poignant, passionate music; a lamentation incarnate, a voice of weeping in the wilderness, a bubble blown of tears, a dream, a mist, a nobody—in short, Peloni!

The dead generations drew him. He fell, weeping passionately, upon a tomb.

II

There seemed an unwonted stir in the Judengasse when Peloni returned to it. Was there another riot threatening? he thought, as he passed along the narrow street of three-storied frame houses, most of them gabled, and all marked by peculiar signs and figures—the Bear or the Lion or the Garlic or the Red Shield (Rothschild)!

Outside the synagogue loitered a crowd, and as he drew near he perceived that there was a long Proclamation in a couple of folio sheets nailed on the door. It was doubtless this which was being discussed by the little groups he had already noted. About the synagogue door the throng was so thick that he could not get near enough to read it himself. But fortunately some one was engaged in reading it aloud for the benefit of those on the outskirts.

"'Wherefore I, Mordecai Manuel Noah, Citizen of the United States of America, late Consul of said States to the City and Kingdom of Tunis, High Sheriff of New York, Counsellor-at-Law, and by the Grace of God Governor and Judge of Israel, have issued this my proclamation.'"

A derisive laugh from a dwarfish figure in the crowd interrupted the reading. "Father Noah come to life again!" It was the Possemacher, or wedding-jester, who was not sparing of his wit, even when not professionally engaged.

"A foreigner—an American!" sneered a more serious voice. "Who made him ruler in Israel?"

"That's what the wicked Israelite asked Moses!" cried Peloni, curiously excited.

"Nun, nun! Go on!" cried others.

"'Announcing to the Jews throughout the world, that an asylum is prepared and hereby offered to them, where they can enjoy that Peace, Comfort, and Happiness which have been denied them through the intolerance and misgovernment of former ages. An asylum in a free and powerful country, where ample protection is secured to their persons, their property, and religious rights; an asylum in a country remarkable for its vast resources, the richness of its soil, and the salubrity of its climate; where industry is encouraged, education promoted, and good faith rewarded. "A land of Milk and Honey," where Israel may repose in Peace, under his "Vine and Fig tree," and where our People may so familiarize themselves with the science of government and the lights of learning and civilization, as may qualify them for that great and final Restoration to their ancient heritage, which the times so powerfully indicate.'"

The crowd had grown attentive. Peloni's face was pale as death. What was this great thing, fallen so unexpectedly from the impassive heaven his hopelessness had challenged?

But the Possemacher captured the moment. "Father Noah's drunk again!"

A great laugh shook the crowd. But Peloni dug his nails into his palms. "Read on! Read on!" he cried hoarsely.

"'The Place of Refuge is in the State of New York, the largest in the American Union, and the spot to which I invite my beloved People from the whole world is called Grand Island.'"

Peloni drew a deep breath. His face had now changed to the other extreme and was flushed with excitement.

"Noah's Ark!" shot the Possemacher dryly, and had his audience swaying hysterically.

"For God's sake, brethren!" cried Peloni. "This is no joke. Have you forgotten already that here we are only animals?"

"And they went in two by two," said the Possemacher, "the clean beasts, and the unclean beasts!"

"Hush, hush, let us hear!" from some of the crowd.

"'Here I am resolved to lay the foundation of a State, named Ararat.'"

"Ah! what did I say?" the exultant Possemacher shrieked at Peloni.

"Ha! ha! ha!" laughed the crowd. "Noah's Ark resting on Ararat!" The dullest saw that.

Peloni was taken aback for a moment.

"But why should not the place of Israel's Ark of Refuge be named Ararat?" he asked of his neighbours.

"If only his name wasn't Noah!" they answered.

"That makes it even more appropriate," he murmured.

But "Noah's Ark" was the nickname that kills. Though the reader continued, it was only to an audience exhilarated by a sense of Arabian Nights fantasy. But the elaborate description of the grandeurs of this Grand Island, and the eloquent passages about the Century of Right, and the ancient Oracles, restored Peloni's enthusiasm to fever heat.

"It is too long," said the reader, wearying at last.

Peloni rushed forward and took up the task. The first sentence exalted him still further.

"'In God's name I revive, renew, and reëstablish the government of the Jewish Nation, under the auspices and protection of the Constitution and the Laws of the United States, confirming and perpetuating all our Rights and Privileges, our Name, our Rank, and our Power among the nations of the Earth, as they existed and were recognized under the government of the Judges of Israel.'" Peloni's voice shook with fervour. As he began the next sentence, "'It is my will,'" he stretched out his hand with an involuntary regal gesture. The spirit of Noah was entering into him, and he felt almost as if it was he who was re-creating the Jewish nation—"'It is my will that a Census of the Jews throughout the world be taken, that those who are well treated and wish to remain in their respective countries shall aid those who wish to go; that those who are in military service shall until further orders remain true and loyal to their rulers.

"'I command'"—Peloni read the words with expansive magnificence, his poet's soul vibrating to that other royal dreamer's across the great Atlantic—"'that a strict Neutrality be maintained in the pending war betwixt Greece and Turkey.

"'I abolish forever'"—Peloni's hand swept the air—"'Polygamy among the Jews.'"

"But where have we polygamy?" interrupted the Possemacher.

"'As it is still practised in Africa and Asia,'" read on Peloni severely.

"I'm off at once for Africa and Asia!" cried the marriage-jester, pretending to run. "Good business for me there."

"You'll find better business in America," said Peloni scathingly. "For do not all our Austrian young men fly thither to marry, seeing that at home only the eldest son may found a family? A pretty fatherland indeed to be a citizen of—a step-fatherland. Listen, on the contrary, to the noble tolerance of the Jew. 'Christians are freely invited.'"

"Ah! Do you know who'll go?" broke in a narrow-faced zealot. "The missionaries."

Peloni continued hastily: "'Ararat is open, too, to the Caraites and the Samaritans. The Black Jews of India and Africa shall be welcome; our brethren in Cochin-China and the sect on the coast of Malabar; all are welcome.'"

"Ha! ha! ha!" laughed a burly Jew. "So we're to live with the blacks. Enough of this joke!"

But Peloni went on solemnly: "'A Capitation-tax on every Jew of Three Silver Shekels per annum—'"

"Ah, now we have got to it!" and a great roar broke from the crowd. "Not a bad Geschäft, eh?" and they winked. "He is no fool, this Noah."

Peloni's blood boiled. "Do you believe everybody is like yourselves?" he cried. "Listen!"

"'I do appoint the first day of next Adar for a Thanksgiving Day to the God of Israel, for His divine protection and the fulfilment of His promises to the House of Israel. I recommend Peace and Union among ourselves, Charity and Good-will to all, Toleration and Liberality toward our Brethren of all Religions—'"

"Didn't I say a missionary in disguise?" murmured the zealot.

Peloni ended, with tremulous emotion: "'I humbly entreat to be remembered in your prayers, and earnestly do I enjoin you to "keep the charge of the Holy God," to walk in His ways, to keep His Statutes and His commandments and His judgments and Testimonies, as written in the Laws of Moses; "that thou mayest prosper in all thou doest and whithersoever thou turnest thyself."

"'Given under our hand and seal in the State of New York, on the 2d of Ab 5586 in the Fiftieth Year of American Independence.'"

Peloni's efforts to organize a company of pilgrims to the New Jerusalem brought him only heart-ache. The very rabbi who had good-naturedly consented to circulate the fantastic foreigner's invitation, tapped his forehead significantly: "A visionary! of good intentions, doubtless, but still—a visionary. Besides, according to our dogmas, God alone knows the epoch of the Israelitish restoration; He alone will make it known to the whole universe, by signs entirely unequivocal; and every attempt on our part to reassemble with any political, national design, is forbidden as an act of high treason against the Divine Majesty. Mr. Noah has doubtless forgotten that the Israelites, faithful to the principles of their belief, are too much attached to the countries where they dwell, and devoted to the governments under which they enjoy liberty and protection, not to treat as a mere jest the chimerical consulate of a pseudo-restorer."

"Noah's a madman, and you're an infant," Peloni's friends told him.

"Since the destruction of the Temple," he quoted in retort, "the gift of prophecy has been confined to children and fools."

"You are giving up a decent livelihood," they warned him. "You are throwing it into the Atlantic."

"'Cast thy bread upon the waters and it shall return to thee after many days.'"

"But in the meantime?"

"'Man doth not live by bread alone.'"

"As you please. But don't ask us to throw up our comfortable home here."

"Comfortable home!" and Peloni grew almost apoplectic as he reminded them of their miseries.

"Persecution?" They shrugged their shoulders. "It comes only now and again, like a snow-storm, and we crawl through it."

"That's just it—the lack of manliness—the poisoned atmosphere!"

"Bah! The Goyim refuse us equal rights because they know we're their superiors. Let us not jump from the frying-pan into the fire."

So Peloni sailed for New York alone.

He was rather disappointed to find no other pilgrim even on the ship. True, there was one Jew, but the business Paradise of New York was his goal across this waste of waters, and of Noah's Ark he had never heard. Peloni's panegyric of Grand Island was rendered ineffective by his own nebulous conception of its commercial possibilities. He passed the slow days in the sailing-vessel polishing up his English, the literature of which he had long studied.

In New York Peloni's hopes revived. Major Noah—for it appeared he was an officer of militia likewise—was in everybody's mouth. Editor of the National Advocate, the leading organ of the Bucktails, or Tammany party, a journalist whose clever sallies and humorous paragraphs were widely enjoyed, an author of excellent "Travels," a playwright of the first distinction, whose patriotic dramas were always given on the Fourth of July, a critic regarded as Sir Oracle, a politician, lawyer, and man of the world, a wit, the gay centre of every gathering—surely in this lion of New York, who was also the Lion of David, Israel had at last found a deliverer. They called him madman down in Frankfort, did they? Well, let them come here and see.

He wrote home to the scoffers of the Judengasse all the information about the great man that was in the very air of the American city, though the man himself he had only as yet corresponded with. He told the famous story of how when Noah was canvassing for the office of High Sheriff of New York, it was urged that no Jew should be put into an office where he might have to hang a Christian, to which Noah had retorted wittily, "Pretty Christian, to have to be hanged!" "And you all fancied 'Father Noah' would fall to pieces before the Possemacher's wit!" Peloni commented with vengeful satisfaction. "I rejoice to say that Noah will never have anything to do with a Possemacher, for he is President of the Old Bachelors' Club, the members of which are pledged never to marry." He told of Noah's adventurous career: of how when he was a mere boy clerk in the auditor's office of his native Philadelphia, Congress had voted him a hundred dollars for his precocious preparation of the actuary tables for the eight-per-cent loan; of the three duels at Charleston, in which he had vindicated at once the courage of the Jew and the policy of American resistance to Great Britain; of his consulate in Tunis, his capture at sea by the British fleet during the war, his release on parole that enabled him to travel about England; of his genius for letters—a very David in Israel; of his generosity to hundreds of strugglers; of his quixotic disdain of money; of his impoverishing himself by paying two hundred thousand dollars of other people's debts as the price of his impulsive shrieval action in throwing open the doors of the Debtor's Jail when the yellow fever broke out within. "Yes," wrote Peloni exultantly, "in New York they talk no more of Shylock. And with all the temptations to Christian fellowship or Pagan free-living, a pillar of the synagogue—nay, Israel's one hope in all the world!"

It was a wonderful moment when Peloni, at last invited to call on the Judge of Israel, palpitated on the threshold of his study and gazed blinkingly at the great man enthroned before his writing-table amid elegant vistas of books and paintings. What a noble poetic vision it seemed to him: the broad brow, with the tumbled hair; the long, delicate-featured face tapering to a narrow chin environed with whiskers, but clean of beard or even of mustache, so that the mobile, sensitive mouth was laid bare. Peloni's glance also took in a handsome black coat, with a decoration on the lapel, a high-peaked collar, a black puffy bow, a frilled shirt, and a very broad jewelled cuff over a white, long-fingered hand, that held a tall quill with a great breadth of feather.

"Ah, come in," said the Governor of Israel, waving his quill. "You are Peloni of Frankfort."

"Come three thousand miles to kiss the hem of your garment."

Noah permitted the attention. "I am obliged to you for your Hebrew poem in honour of my project," he said urbanely. "I approve of Hebrew—it is a link that binds us to our forefathers. I am myself editing a translation of the Book of Jasher."

"You will have found my verses a very poor expression of your divine ideas."

"You use a difficult Hebrew. But the general drift seemed to show you had caught the greatness of my conception."

"Ah, yes! I have lived in Judengasse, oppressed and derided."

"But there is worse than oppression—there is inward stagnation of the spiritual life. My idea came to me in Tunis, where the Jews are little oppressed. You know President Madison appointed me consul of the United States for the city and kingdom of Tunis, one of the most respectable and interesting stations in the regencies of Barbary. I had long desired to visit the country of Dido and Hannibal, to trace the field of Zama, and seek out the ruins of Utica—whose sites I believe I have now successfully established—but it was my main design to investigate the condition of the Barbary Jews, of whom, you will remember, we have no account later than Benjamin of Tudela's in the thirteenth century. But do not stand — take a chair. Well, I found our brethren—to the number of seven hundred thousand—controlling everything in Barbary, farming the revenue, regulating the coinage, keeping the Dey's jewels and almost his person— in short, anything but persecuted, though, of course, the majority were miserably poor. They did not know I was a Jew—though Secretary Monroe recalled me because I was, and it was Monroe's doctrine that Judaism would be an obstacle to the discharge of my functions. Absurd! The Catholic priest was allowed to sprinkle the Consulate with holy water: the barefooted Franciscan received an alms, nor did I fail to acknowledge by a donation the decorated branch sent on Palm Sunday by the Greek Bishop. And as for the slaves, I assure you they were not backward in coming to ask favours. The only people who never came to me were precisely the Jews. I went about among them incognito, so to speak, like Haroun Alraschid among his subjects; hence I was able to see all the evils that will never be eliminated till Israel is again a nation."

"Ah! your words are the words of wisdom. You touch the root of the evil. It is what I have always told them."

Noah rose to his feet, displaying a royal stature in harmony with his broad shoulders. "Yes, I resolved it should be mine to elevate my people, to make them hold up their heads worthily in this century of freedom and enlightenment."

"It is the Ark of the Convenant, as well as of the Deluge, which will rest on Ararat!"

"True—and like the first Noah, I may become the progenitor of a new world. I have communications from the four corners of the earth. You are the type of thousands who will flee from the rotting tyrannies of Europe into the great free republic which I shall direct."

He began to pace the room. Peloni had visions of great black lines of pilgrims converging from every quarter of the compass.

"But this Grand Island—is it yours?" he inquired timidly.

"I have bought thousands of acres of it—I and a few others who believe in the great future of our people."

"Jews?"

"No, not Jews—capitalists who know that we shall become the commercial centre of the new world—that is, of the world of the future."

Peloni groaned. "And Jews will not believe? We must go to the Gentiles. Jews will only put their money into Gentile schemes; will build always for others, never for themselves. It is the same everywhere. Alas for Israel!"

"It is what I preach. Why administer Barbary for a savage Dey when you can administer Grand Island for yourself? Seven hundred thousand Jews in savage Barbary, and throughout these vast free States not seven thousand. Ah, but they will come; they will come. Ararat will gather its millions."

"But will there be room?"

"The State of New York," replied Noah, impressively, "is the largest in the Union, containing forty-three thousand two hundred and fourteen square miles divided into fifty-five counties and having six thousand and eighty-seven post-towns and cities together with six million acres of cultivated land. The constitution is founded on equality of rights. We recognize no religious differences. In our seven thousand free schools and gymnasia, four hundred thousand children of every religion are being educated. Here in this great and progressive State the long wandering of my beloved people shall end."

"But Grand Island itself?" murmured Peloni feebly.

"Come here," and Noah unrolled a great map. "See, how nobly it is situated in the Niagara River, near the world-famed Falls, which will supply water-power for our machinery. It is twelve miles long and from three to seven broad, and contains seventeen thousand acres. Lake Erie is two hundred and seventy miles long and borders New York, Pennsylvania, and Ohio, as well as Canada. And see! by navigable streams this great lake is connected with all that wonderful chain of lakes. By short canals we shall connect with the Illinois and Mississippi, and trade with New Orleans and the Gulf of Mexico. Through the Ontario—see here!—we traffic with Quebec, Montreal, and touch the great Atlantic. The Niagara Falls, as I said, turn our machinery. The fur trade, the lumber trade, all is ours. Our cattle multiply, our lands wave with harvests. We are the centre of the world, the capital of the future. And look! See what the Albany Gazette says: 'Here the Hebrews can have their Jerusalem without fearing the legions of Titus. Here they can erect their Temple without dreading the torches of frenzied soldiers. Here they can lay their heads on their pillows at night without fear of mobs, of bigotry and persecution.'"

Peloni drew a long breath, enraptured by this holy El Dorado, sparkling on the map, amid its tributary lakes and rivers.

"You will see the eighteenth chapter of Isaiah fulfilled," Noah went on. "For what is the 'land shadowing with wings, which is beyond the rivers of Ethiopia,' which shall send messengers to a nation scattered and peeled? What but America, shadowing us with the wings of its eagle? As it is written elsewhere, 'I will bear thee on eagle's wings.' It is true the English Bible translates 'Woe to the land,' but this is a mistranslation. It should be 'Hail to the land!' Also the word 'goumey' they translate 'bulrushes'—'that sendeth messengers in vessels of bulrushes!' But does not 'goumey' also mean 'rush, impetus?' And is it not therefore a prophecy of those new steam-vessels that are beginning to creep up, one of which has just crossed from England to India? Erelong they will be running between America and all the world. It is the Lord making ready for the easy ingathering of His people. Ay, and along these lakes"—the Prophet's finger swept the map—"will be heard the panting of mighty steam-monsters, all making for Ararat. By the way, Ararat lies here," and he indicated a spot of the island opposite Tonawanda on the mainland.

Peloni bent down and poetically pressed his lips to the spot, like Jehuda Halevi kissing the holy soil.

"There is no one in possession there?" he inquired anxiously.

"Maybe a few Iroquois Indians," said Noah. "But they will not have to be turned out like the Hittites and Amorites and Jebusites by our ancestors."

"No?" murmured Peloni.

"Of course not. They are our own brothers, carried away by the King of Assyria. There can be not the slightest doubt that the Red Indians are the Lost Ten Tribes of Israel."

"What?" cried Peloni, vastly excited.

"I shall publish a book on the subject. Yes, in worship, dialect, language, sacrifices, marriages, divorces, burials, fastings, purifications, punishments, cities of refuge, divisions of tribes, High-Priests, wars, triumphs—'tis our very tradition."

"Then I suppose one could lodge with them. I am anxious to settle in Ararat at once."

"You can scarcely settle there till the forest is cleared," said the great man, arching his eyebrows.

"The forest!" repeated Peloni, taken aback.

"Ah, you are dismayed. You are a European, accustomed to ready-made cities. We Americans, we change continents while you wait, build up Aladdin's palaces over-night. As soon as I can manage to go over the ground I will plan out the city."

"You haven't been there yet?" gasped Peloni.

"Ah, my dear Peloni. When should I find time to travel all the way to Buffalo—a busy editor, lawyer, playwright, what not? True, the time that other men give to domestic happiness the President of the Old Bachelors' Club is able to give to his fellow-men. But the slow canal voyage—"

At this moment there was a knock at the door, and a servant inquired if Major Noah could see his tailor.

"Ah, a good augury!" cried the major. "Here is the tailor come to try on my Robe of Governor and Judge of Israel."

The man bore an elaborate robe of crimson silk trimmed with ermine, which he arranged about Noah's portly person, making marks with pins and chalk where it could be made to fit better.

"Do you like it?" said Noah, puffing himself out regally.

Peloni's uneasiness vanished. Doubt was impossible before these magnificent realities. Ah! the Americans were wonderful.

"I had to go through our annals," Noah explained, "to find which period of our government we could revive. Kingship was opposed to the sentiment of these States: in the epoch of the Judges I found my ideal. Indeed, what is the President of the United States but a Shophet, a Judge of Israel? Ah, you are looking at that painting of me—I shall have to be done again in my new robes. That elegant creature who hangs beside me is Miss Leesugg, the Hebe of English actresses, as she appeared in my 'She would be a Soldier, or the Plains of Chippewa.' There is a caricature of my uncle, Aaron J. Phillips, as the Turkish Commander in my 'Grecian Captive.' Dear me, shall I ever forget how he tumbled off that elephant! Ha! ha! ha! That is Miss Johnson, in my 'Yusef Carmatti, or the Siege of Tripoli.' The black and white is a fancy sketch of 'Marion, or the Hero of Lake George,' a play I wrote for the reopening of the Park Theatre and to celebrate the evacuation of New York by the British in 1783."

"Ah, I was there, Major," said the tailor. "It was bully. But the house was so full of generals and colonels you could hardly hear a word."

"Fortunately for me," laughed Noah. "Yes, I asked them to come in full uniform for the éclat of the occasion. Which reminds me—here is a ticket for you."

"For the play?" murmured Peloni, as he took it.

Noah started and looked at him keenly. But his flush of anger faded before Peloni's innocent eyes. "No, no," he explained; "for the opening ceremony of the foundation of Ararat."

Peloni's black eyes shone.

"There will be a great crush and only ticket-holders can be admitted into the church."

"Into the church!" echoed Peloni, paling.

"Yes," said the Judge of Israel impressively, as he stood before a glass to adjust the graceful folds of his crimson robe. "Our fellow-citizens in Buffalo have been good enough to lend us the Episcopal Church for the ceremony."

"What ceremony?" he faltered, as horrid images swept before him, and he heard all the way from Frankfort the taunting cry of "Missionary!"

"The laying of the foundation-stone of Ararat."

"Laying the foundation-stone in a church!" Peloni was puzzled.

"Ah," said the Major, misunderstanding him; "it seems strange to you, nursed in the musty lap of Europe. But here in this land of freedom and this century of enlightenment all men are brothers."

"But surely the foundation-stone should be laid on Grand Island."

"It would have been desirable. But so many will wish to be present at this great celebration. Buffalo alone has some thirteen hundred inhabitants. How should we get them across? There are scarcely any boats to be had—and Ararat is twelve miles away. No, no, it is better to hold our ceremony in Buffalo. It is, after all, only a symbolism. The corner-stone is already being inscribed in Hebrew and English. 'Hear, O Israel, the Lord is our God. Ararat, a City of Refuge for the Jews, founded by Mordecai M. Noah in the month Tishri, corresponding with September, 1825, in the fiftieth year of American Independence.'"

The sonorous recitation by the Shophet in his crimson and ermine robe somewhat restored Peloni's equanimity.

"But when will the actual city be begun?" he asked.

The Shophet waved his hand airily. "A matter of days."

"But are you sure we can build there?"

"Look at the map. Here is Grand Island—ours! Here is the site of Ararat. It is all as plain as a pikestaff. And, talking of pikestaffs, it would not be a bad idea to plant a staff on Ararat with the flag of Israel."

Peloni took fire: "Yes, yes, let me go and plant it. I'll journey night and day."

"You shall plant it," said the Shophet graciously. "Yes, I'll have the flag made at once. The property man at the Park Theatre will attend to it for me. The Lion of Judah and seven stars."

"It shall be waving on Grand Island before you open the celebration in Buffalo."

Peloni went out like a lion, his head in the seven stars. Could it be possible that to him—Peloni—had fallen the privilege of proclaiming the New Jerusalem!

IV

After the bustle of New York, the scattered village of Buffalo was restful but somewhat chilling to the Ghetto-bred poet, with his quick brain, unaccustomed to the slow processes of nature. Buffalo—with its muddy, unpaved streets, and great trees, up which squirrel and chipmunk ran—was still half in and half out of mother earth; man's artifice ruled in the high street with its stores and inns, some of which were even of brick; but in the byways every now and then a primitive log cabin broke the line of frame cottages, and in the outskirts cows and pigs walked about unconcernedly. It was a reminder of all that would have to be done in Ararat ere a Temple could shine, like a lighthouse of righteousness to the tossing nations. But when Peloni learned that it was only twelve years since the scarcely born village had been burnt down by the British and Indians in the war, he felt reëncouraged, warming himself at the flame, so to speak. And when he found that the citizens were all agog about Ararat and the church celebration—that it divided interest with the Erie Canal, the hanging of the three Thayers, and the recent reception of General Lafayette at the Eagle Tavern—his heart expanded in a new poem.

It was indeed an auspicious moment for Noah's scheme. All eyes were turned on the coming celebration of the opening of the great canal, to be the terminus of which Buffalo had fought victoriously against Black Rock. Golden visions of the future gleamed almost tangibly; and amid the general magnificence Noah's ornate dream took on equal solidity. Endless capital would be directed into the neighbourhood of Buffalo—for Ararat was only twelve miles away. Besides, all the great men of Buffalo—and there were many—had been honoured with elaborate cards of invitation to the grand ceremony of the foundation-stone. A few old Baptist farmers were surly about the threatened vast Jewish immigration, but the majority proclaimed with righteous warmth that the glorious American Constitution welcomed all creeds, and that there was money in it.

Peloni looked about for a Jew to guide him, but could find none. Finally a Seneca Indian from the camp just below Buffalo undertook to look for the spot. It was with a strange thrill that Peloni's eyes rested for the first time on a red Indian. Was this indeed a long-lost brother of his? He cried "Shalom Aleikhem" in Hebrew, but the Indian, despite Noah's theories, did not seem to understand. Ultimately the dialogue was carried on in the few words of broken English which the Indian had picked up from the trappers, and in the gesture-language, in which, with his genius for all languages, Peloni was soon at home. And in truth he did find at heart some subtle sympathy with this copper-coloured savage which was not called out by the busy citizens of Buffalo. On a sunlit morning, bearing his flagstaff with the flag wrapped round it, a blanket, and a little store of provisions for camping out over-night, Peloni slipped into the birch canoe and the Indian paddled off. For miles they glided in silence along the sparkling Niagara, lone denizens of a lonely world.

Suddenly Peloni thought of the Judengasse of Frankfort, and for a moment it seemed to him that he must be dreaming. What! a few short months ago he was selling prayer-books and phylacteries in the shadow of the old high-gabled houses, and now, in a virgin district of the New World, in company with a half-naked red Indian, he was going to plant the flag of Judah on an island forest and to found the New Jerusalem. What would they say, his old friends, if they could see him now? And he—the Possemacher—what winged jest would he let fly? A perception of the monstrous fantasy of the thing stole on poor Peloni. Was he, perhaps, dreaming after all? No, there was the Niagara River, the village of Black Rock on his right hand, and on the other side of the gorge the lively Fort Erie and the poplar-fringed Canadian shore, and there too—on the map Noah had given him—Ararat lay waiting.

The Indian paddled imperturbably, throwing back the sparkling water with a soft, soothing sound. Peloni lapsed into more pleasurable reflections. How beautiful was this great free place of sun and wind, of water and forest, after the noisome Jew-street! He was not dreaming, nor—thank God!—was Noah. Strange, indeed, that thus should deliverance for Israel be wrought; yet what was Israel's history but a series of miracles? And his—Peloni's—humble hand was to plant the flag that had lain folded and inglorious these twenty centuries!

They glided by a couple of little islands, duly marked on the map, and then a great, wooded, dark purple mass rose to meet them with a band of deep orange on the low coast-line.

It was Grand Island.

Peloni whispered a prayer.

Obeying the map marked by Noah, the canoe glided round the island, keeping to the American side. As they shot past a third little island, a dull booming began to be audible.

"What is that?" Peloni's face inquired.

The Indian smiled. "Not go many miles farther," he indicated. "The Rapids soon. Then—whizz! Then big jump! Niagara. Dead."

Fortunately Ararat was due much sooner than Niagara. As they drew near the fourth of the little islands, which lay betwixt Grand Island and the mainland of the States, and saw the Tonawanda Creek emptying itself into the river, Peloni signed to the Indian to land; for it was here that Ararat was to arise.

The landing was easy, the river here being shallow and the bank low. The beauty of the spot, as it lay wild and fresh from God's hand in the golden sunlight, moved Peloni to tears. The Indian, who seemed curious as to his movements and willing to share his mid-day meal, tied his canoe to a basswood tree and followed the standard-bearer. There was a glorious medley of leafy life—elm, oak, maple, linden, pine, wild cherry, wild plum—which Peloni could only rejoice in without differentiating it by names; and as the oddly assorted couple walked through the sun-dappled glades they startled a world of scurrying animal life—snipe and plover and partridges and singing-birds, squirrels and rabbits and even deer, that frisked and fluttered unprescient of the New Jerusalem that menaced their immemorial inheritance. The joy of city-building had begun at last to dawn on Peloni, the immense pleasure to the human will of beginning afresh, of shaking off the pressure of the ages, of inscribing free ideas on the plastic universe. As he wandered at random in search of a suitable spot on which to plant the flagstaff, the romance of this great American world thrilled him, of this vast continent won acre by acre from nature and the savage, covering itself with splendid cities; a retrospective sympathy with the citizens of Buffalo and their coming canal warmed his breast.

Of a sudden he heard a screaming, and looking up he observed two strange, huge birds upon a blasted pine.

"Eagles," said the laconic Indian.

"Eagles!" And Peloni's heart leaped with a remembrance of Noah's words. "Here under their wings shall our flag be unfurled. And that blasted tree is Israel, that shall flourish again."

He dug the pole into the earth. A breeze caught the flag, and the folds flew out, and the Lion of Judah and the seven stars flapped in the face of an inattentive universe. Peloni intoned the Hebrew benediction, closing his eyes in pious ecstasy. "Blessed art Thou, O Lord our God, who hast kept us alive, and preserved us, and enabled us to reach this day!"

As he opened his eyes, he perceived in the distance high in air, rising far above the Island, a great mist of shining spray, amid which rainbows netted and tangled themselves in ineffable dream-like loveliness. At the same instant his ear caught—over the boom of the rapids—the first hint of another, a mightier, a more majestic roar.

"Niagara," murmured the Indian.

But Peloni's eyes were fixed on the celestial vision.

"The Shechinah!" he whispered. "The divine presence that rested on the Tabernacle, and on Solomon's Temple, and that has returned at last—to Ararat."

V

The booming of cannon from the Court House, and from the Terrace facing the lake, saluted the bright September dawn and reminded the citizens of Buffalo that the Messianic day was here. But they needed no reminding. The great folk had laid out their best clothes; military insignia and Masonic regalia had been furbished up. Troops guarded St. Paul's Church and kept off the swarming crowd.

The first act of the great historic drama—"Mordecai Manuel Noah; or, The Redemption of Israel"— passed off triumphantly, to the music of patriotic American airs. The procession, which marched at eleven from the Lodge through the chief streets, did honour to this marshaller of stage pageants.

ORDER OF PROCESSION

Grand Marshal, Col. Potter, on horseback.
Music.
Military.
Citizens.
Civil Officers.
State Officers in Uniform.
President and Trustees of the Corporation.
Tyler.
Stewards.
Entered Apprentices.
Fellow Crafts.
Master Masons.
Senior and Junior Deacons.
Secretary and Treasurer.
Senior and Junior Wardens.
Master of Lodges.
Past Masters.
Rev. Clergy.
Stewards, with corn, wine, and oil.

Principal Architect, with square, level, and plumb.
Bible.
Square and Compass, borne by a Master Mason.
The Judge of Israel
In black, wearing the judicial robes of crimson silk, trimmed with ermine, and a richly embossed golden medal suspended from the neck.
A Master Mason.
Royal Arch Masons.

Knights Templars.

At the church door there was a halt. The troops parted to right and left, the pageant passed through into the crowded church, gay with the summer dresses of the ladies, the band played the grand march from "Judas Maccabæus," the organ pealed out the "Jubilate." On the communion-table lay the corner-stone of Ararat!

The morning service was read by the Rev. Mr. Searle in full canonicals; the choir sang "Before Jehovah's Awful Throne"; then came a special prayer for Ararat, and passages from Jeremiah, Zephaniah, and the Psalms, charged with divine promises and consolations for the long suffering of Israel, idyllic pictures of the Messianic future, symbolized by the silver cups with wine, corn, and oil, that lay on the corner-stone. At last arose, with that crimson silk robe trimmed with ermine thrown over his stately black attire, and with the richly embossed golden medal hanging from his neck—the Master of the Show, the Dramatist of the Real, the Humorist without a sense of Humour, the Dreamer of the Ghetto and American Man of Action, the Governor and Judge of Israel, the Shophet—in brief, Mordecai Manuel Noah. He delivered a great discourse on the history of Israel and its present reorganization, which filled more than five columns of the newspapers, and was heard with solemn attention by the crowded Christian audience. Save a few Indians and his own secretary, not a single Jew was present to hold in check the orator's oriental imagination. Then the glittering procession filed back to the Lodge, and the brethren and the military dined joyously at the Eagle Tavern, and Noah's wit and humour returned for the after-dinner speech. He withdrew early in order to write a full account of the proceedings for the Buffalo Patriot Extra.

A salvo of twenty-four guns rounded off the great day of Israel's restoration.

VI

Meantime Peloni on his island awaited the coming of its Ruler. He heard faintly the cannonade that preceded and concluded the laying of the foundation-stone in the chancel of the church, and he expected Noah the next day at the latest. But the next day passed, and no Noah. Peloni fed on the remains of his corn and drank from the river, but though his Indian guide was gone and he was a prisoner, he had no fear of starvation, because he saw the wigwams of another Indian encampment across the river and occasionally a party of them would glide past in a large canoe. Despite hunger, his sensations on this first day were delicious. The poet in him responded rapturously to the appeal of all this new life; to feel the brotherhood of wild creatures, to sleep under the stars in the vast night, to watch the silent, passionate beauty of the sunrise, ripening to the music of the birds.

On the second day his eyes were gladdened by the oncoming of a boat rowed by two whites. They proved to be a stone mason and his man, and they bore provisions, a letter, and newspapers from Noah:—

"MY DEAR PELONI:

"A hurried line to report a glorious success, thank Heaven! A finer day and more general satisfaction has not been known on any similar occasion. All the dignity and talent of the neighbourhood for miles was present. I hear that a vast concourse also assembled at Tonawanda, expecting that the ceremonies would be at Grand Island, but that many of them came up in carriages in time to hear my Inaugural

Speech. You will see that the newspapers, especially the Buffalo Patriot Extra, have reported me fully, showing how they realize the importance of this world-stirring episode in Israel's history. Their comments, too, are for the most part highly sympathetic. Of course the New York Herald will sneer; but then Bennett was once in my employ on the Courier and Enquirer. They tell me that you duly set out to plant the flag of Judah, and I assume it is now by God's grace waving over Ararat. Heaven bless you! my heart is too full for words. I had hoped to find time to-day to behold the sublime spectacle myself, but urgent legal business calls me back to New York. But I am resolved to start the city without delay, and the bearers of this have my plan for a little monument of brick and wood with the simple inscription— 'Ararat founded by Mordecai Manuel Noah, 1825'—from the summit of which the flag can wave. I leave you to superintend the same, and take any measures you please to promote the growth of the city and to receive, as my representative, the inflowing immigrants from the Ghettos of the world. I appoint you, moreover, Keeper of the Records. To you shall be given to write the new Book of the Chronicles of Israel. My friend Mr. Smith, one of the proprietors of the island, will communicate with you on behalf of the Shareholders, as occasion arises. Expect me shortly (perhaps with my bride, for I am entering into holy wedlock with the most amiable and beautiful of her sex) and meantime receive my blessing.

"MORDECAI MANUEL NOAH, Judge of Israel, "pro A.B. SEIXAS, Secr. pro tem."

While the little monument was building, and the men were coming to and fro in boats, Peloni made friends with the Indians, the smoke-wreaths of whose lodges hovered across the river, and he picked up a little of their language. Also he explored his island, drawn by the crescendo roar of Niagara. It was at Burnt Island Bay that he had his first, if distant, view of the Falls themselves. The rapids, gurgling and plunging with foam and swirl and eddy, quickened his blood, but the cataracts disappointed him, after that rainbow glimpse of the upper spray, and it was not till he got himself landed on the Canadian shore and saw the monstrous rush of the vast tameless flood toward the great leap that he felt the presence and the power that were to be with him for the rest of his days. The bend of the Horse-Shoe was hidden by a white spray mountain that rose above its topmost waters, as they hurled themselves from green solidity to creamy mist. And as he looked, lo! the enchanting rainbows twinkled again, and he had a sense as of the smile of God, of the love of that awful, unfathomable Being, eternally persistent, while the generations rise and fall like vaporous spray.

The tide was low and, drawn by an irresistible fascination, he adventured down among the rocks near the foot of the Fall. But a tingling storm of spray smote him half blind and wholly breathless, and all he could see was a monstrous misty Brocken-spirit upreared and in his ears were a thousand thunders. A wild elemental passion swelled and lifted him. Yes, Force, Force, was the secret of things: the vast primal energies that sent the stars shining and the seas roaring. Force, Life, Strength, that was what Israel needed. It had grown anæmic, slouching along its airless Judengassen. Oh, to fight, to fight, like the warriors who went out against the Greeks, who defended the Holy City against the Romans. "For the Lord is a Man of War." And he shouted the cry of David, "Blessed be the Lord, my Rock, who teacheth my hands to war, and my fingers to fight." But he stopped, smitten by an ironic memory. This very blessing was uttered every Sabbath twilight, in every Ghetto, by every bloodless worshipper, to a melancholy despairing melody, in the lightless dusk of the synagogues.

The monument was speedily erected and, being hollow, proved useful for Peloni to sleep in, as the October nights grew chilly. And thus Peloni lived, a latter-day Crusoe. He had now procured fishing-tackle, and grew dexterous in luring black bass and perch and whitefish from the river. Also he had found out what berries he might eat. Occasionally a boat would sell him cornmeal from Buffalo, but his savings were melting away and he preferred to forage for himself, relishing the wild flavour of uncivilized living. He even wished it were possible to eat the birds or the rabbits he could have killed: but as various points of Jewish law forbade such diet, there was no use in buying a musket or a bow and arrow. So his relations with the animal world remained purely amicable. The robins and bluebirds and thrushes sang for him. The woodpeckers tapped on his monument to wake him in the morning. The blue jays screamed without wrath, and the partridges drummed unmartially. The squirrels frolicked with him, and the rabbits lost their shyness. One would have said these were the Lost Ten Tribes he had found.

Peloni had become, not the Keeper of the Records, but the Keeper of Noah's Ark.

VII

So winter came, and there was still nothing to record, save the witchery of the muffled white world with its blue shadows and fantastic ice friezes and stalactites. Great icicles glittered on the rocks, showing all the hues beneath. Peloni, wrapped in his blanket, crouched on his monument over a log that burnt in an improvised grate. It was very lonely. He had heard from no one, neither from Noah, nor Smith, nor any Jewish or Indian pilgrim to the New Jerusalem, and the stock of winter provisions had exhausted his little hoard of coin. The old despair began to twine round him like some serpent of ice. As he listened in such moods to the distant thunder of Niagara—which waxed louder as the air grew heavier, till it quite dominated the ever present rumble of the rapids—the sound took on endless meanings to his feverish brain. Now it was no longer the voice of the Eternal Being, it was the endless plaint of Israel beseeching the deaf heaven, the roar of prayer from some measureless synagogue; now it was the raucous voice of persecution, the dull bestial roar of malicious multitudes; and again it was the voice of the whole earth, groaning and travailing. And the horror of it was that it would not stop. It dropped on his brain, this falling water, as on the prisoner's in the mediæval torture chamber. Could no one stop this turning wheel of the world, jar it grindingly to a standstill?

Spring wore slowly round again. The icicles melted, the friezes dripped away, the fantastic mufflers slipped from the trees, and the young buds peeped out and the young birds sang. The river flowed uncurdled, the cataracts fell unclogged.

In Peloni's breast alone the ice did not melt: no new sap stirred in his veins. The very rainbows on the leaping mist were now only reminders of the Biblical promise that the world would go on forever; forever the wheel would turn, and Israel wander homeless.

And at last one sunny day a boat arrived with a message from the Master. Alas! even Noah had abandoned Ararat. "I am beginning to see," he wrote, "that our only hope is Palestine. Zion alone has magnetism for the Jew. The great war against Gog prophesied in Ezekiel will be in Palestine. Gog is Russia, and the Russians are the descendants of the joint colony of Meshech and Tubal and the little horn of Daniel. Russia in an attempt to wrest India and Turkey from the English and the Turks will make the Holy Land the theatre of a terrible conflict. But yet in the end in Jerusalem shall we reërect Solomon's Temple. The ports of the Mediterranean will be again open to the busy hum of commerce; the fields will again bear the fruitful harvest, and Christian and Jew will together, on Mount Zion, raise their voices in praise of Him whose covenant with Abraham was to endure forever, in whose seed all the nations of the earth are to be blessed. This is our destiny."

Peloni wandered automatically to the apex of the island at Burnt Ship Bay, and stood gazing meaninglessly at the fragments of the sunken ships. Before him raced the rapids, frenziedly anxious for the great leap. Even so, he thought, had Noah and he dreamed Israel would haste to Ararat. And Niagara maintained its mocking roar—its roar of gigantic laughter.

Reërect Solomon's Temple in Palestine! A ruined country to regenerate a ruined people! A land belonging to the Turks, centre of the fanaticisms of three religions and countless sects! A soil which even to Noah was the destined theatre of world-shaking war!

As he lifted his swimming eyes he saw to his astonishment that he was no longer alone. A tall majestic figure stood gazing at him: a grave, sorrowful Indian, feathered and tufted, habited only in buckskin leggings, and girdled by a belt of wampum. A musket in his hand showed he had been hunting, and a canoe Peloni now saw tethered to the bank indicated he was going back to his lodge. Peloni knew from his talks with the Tonawanda Indians opposite Ararat that this was Red Jacket, the famous chief of the Iroquois, the ancient lords of the soil. Peloni tendered the salute due to the royalty stamped on the man. Red Jacket ceremoniously acknowledged the obeisance. Then they gazed silently at each other, the puny, stooping scholar from the German Ghetto, and the stalwart, kingly savage.

"Tell me," said Red Jacket imperiously, "what nation are you that build a monument but never a city like the other white men, nor even a camp like my people?"

"Great Chief," replied Peloni in his best Iroquois, "we are a people that build for others."

"I would ye would build for my people then. For these white men sweep us back, farther, farther, till there is nothing but"—and he made an eloquent gesture, implying the sweep into the river, into the jaws of the hurrying rapids. "Yet, methinks, I heard of a plan of your people—of a great pow-wow of your chiefs in a church, of a great city to be born here."

"It is dead before birth," said Peloni.

"Strange," mused Red Jacket. "Scarce twenty summers ago Joseph Elliott came here to plan out his city on a soil that was not his, and lo! this Buffalo rises already mighty and menacing. To-morrow it will be at my wigwam door—and we"—another gesture, hopeless, yet full of regal dignity, rounded off the sentence.

And in that instant it was borne in upon Peloni that they were indeed brothers: the Jew who stood for the world that could not be born again, and the Red Indian who stood for the world that must pass away. Yes, they were both doomed. Israel had been too bent and broken by the long dispersion and the long persecution: the spring was snapped; he could not recover. He had been too long the pliant protégé of kings and popes: he had prayed too many centuries in too many countries for the simultaneous welfare of too many governments, to be capable of realizing that government of his own for which he likewise prayed. This pious patience—this rejection of the burden on to the shoulders of Messiah and Miracle—was it more than the veil of unconscious impotence? Ah, better sweep oneself away than endure the long ignominy. And Niagara laughed on.

"May I have the privilege of crossing in your canoe?" he asked.

"You are not afraid?" said Red Jacket. "The rapids are dangerous here."

Afraid! Peloni's inward laughter seemed to himself to match Niagara's.

When he got to the mainland, he made straight for the Fall. He was on the American side, and he paused on the sward, on the very brink of the tameless cataract, that had for immemorial ages been driving itself backward by eating away its own rock. His fascinated eyes watched the curious smooth, purring slide of the vast mass of green water over the sharp edges, unending, unresting, the eternal revolution of a maddening, imperturbable wheel. O that blind wheel, turning, turning, while the generations waxed and waned, one succeeding the other without haste or rest or possibility of pause: creatures of meaningless majesty, shadows of shadows, dreaming of love and justice, and fading into the kindred mist, while this solid green cataract roared and raced through æons innumerable, stable as the stars, thundering in majestic meaninglessness. And suddenly he threw himself into its remorseless whirl and was sucked down into the monstrous chaos of seething waters and whirled and hurled amid the rocks, battered and shapeless, but still holding Noah's letter in his convulsively clinched hand, while the rainbowed spray leapt impassively heavenward.

The corner-stone of Ararat lies in the rooms of the Buffalo Historical Society, and no one who copies the inscription dreams that it is the gravestone of Peloni.

And while the very monument has mouldered away in Ararat, Buffalo sits throned amid her waters, the Queen City of the Empire State, with the world's commerce at her feet. And from their palaces of Medina sandstone the Christian railroad kings go out to sail in their luxurious yachts—vessels not of bulrushes but driven by steam, as predicted by Mordecai Manuel Noah, Governor and Judge of Israel.

IV

THE LAND OF PROMISE

I

"Telegraph how many pieces you have."

In this wise did the Steamship Company convey to the astute agent its desire to know how many Russian Jews he was smuggling out of the Pale into the steerage of its Atlantic liner.

The astute agent's task was simple enough. The tales he told of America were only the clarification of a nebulous vision of the land flowing with milk and honey that hovered golden-rayed before all these hungry eyes. To the denizens of the Pale, in their cellars, in their gutter-streets, in their semi-subterranean shops consisting mainly of shutters and annihilating one another's profits; to the congested populations newly reinforced by the driving back of thousands from beyond the Pale, and yet multiplying still by an improvident reliance on Providence; to the old people pauperized by the removal of the vodka business to Christian hands, and the young people dammed back from their natural outlets by Pan-Slavic ukases, and clogged with whimsical edicts and rescripts—the astute agent's offer of getting you through Germany, without even a Russian passport, by a simple passage from Libau to New York, was peculiarly alluring.

It was really almost an over-baiting of the hook on the part of the too astute agent to whisper that he had had secret information of a new thunderbolt about to be launched at the Pale; whereby the period of service for Jewish conscripts would be extended to fifteen years, and the area of service would be extended to Siberia.

"Three hundred and seventy-seven pieces," ran his telegram in reply. In a letter he suggested other business he might procure for the line.

"Confine yourself to freight," the Company wrote cautiously, for even under sealed envelopes you cannot be too careful. "The more the better."

Freight! The word was not inexact. Did not even the Government reports describe these exploiters of the Muzhik as in some places packed in their hovels like salt herrings in a barrel; as sleeping at night in serried masses in sties which by day were tallow or leather factories?

To be shipped as cargo came therefore natural enough. Nevertheless, each of these "pieces," being human after all, had a history, and one of these histories is here told.

II

Nowhere was the poverty of the Pale bitterer than in the weavers' colony, in which Srul betrothed himself to Biela. The dowries, which had been wont to kindle so many young men's passions, had fallen to freezing-point; and Biela, if she had no near prospect of marriage, could console herself with the knowledge that she was romantically loved. Even the attraction of kest—temporary maintenance of the young couple by the father-in-law—was wanting in Biela's case, for the simple reason that she had no father, both her parents having died of the effort to get a living. For marriage-portion and kest, Biela could only bring her dark beauty, and even that was perhaps less than it seemed. For you scarcely ever saw Biela apart from her homely quasi-mother, her elder sister Leah, who, like the original Leah, had "tender eyes," which combined with a pock-marked face to ensure for her premature recognition as an old maid. The inflamed eyelids were the only legacy Leah's father had left her.

From Srul's side, though his parents were living, came even fainter hope of the wedding-canopy. Srul's father was blind—perhaps a further evidence that the local hygienic conditions were nocuous to the eye in particular—and Srul himself, who had occupied most of his time in learning to weave Rabbinic webs, had only just turned his attention to cloth, though Heaven was doubtless pleased with the gear of Gemara he had gathered in his short sixteen years. The old weaver had—in more than one sense—seen better days before his affliction and the great factories came on: days when the independent hand-weaver might sit busily before the loom from the raw dawn to the black midnight, taking his meals at the bench; days when, moreover, the "piece" of satin-faced cloth was many ells shorter. "But they make up for the extra length," he would say with pathetic humour, "by cutting the pay shorter."

The same sense of humour enabled him to bear up against the forced rests that increasing slackness brought the hand-weavers, while the factories whirred on. "Now is the proverb fulfilled," he cried to his unsmiling wife, "for there are two Sabbaths a week." Alas! as the winter grew older and colder, it became a week of Sabbaths. The wheels stood still; in all the colony not a spool was reeled. It was unprecedented. Gradually the factories had stolen the customers. Some sat waiting dazedly for the raw yarns they knew could no longer come at this season; others left the suburb in which the colony had drowsed from time immemorial, and sought odd jobs in the town, in the frowning shadows of the factories. But none would enter the factories themselves, though these were ready to suck them in on one sole condition.

Ah! here was the irony of the tragedy. The one condition was the one condition the poor weavers could not accept. It was open to them to reduce the week of Sabbaths to its ancient and diurnal dimensions, provided the Sabbath itself came on Sunday. Nay, even the working-day offered them was less, and the wage was more than their own. The deeper irony within this irony was that the proprietor of every one of these factories was a brother in Israel! Jeshurun grown fat and kicking.

Even the old blind man's composure deserted him when it began to be borne in on his darkness that the younger weavers meditated surrender. The latent explosives generated through the years by their perusal of un-Jewish books in insidious "Yiddish" versions, now bade fair to be touched to eruption by this paraded prosperity of wickedness; wickedness that had even discarded the caftan and shaved the corners of its beard.

"But thou, apple of my eye," the old man said to Srul, "thou wilt die rather than break the Sabbath?"

"Father," quoted the youth, with a shuddering emotion at the bare idea, "I have been young and now I am old, but never have I seen the righteous forsaken, nor his seed begging for bread."

"My son! A true spark of the Patriarchs!" And the old man clasped the boy to his arms and kissed him on the pious cheeks down which the ear-locks dangled.

"But if Biela should tempt thee, so that thou couldst have the wherewithal to marry her," put in his mother, who could not keep her thoughts off grandchildren.

"Not for apples of gold, mother, will I enter the service of these serpents."

"Nevertheless, Biela is fair to see, and thou art getting on in years," murmured the mother.

"Leah would not give Biela to a Sabbath-breaker," said the old man reassuringly.

"Yes, but suppose she gives her to a bread-winner," persisted the mother. "Do not forget that Biela is already fifteen, only a year younger than thyself."

But Leah kept firm to the troth she had plighted on behalf of Biela, even though the young man's family sank lower and lower, till it was at last reduced from the little suburban wooden cottage, with the spacious courtyard, to one corner of a large town-cellar, whose population became amphibious when the Vistula overflowed.

And Srul kept firm to the troth Israel had plighted with the Sabbath-bride, even when his father's heart no longer beat, so could not be broken. The old man remained to the last the most cheerful denizen of the cellar: perhaps because he was spared the vision of his emaciated fellow-troglodytes. He called the cellar "Arba Kanfôs," after the four-cornered garment of fringes which he wore: and sometimes he said these were the "Four Corners" from which, according to the Prophets, God would gather Israel.

III

In such a state of things an agent scarcely needed to be astute. "Pieces" were to be had for the picking up. The only trouble was that they were not gold pieces. The idle weavers could not defray the passage-money, still less the agent's commission for smuggling them through.

"If I only had a few hundred roubles," Srul lamented to Leah, "I could get to a land where there is work without breaking the Sabbath, a land to which Biela could follow me when I waxed in substance."

Leah supported her household of three—for there was a younger sister, Tsirrélé, who, being only nine, did not count except at meal-times—on the price of her piece-work at the Christian umbrella factory, where, by a considerate Russian law, she could work on Sunday, though the Christians might not. Thus she earned, by literal sweating in a torrid atmosphere, three roubles, all except a varying number of kopecks, every week. And when you live largely on black bread and coffee, you may, in the course of years, save a good deal, even if you have three mouths. Therefore, Leah had the sum that Srul mentioned so wistfully, put by for a rainy day (when there should be no umbrellas to make). And as the sum had kept increasing, the notion that it might form the nucleus of an establishment for Biela and Srul had grown clearer and clearer in her mind, which it tickled delightfully. But the idea that now came to her of staking all on a possible future was agitating.

"We might, perhaps, be able to get together the money," she said tentatively. "But—" She shook her head, and the Russian proverb came to her lips. "Before the sun rises the dew may destroy you."

Srul plunged into an eager recapitulation of the agent's assurances. And before the eyes of both the marriage-canopy reared itself splendid in the Land of Promise, and the figure of Biela flitted, crowned with the bridal wreath.

"But what will become of your mother?" Leah asked.

Srul's soap-bubbles collapsed. He had forgotten for the moment that he had a mother.

"She might come to live with us," Leah hastened to suggest, seeing his o'erclouded face.

"Ah, no, that would be too much of a burden. And Tsirrélé, too, is growing up."

"Tsirrélé eats quite as much now as she will in ten years' time," said Leah, laughing, as she thought fondly of her dear, beautiful little one, her gay whimsies and odd caprices.

"And my mother does not eat very much," said Srul, wavering.

In this way Srul became a "piece," and was dumped down in the Land of Promise.

IV

To the four females left behind—odd fragments of two families thrown into an odder one—the movements of the particular piece, Srul, were the chief interest of existence. The life in the three-roomed wooden cottage soon fell into a routine, Leah going daily to the tropical factory, Biela doing the housework and dreaming of her lover, little Tsirrélé frisking about and chattering like the squirrel she was, and Srul's mother dozing and criticising and yearning for her lost son and her unborn grandchildren. By the time Srul's first letter, with its exciting pictorial stamp, arrived from the Land of Promise, the household seemed to have been established on this basis from time immemorial.

"I had a lucky escape, God be thanked," Srul wrote. "For when I arrived in New York I had only fifty-one roubles in my pocket. Now it seems that these rich Americans are so afraid of being overloaded with paupers that they will not let you in, if you have less than fifty dollars, unless you can prove you are sure to prosper. And a dollar, my dear Biela, is a good deal more than a rouble. However, blessed be the Highest One, I learned of this ukase just the day before we arrived, and was able to borrow the difference from a fellow-passenger, who lent me the money to show the Commissioners. Of course, I had to give it back as soon as I was passed, and as I had to pay him five roubles for the use of it, I set foot on the soil of freedom with only forty-six. However, it was well worth it; for just think, beloved Biela, if I had been shipped back and all that money wasted! The interpreter also said to me, 'I suppose you have got some work to do here?' 'I wish I had,' I said. No sooner had the truth slipped out than my heart seemed turned to ice, for I feared they would reject me after all as a poor wretch out of work. But quite the contrary; it seemed this was only a trap, a snare of the fowler. Poor Caminski fell into it—you remember the red-haired weaver who sold his looms to the Maggid's brother-in-law. He said he had agreed to take a place in a glove factory. It is true, you know, that some Polish Jews have made a glove town in the north, so the poor man thought that would sound plausible. Hence you may expect to see Caminski's red hair back again, unless he takes ship again from Libau and tells the truth at the second attempt. I left him howling in a wooden pen, and declaring he would kill himself rather than face his friends at home with the brand on his head of not being good enough for America. He did not understand that contract-labourers are not let in. Protection is the word they call it. Hence, I thank God that my father—his memory for a blessing!—taught me to make Truth the law of my mouth, as it is written. Verily was the word of the Talmud (Tractate Sabbath) fulfilled at the landing-stage: 'Falsehood cannot stay, but truth remains forever.' With God's help, I shall remain here all my life, for it is a land overflowing with milk and honey. I had almost forgotten to tell my dove that the voyage was hard and bitter as the Egyptian bondage; not because of the ocean, over which I passed as easily as our forefathers over the Red Sea, but by reason of the harshness of the overseers, who regarded not our complaints that the meat was not kosher, as promised by the agent. Also the butter and meat plates were mixed up. I and many with me lived on dry bread, nor could we always get hot water to make coffee. When my Biela comes across the great waters—God send her soon—she must take with her salt meat of her own."

From the first, Srul courageously assumed that the meat would soon have to be packed; nay, that Leah might almost set about salting it at once. Even the slow beginnings of his profits as a peddler did not daunt him. "A great country," he wrote on paper stamped with the Stars and Stripes, with an eagle screaming on the envelope. "No special taxes for the Jews, permission to travel where you please, the schools open freely to our children, no passports and papers at every step, above all, no conscription. No wonder the people call it God's own country. Truly, as it is written, this is none other but the House of God, this is the Gate of Heaven. And when Biela comes, it will be Heaven." Letters like this enlarged the little cottage as with an American room, brightened it as with a fresh wash of blue paint. Despite the dreary grind of the week, Sabbaths and festivals found the household joyous enough. The wedding-canopy of Srul and Biela was a beacon of light for all four, which made life livable as they struggled toward it. Nevertheless, it came but slowly to meet them: nearly three years oozed by before Srul began to lift his eye toward a store. The hereditary weaver of business combinations had emerged tardily from beneath the logic-weaver and the cloth-weaver, but of late he had been finding himself. "If I could only get together five hundred dollars clear," he wrote to Leah. "For that is all I should have to pay down for a ladies' store near Broadway, and just at the foot of the stairs of the Elevated Railway. What a pity I have only four hundred and thirty-five dollars! Stock and goodwill, and only five hundred dollars cash! The other five hundred could stand over at five per cent. If I were once in the store I could gradually get some of the rooms above (there is already a parlour, in which I shall sleep), and then, as soon as I was making a regular profit, I could send Biela and mother their passage-money, and my wife could help 'the boss' behind the counter."

To hasten the rosy day Leah sent thirty-five roubles, and presently, sure enough, Srul was in possession, and a photograph of the store itself came over to gladden their weary eyes and dilate those of the neighbours. The photograph of Srul, which had come eighteen months before, was not so suited for display, since his peaked cap and his caftan had been replaced by a jacket and a bowler, and, but for the ear-locks which were still in the picture, he would have looked like a factory-owner. In return, Srul received a photograph of the four—taken together, for economy's sake—Leah with her arm around Biela's waist, and Tsirrélé sitting in his mother's lap.

V

But a long, wearying struggle was still before the new "boss," and two years crept along, with their turns of luck and ill-luck, of bargains and bad debts, ere the visionary marriage-canopy (that seemed to span the Atlantic) began to stand solidly on American soil. The third year was not half over ere Srul actually sent the money for Biela's passage, together with a handsome "waist" from his stock, for her to wear. But Biela was too timid to embark alone without Srul's mother, whose fare Srul could not yet manage to withdraw from his capital. Leah, of course, offered to advance it, but Biela refused this vehemently, because a new hope had begun to spring up in her breast. Why should she be parted from her family at all? Since her marriage had been delayed these five and a half years, a few months more or less could make no difference. Let Leah's savings, then, be for Leah's passage (and Tsirrélé's) and to give her a start in the New World. "It rains, even in America, and there are umbrella factories there, too," she urged. "You will make twice the living. Look at Srul!"

And there was a new fear, too, which haunted Biela's aching heart, but which she dared not express to Leah. Leah's eyes were getting worse. The temperature of the factory was a daily hurt, and then, too, she had read so many vilely printed Yiddish books and papers by the light of the tallow candle. What if she were going blind? What if, while she, Biela, was happy with Srul, Leah should be starving with Tsirrélé? No, they must all remain together: and she clung to her sister, with tears.

To Leah the prospect of witnessing her sister's happiness was so seductive that she tried to take the lowest estimate of her own chances of finding work in New York. Her savings, almost eaten up by the journey, could not last long, and it would be terrible to have to come upon Srul for help, a man with a wife and (if God were good) children, to say nothing of his old mother. No, she could not risk Tsirrélé's bread.

But the increased trouble with her eyes turned her in favour of going, though, curiously enough, for a side reason quite unlike Biela's. Leah, too, was afraid of a serious breakdown, though she would not hint her fears to any one else. From her miscellaneous Yiddish reading she had gathered that miraculous eye-doctors lived in Königsberg. Now a journey to Germany was not to be thought of; if she went to America, however, it could be taken en route. It would be a sort of saving, and few things appealed to Leah as much as economy. This was why, some four months later, the ancient furniture of the blue-washed cottage was sold off, and the quartette set their faces for America by way of Germany. The farewell to the home of their youth took place in the cemetery among the high-shouldered Hebrew-speaking stones. Leah and Biela passionately invoked the spirits of their dead parents and bade them watch over their children. The old woman scribbled Srul and Biela's interlinked names over the flat tomb of a holy scholar. "Take their names up to the Highest One," she pleaded. "Entreat that their quiver be full, for the sake of thy righteousness."

More dead than alive, the four "pieces" with their bundles arrived at Hamburg. Days and nights of travelling, packed like "freight" in hard, dirty wooden carriages, the endless worry of passports, tickets, questions, hygienic inspections and processes, the illegal exactions of petty officials, the strange phantasmagoria of places and faces—all this had left them dazed. Only two things kept up their spirits—the image of Srul waiting on the Transatlantic wharf in hymeneal attire, and the "pooh-pooh" of the miraculous Königsberg doctor, reassuring Leah as to her eyes. There was nothing radically the matter. Even the inflamed eyelids—though incurable, because hereditary—would improve with care. Peasant-like, Leah craved a lotion. "The sea voyage and the rest will do you more good than my medicines. And don't read so much." Not a groschen did Leah have to pay for the great specialist's services. It was the first time in her hard life anybody had done anything for her for nothing, and her involuntary weeping over this phenomenon tended to hurt the very eyelids under attention. They were still further taxed by the kindness of the Jewish committee at Hamburg, on the look-out to smooth the path of poor emigrants and overcome their dietary difficulties. But it was a crowded ship, and our party reverted again to "freight." With some of the other females, they were accommodated in hammocks swung over the very dining-tables, so that they must needs rise at dawn and be cleared away before breakfast. The hot, oily whiff of the cooking-engines came through the rocking doorway. Of the quartette, only Tsirrélé escaped sea-sickness, but "baby" was too accustomed to be petted and nursed to be able suddenly to pet and nurse, and she would spend hours on the slip of lower deck, peering into the fairy saloons which were vivified by bugle instead of bell, and in which beautiful people ate dishes fit for the saints in Heaven. By an effort of will, Leah soon returned to her rôle of factotum, but the old woman and Biela remained limp to the end. Fortunately, there was only one day of heavy rolling and battened-down hatches. For the bulk of the voyage the great vessel brushed the pack of waves disdainfully aside. And one wonderful day, amid unspeakable joy, New York arrived, preceded by a tug and by a boat that conveyed inquiring officials. The great statue of Liberty, on Bedloe's Island, upheld its torch to light the new-comers' path. Srul—there he is on the wharf, dear old Srul!—God bless him! despite his close-cropped hair and his shaven ear-locks. Ah! Heaven be praised! Don't you see him waving? Ah, but we, too, must be content with waving. For here only the tschinovniks of the gilded saloon may land. The "freight" must be packed later into rigid gangs, according to the ship's manifest, transferred to a smaller steamer and discharged on Ellis Island, a little beyond Bedloe's.

VI

And at Ellis Island a terrible thing happened, unforeseen—a shipwreck in the very harbour.

As the "freight" filed slowly along the corridor-cages in the great bare hall, like cattle inspected at ports by the veterinary surgeon, it came into the doctor's head that Leah's eye-trouble was infectious. "Granular lids—contagious," he diagnosed it on paper. And this diagnosis was a flaming sword that turned every way, guarding against Leah the Land of Promise.

"But it is not infectious," she protested in her best German. "It is only in the family."

"So I perceive," dryly replied America's Guardian Angel, who was now examining the obvious sister clinging to Leah's skirts. And in Biela, heavy-eyed with sickness and want of sleep, his suspicious vision easily discovered a reddish rim of eyelid that lent itself to the same fatal diagnosis, and sent her to join Leah in the dock of the rejected. The fresh-faced Tsirrélé and the wizen-faced mother of Srul passed unscrutinized, and even the dread clerk at the desk who asked questions was content with their oath that the wealthy Srul would support them. Srul was, indeed, sent for at once, as Tsirrélé was too pretty to be let out under the mere protection of a Polish crone.

When the full truth that neither she nor Biela was to set foot in New York burst through the daze in Leah's brain, her protest grew frantic.

"But my sister has nothing the matter with her—nothing. O gnädiger Herr, have pity. The Königsberg doctor—the great doctor—told me I had no disease, no disease at all. And even if I have, my sister's eyes are pure as the sunshine. Look, mein Herr, look again. See," and she held up Biela's eyelids and passionately kissed the wet bewildered eyes. "She is to be married, my lamb—her bridegroom awaits her on the wharf. Send me back, gnädiger Herr; I ought not to have come. But for God's sake, don't keep Biela out, don't." She wrung her hands. But the marriage card had been played too often in that hall of despairing dodges. "Oh, Herr Doktor," and she kissed the coat-tail of the ship's doctor, "plead for us; speak a word for her."

The ship's doctor spoke a word on his own behalf. It was he who had endorsed the two girls' health-certificates at Hamburg, and he would be blamed by the Steamship Company, which would have to ship the sisters back free, and even defray their expenses while in quarantine at the dépôt. He ridiculed the idea that the girls were suffering from anything contagious. But the native doctor frowned, immovable.

Leah grew hysteric. It was the first time in her life she had lost her sane standpoint. "Your own eye is affected," she shrieked, her dark pock-marked face almost black with desperate anger, "if you cannot see that it is only because my sister has been weeping, because she is ill from the voyage. But she carries no infection—she is healthy as an ox, and her eye is the eye of an eagle!" She was ordered to be silent, but she shrieked angrily, "The German doctors know, but the Americans have no Bildung."

"Oh, don't, Leah," moaned Biela, throwing her arms round the panting breast. "What's the use?" But the irrepressible Leah got an S.I. ticket of Special Inquiry, forced a hearing in the Commissioners' Court.

"Let her in, kind gentlemen, and send back the other one. Tsirrélé will go back with me. It does not matter about the little one."

The kind gentlemen on the bench were really kind, but America must be protected.

"You can take the young one and the old one both back with you," the interpreter told her. "But they are the only ones we can let in."

Leah and Biela were driven back among the damned. The favoured twain stood helplessly in their happier compartment. Even Tsirrélé, the squirrel, was dazed. Presently the spruce Srul arrived—to find the expected raptures replaced by funeral misery. He wormed his way dizzily into the cage of the rejected. It was not the etiquette of the Pale to kiss one's betrothed bride, but Srul stared dully at Biela without even touching her hand, as if the Atlantic already rolled again between them. Here was a pretty climax to the dreams of years!

"My poor Srul, we must go back to Hamburg to be married," faltered Biela.

"And give up my store?" Srul wailed. "Here the dollar spins round. We have now what one names a boom. There is no land on earth like ours."

The forlornness of the others stung Leah to her senses.

"Listen, Srul," she said hurriedly. "It is all my fault, because I wanted to share in the happiness. I ought not to have come. If we had not been together they never would have suspected Biela's eyes—who would notice the little touch of inflammation which is the most she has ever suffered from? She shall come again in another ship, all alone—for she knows now how to travel. Is it not so, Biela, my lamb? I will see you on board, and Srul will meet you here, although not till you have passed the doctor, so that no one will have a chance of remembering you. It will cost a heap, alas! but I can get some work in Hamburg, and the Jews there have hearts of gold. Eh, Biela, my poor lamb?"

"Yes, yes, Leah, you can always give yourself a counsel," and Biela put her wet face to her sister's, and kissed the pock-marked cheek.

Srul acquiesced eagerly. No one remembered for the moment that Leah would be left alone in the Old World. The problem of effecting the bride's entry blocked all the horizon.

"Yes, yes," said Srul. "The mother will look after Tsirrélé, and in less than three weeks Biela will slip in."

"No, three weeks is too soon," said Leah. "We must wait a little longer till the doctor forgets."

"Oh, but I have already waited so long!" whimpered Srul.

Leah's eyes filled with sympathetic tears. "I ought not to have made so much fuss. Now she will stick in the doctor's mind. Forgive me, dear Srul, I will do my best and try to make amends."

Leah and Biela were taken away to the hospital, where they remained isolated from the world till the steamer sailed back to Hamburg. Herein, generously lodged, they had ample leisure to review the situation. Biela discovered that the new plan would leave Leah deserted, Leah remembered that she would be deserting little Tsirrélé. Both were agreed that Tsirrélé must go back with them, till they bethought themselves that her passage would have to be paid for, as she was not refused. And every kopeck was precious now. "Let the child stay till I get back," said Biela. "Then I will send her to you."

"Yes, it is best to let her stay awhile. I myself may be able to join you after all. I will go back to Königsberg, and the great doctor will write me out a certificate that my affliction is not contagious."

At the very worst—if even Biela could not get in—Srul should sell his store and come back to the Old World. It would put off the marriage again. But they had waited so long. "So let us cheer up after all, and thank the Lord for His mercies. We might all have been drowned on the voyage."

Thus the sisters' pious conclusion.

But though Srul and his mother and Tsirrélé got on board to see them off, and Tsirrélé gave graphic accounts of the wonders of the store and the rooms prepared for the bride, to say nothing of the great city itself, and Srul brought Biela and Leah splendid specimens of his stock for their adornment, yet it was a horrible thing for them to go back again without having once trodden the sidewalks of the Land of Promise. And when the others were tolled off, as by a funeral bell, and became specks in a swaying crowd; when the dock receded and the cheers and good-byes faded, and the waving handkerchiefs became a blur, and the Statue of Liberty dwindled, and the lone waste of waters faced them once more, Leah's optimism gave way, a chill sinister shadow fell across her new plan, some ominous intuition traversed her like a shudder, and she turned away lest Biela should see her tears.

VII

This despair did not last long. It was not in Leah's nature to despair. But her wildest hopes were exceeded when she set foot again in Hamburg and explained her hard case to the good committee, and a member gave her an informal hint which was like a flash of light from Heaven—its answer to her ceaseless prayer. Ellis Island was not the only way of approaching the Land of Promise. You could go round about through Canada, where they were not so particular, and you could slip in by rail from Montreal without attracting much attention. True, there was the extra expense.

Expense! Leah would have gladly parted with her last rouble to unite Biela with her bridegroom. There must be no delay. A steamer for Canada was waiting to sail. What a fool she had been not to think that out for herself! Yes, but there was Biela's timidity again to consider. Travel by herself through this unknown Canada! And then if they were not so particular, why could not Leah slip through likewise?

"Yes, but my eyes are more noticeable. I might again do you an injury."

"We will separate at the landing-stage and the frontier. We will pretend to be strangers." Biela's wits were sharpened by the crisis.

"Well, I can only lose the passage-money," said Leah, and resolved to take the risk. She wrote a letter to Srul explaining the daring invasion of New York overland which they were to attempt, and was about to post it, when Biela said:—

"Poor Srul! And if I shall not get in after all!" Leah's face fell.

"True," she pondered. "He will have a more heart-breaking disappointment than before."

"Let us not kindle their hopes. After all, if we get in, we shall only be a few days later than our letter. And then think of the joy of the surprise."

"You are right, Biela," and Leah's face glowed again with the anticipated joy of the surprise.

The journey to Canada was longer than to the States, and the "freight" was less companionable. There were fewer Jews and women, more stalwart shepherds, miners, and dock-labourers. When after eleven days, land came, it was not touched at, but only remained cheeringly on the horizon for the rest of the voyage. At last the sisters found themselves unmolested on one of the many wharves of Montreal. But they would not linger a day in this unhomely city. The next morning saw them, dazed and worn out but happy-hearted, dodging the monstrous catapults of the New York motor-cars, while a Polish porter helped them with their bundles and convoyed them toward Srul's store. Ah, what ecstasy to be unregarded units of this free chaotic crowd. Outside the store—what a wonderful store it was, larger than the largest in the weavers' colony!—the sisters paused a moment to roll the coming bliss under their tongues. They peeped in. Ah, there is Srul behind the counter, waiting for customers. Ah, ah, he little knows what customers are waiting for him! They turned and kissed each other for mere joy.

"Draw your shawl over your face," whispered Leah merrily. "Go in and ask him if he has a wedding-veil." Biela slipped in, brimming over with mischief and tears.

"Yes, Miss?" said Srul, with his smartest store manner.

"I want a wedding-veil of white lace," she said in Yiddish. At her voice Srul started. Biela could keep up the joke no longer. "Srul, my darling Srul!" she cried hysterically, her arms yearning to reach him across the counter.

He drew back, pale, gasping for breath.

"Ah, my dear ones!" blubbered Leah, rushing in. "God has been good to you, after all."

"But—but—how did you get in?" he cried, staring.

"Never mind how we got in," said Leah, every pock-mark glistening with smiles and tears. "And where is Tsirrélé—my dear little Tsirrélé?"

"She—she is out marketing, with the mother."

"And the mother?"

"She is well and happy."

"Thank God!" said Leah fervently, and beckoned the porter with the bundles.

"But—but I let the room," he said, flushing. "I did not know that—I could not afford—"

"Never mind, we will find a room. The day is yet high." She settled with the porter.

Meantime Srul had begun playing nervously with a pair of scissors. He snipped a gorgeous piece of stuff to fragments.

"What are you doing?" said Biela at last.

"Oh—I—" he burst into a nervous laugh. "And so you ran the blockade after all. But—but I expect customers every minute—we can't talk now. Go inside and rest, Biela: you will find a sofa in the parlour. Leah, I want—I want to talk to you."

Leah flashed a swift glance at him as Biela, vaguely chilled, moved through the back door into the revivifying splendours of the parlour.

"Something is wrong, Srul," Leah said hoarsely. "Tsirrélé is not here. You feared to tell us."

He hung his head. "I did my best."

"She is ill—dead, perhaps! My beautiful angel!"

He opened his eyes. "Dead? No. Married!"

"What! To whom?"

He turned a sickly white. "To me."

In all that long quest of the canopy, Leah had never come so near fainting as now. The horror of Ellis Island was nothing to this. That scene resurged, and Tsirrélé's fresh beauty, unflecked by the voyage, came up luridly before her; the "baby," whom the unnoted years had made a young woman of fifteen, while they had been aging and staling Biela.

"But—but this will break Biela's heart," she whispered, heart-broken.

"How was I to know Biela would ever get in?" he said, trying to be angry. "Was I to remain a bachelor all my life, breaking the Almighty's ordinance? Did I not wait and wait faithfully for Biela all those years?"

"You could have migrated elsewhere," she said faintly.

"And ruin my connection—and starve?" His anger was real by now. "Besides I have married into the family—it is almost the same thing. And the old mother is just as pleased."

"Oh, she!" and all the endured bitterness of the long years was in the exclamation. "All she wants is grandchildren."

"No, it isn't," he retorted. "Grandchildren with good eyes."

"God forgive you," was all the lump in Leah's throat allowed her to reply. She steadied herself with a hand on the counter, striving to repossess her soul for Biela's sake.

A customer came in, and the tragic universe dwindled to a prosaic place in which ribbons existed in unsatisfactory shades.

"Of course we must go this minute," Leah said, as Srul clanked the coins into the till. "Biela cannot ever live here with you now."

"Yes, it is better so," he assented sulkily. "Besides, you may as well know at once. I keep open on the Sabbath, and that would not have pleased Biela. That is another reason why it was best not to marry Biela. Tsirrélé doesn't seem to mind."

The very ruins of her world seemed toppling now. But this new revelation of Tsirrélé's and his own wickedness seemed only of a piece with the first—indeed, went far to account for it.

"You break the Sabbath, after all!"

He shrugged his shoulders. "We are not in Poland any longer. No dead flies here. Everybody does it. Shut the store two days a week! I should get left."

"And you bring your mother's gray hairs down with sorrow to the grave."

"My mother's gray hairs are no longer hidden by a stupid black Shaitel. That is all. I have explained to her that America is the land of enlightenment and freedom. Her eyes are opened."

"I trust to God, your father's—peace be upon him!—are still shut!" said Leah as she walked with slow steady steps into the parlour, to bear off her wounded lamb.

V

TO DIE IN JERUSALEM

I

The older Isaac Levinsky grew, and the more he saw of the world after business hours, the more ashamed he grew of the Russian Rabbi whom Heaven had curiously chosen for his father. At first it seemed natural enough to shout and dance prayers in the stuffy little Spitalfields synagogue, and to receive reflected glory as the son and heir of the illustrious Maggid (preacher) whose four hour expositions of Scripture drew even West End pietists under the spell of their celestial crookedness. But early in Isaac's English school-life—for cocksure philanthropists dragged the younger generation to anglicization—he discovered that other fathers did not make themselves ridiculously noticeable by retaining the gabardine, the fur cap, and the ear-locks of Eastern Europe: nay, that a few—O, enviable sons!—could scarcely be distinguished from the teachers themselves.

When the guardian angels of the Ghetto apprenticed him, in view of his talent for drawing, to a lithographic printer, he suffered agonies at the thought of his grotesque parent coming to sign the indentures.

"You might put on a coat to-morrow," he begged in Yiddish.

The Maggid's long black beard lifted itself slowly from the worm-eaten folio of the Babylonian Talmud, in which he was studying the tractate anent the payment of the half-shekel head-tax in ancient Palestine. "If he took the money from the second tithes or from the Sabbatical year fruit," he was humming in his quaint sing-song, "he must eat the full value of the same in the city of Jerusalem." As he encountered his boy's querulous face his dream city vanished, the glittering temple of Solomon crumbled to dust, and he remembered he was in exile.

"Put on a coat?" he repeated gently. "Nay, thou knowest 'tis against our holy religion to appear like the heathen. I emigrated to England to be free to wear the Jewish dress, and God hath not failed to bless me."

Isaac suppressed a precocious "Damn!" He had often heard the story of how the cruel Czar Nicholas had tried to make his Jews dress like Christians, so as insidiously to assimilate them away; how the police had even pulled off the unsightly cloth-coverings of the shaven polls of the married women, to the secret delight of the pretty ones, who then let their hair grow in godless charm. And, mixed up with this story, were vaguer legends of raw recruits forced by their sergeants to kneel on little broken stones till they perceived the superiority of Christianity.

How the Maggid would have been stricken to the heart to know that Isaac now heard these legends with inverted sympathies!

"The blind fools!" thought the boy, with ever growing bitterness. "To fancy that religion can lie in clothes, almost as if it was something you could carry in your pockets! But that's where most of their religion does lie—in their pocket." And he shuddered with a vision of greasy, huckstering fanatics. "And just imagine if I was sweet on a girl, having to see all her pretty hair cut off! As for those recruits, it served them right for not turning Christians. As if Judaism was any truer! And the old man never thinks of how he is torturing me—all the sharp little stones he makes me kneel on." And, looking into the future with the ambitious eye of conscious cleverness, he saw the paternal gabardine over-glooming his life.

II

One Friday evening—after Isaac had completed his 'prentice years—there was anxiety in the Maggid's household in lieu of the Sabbath peace. Isaac's seat at the board was vacant. The twisted loaves seemed without salt, the wine of the consecration cup without savour.

The mother was full of ominous explanations.

"Perturb not the Sabbath," reproved the gabardined saint gently, and quoted the Talmud: "'No man has a finger maimed but 'tis decreed from above."

"Isaac has gone to supper somewhere else," suggested his little sister, Miriam.

"Children and fools speak the truth," said the Maggid, pinching her cheek.

But they had to go to bed without seeing him, as though this were only a profane evening, and he amusing himself with the vague friends of his lithographic life. They waited till the candles flared out, and there seemed something symbolic in the gloom in which they groped their way upstairs. They were all shivering, too, for the fire had become gray ashes long since, the Sabbath Fire-Woman having made her last round at nine o'clock and they themselves being forbidden to touch even a candlestick or a poker.

The sunrise revealed to the unclosed eyes of the mother that her boy's bed was empty. It also showed—what she might have discovered the night before had religion permitted her to enter his room with a light—that the room was empty, too: empty of his scattered belongings, of his books and sketches.

"God in Heaven!" she cried.

Her boy had run away.

She began to wring her hands and wail with oriental amplitude, and would have torn her hair had it not been piously replaced by a black wig, neatly parted in the middle and now grotesquely placid amid her agonized agitation.

The Maggid preserved more outward calm. "Perhaps we shall find him in synagogue," he said, trembling.

"He has gone away, he will never come back. Woe is me!"

"He has never missed the Sabbath service!" the Maggid urged. But inwardly his heart was sick with the fear that she prophesied truly. This England, which had seduced many of his own congregants to Christian costume, had often seemed to him to be stealing away his son, though he had never let himself dwell upon the dread. His sermon that morning was acutely exegetical: with no more relation to his own trouble than to the rest of contemporary reality. His soul dwelt in old Jerusalem, and dreamed of Israel's return thither in some vague millennium. When he got home he found that the postman had left a letter. His wife hastened to snatch it.

"What dost thou?" he cried. "Not to-day. When Sabbath is out."

"I cannot wait. It is from him—it is from Isaac."

"Wait at least till the Fire-Woman comes to open it."

For answer the mother tore open the envelope. It was the boldest act of her life—her first breach with the traditions. The Rabbi stood paralyzed by it, listening, as without conscious will, to her sobbing delivery of its contents.

The letter was in Hebrew (for neither parent could read English), and commenced abruptly, without date, address, or affectionate formality. "This is the last time I shall write the holy tongue. My soul is wearied to death of Jews, a blind and ungrateful people, who linger on when the world no longer hath need of them, without country of their own, nor will they enter into the blood of the countries that stretch out their hands to them. Seek not to find me, for I go to a new world. Blot out my name even as I shall blot out yours. Let it be as though I was never begotten."

The mother dropped the letter and began to scream hysterically. "I who bore him! I who bore him!"

"Hold thy peace!" said the father, his limbs shaking but his voice firm. "He is dead. 'The Lord giveth and the Lord taketh away. Blessed be the name of the Lord.' To-night we will begin to sit the seven days' mourning. But to-day is the Sabbath."

"My Sabbath is over for aye. Thou hast driven my boy away with thy long prayers."

"Nay, God hath taken him away for thy sins, thou godless Sabbath-breaker! Peace while I make the Consecration."

"My Isaac, my only son! We shall say Kaddish (mourning-prayer) for him, but who will say Kaddish for us?"

"Peace while I make the Consecration!"

He got through with the prayer over the wine, but his breakfast remained untasted.

III

Re-reading the letter, the poor parents agreed that the worst had happened. The allusions to "blood" and "the new world" seemed unmistakable. Isaac had fallen under the spell of a beautiful heathen female; he was marrying her in a church and emigrating with her to America. Willy-nilly, they must blot him out of their lives.

And so the years went by, over-brooded by this shadow of living death. The only gleam of happiness came when Miriam was wooed and led under the canopy by the President of the congregation, who sold haberdashery. True, he spoke English well and dressed like a clerk, but in these degenerate days one must be thankful to get a son-in-law who shuts his shop on the Sabbath.

One evening, some ten years after Isaac's disappearance, Miriam sat reading the weekly paper—which alone connected her with the world and the fulness thereof—when she gave a sudden cry.

"What is it?" said the haberdasher.

"Nothing—I thought—" And she stared again at the rough cut of a head embedded in the reading matter.

But no, it could not be!

"Mr. Ethelred P. Wyndhurst, whose versatile talents have brought him such social popularity, is rumoured to have budded out in a new direction. He is said to be writing a comedy for Mrs. Donald O'Neill, who, it will be remembered, sat to him recently for the portrait now on view at the Azure Art Club. The dashing comédienne will, it is stated, produce the play in the autumn season. Mr. Wyndhurst's smart sayings have often passed from mouth to mouth, but it remains to be seen whether he can make them come naturally from the mouths of his characters."

What had these far-away splendours to do with Isaac Levinsky? With Isaac and his heathen female across the Atlantic?

And yet—and yet Ethelred P. Wyndhurst was like Isaac—that characteristic curve of the nose, those thick eyebrows! And perhaps Isaac had worked himself up into a portrait-painter. Why not? Did not his old sketch of herself give distinction to her parlour? Her heart swelled proudly at the idea. But no! more probably the face in print was roughly drawn—was only accidentally like her brother. She sighed and dropped the paper.

But she could not drop the thought. It clung to her, wistful and demanding satisfaction. The name of Ethelred P. Wyndhurst, whenever it appeared in the paper—and it was surprising how often she saw it now, though she had never noticed it before—made her heart beat with the prospect of clews. She bought other papers, merely in the hope of seeing it, and was not unfrequently rewarded. Involuntarily, her imagination built up a picture of a brilliant romantic career that only needed to be signed "Isaac." She began to read theatrical and society journals on the sly, and developed a hidden life of imaginative participation in fashionable gatherings. And from all this mass of print the name Ethelred P. Wyndhurst disengaged itself with lurid brilliancy. The rumours of his comedy thickened. It was christened The Sins of Society. It was to be put on soon. It was not written yet. Another manager had bid for it. It was already in rehearsal. It was called The Bohemian Boy. It would not come on this season. Miriam followed feverishly its contradictory career. And one day there was a large picture of Isaac! Isaac to the life! She soared skywards. But it adorned an interview, and the interview dropped her from the clouds. Ethelred was born in Brazil of an English engineer and a Spanish beauty, who performed brilliantly on the violin. He had shot big game in the Rocky Mountains, and studied painting in Rome.

The image of her mother playing the violin, in her preternaturally placid wig, brought a bitter smile to Miriam's lips. And yet it was hard to give up Ethelred now. It seemed like losing Isaac a second time. And presently she reflected shrewdly that the wig and the gabardine wouldn't have shown up well in print, that indeed Isaac in his farewell letter had formally renounced them, and it was therefore open to him to invent new parental accessories. Of course—fool that she was!—how could Ethelred P. Wyndhurst acknowledge the same childhood as Isaac Levinsky! Yes, it might still be her Isaac.

Well, she would set the doubt at rest. She knew, from the wide reading to which Ethelred had stimulated her, that authors appeared before the curtain on first nights. She would go to the first night of The Whirligig (that was the final name), and win either joy or mental rest.

She made her expedition to the West End on the pretext of a sick friend in Bow, and waited many hours to gain a good point of view in the first row of the gallery, being too economical to risk more than a shilling on the possibility of relationship to the dramatist.

As the play progressed, her heart sank. Though she understood little of the conversational paradoxes, it seemed to her—now she saw with her physical eye this brilliant Belgravian world, in the stalls as well as on the stage—that it was impossible her Isaac could be of it, still less that it could be Isaac's spirit which marshalled so masterfully these fashionable personages through dazzling drawing-rooms; and an undercurrent of satire against Jews who tried to get into society by bribing the fashionables, contributed doubly to chill her. She shared in the general laughter, but her laugh was one of hysterical excitement.

But when at last amid tumultuous cries of "Author!" Isaac Levinsky really appeared—Isaac, transformed almost to a fairy prince, as noble a figure as any in his piece, Isaac, the proved master-spirit of the show, the unchallenged treader of all these radiant circles—then all Miriam's effervescing emotion found vent in a sobbing cry of joy.

"Isaac!" she cried, stretching out her arms across the gallery bar.

But her cry was lost in the applause of the house.

IV

She wrote to him, care of the theatre. The first envelope she had to tear up because it was inadvertently addressed to Isaac Levinsky.

Her letter was a gush of joy at finding her dear Isaac, of pride in his wonderful position. Who would have dreamed a lithographer's apprentice would arrive at leading the fashions among the nobility and gentry? But she had always believed in his talents; she had always treasured the water-colour he had made of her, and it hung in the parlour behind the haberdasher's shop into which she had married. He, too, was married, they had imagined, and gone to America. But perhaps he was married, although in England. Would he not tell her? Of course, his parents had cast him out of their hearts, though she had heard mother call out his name in her sleep. But she herself thought of him very often, and perhaps he would let her come to see him. She would come very quietly when the grand people were not there, nor would she ever let out that he was a Jew, or not born in Brazil. Father was still pretty strong, thank God, but mother was rather ailing. Hoping to see him soon, she remained his loving Miriam.

She waited eagerly for his answer. Day followed day, but none came.

When the days passed into weeks, she began to lose hope; but it was not till The Whirligig, which she followed in the advertisement columns, was taken off after a briefer run than the first night seemed to augur, that she felt with curious conclusiveness that her letter would go unanswered. Perhaps even it had miscarried. But it was now not difficult to hunt out Ethelred P. Wyndhurst's address, and she wrote him anew.

Still the same wounding silence. After the lapse of a month, she understood that what he had written in Hebrew was final; that he had cut himself free once and forever from the swaddling coils of gabardine, and would not be dragged back even within touch of its hem. She wept over her second loss of him, but the persistent thought of him had brought back many tender childish images, and it seemed incredible that she would never really creep into his life again. He had permanently enlarged her horizon, and she continued to follow his career in the papers, worshipping it as it loomed grandiose through her haze of ignorance. Gradually she began to boast of it in her more English circles, and so in course of time it became known to all but the parents that the lost Isaac was a shining light in high heathendom, and a vast secret admiration mingled with the contempt of the Ghetto for Ethelred P. Wyndhurst.

V

In high heathendom a vast secret contempt mingled with the admiration for Ethelred P. Wyndhurst. He had, it is true, a certain vogue, but behind his back he was called a Jew. He did not deserve the stigma in so far as it might have implied financial prosperity. His numerous talents had only availed to prevent one another from being seriously cultivated. He had had a little success at first with flamboyant pictures, badly drawn, and well paragraphed; he had written tender verses for music, and made quiet love to ugly and unhappy society ladies; he was an assiduous first-nighter, and was suspected of writing dramatic criticisms, even of his own comedy. And in that undefined social segment where Kensington and Bohemia intersect, he was a familiar figure (a too familiar figure, old fogies grumbled) with an unenviable reputation as a diner-out—for the sake of the dinner.

Yet some of the people who called him "sponge" were not averse from imbibing his own liquids when he himself played the gracious host. He was appearing in that rôle one Sunday evening before a motley assembly in his dramatically furnished studio, nay, he was in the very act of biting into a sandwich scrupulously compounded with ham, when a telegram was handed to him.

"Another of those blessed actresses crying off," he said. "I wonder how they ever manage to take up their cues!"

Then his face changed as he hurriedly crumpled up the pinkish paper.

"Mother is dying. No hope. She cries to see you. Have told her you are in London. Father consents. Come at once.—MIRIAM."

He put the crumpled paper to the gas and lit a new cigarette with it.

"As I thought," he said, smiling. "When a woman is an actress as well as a woman—"

VI

After his wife died—vainly calling for her Isaac—the old Maggid was left heart-broken. It was as if his emotions ran in obedient harmony with the dictum of the Talmud: "Whoso sees his first wife's death is as one who in his own day saw the Temple destroyed."

What was there for him in life now but the ruins of the literal Temple? He must die soon, and the dream that had always haunted the background of his life began to come now into the empty foreground. If he could but die in Jerusalem!

There was nothing of consequence for him to do in England. His Miriam was married and had grown too English for any real communion. True, his congregation was dear to him, but he felt his powers waning: other Maggidim were arising who could speak longer.

To see and kiss the sacred soil, to fall prostrate where once the Temple had stood, to die in an ecstasy that was already Gan-Iden (Paradise)—could life, indeed, hold such bliss for him, life that had hitherto proved a cup of such bitters?

Life was not worth living, he agreed with his long-vanished brother-Rabbis in ancient Babylon, it was only a burden to be borne nobly. But if life was not worth living, death—in Jerusalem—was worth dying. Jerusalem! to which he had turned three times a day in praying, whose name was written on his heart, as on that of the mediæval Spanish singer, with whom he cried:—

"Who will make to me wings that I may fly ever Eastward, Until my ruined heart shall dwell in the ruins of thee? Then will I bend my face to thy sacred soil and hold precious Thy very stones, yea e'en to thy dust shall I tender be.

"Life of the soul is the air of thy land, and myrrh of the purest Each grain of thy dust, thy waters sweetest honey of the comb. Joyous my soul would be, could I even naked and barefoot, Amid the holy ruins of thine ancient Temple roam, Where the Ark was shrined, and the Cherubim in the Oracle had their home."

To die in Jerusalem!—that were success in life.

Here he was lonely. In Jerusalem he would be surrounded by a glorious host. Patriarchs, prophets, kings, priests, rabbonim—they all hovered lovingly over its desolation, whispering heavenly words of comfort.

But now a curious difficulty arose. The Maggid knew from correspondence with Jerusalem Rabbis that a Russian subject would have great difficulty in slipping in at Jaffa or Beyrout, even aided by bakhshîsh. The only safe way was to enter as a British subject. Grotesque irony of the fates! For nigh half a century the old man had lived in England in his gabardine, and now that he was departing to die in gabardine lands, he was compelled to seek naturalization as a voluntary Englishman! He was even compelled to account mendaciously for his sudden desire to identify himself with John Bull's institutions and patriotic prejudices, and to live as a free-born Englishman. By the aid of a rich but pious West End Jew, who had sometimes been drawn Eastwards by the Maggid's exegetical eloquence, all difficulties were overcome. Armed with a passport, signed floridly as with a lion's tail rampant, the Maggid—after a quasi-death-bed blessing to Miriam by imposition of hands from the railway-carriage window upon her best bonnet—was whirled away toward his holy dying-place.

VII

Such disappointment as often befalls the visionary when he sees the land of his dreams was spared to the Maggid, who remained a visionary even in the presence of the real; beholding with spiritual eye the refuse-laden alleys and the rapacious Schnorrers (beggars). He lived enswathed as with heavenly love, waiting for the moment of transition to the shining World-To-Come, and his supplications at the Wailing Wall for the restoration of Zion's glory had, despite their sympathetic fervour, the peaceful impersonality of one who looks forward to no worldly kingdom. To outward view he lived—in the rare intervals when he was not at a synagogue or a house-of-learning—somewhere up a dusky staircase in a bleak, narrow court, in one tiny room supplemented by a kitchen in the shape of a stove on the landing, itself a centre of pilgrimage to Schnorrers innumerable, for whom the rich English Maggid was an unexpected windfall. Rich and English were synonymous in hungry Jerusalem, but these beggars' notion of charity was so modest, and the coin of the realm so divisible, that the Maggid managed to gratify them at a penny a dozen. At uncertain intervals he received a letter from Miriam, written in English. The daughter had not carried on the learned tradition of the mother, and so the Maggid was wont to have recourse to the head of the philanthropic technical school for the translation of her news into Hebrew. There was, however, not much of interest; Miriam's world had grown too alien: she could scrape together little to appeal to the dying man. And so his last ties with the past grew frailer and frailer, even as his body grew feebler and feebler, until at last, bent with great age and infirmity, so that his white beard swept the stones, he tottered about the sacred city like an incarnation of its holy ruin. He seemed like one bent over the verge of eternity, peering wistfully into its soundless depths. Surely God would send his Death-Angel now.

Then one day a letter from Miriam wrenched him back violently from his beatific vision, jerked him back to that other eternity of the dead past.

Isaac, Isaac had come home! Had come home to find desolation. Had then sought his sister, and was now being nursed by her through his dying hours. His life had come to utter bankruptcy: his possessions—by a cruel coincidence—had been sold up at the very moment that the doctors announced to him that he was a doomed man. And his death-bed was a premature hell of torture and remorse. He raved incessantly for his father. Would he not annul the curse, grant him his blessing, promise to say Kaddish for his soul, that he might be saved from utter damnation? Would he not send his forgiveness by return, for Isaac's days were numbered, and he could not linger on more than a month or so?

The Maggid was terribly shaken. He recalled bitterly the years of suffering, crowned by Isaac's brutal heedlessness to the cry of his dying mother: but the more grievous the boy's sin, the more awful the anger of God in store for him.

And the mother—would not her own Gan-Iden be spoilt by her boy's agonizing in hell? For her sake he must forgive his froward offspring; perhaps God would be more merciful, then. The merits of the father counted: he himself was blessed beyond his deserts by the merits of the Fathers—of Abraham, Isaac, and Jacob. He had made the pilgrimage to Jerusalem; perhaps his prayers would be heard at the Mercy-Seat.

With shaking hand the old man wrote a letter to his son, granting him a full pardon for the sin against himself, but begging him to entreat God day and night. And therewith an anthology of consoling Talmudical texts: "A man should pray for Mercy even till the last clod is thrown upon his grave.... For Repentance and Prayer and Charity avert the Evil Decree." The Charity he was himself distributing to the startled Schnorrers.

The schoolmaster wrote out the envelope, as usual, but the Maggid did not post the letter. The image of his son's death-bed was haunting him. Isaac called to him in the old boyish tones. Could he let his boy die there without giving him the comfort of his presence, the visible assurance of his forgiveness, the touch of his hands upon his head in farewell blessing? No, he must go to him.

But to leave Jerusalem at his age? Who knew if he would ever get back to die there? If he should miss the hope of his life! But Isaac kept calling to him—and Isaac's mother. Yes, he had strength for the journey. It seemed to come to him miraculously, like a gift from Heaven and a pledge of its mercy.

He journeyed to Beyrout, and after a few days took ship for Marseilles.

VIII

Meantime in the London Ghetto the unhappy Ethelred P. Wyndhurst found each day a year. He was in a rapid consumption: a disorderly life had told as ruinously upon his physique as upon his finances. And with this double collapse had come a strange irresistible resurgence of early feelings and forgotten superstitions. The avenging hand was heavy upon him in life—what horrors yet awaited him when he should be laid in the cold grave? The shadow of death and judgment over-brooded him, clouding his brain almost to insanity.

There would be no forgiveness for him—his father's remoteness had killed his hope of that. It was the nemesis, he felt, of his refusal to come to his dying mother. God had removed his father from his pleadings, had wrapped him in an atmosphere holy and aloof. How should Miriam's letter penetrate through the walls of Jerusalem, pierce through the stonier heart hardened by twenty years of desertion!

And so the day after she had sent it, the spring sunshine giving him a spurt of strength and courage, a desperate idea came to him. If he could go to Jerusalem himself! If he could fall upon his father's neck, and extort his blessing!

And then, too, he would die in Jerusalem!

Some half-obliterated text sounded in his ears: "And the land shall forgive sin."

He managed to rise—his betaking himself to bed, he found, as the sunshine warmed him, had been mere hopelessness and self-pity. Let him meet Death standing, aye, journeying to the sun-lands. Nay, when Miriam, getting over the alarm of his up-rising, began to dream of the Palestine climate curing him, he caught a last flicker of optimism, spoke artistically of the glow and colour of the East, which he had never seen, but which he might yet live to render on canvas, winning a new reputation. Yes, he would start that very day. Miriam pledged her jewellery to supply him with funds, for she dared not ask her husband to do more for the stranger.

But long before Ethelred P. Wyndhurst reached Jaffa he knew that only the hope of his father's blessing was keeping him alive.

Somewhere at sea the ships must have passed each other.

IX

When the gabardined Maggid reached Miriam's house, his remains of strength undermined by the long journey, he was nigh stricken dead on the door-step by the news that his journey was vain.

"It is the will of God," he said hopelessly. The sinner was beyond mercy. He burst into sobs and tears ran down his pallid cheeks and dripped from his sweeping white beard.

"Thou shouldst have let us know," said Miriam gently. "We never dreamed it was possible for thee to come."

"I came as quickly as a letter could have announced me."

"But thou shouldst have cabled."

"Cabled?" The process had never come within his ken. "But how should I dream he could travel? Thy letter said he was on his death-bed. I prayed God I might but arrive in time."

He was for going back at once, but Miriam put him to bed—the bed Isaac should have died in.

"Thou canst cable thy forgiveness, at least," she said, and so, without understanding this new miracle, he bade her ask the schoolmaster to convey his forgiveness to his son.

"Isaac will inquire for me, if he arrives alive," he said. "The schoolmaster will hear of him. It is a very small place, alas! for God hath taken away its glory by reason of our sins."

The answer came the same afternoon. "Message just in time. Son died peacefully."

The Maggid rent his bed-garment. "Thank God!" he cried. "He died in Jerusalem. Better he than I! Isaac died in Jerusalem! God will have mercy on his soul."

Tears of joy sprang to his bleared eyes. "He died in Jerusalem," he kept murmuring happily at intervals. "My Isaac died in Jerusalem."

Three days later the Maggid died in London.

VI

BETHULAH

I

The image of her so tragically trustful in that mountain village of Bukowina still haunts my mind, and refuses to be exorcised, as of yore, by the prose of life. One who is very dear to me advises driving her out at the point of the pen. Whether such recording of my life's strangest episode will lay these memories or not, the story itself may at least instruct my fellow-Jews in New York how variously their religion has manifested itself upon this perplexing planet. Doubtless many are still as ignorant as I was respecting their mediæval contemporaries in Eastern Europe. True, they have now opportunities in their own Ghetto—which is, for cosmopolitanism, a New York within a New York—of studying strata from other epochs of Judaism spread out on the same plane of time as their own, even as upon the white sheet of that wonderful invention my aged eyes have lived to see, sequent events may be pictured simultaneously. In my youth these opportunities did not exist. Only in Baltimore and a few of the great Eastern cities was there any aggregation of Jews, and these were all—or wanted to be—good Yankees; while beyond the Mississippi, where my father farmed and hunted like a Christian, and where you might have scoured a thousand square miles to get minyan (ten Jews for worship), our picturesque customs and ceremonies dwindled away from sheer absence of fellowship. My father used to tell of a bronzed trapper he breakfasted with on the prairie, who astonished him by asking him over their bacon if he were a Jew. "Yes," said my father. "Shake!" said the trapper. "You're the first fellow-Jew I've met for twenty years." Though in my childhood my father taught me the Hebrew he had brought from Europe, and told me droll Jewish stories in his native German, it will readily be understood that the real influences I absorbed were the great American ideals of liberty and humanity, emancipation and enlightenment, and that therefore the strange things I witnessed among the Carpathians were far more startling to me than they can be to the Jews of to-day upon whom the Old World has poured its archaic inhabitants. Nevertheless, I cannot but think that even those who have met strange drifts of sects in New York will be astonished by the tradition which I stumbled upon so blindly in my first European tour. For, so far as I can gather, the Zloczszol legend is unique in Jewish history and confined exclusively to this out-of-the-way corner, however near other heresies may have approached to some of the underlying conceptions. My landlord Yarchi's view that it was a mere piece of local commercial myth-making, a gross artifice, would have at least the merit of explaining this uniqueness. It has, in my eyes, no other.

This tour of mine was to make not a circle, but a half-circle, for, landing at Hamburg I was to return by the Baltic, after a circuit through Berlin, Prague, Vienna, Buda-Pesth, Lemberg, (where my grandfather had once been a rabbi of consideration), Moscow, and St. Petersburg. I did not linger at Hamburg; purchasing a stout horse, I started on my long ride. Of course it did not seem so long to me—who had already ridden from Kansas to both of our seaboards—as it would to a young gentleman of to-day accustomed to parlour cars, though the constant change of dialects and foods was somewhat unsettling.

But money speaks all languages, and a good Western stomach digests all diets. Bad water, however, no stomach can cope with; and I was laid up at Prague with a fever, which left me too weak to hurry on. I rambled about the Ghetto—the Judenstadt—which gave me my first insight into mediæval Judaism, and was fascinated by the quaint alleys and houses, the Jewish town-hall, and the cellarlike Alt-Neu synagogue with its miraculous history of unnumbered centuries. I heard the story of the great red flag on the pillar, with its "shield of David" and the Swede's hat, and was shown on the walls the spatterings of the blood of the martyrs of 1389.

What emotions I had in the old graveyard—a Ghetto of the dead—where the graves were huddled together, three and four deep, and the very tombstones and corpses had undergone Ghetto persecution! A whole new world opened out to me, crooked as the Ghetto alleys—so alien from the free life of the flowering prairies—as I walked about this "Judengarten," studying the Hebrew inscriptions and the strange symbolic sculptures—the Priest's hands of blessing, the Levite's ewer, the Israelites' bunch of grapes, the Virgin with roses—and trying to reconstruct the life these dead had lived. Strange ancestral memories seemed thrilling through me, helping me to understand. Many stories did I hear, too, of the celebrated Rabbi Löw, and of the golem he created, which brought him his meals: in sign whereof I was shown his grave, and his house marked with a lion on a blue background. I listened with American incredulity but hereditary sympathy. I was astonished to find men who still believed in a certain Sabbataï Zevi, Messiah of the Jews, and one showed me a Sabbatian prayer-book with a turbaned head of this Redeemer side by side with King David's, and another who scoffed at this seventeenth-century impostor, yet told me the tradition in his own family, how they had sold their business and were about to start for Palestine, when the news reached them that so far from deposing the Sultan, this Redeemer of Israel had become his doorkeeper and a Mohammedan.

The year was passing toward the Fall ere I got to Buda-Pesth (in those days the enchanted gateway of the Orient, resounding with gypsy music, and not the civilized capital I found it the other day), and I had not proceeded far on the northerly bend of my journey when, soon after crossing the Carpathians, I was imprisoned in the mountain village of Zloczszol by the sudden overflow of the Dniester. The village itself was sheltered from the floods by a mountain between it and the tributary of the Dniester; but all the roads northward were impassable, and the water came round by clefts and soused our bordering fields and oozed very near the maize-garden of Yarchi's pine cottage, to which I had removed from the dirty inn, where a squalling baby in a cradle had shared the private sitting-room. It was a very straggling village, which began to straggle at the mountain-foot, but, for fear of avalanches, I was told, the houses did not grow companionable till some half a mile down the plain.

In the centre of the village was a cobble-paved "Ring-Place" and market-place, on which gave a few streets of shops (the provision-shops benefiting hugely by the floods, which made imports difficult). It was a Jewish colony, with the exception of a few outlying farms, whose peasants brought touches of gorgeous colour into the procession of black gabardines. It was strange to me to live in a place in which every door-post bore a Mezuzah. It gave me a novel sense of being in a land of Israel, and sometimes I used to wonder how these people could feel such a sense of local patriotism as seemed to possess them. And yet I reflected that, like the giant cedar of Lebanon which rose from the plain in such strange contrast with the native trees of Zloczszol, Israel could be transplanted everywhere, and was made of as enduring and undying a wood—nay, that, even like this cedar-wood, it had strange properties of conserving other substances and arresting putrefaction. Hence its ubiquitous patriotism was universally profitable. Nevertheless, this was one of the surprises of my journey—to find Jews speaking every language under the European sun, regarding themselves everywhere as part of the soil, and often patriotic to the point of resenting immigrant Jews as foreigners. I myself was popularly known as "the Stranger," though I was not resented, because the couple of dollars at which I purchased the privilege of "ark-opening" on my first visit to the synagogue—a little Gothic building standing in a court-yard—gave me a further reputation as "the rich stranger." Once I blushed to overhear myself called "the handsome stranger," and I looked into my cracked mirror with fresh interest. But I told myself modestly a stalwart son of the prairies had an unfair advantage in such a world of stooping sallow students. Certainly I felt myself favoured both in youth and looks when I stepped into the Beth-Hamedrash, the house of study (which I had at first taken for a little mosque, like those I had seen on the slopes of Buda), and watched the curious gnarled graybeards crooning and rocking the livelong day over worm-eaten folios.

Despite such odd glimpses of the interesting, I grew as tired of waiting for the waters to abate as Noah himself must have felt in his zoological institute.

One day as I was gazing from my one-story window at the melancholy marsh to which the flood had reduced the landscape, I said glumly to my hunchbacked landlord, who stood snuffing himself under the porch, "I suppose it will be another week before I can get away."

"Alas! yes," Yarchi replied.

"Why alas?" I asked. "It's an ill wind that blows nobody any good, and the longer I stay the better for you."

He shook his head. "The flood that keeps you here keeps away the pilgrims."

"The pilgrims!" I echoed.

"Ay," said he. "There will be three in that bed of yours."

"But what pilgrims?"

He stared at me. "Don't you know the New Year is nigh?"

"Of course," I said mendaciously. I felt ashamed to confess my ignorant unconcern as to the proximity of the solemn season of ram's-horn blasts and penitence.

"Well, it is at New Year the pilgrims flock to their Wonder Rabbi, that he may hear their petitions and bear them on high, likewise wrestle with Satan, and entreat for their forgiveness at the throne of Grace." There was a twinkle in Yarchi's eyes not quite consistent with the gravity of his words.

"Do Wonder Rabbis live nowadays?" I asked.

A pinch of snuff Yarchi was taking fell from between his fingers. "Do they live!" he cried. "Yes—and off white bread, for poverty!"

"We have none in America. I only heard of one in Prague," I murmured apologetically, fearing the genus might be of the very elements of Judaism.

"Ah, yes, the high Rabbi Löw, his memory for a blessing," he said reverently. "But these new Wonder Rabbis can only work one miracle."

"What is that?" I asked.

"The greatest of all—making their worshippers support them like princes." And he laughed in admiration of his own humour.

"Then you are a heretic?" I said.

"Heretic!" Yarchi's black eyes exchanged their twinkle for a flash of resentment. "Nay; they are the heretics, breeding dissension in Israel. Did they not dance on the grave of the sainted Elijah Wilna?"

Tired of tossing the ball of conversation up and down, I left the window and joined the philosopher under his porch, where I elicted from him his version of the eighteenth-century movement of Chassidim, (the pious ones), which, in these days of English books on Judaism, will not be so new to American Jews as it was to me. These Shakers (or, as we should perhaps say nowadays, Salvationists), these protestants against cut-and-dried Judaism, who arose among the Carpathians under the inspiration of Besht (a word which Yarchi explained to me was made out of the initials of Baal Shem Tob—the Master of the Good Name), had, it seemed, pullulated into a thousand different sects, each named after the Wonder Rabbi whom it swore by, and in whose "exclusive divine right" (the phrase is Yarchi's) it believed.

"But we have the divinest chief," concluded Yarchi, grinning.

"That's what they all say, eh?" I said, smiling in response.

"Yes; but the Zloczszol rabbi is stamped with the royal seal. He professes to be of the Messianic seed, a direct descendant of David, the son of Jesse." And the hunchback chuckled with malicious humour.

"I should like to see him," I said, feeling as if Providence had provided a new interest for my boredom.

Yarchi pointed silently with his discoloured thumb over the plain.

"You don't mean he is kept in that storehouse!" I said.

Yarchi guffawed in high good-humour.

"That! That's the Klaus!"

"And what's the Klaus?"

"The Chassidim Stubele (little room)."

"Is that where the miracles are done?"

"No; that's their synagogue."

"Oh, they just pray there!"

"Pray? They get as drunk as Lot."

II

I returned to my window and gazed curiously at the Klaus, and now that my eye was upon it I saw it was astir with restless life. Men came and went continually. I looked toward the synagogue, and the more pretentious building seemed dead. Then I remembered what Yarchi had told me, that the Chassidim had revolted against set prayer-times. ("They pray and drink at all hours," was his way of putting it.) Something must always be forward in the Klaus, I thought, as I took my hat and stick, on exploring bent. Instinctively I put my pistol in my hip pocket, then bethought myself with a laugh that I was not likely to be molested by the "pious ones." But as it was unloaded, I let it remain in the pocket.

I slipped into the building and on to a bench near the door. But for the veiled Ark at the end, I should not have known the place for a house of worship. True, some men were sitting or standing about, shouting and singing, with odd spasmodic gestures, but the bulk were lounging, smoking clay pipes, drinking coffee, and chattering, while a few, looking like tramps, lay snoring on the hard benches, deaf to all the din. My eye sought at once for the Wonder Rabbi himself, but amid the many quaint physiognomies there was none with any apparent seal of supremacy. The note of all the faces was easy-going good-will, and even the passionate contortions of melody and body which the worshippers produced, the tragic clutchings at space, the clinching of fists, and the beating of breasts had an air of cheery impromptu. They seemed to enjoy their very tears. And every now and then the inspiration would catch one of the gossipers and contort him likewise, while a worshipper would as suddenly fall to gossiping.

Very soon a frost-bitten old man I remembered coming across in the cemetery on the mountain-slope, where he was sweeping the fallen leaves from a tomb, and singing like the grave-digger in Hamlet, sidled up to me and asked me if I needed vodka. I thought it advisable to need some, and was quickly supplied from a box the old fellow seemed to keep under the Ark. The price was so moderate that I tipped him with as much again, doubtless to the enhancement of the "rich stranger's" reputation. Sipping it, I was able to follow with more show of ease the bursts of rambling conversation. Sometimes they talked about the floods, anon about politics, then about sacred texts and the illuminations of the Zohar. But there was one topic which ran like a winding pattern through all the talk, bursting in at the most unexpected places, and this was the wonders wrought by their rabbi.

As they dilated "with enkindlement" upon miracle after miracle, some wrought on earth and some in the higher spheres to which his soul ascended, my curiosity mounted, and calling for more vodka, "Where is the rabbi?" I asked the sexton.

"He may perhaps come down to lunch," said he, in reverent accents, as if to imply that the rabbi was now in the upper spheres. I waited till tables were spread with plain fare in the Klaus itself. At the savour the fountain of worship was sealed; the snorers woke up. I was invited to partake of the meal, which, I was astonished to find, was free to all, provided by the rabbi.

"Truly royal hospitality," I thought. But our royal host himself did not "come down."

My neighbour, of whom I kept inquiring, at last told me, sympathetically, to have patience till Friday evening, when the rabbi would come to welcome in the Sabbath. But as it was then Tuesday, "Cannot I call upon him?" I asked.

He shook his head. "Ben David holds his court no more this year," he said. "He is in seclusion, preparing for the exalted soul-flights of the pilgrim season. The Sabbath is his only public day now."

There was nothing for it but to wait till the Friday eve, though in the meantime I got Yarchi to show me the royal palace—a plain two-storied Oriental-looking building with a flat roof, and a turret on the eastern side, whose high, ivy-mantled slit of window turned at the first rays of the sun into a great diamond.

"He couldn't come down, couldn't he?" Yarchi commented. "I daresay he wasn't sober enough."

Somehow this jarred upon me. I was beginning to conjure up romantic pictures, and assuredly my one glimpse of the sect had not shown any intoxication save psychic.

"He is very generous, anyhow," I said. "He supplies a free lunch."

"Free to him," retorted the incorrigible Yarchi. "The worshippers fancy it is free, but it is they who pay for it." And he snuffed himself, chuckling. "I'll tell you what is free," he added. "His morals!"

"But how do you know?"

"Oh, all those fellows go in for the Adamite life."

"What is the Adamite life?"

He winked. "Not the pre-Evite."

I saw it was fruitless to reason with his hunchbacked view of the subject.

On the Friday eve I repaired again to the Klaus, but this time it was not so easy to find a seat. However, by the grace of my friend the sexton, I was accommodated near the Ark, where, amid a congregation clad in unexpected white, I sat, a conscious black discord. There was a certain palpitating fervour in the air, as though the imminence of the New Year and Judgment Day had strung all spirits to a higher tension. Suddenly a shiver seemed to run through the assemblage, and all eyes turned to the door. A tall old man, escorted by several persons of evident consideration, walked with erect head but tottering gait to the little platform in front of the Ark, and, taking a praying-shawl from the reverential hand of the sexton, held it a moment, as in abstraction, before drawing it over his head and shoulders. As he stood thus, almost facing me, yet unconscious of me, his image was photographed on my excited brain. He seemed very aged, with abundant white locks and beard, and he was clothed in a white satin robe cut low at the neck and ornamented at the breast with gold-laced, intersecting triangles of "the Shield of David."

On his head was a sort of white biretta. I noted a curious streak of yellow in the silvered eyebrows, as if youth clung on, so to speak, by a single hair, and underneath these arrestive eyebrows green pupils alternately glowed and smouldered. On his forefinger he wore a signet ring, set with amethysts and with a huge Persian emerald, which, as his hand rose and fell, and his fingers clasped and unclasped themselves in the convulsion of prayer, seemed to glare at me like a third green eye. And as soon as he began thus praying, every trace of age vanished. He trembled, but only from emotion; and his passion mounted, till at last his whole body prayed. And the congregation joined in with shakings and quiverings and thunderings and ululations. Not even in Prague had I experienced such sympathetic emotion. After the well-regulated frigidities of our American services, it was truly warming to be among worshippers not ashamed to feel. Hours must have passed, but I sat there as content as any. When the service ended, everybody crowded round the Wonder Rabbi to give the "Good Sabbath" handshake. The scene jarred me by its incongruous suggestion of our American receptions at which the lion of the evening must extend his royal paw to every guest. But I went up among the rest, and murmured my salutation. The glow came into his eyes as they became conscious of me for the first time, and his gaunt bloodless hand closed crushingly on mine, so that I almost fancied the signet ring was sealing my flesh.

"Good Sabbath, stranger," he replied. "You linger long here."

"As long as the floods," I said.

"Are you as dangerous to us?" he flashed back.

"I trust not," I said, a whit startled.

His jewelled forefinger drummed on the reading-stand, and his eyes no longer challenged mine, but were lowered as in abstraction.

"Your grandfather, who lies in Lemberg, was no friend to the followers of Besht. He laid the ban even on white Sabbath garments, and those who but wept in the synagogues he classed with us."

I was more taken aback by his knowledge of my grandfather than by that ancient gentleman's hostility to the emotional heresy of his day.

"I never saw my grandfather," I replied simply.

"True. The son of the prairies should know more of God than the bookworms. Will you accept a seat at my table?"

"With pleasure, Rabbi," I murmured, dazed by his clairvoyant air.

They were now arranging the two tables, one with a white cloth for the master and his circle in strict order of precedence; and the other of bare wood for such of the rabble as could first scramble into the seats. I was placed on his right hand, and became at once an object of wonder and awe. The Kiddush which initiated the supper was not a novel ceremony to me, but what I had never seen before was the eagerness with which each guest sipped from the circulating wine-cup of consecration, and the disappointment of such of the mob as could find no drop to drain. Still fiercer was the struggle for the Wonder Rabbi's soup, after he had taken a couple of spoonfuls; even I had no chance of distinction before this sudden simultaneous swoop, though of course I had my own plateful to drink. As sudden was the transition from soup to song, the whole company singing and swaying in victorious ecstasy. I turned to speak to my host, but his face awed me. The eyes had now their smouldering inward fire. The eyebrows seemed wholly white; the features were still. Then as I watched him his whole body grew rigid, he closed his eyes, his head fell back. The singing ceased; as tense a silence reigned as though the followers too were in a trance. My eyes were fixed on the Master's blind face, which had now not the dignity of death, but only the indignity of lifelessness, and, but for the suggestion of mystery behind, would have ceased to impress me. For there was now revealed a coarseness of lips, a narrowness of forehead, an ugliness of high cheek-bone, which his imperial glance had transfigured, and which his flowing locks still abated. But as I gazed, the weird stillness took possession of me. I could not but feel with the rest that the Master was making a "soul-ascension."

It seemed very long—yet it may have been only a few minutes, for in absolute silence one's sense of time is disconcerted—ere waves of returning life began to traverse the cataleptic face and form. At last the Wonder Rabbi opened his eyes, and the hush grew profounder. Every ear was astrain for the revelations to come.

"Children," said he slowly, "as I passed through the circles the souls cried to me. 'Haste, haste, for the Evil One plotteth and the Messianic day will be again delayed.' So I rose into the ante-chamber of Grace where the fiery wheels sang 'Holy, holy,' and there I came upon the Poison God waiting to see the glory of the Little Face. And with him was a soul, very strange, such as I had never seen, living neither in heaven nor hell, perchance created of Satan himself for his instrument. Then with a great cry I uttered the Name, and the Poison God fled with a great fluttering, leaving the nameless, naked soul helpless amid the consuming, dazzling wheels. So I returned through the circles to reassure the souls, and they shouted with a great shout."

"Hallelujah!" came in a great shout from the wrought-up listeners, and then they burst into a lilting chant of triumph. But by this time my mood had changed. The spell of novelty had begun to wear off; perhaps also I was fatigued by the long strain. I recalled the coarser face of the comatose saint, and I found nothing but gibberish in the oracular "revelation" which he had brought down with such elaborate pains from the circles amid which he seemed to move.

Thanking him for his hospitality, I slipped from the hot, roaring room.

Ah! what a waft of fresh air and sense of starlit space! The young moon floated in the star-sprinkled heavens like a golden boat, with a faint suggestion of the full-sailed orb. The true glamour and mystery of the universe were again borne in upon me, as in our rich, constellated prairie nights, and all the artificial abracadabra of the Klaus seemed akin to its heated, noisy atmosphere. The lights of the village were extinguished, and, looking at my watch, I found it was close upon midnight. But as I passed the saint's "palace" I was astonished to find a light twinkling from the turret window. I wondered who kept vigil. Then I bethought me it was Friday night when no light could be struck, and this must be Ben David's bed-room lamp, awaiting his return.

"I thought he had taken you up in his fiery chariot," grumbled Yarchi sleepily, as he unbarred the door.

"The fiery chariot must not run on the Sabbath," I said smiling. "And, moreover, Ben David takes no passengers to the circles."

"Circles! He ought to have a circle of rope round his neck."

"The soup was good," I pleaded, as I groped my way toward my quaint, tall bed.

III

I cannot explain why, when Yarchi asked me sarcastically, over the Sabbath dinner, whether I was going to the "Supper of the Holy Queen," I knew at once that I should be found at this mysterious meal. Perhaps it was that I had nothing better to do; perhaps my sympathy was returning to those strange, good-humoured, musical loungers, so far removed from the New York ideal of life. Or perhaps I was vaguely troubled by the dream I had wrestled with more or less obscurely all night long—that I stood naked in a whirl of burning wheels that sang, as they turned, the melody of the Chassidim. Was I this nondescript soul, I wondered, half smilingly, fashioned of the Evil One to delay the Messianic era?

The sun was set, the three stars already in the sky, and my pious landlord had performed the Ceremony of Division ere I set out, declining the bread and fish Yarchi offered to make up in a package.

"Saturday nights every man must bring his own meal," he said

I replied that I went not to eat, but to look on. However, I was so late in arriving that, as there were no lights, looking on was well-nigh reduced to listening. In the gray twilight the Klaus seemed full of uncanny forms rocking in monotonous sing-song. Through the gathering gloom the old Wonder Rabbi's face loomed half ghostlike, half regal. As the mystic dusk grew deeper and darkness fell, the fascination of it all began to overcome me: the dim, tossing, crooning figures, divined rather than seen, washed round lappingly and swayingly by their own rhythmic melody, full of wistful sweetness. My soul too tossed in this circumlapping tide. The complex world of modern civilization fell away from me as garments fall from a bather. Even this primitive mountain village passed into nothingness, and in a timeless, spaceless universe I floated in a lulling, measureless music.

Æons might have elapsed ere the glare of light dazzled my eyes when the week-day candles were lit, and the supper to escort the departing Holy Queen—the Sabbath—began. Again I was invited to the upper table, despite Yarchi's warning. But I had no appetite for earthly things, was jarred by the prosaic gusto with which the mystics threw themselves upon the tureen of red Borsch and the black pottle of brandy.

"Der Rabbi hat geheissen Branntwein trinken," hummed the sexton joyously. But little by little, as their stomachs grew satiate, the holy singing started afresh, and presently they leaped up, pulled aside the table, and made a whirling ring. I was caught up into the human cyclone, and round and round we flew, our hands upon one another's shoulders, with blind ecstatic faces, our legs kicking out madly, to repel, I understood, the embryonic demons outside the magic circle. And again methought I made a "soul-ascension," or at least hovered as near to the ineffable mysteries as the demoniacles to our magic circle.

Oh, what inexpressible religious raptures were mine! What no gorgeous temple, nor pealing organ, nor white-robed minister had ever wrought for me was wrought in this barracklike room with its rude benches and wooden ark. "Children of the Palace" we sang, and as I strove to pick up the words I thought we were indeed sons of our Father who is in Heaven.

CHILDREN OF THE PALACE

Children of the Palace, haste—
All who yearn the bliss to taste
Of the glorious Little-Faced,
Where, within the King's house placed,
Shines the sapphire throne enchased.
Come, in joyful dance enlaced,
Mock the cold and primly chaste.
See no sullen nor straitlaced
In our circle may be traced.
Here with th' Ancient One embraced
Inmost truth 'tis ours to taste,
Outer husks are shred to waste.
Children of the Palace, haste,
With the glory to be graced,
Come, behold the Little-Faced.

We broke up some hours earlier than the previous evening, but I hurried away from my sauntering fellow-worshippers, not now because I was disgusted, but because I feared to be. I needed solitude—communion with my own soul. The same crescent moon hung in the heavens, the same endless stars drew on the thoughts to a material infinity.

But now I felt there was another and a truer universe encompassing this painted vision—a spiritual universe of which I had hitherto known nothing, though I had glibly prated of it and listened well-satisfied to sermons about it.

The air was warm and pleasant, and, still thrilling with the sense of the Over-Soul, I had passed the outposts of the village almost unconsciously, and walked in the direction of the cemetery on the other slope of the mountain (for the dead feared neither floods nor avalanches). On my left ran the river, still turbulent and encumbered with wreckage and logs, but now at low tide some feet below the level of its steep banks. The road gradually narrowed till at last I was walking on a mere strip of path between the starlit water and the base of the mountain, which rose ineffably solemn with its desolate rock at my side and its dark pines higher up. And suddenly lifting my eyes, I saw before me a mystic moonlit figure that set my heart beating with terror and surprise.

It was the figure of a woman, or rather of a girl, tall, queenly, shining in a strange white robe, with a crown of roses and olive branches. For a moment she seemed like some spirit of moonlight. But though the eyes were misted with sadness and dream, the face was of the most beautiful Jewish oval, glowing with dark creamy flesh.

A wild idea rose to my mind, and, absurdly enough, stilled my beating heart. This was the Holy Queen Sabbath whose departure we had just been celebrating, and in this unfrequented haunt she abode till the twilight of the next Friday.

"Hail, Holy Queen!" I said, almost involuntarily.

I saw her large beautiful eyes grow larger as she woke with a start to my presence, but she only inclined her head with a sovereign air, as one used to adoration, and floated on—for so her gracious motion seemed to me.

And as she passed by, it flashed upon me that the strange white robe was nothing but a shroud. And again a great horror seized me. But struggling with my failing senses, I told myself that at worst it was some poor creature buried alive in the graveyard, who had forced the coffin lid, and now wandered half insanely homewards.

"May I not escort you, lady?" I cried after her. "The way is lonely."

She turned her face again upon me. I saw it had fire as well as mystery.

"Who dare molest the Holy Queen?" she said.

Again I was plunged into the wildest bewilderment. Was my first fancy true? Or had I stumbled upon some esoteric title she bore? Or had she but seized on my own phrase?

"But you go far?" I persisted.

"Unto my father's house."

"Pardon me. I am a stranger."

She turned round wholly now and looked at me. "Oh, are you the Stranger?" she said. The question rippled like music from her lips and was as sweet to my ear, linking her to me by the suggestion that I was not new to her imagination.

"I am the Stranger," I answered, moving slowly toward her, "and therefore afraid for your sake, and startled by the shroud you wear."

"Since the dawn of my thirteenth year it has been my daily robe. It should be in lamentation for Zion laid waste. But me, I fear, it reminds more of my dead mother and sisters."

"You had sisters?"

"Two beautiful lives, blown out one after the other like candles, making our home dark, when I was but a child. They too wore shrouds in life and death, first the elder, then the younger; and when I draw mine over my dress, it is of them I think always. I feel we are truly sisters—sisters of the shroud."

I shivered as from some chill graveyard air, despite her sweet corporeality.

"But the crown—the crown of joy?" I murmured, regarding now with closer vision the intertangled weaving of roses and myrtle and olive branches, with gold and crimson threads wound about salt stones and the pale yellow of pyrites.

"I do not know what it signifies," she said simply.

"Are you not the Holy Queen?" I asked, beginning to scent some Cabalistic or Chassidic mystery.

"Men worship me. But I know not of what I am queen." And a wistful smile played about the sweet mouth. "Peace and sweet dreams to you, sir." And she turned her face to the village.

She knew not of what she was queen. There, all in one sentence, was the charm, the wonder, the pathos, of her. Yet there was still much that she knew that would enlighten me. And it was not wholly curiosity that provoked me to hold the vision. I hated to see the enchantment of her presence dissolve, to be robbed of the liquid notes of her voice.

"You are queen of me at least," I said, following her, and throwing all my republican principles into the river among the other wreckage. "And your Majesty's liege cannot endure to see you walk unattended so late in the night."

"I have God's company," she answered quietly.

"True; He is always with us. Nevertheless, at night and in the mountains—"

"He may be perceived more clearly. My father makes soul-ascensions at any hour by force of prayer. But for me the divine ecstasy comes only under God's heaven, and most clearly at night and among the graves. By day God is invisible, like the stars."

"They may be perceived from a well," I said, mechanically, for my brain was busy with the intuition that she was Ben David's daughter, that her "queendom" was somehow bound up with his alleged royal descent.

"Even so is God visible from the deeps of the spirit," she answered. "But these depths are not mine, and day speaks to me less surely of Him."

"The day is divine too," I urged. "God speaks also through joy, through sunshine."

"It is but the gilding of sorrow."

"Nay, that is too hard a saying. How can you know that? You"—I made a bold guess, for my brain had continued to work feverishly—"who live cloistered in a turret, who are kept sequestered from man, who walk at night, and only among the dead. How can you know that life is so sad?"

"I feel it. Is not every stone in the graveyard hewn from the dead heart of the mourners?"

All the sadness of the world was in her eyes, yet somehow all the sweet solace. Again she bade me good-night, and I was so under the spell of her strange reply that I made no further effort to follow her, as she was swallowed up in the gloom of the firs where the path wound back round the mountain.

IV

The floods abated before the New Year dawned, as was testified by the arrival, not of doves with olive leaves, but of pilgrims from the north with shekels. The road was therefore open for me to go, yet I lingered. I told myself it was the fascination of the pilgrims, that curious new population which brought quite a bustle into the "Ring-Place" of Zloczszol, and gave even the shops of the native Chassidim a live air. There were unpleasant camp-followers in the train of the invading army, cripples and consumptives, both rich and poor; but, on the whole, it was a cheery, well-to-do company. I retained my room by paying the rent of three lodgers, and even then Yarchi would come in and look at the big, tall bed wistfully, as if it were a waste of sleeping material.

The great episode of each day was now the royal levee. Crowds besieged the door of the "palace," in quest of health, wealth, and happiness, and the proprietor of fields had to squeeze in with the tramp, and the peasant woman and her neglected brat jostled the jewelled dame from the towns. I was glad to think that the "Holy Queen" was hidden safely away in her turret, and this consoled me for not meeting her again, though I walked or trotted about on my bay mare at all hours and in all places in quest of her.

It may seem curious that I did not boldly call and ask to see her, but that would bring the commonplace into our so poetic relation. Besides which, I divined that she would not be easily on view. Beyond indirectly justifying my intuition that she was Ben David's daughter by satisfying myself that the Wonder Rabbi had once had three girls, two of whom had died, I would not even make inquiries. I feared to dissipate the mystery and sacredness of our relation by gossip. Perhaps Yarchi would tell me she was mad, or treat me to some other coarse misconception due to the callous feelers with which he apprehended the world.

I did not even know for certain that the light I saw in the turret was hers. But when at night it was out, I hastened to the river-side, to see only my own shadow on the hushed mountain slope or on the white tombs. It seemed clear that she was being kept sacred from the pilgrims' gaze; perhaps, too, the deserted, untravelled road which was safe as her own home in normal times, was less secure now.

When I at last ventured to say casually to Yarchi that Ben David's daughter seemed to be kept strictly to the house, the ribald grin I had feared distorted his malicious mouth.

"Oh, you have seen Bethulah!" he said.

"Yes," I murmured, turning my flushed face away, but glad to learn her name. Bethulah! Bethulah! my heart seemed to beat to the music of it.

"Does she still stalk about in a shroud?" He did not wait for an answer, but went off into unending laughter, which doubled him up till his hunch protruded upward like a camel's.

"She does not go about at all now," I said freezingly. But this set Yarchi cachinnating worse than ever.

"He daren't trust even his own disciples, you see! Ha! ha! ha!"

"Yarchi!" I cried angrily, "you know Bethulah must be kept sacred from this rabble," and I switched with my riding-whip at the poppies that grew among the maize in the little front garden, as if they were pilgrims and I a Tarquin.

"Yes, I know that's Ben David's game. But I wish some man would marry her and ruin his business. Ha! ha! ha!"

"It would ruin yours too," I reminded him, more angrily. "You are ready enough to let lodgings to the pilgrims."

Yarchi shrugged his hump. "If fools are fools, wise men are wise men," he replied oracularly.

I strode away, but he had heated my brain with a new idea, or one that I now allowed myself to see clearly. Some man might marry her. Then why should I not be that man? Why should I not carry Bethulah back to America with me—the most precious curiosity of the Old World—a frank, virginal creature with that touch of the angel which I had dreamed of but had never met among our smart girls—up to then. And even if it were true that Ben David was a fraud, and needed the girl for his Cabalistic mystifications, even so I was rich enough to recoup him. The girl herself was no conscious accessory; of that I felt certain.

When my brain cooled, suggestions of the other aspects of the question began to find entrance. What of Bethulah herself? Why should she care to marry me? Or to go to the strange, raw country? And such a union—was it not too incongruous, too fantastic, for practical life? Thus I wrestled with myself for three days, all the while watching Bethulah's turret or the roads she might come by. On the third night I saw a wild mob of men at the turret end of the house, dancing in a ring and singing, with their eyes turned upward to the light that burnt on high. Their words I could not catch at first through the tumultuous howl, but it went on and on, like their circumvolutions, over and over again, till my brain reeled. It seemed to be an appeal to Bethulah to plead their cause on the coming Yom-Hadin (New-Year day of Judgment):—

"By thy soul without sin, Enter heaven within, This divine Yom-Hadin, Holy Maid.

"Undertake thou our plea; Let the Poison God be Answered stoutly by thee, Holy Queen."

When I came to write this down afterward, I discovered it was an acrostic on her name, as is customary with festival prayers. And this I have preserved in my rough translation.

V

Despite my new spiritual insight, I could not bring myself to sympathize with such crude earthly visionings of the heavenly judgment bar (doubtless borrowed from the book of Job, which our enlightened Western rabbis rightly teach to be allegorical). Temporary absorption into the Over-Soul seemed to me to sum up the limits of Chassidic experience. Besides, Bethulah was not a being to be employed as a sort of supernatural advocate, but a sad, tender creature needing love and protection.

This mob howling outside my lady's chamber added indignation to my strange passion for this beautiful "sister of the shroud." I would rescue her from this grotesque environment. I would go to her father and formally demand her hand, as, I had learnt, was the custom among these people. I slept upon the resolution, yet in the morning it was still uncrumpled; and immediately after breakfast I took my stand among the jostling crowd outside the turreted house, and unfairly secured precedence by a gold piece slipped into the palm of the doorkeeper. The scribe I found stationed in the ante-chamber made me write my wish on a piece of paper, which, however, I was instructed to carry in myself.

Ben David was seated in a curious soft-cushioned, high-backed chair, with the intersecting triangles making a carved apex to it, but otherwise there was no mark of what Yarchi would have called charlatanism. His face, set between a black velvet biretta and the white masses of his beard, had the dignity with which it had first impressed me, and his long, fur-trimmed robe gave him an air of mediæval wisdom.

"Peace be to you, long-lingering stranger," he said, though his green eyes glittered ominously.

"Peace," I murmured uneasily.

With his left hand he put the still folded paper to his brow. I watched the light playing on the Persian emerald seal of the ring on the forefinger of his right hand. Suddenly I perceived he too was looking at the stone—nay, into it—and that while that continued to glitter, his own eyes had grown glazed.

"Strange, strange," he muttered. "Again I see the fiery wheels, and the strange soul fashioned of Satan that dwells neither in heaven nor in hell." And his eyes lit up terribly again and rolled like fiery wheels.

"What do you want?" he cried harshly.

"It is written on the paper," I faltered, "just two words."

He opened the paper and read out, "Your daughter!" His eyes rolled again. "What know you of my daughter?"

"Oh, I know all about her," I said airily.

"Then you know that my daughter does not receive pilgrims."

"Nay, 'tis I that wish to receive your daughter," I ventured jocosely, with a touch of levity I did not feel. He raised his clinched hand as if to strike me, and I had a lurid sense of three green eyes glaring at me. I stood my ground as coolly as possible, and said, in dry, formal tones, "I wish to make application for her hand."

A great blackness came over the frosted visage, as if his black biretta had been suddenly drawn forward, and his erst blanched eyebrows gloomed like a black lightning-cloud over the baleful eyes.

I shrank back, then I had a sudden vision of the wagons clattering down Broadway in a live, sunlit, go-ahead world, and the Wonder Rabbi turned into an absurd old parent with a beautiful daughter and a bad temper.

"I am a man of substance," I went on dryly. "In my country I have fat lands."

The horribleness of thus bidding for Bethulah flashed on me even as I spoke. To mix up a creature of mist and moonlight with substance and fat lands! Monstrous! And yet I knew that thus, and thus only, by honourable talk with her guardian, could a Zloczszol bride be won.

But the Wonder Rabbi sprang to his feet so vehemently that his high-backed chair rocked as in a gale.

"Dog!" he shrieked. "Blasphemer!"

I summoned all my American sang-froid.

"Dog," I agreed, "inasmuch as I follow your daughter like a dog, humbly, lovingly. But blasphemer? Say rather worshipper. For I worship Bethulah."

"Then worship her like the others," he roared. Had I not heard him pray, I should have expected the hoary patriarch to collapse after such an outburst.

"Thank you," I said. "I don't want her to fly up to heaven for me. I want her to come down to earth— from her turret."

"She will not come down to any earthly spouse," he said more gently. "Quite the reverse."

"Then I will make a soul-ascension," I said defiantly.

"Get back to hell, spawn of Satan!" he thundered again. "Or since, strange son of the New World, you neither believe nor disbelieve, hover eternally between hell and heaven!"

"Meantime I am here," I said good-humouredly, "between you and your daughter. Come, come, be sensible; you are a very old man. Where in Zloczszol will you find a superior husband for your child?"

"The Lord, to whom she is consecrated, forgive you your blasphemy," he said, in a changed voice, and rang his bell, so that the next applicant came in and I had to go.

It was plain the girl was kept as a sacred celibate, a sort of vestal virgin—Bethulah was the very Hebrew for virgin, it suddenly flashed upon me. But how came such practices into Judaism—Judaism, with its cheery creed, "increase and multiply?" And Chassidism, I had hitherto imagined, was the cheeriness of Judaism concentrated! In Yarchi's version it was even license—"the Adamite life." I raked up my memories of the Bible—remembered Jephtha's daughter. But no! there could be no question of a vow; this was some new Chassidic mystery. The crown and the shroud! The shroud of renunciation, the crown of victory!

And for some fantastic shadow-myth a beautiful young life was to be immolated. My respect for Chassidism vanished as suddenly as it came.

But I was powerless. I could only wait till the flood of pilgrims oozed back, even as the waters had done. Then perhaps Bethulah might walk again upon the moonlit mountain-peak, or in the "house of life," as the cemetery was mystically called.

The penitential season, with its trumpets and terrors, judgment-writings and sealings, was over at last, and Tabernacles came like a breath of air and nature. Yarchi hammered up a little wooden booth in the corner of his front garden, and hung grapes and oranges and flowers from its loose roof of boughs, through which the stars peeped at us as we ate. It struck me as a very pretty custom, and I wondered why American Judaism had let it fall into desuetude. Ere the break-up of these booths the pilgrims had begun to melt away, the old sleepiness to fall upon Zloczszol.

Hence I was startled one morning by the passage of a joyous procession that carried torches and played on flutes and tambourines. I ran out and discovered that I was part of a wedding procession escorting a bride. As this was a company not of Chassidim, but of everyday Jews, bound for the little Gothic synagogue, I was surprised, despite my experience of the Tabernacles, to find such picturesque goings-on, and I went all the way to the courtyard, where the rabbi came out to meet us with the bridegroom, who, it seemed, had already been conducted hither with parallel pomp. The happy youth—for he could only have been sixteen—was arrayed in festival finery, with white shoes on his feet and black phylacteries on his forehead, which was further over-gloomed by a cowl. He took the bride's hand, and then we all threw wheat over their heads, crying three times, "Peru, Urvu" (Be fruitful and multiply). But just when I expected the ceremony to begin, the bride was snatched away, and we all filed into the synagogue to await her return.

I had fallen into a mournful reverie—perhaps the suggestion of my own infelicitous romance was too strong—when I felt a stir of excitement animating my neighbours, and, looking up, lo! I saw a tall female figure in a white shroud, with a veiled face, and on her head a crown of roses and myrtles and olive branches. A shiver ran through me. "Bethulah!" I cried half-aloud. My neighbours smiled, and as I continued to stare at the figure, I saw it was only the bride, thus transmogrified for the wedding canopy. And then some startling half comprehension came to me. Bethulah's dress was a bride's dress, then. She was made to appear a perpetual bride. Of whom? To what Cabalistic mystery was this the key? The Friday night hymn sprang to my mind.

"Oh, come, my beloved, to meet the Bride, The face of the Sabbath let us welcome."

For a moment I thought I held the solution, and that my very first conjecture had been warranted. The Holy Queen Sabbath was also typified as the Sabbath Bride, and this dual allegory it was that Bethulah incarnated. Or perchance it was Israel, the Bride of God!

But I was still dissatisfied. I felt that the truth lay deeper than a mere poetic metaphor or a poetical masquerading. I discovered it at last, but at the risk of my life.

VI

I continued to walk nightly on the narrow path between the mountain and the river, like the ghost of one drowned, but without a glimpse of Bethulah. At last it grew plain that her father had warned her against me, that she had changed the hour of her exercise and soul-ascension, or even the place. I was indebted to accident for my second vision of this strange creature.

I had diverted myself by visiting the neighbouring village, a refreshing contrast to Jewish Zloczszol, from the rough garland-hung wayside crosses (which were like sign-posts to its gilt-towered church) to the peasant women in pink aprons and top boots.

A marvellous sunset was well-nigh over as I struck the river-side that curved homewards. The bank was here very steep, the river running as between cliffs. In the sky great drifts of gold-flushed cloud hung like relics of the glory that had been, and the autumn leaves that muffled my mare's footsteps seemed to have fallen from the sunset. In the background the white peak of the mountain was slowly parting with its volcanic splendour. And low on the horizon, like a small lake of fire in the heart of a tangled bush, the molten sun showed monstrous and dazzling.

And straight from the sunset over the red leaves Bethulah came walking, rapt as in prophetic thought, shrouded and crowned, preceded by a long shadow that seemed almost as intangible.

I reined in my horse and watched the apparition with a great flutter at my heart. And as I gazed, and thought of her grotesque worshippers, it was borne in upon me how unbefittingly Nature had peopled her splendid planet. The pageantry of dawn and sunset, of seas and mountains, how incongruous a framework for our petty breed, sordidly crawling under the stars. Bethulah alone seemed fitted to the high setting of the scene. She matched this lone icy peak, this fiery purity.

"Bethulah!" I said, as she was almost upon my horse.

She looked up, and a little cry that might have been joy or surprise came from her lips. But by the smile that danced in her eyes and the blood that leapt to her cheeks, I saw with both joy and surprise that this second meeting was as delightful to her as to me.

But the conscious Bethulah hastened to efface what the unconscious had revealed. "It is not right of you, stranger, to linger here so long," she said, frowning.

"I am your shadow," I replied, "and must linger where you linger."

"But you are indeed a shadow, my father says—a being fashioned of the Poison God to work us woe."

"No, no," I said, laughing; "my horse bears no shadow. And the Poison God who fashioned me is not the absurd horned and tailed tempter you have been taught to believe in, but a little rosy-winged god, with a bow and poisoned arrows."

"A little rosy-winged god?" she said. "I know of none such."

"And you know not of what you are queen," I retorted, smiling.

"There is but one God," she insisted, with sweet seriousness. "See, He burns in the bush, yet it is not consumed."

She pointed to where the red sinking sun seemed to eat out the heart of the bush through which we saw it.

"Thus this love-god burns in our hearts," I said, lifted up into her poetic strain, "and we are not consumed, only glorified."

I strove to touch her hand, which had dropped caressingly on my horse's neck. But she drew back with a cry.

"I may not listen. This is the sinful talk my father warned me of. Fare you well, stranger." And with swift step she turned homewards.

I sat still a minute or two, half-disconcerted, half-content to gaze at her gracious motions; then I touched the mare with my heel, and she bounded off in pursuit. But at this instant three men in long gabardines and great round velvet hats started forward from the thicket, shouting and waving lighted pine-branches, and my frightened animal reared and plunged, and then broke into a mad gallop, making straight for the river curve between the cliffs. I threw myself back in the saddle, tugging desperately at the creature's mouth; but I might have been a child pulling at an elephant. I shook my feet free of the stirrups and prepared to tumble off as best I could, rather than risk the plunge into the river, when a projecting bough made me duck my head instinctively; but as I passed under it, with another instinctive movement I threw out my hands to clasp it, and, despite a violent wrench that seemed to pull my arms out of their sockets and swung my feet high forward, I hung safely. The mare, eased of my weight, was at the river-side the next instant, and with a wild, incredible leap alighted with her forefeet and the bulk of her body on the other bank, up which she scraped convulsively, and then stood still, trembling and sweating. I could not get at her, so, trusting she would find her way home safely, I dropped to the ground and ran back, with a mixed idea of finding Bethulah and chastising the three scoundrels. But all were become invisible.

I walked half a mile across the plain to get to the rough pine bridge; and, once on the other bank, I had no difficulty in recovering the mare. She cantered up to me, indeed, and put her soft and still perspiring nose in my palm and whinnied her apologetic congratulations on our common escape.

I rode slowly home, reflecting on the new turn in my love affairs, for it was plain that Bethulah had now been provided with a body-guard, of which she was as unconscious as of her body itself.

But for the apparent necessity of her making soul-ascensions under God's heaven, I supposed she would not have been allowed to take the air at all with such a creature of Satan hovering.

I stood sunning myself the next day on the same pine bridge, looking down on the swift current, and regretting there was no rail to lean on as one watched the fascinating flow of the beautiful river. It struck me as inordinately blue—perhaps, I analyzed, by contrast with the long, sinuous weeds which here glided and tossed in the current like green water-snakes. These flexible greens reminded me of the Wonder Rabbi's eyes and his emerald seal; and I turned, with some sudden premonition of danger, just in time to dodge the attack of the same three ruffians, who must have been about to push me over.

In an instant I had whipped out my pistol from my hip pocket, and cried, "Stand, or I fire!"

The trio froze instantly in odd attitudes, which was lucky, as my pistol was unloaded. They looked almost comical in their air of abject terror. Their narrow, fanatical foreheads, with ringlets of piety hanging down below the velvet, fur-trimmed hats, showed them more accustomed to murdering texts than men. Had I not been still smouldering over yesterday's trick, I could have pitied them for the unwelcome job thrust upon their unskilled and apparently even unweaponed hands by the machinations of the Poison God and the orders of Ben David. One of them seemed quite elderly, and one quite young. The middle-aged one had a goitre, and perhaps that made me fancy him the most sinister, and keep my eye most warily upon him.

"Sons of Belial," I said, recalling a biblical phrase that might be expected to prick, "why do you seek my life?"

Two of them cowered under my gaze, but the elderly Chassid, seeing the shooting was postponed, spoke up boldly: "We are no sons of Belial. You are the begotten of Satan; you are the arch enemy of Israel."

"I?" I protested in my turn. "I am a plain God-fearing son of Abraham."

"A precious scion of the Patriarch's seed, who would delay the coming of the Messiah!"

Again that incomprehensible accusation.

"You speak riddles," I said.

"How so? Did you not tell Ben David—his horn be exalted—that you knew all concerning Bethulah? Then must you know that of her immaculacy will the Messiah be born, one ninth of Ab."

A flood of light burst upon me—mystic, yet clarifying; blinding, yet dissipating my darkness. My pistol drooped in my hand. My head swam with a whirl of strange thoughts, and Bethulah, already divine to me, took on a dazzling aureola, sailed away into some strange supernatural ether.

"Have we not been in exile long enough?" said the youngest. "Shall a godless stranger tamper with the hope of generations?"

"But whence this mad hope?" I said, struggling under the mystic obsession of his intensity.

"Mad?" began the first, his eyes spitting fire; but the younger interrupted him.

"Is not our saint the sole scion of the house of David? Is not his daughter the last of the race?"

"And what if she is?"

"Then who but she can be the destined mother of Israel's Redeemer?"

The goitred Chassid opened his lips and added, "If not now, when? as Hillel asked."

"In our days at last must come the crowning glory of the house of Ben David," the young man went on. "For generations now, since the signs have pointed to the millennium, have the daughters of the house been kept unwedded."

"What!" I cried. "Generations of Bethulahs have been sacrificed to a dream!"

Again the eyes of the first Chassid dilated dangerously. I raised my pistol, but hastened to ask, in a more conciliatory tone, "Then how has the line been carried on?"

"Through the sons, of course," said the young Chassid. "Now for the first time there are no sons, and only one daughter remains, the manifest vessel of salvation."

I tried to call up that image of bustling Broadway that had braced me in colloquy with the old Wonder Rabbi, but it seemed shadowy now, compared with this world of solid spiritualities which begirt me.

Could it be the same planet on which such things went on simultaneously? Or perhaps I was dreaming, and these three grotesque creatures were the product of Yarchi's cookery.

But their hanging curls had a daylight definiteness, and down in the sunlit, translucent river I could see every shade of colour, from the green of the sinuous reed-snakes to the brown of the moss patches.

On the bank walked two crows, and I noted for the first time with what comic pomposity they paced, their bodies bent forward like two important old gentlemen with their hands in the pockets of their black coat tails. They brought a smile to my face, but a menacing movement of the Chassidim warned me to be careful.

"And does the girl know all this?" I asked hurriedly.

"She did not yesterday," said the elderly fellow. "Now she has been told."

There was another long pause. I meditated rapidly but disjointedly, having to keep an eye against a sudden rush of my assailants, and mistrusting the goitred saint yet the more because he was so silent.

"And is Bethulah content with her destiny?" I asked.

"She is in the seventh heaven," said the elderly saint.

I had a poignant shudder of incredulous protest. I recalled the flush of her sweet face at the sight of me, and brief as our meetings had been, I dared to feel that the irrevocable thrill had passed between us; that the rest would have been only a question of time.

"Let Bethulah tell me so herself," I cried, "and I will leave her in her heaven."

The men looked at one another. Then the eldest shook his head. "No; you shall never speak to her again."

"We have maidens more beautiful among us," said the young man. "You shall have your choice. Ay, even my own betrothed would I give you."

I flicked aside his suggestion. "But you cannot prevent Bethulah walking under God's heaven." They looked dismayed. "I will meet her," I said, pursuing my advantage. "And Yarchi and other good Jews shall be at hand."

"She shall be removed elsewhere," said the first.

"I will track her down. Ah, you are afraid," I said mockingly. "You see it is not true that she is content to be immolated."

"It is true," they muttered.

"True as the Torah," added the elderly man.

"Then there is no harm in her telling me so."

"You may bear her off on your horse," said he of the goitre.

"I will go on foot. Let her bid me go away, and I will leave Zloczszol."

Again they looked at one another, and the relief in their eyes brought heart-sinking into mine. Yes, it was true. Bethulah was in the glow of a great surrender; she was still tingling with the revelation of her supreme destiny. To put her to the test now would be fatal. No; let her have time to meditate; ay, even to disbelieve.

"To-morrow you shall speak with her, and no man shall know," said the oldest Chassid.

"No, not to-morrow. In a week or two."

"Ah, you wish to linger among us," he replied suspiciously.

"I will go away till the appointed day," I replied readily.

"Good. Continue your travels. Let us say a month, or even two."

"If you will not spirit her away in my absence."

"It is as easy to do so in your presence."

"So be it."

"Shall we say—the eve of Chanukah?" he suggested.

It was my turn to regard him suspiciously. But I could see nothing to cavil at. He had merely mentioned an obvious date—that of the next festival landmark. Chanukah—the feast of rededication of the Temple after the Grecian pollution—the miracle of the unwaning oil, the memorial lighting of lights; there seemed nothing in these to work unduly upon the girl's soul, except in so far as the inspiring tradition of Judas Maccabæus might attach her more devotedly to her conceptions of duty and self-dedication. Perhaps, I thought, with a flash of jealous anger, they meditated a feast of rededication of her after the pollution of my presence had been removed. Well, we should see.

"The eve of Chanukah," I agreed, with a nonchalant air. "Only let the place be where I first met her—the path 'twixt mountain and river as you go to the cemetery."

That would at least be a counter-influence to Chanukah! As they understood none of the subtleties of love, they agreed to this, and I made them swear by the Name.

When they went their way I stood pondering on the bridge, my empty pistol drooping in my hand, till sky and river glowed mystically as with blood, and the chill evening airs reminded me that November was nigh.

VII

I got to Warsaw and back in the time at my disposal, but not all the freshness and variety of my experiences could banish the thought of Bethulah. There were days when I could absorb myself in the passing panorama, but I felt always, so to speak, in the ante-chamber of the great moment of our third and decisive meeting.

And with every shortening day of December that moment approached. Yet I all but missed it when it came. A snowfall I might easily have foreseen retarded my journey at the eleventh hour, but my faithful mare ploughed her way through the white morasses. As she munched her mid-day corn in that quaint Christian village that neighboured Zloczszol, and in which I had agreed to stable her, it was borne in on me for the first time that the eve of Chanukah was likewise Christmas eve. I wondered vaguely if there was any occult significance in the coincidence or in the Chassidic choice of dates; but it was too late now to protest, and loading my pistol against foul play, I hurried to the rendezvous.

On the dark barren base of the mountain, patches of snow gleamed like winter blossoms; the gargoyle-like faces of the jags of rock on the river-bank were white-bearded with icicles. Down below the stream raced, apparently as turbid as ever, but suddenly, as it made a sharp curve and came under a thick screen of snow-laden boughs interarching over the cleft, it grew glazed in death.

The sight of Bethulah was as of a spirit of sunshine moving across the white desolation. Her tall lone shadow fell blue upon the snowy path. She was swathed now in splendid silver furs, from which her face shone out like a tropical flower beneath its wreathed crown.

Dignity and sovereignty had subtly replaced the grace of her movement, her very stature seemed aggrandized by the consciousness of her unique mission.

She turned, and her virginal eyes met mine with abashing purity, and in that instant of anguished rapture I knew that my quest was vain. The delicate flush of joy and surprise touched her cheeks, indeed, as before, but this time I felt it would not be succeeded by terror. Self-conscious now, self-poised, she stood regally where she had faltered and fled.

"You return to spend Chanukah with us," she said.

"I came," I said, with uneasy bravado, "in the hope of spending it elsewhere—with you."

"But you know that cannot be," she said gently.

Ah, now she knew of what she was queen. But revolt was hot in my heart.

"Then they have made you share their dream," I said bitterly.

"Yes," she replied, with unruffled sweetness. "How beautiful upon the mountains are the feet of those that bring good tidings!" And her eyes shone in exultation.

"They were messengers of evil," I said—"whisperers of untruth. Life is for love and joy."

"Ah, no!" she urged tremulously. "Surely you know the world—how full it is of suffering and sin." And as with an unconscious movement, she threw back her splendid furs, revealing the weird shroud. "Ah, what ecstasy to think that the divine day will come, ere I am old, when, as it is written in the twenty-fifth chapter of Isaiah, 'He will destroy in this mountain the face of the covering cast over all people, and the vail that is spread over all nations. He will swallow up death in victory: and the Lord God will wipe away tears from off all faces; and the rebuke of His people shall He take away from off all the earth: for the Lord hath spoken.'"

Her own eyes were full of tears, which I yearned to kiss away.

"But your own life meantime?" I said softly.

"My life—does it not already take on the glory of God as this mountain the coming day?"

She seemed indeed akin to the cold white peak as I had seen it flushed with sunrise. My passion seemed suddenly prosaic and selfish. I was lifted up into the higher love that worships and abnegates.

"God bless you!" I said, and turning away with misty vision, saw, creeping off, the three dark fanatical figures.

VIII

Half a century later I was startled to find the name of Zloczszol in a headline of the Sunday edition of my American paper.

I had married, and was even a grandfather; for after my return to America the world of Bethulah had grown fantastic, stupidly superstitious, and, finally, shadowy and almost unreal. Years and years of happiness had dissipated and obliterated the delicate fragrant dream of spiritual love.

But that strange long-forgotten name stirred instantly the sleeping past to life. I adjusted my spectacles and read the column eagerly. It was sensational enough, though not more so than a hundred columns of calamities in unknown places that one skips or reads with the mildest of thrills.

The long-threatened avalanche had fallen, and Nature had once more rudely reminded man of his puny place in creation. Rare conditions had at last come together. First a slight fall of snow, covering the mountain—how vividly I pictured it!—then a sharp frost which had frozen this deposit; after that a measureless, blinding snow-storm and a cyclonic wind. When all seemed calm again, the second mass of snow had begun to slide down the frozen surface of the first, quickening to a terrific pace, tearing down the leafless trunks and shooting them at the village like giant arrows of the angry gods. One of these arrows penetrated the trunk of a great cedar on the plain and stuck out on both sides, making a sort of cross, which the curious came from far and near to see. But, alas! the avalanche had not contented itself with such freakish manifestations; it had annihilated the new portion of the village which had dared crawl nearer the mountain when the railroad—a railroad in Zloczszol!—had found it cheaper to pass near the base than to make a circuit round the congested portion!

Alas! the cheapness was illusory. The dépôt with its crowd had been wiped out as by the offended Fury of the mountain; though by another freakish incident, illustrating the Titanic forces at work, yet the one redeeming detail of the appalling catastrophe, a small train of three carriages that had just moved off was lifted up bodily by the terrible wind that raced ahead of the monstrous sliding snowball, and was clapped down in a field out of its reach, as if by a protecting hand. Not a creature on it was injured.

I had passed the years allotted to man by the Psalmist, and my memory of the things of yesterday had begun to be faint and elusive, but the images of my Zloczszol adventure returned with a vividness that grew daily more possessive. What had become of Bethulah? Was she alive? Was she dead? And which were the sadder alternative—to have felt the darkness of early death closing round the great hope, or to have survived its possibility, and old, bent, bitter, and deserted by her followers, to await the lesser disenchantment of the grave?

An irresistible instinct impelled me—aged as I was myself—to revisit alone these scenes of my youth, to see how fate had rounded or broken off its grim ironic story.

I pass over the stages of the journey, at the conclusion of which I found myself again in the mountain village. Alas! The changes on the route had prepared me for the change in Zloczszol. Railroads threw their bridges over the gorges I had climbed, telegraph poles tamed the erst savage forest ways. And Zloczszol itself had now, by the line passing through it, expanded into a trading centre, with vitality enough to recuperate quickly from the avalanche. The hotel was clean and commodious, but I could better have endured that ancient sitting-room in which the squalling baby was rocked. Strange, I could see its red wrinkled face, catch the very timbre of its piping cries! Only the mountain was unchanged, and the pines and firs that had whispered dreams to my youth whispered sleep to my age. Ah, how frail and futile is the life of man! He passes like a shadow, and the green sunlit earth he trod on closes over him and takes the tread of the new generations. What had I to say to these new, smart people in Zloczszol? No, the dead were my gossips and neighbours. For me more than the avalanche had desolated Zloczszol. I repaired to the cemetery. There I should find Yarchi. It was no use looking for him under the porch of the pine cottage. And there, too, I should in all likelihood find Bethulah!

But Ben David's tomb was the first I found, carved with the intersecting triangles. The date showed he had died very soon after my departure; perhaps, I thought remorsefully, my importunities had agitated him too much. Ah! there at last was Yarchi. Under a high white stone he slept as soundly as any straight corpse. His sneering mouth had crumbled to dust, but I would have given much to hear it once more abuse the Chassidim. Propped on my stick and poring over the faded gilt letters, I recalled "the handsome stranger" whom the years had marred. But of Bethulah I saw no sign. I wandered back and found the turreted house, but it had been converted into a large store, and from Bethulah's turret window hung a great advertising sky-sign.

I returned cheerlessly to the hotel, but as the sun began to pierce auspiciously through the bleakness of early March, I was about to sally forth again in the direction of Yarchi's ancient cottage, when the porter directed me—as if I were a mere tourist—to go to see the giant cedar of Lebanon with its Titanic arrow. However, I followed his instructions, and pretty soon I espied the broad-girthed tree towering over its field, with the foreign transpiercing trunk about fifteen feet from the ground, making indeed a vast cross. Leaning against the sunlit cedar was a white-robed figure, and as I hobbled nearer I saw by the shroud and the crown of flowers that I had found Bethulah.

At my approach she drew herself up in statuesque dignity, upright as Ben David of yore, and looked at me with keen unclouded eyes. There was a wondrous beauty of old age in her face and bearing. The silver hair banded on the temples glistened picturesquely against the reds and greens and golds of her crown.

"Ah, stranger!" she said, with a gracious smile. "You return to us."

"You recognize me?" I mumbled, in amaze.

"It is the face I loved in youth," she said simply.

Strange, happy, wistful tears sprang to my old eyes—some blurred sense of youth and love and God.

"Your youth seems with you still," I said. "Your face is as sweet, your voice as full of music."

The old ecstatic look lit up her eyes. "It is God who keeps me ever young, till the great day dawns."

I was taken aback. What! She believed still! That alternative had not figured in my prevision of pathetic closes. I was silent, but the old tumult of thought raged within me.

"But is not the day passed forever?" I murmured at last.

The light in her eyes became queenly fire.

"While there is life," she cried, "in the veins of the house of Ben David!" And as she spoke my eye caught the gleam of the Persian emerald on her forefinger.

"And your worshippers—what of them?" I asked.

Her eyes grew sad. "After my father's death—his memory for a blessing!—the pilgrims fell off, and when the years passed without the miracle, his followers even here in Zloczszol began to weaken. And slowly a new generation arose, impatient and lax, which believed not in the faith of their forefathers and mocked my footsteps, saying, 'Behold! the dreamer cometh!' And then the black fire-monster came, whizzing daily to and fro on the steel lines and breathing out fumes of unfaith, and the young men said lo! there is our true Redeemer. Wherefore, as the years waxed and waned, until at last advancing Death threw his silver shadow on my hair, even the faithful grew to doubt, and they said, 'But a few short years more and death must claim her, her mission unfulfilled, and the lamp of Israel's hope shattered forever. Perchance it is we that have misunderstood the prophecies. Not here, not here, shall God's great miracle be wrought; this is not holy ground. "For the Lord dwelleth in Zion,"' they cried with the Prophets. Only on the sacred soil, outside of which God has never revealed himself, only in Palestine, they said, can Israel's Redeemer be born. As it is written, 'But upon Mount Zion shall be deliverance, and there shall be holiness.'

"Then these and the scoffers persuaded me, seeing that I waxed very old, and I sold my father's house—now grown of high value—to obtain the money for the journey, and I made ready to start for Jerusalem. There had been a whirlwind and a great snow the day before and I would have tarried, but they said I must arrive in the Holy City ere the eve of Chanukah. And putting off my shroud and my crown, seeing that only in Jerusalem I might be a bride, I trusted myself to the fire-monster, and a vast company went with me to the starting-place—both of those who believed that salvation was of Zion and those who scoffed. But the monster had scarcely crawled out under God's free heaven than God's hand lifted me up and those with me—for my blessedness covered them—and put us down very far off, while a great white thunder-bolt fell upon the building and upon the scoffers and upon those who had prated of Zion, and behold! they were not. The multitude of Moab was as straw trodden down for the dunghill, and the high fort of the fire-monster was brought down and laid low and brought to the ground, even to the dust. Then arose a great cry from all the town and the mountain, and a rending of garments and a weeping in sackcloth. And many returned to the faith in me, for God's hand has shown that here, and not elsewhere, is the miracle to be wrought. As it is written, word for word, in the twenty-fifth chapter of Isaiah:—

"'And He will destroy in this mountain the face of the covering cast over all people, and the vail that is spread over all nations. He will swallow up death in victory; and the Lord God shall wipe away tears from off all faces: and the rebuke of His people shall He take away from off all the earth: for the Lord hath spoken it. And it shall be said in that day, Lo, this is our God; we have waited for Him, and He will save us: this is the Lord; we have waited for Him, we will be glad and rejoice in His salvation. For in this mountain shall the hand of the Lord rest, and Moab shall be trodden down under Him, even as straw is trodden down for the dunghill. And He shall spread forth His hands in the midst of them, as he that swimmeth spreadeth forth to swim: and He shall bring down their pride together with the spoils of their hands. And the fortress of the high fort of thy walls shall He bring down, lay low, and bring to the ground, even to the dust.'

"And here in this cedar of Lebanon, transplanted like Israel under the shadow of this alien mountain, the Lord has shot a bolt, for a sign to all that can read. And here I come daily to pray, and to await the divine moment."

She ceased, and her eyes turned to the now stainless heaven. And as I gazed upon her shining face it seemed to me that the fresh flowers and leaves of her crown, still wet with the dew, seen against that garment of death and the silver of decaying life, were symbolic of an undying, ever rejuvenescent hope.

IX

A last surprise awaited me. Bethulah now lived all alone in Yarchi's pine cottage, which the years had left untouched.

Whether accident or purpose settled her there I do not know, but my heart was overcharged with mingled emotion as I went up the garden the next day to pay her a farewell visit. The poppies flaunted riotously amid the neglected maize, but the cottage itself seemed tidy.

It was the season when the cold wrinkled lips of winter meet the first kiss of spring, and death is passing into resurrection. It was the hour when the chill shadows steal upon the sunlit day. In the sky was the shot purple of a rolling moor, merging into a glow of lovely green.

I stood under the porch where Yarchi had been wont to sun and snuff himself, and knocked at the door, but receiving no answer, I lifted the latch softly and looked in.

Bethulah was at her little table, her head lying on a great old Bible which her arms embraced. One long finger of departing sunlight pointed through the window and touched the flowers on the gray hair. I stole in with a cold fear that she was dead. But she seemed only asleep, with that sleep of old age which is so near to death and is yet the renewal of life.

I was curious to see what she had been reading. It was the eighteenth chapter of Genesis, and in the shadow of her crown ran the verses:—

"And the Lord said unto Abraham,
Wherefore did Sarah laugh, saying,
Shalt I of a surety bear a child, which am old?

"Is anything too hard for the Lord?"

VII

THE KEEPER OF CONSCIENCE

I

Salvina Brill walked to and fro in the dingy Hackney Terrace, waiting till her mother should return with the house-key. So far as change of scene was concerned the little pupil-teacher might as well have stood still. Everywhere bow-windows, Venetian blinds, little front gardens—all that had represented domestic grandeur to her after a childhood of apartments in Spitalfields, though her subsequent glimpse of the West End home in which her sister Kitty was governess, had made her dazedly aware of Alps beyond Alps.

Though only seventeen, Salvina was not superficially sweet and could win no consideration from the seated males in the homeward train, and the heat of the weather and the crush of humanity—high hats sandwiched between workmen's tool-baskets—had made her head ache. Her day at the Whitechapel school had already been trying, and Thursday was always heavy with the accumulated fatigues of the week. It was unfortunate that her mother should be late, but she remembered how at breakfast the good creature had promised father to make a little excursion to the Borough and take a packet of tea to the house of some distant relatives of his, who were sitting shivah (seven days' mourning). The non-possession of a servant made it necessary to lock up the house and pull down the blinds, when its sole occupant went visiting.

After a few minutes of vain expectation, Salvina mechanically returned to her Greek grammar, which opened as automatically at the irregular verbs. She had just achieved the greatest distinction of her life, and one not often paralleled in Board School girl-circles, by matriculating at the London University. Hers was only a second-class pass, but gained by private night-study, supplemented by some evening lessons at the People's Palace, it was sufficiently remarkable; especially when one considered she had still other subjects to prepare for the Centres. Salvina was now audaciously aiming at the Bachelorhood of Arts, for which the Greek verbs were far more irregular. It was not only the love of knowledge that animated her: as a bachelor she might become a head-mistress, nay, might even aspire to follow the lead of her dashing elder sister and teach in a wealthy family that treated you as one of itself. Not that Kitty had ever matriculated, but an ugly duckling needs many plumes of learning ere it can ruffle itself like a beautiful swan.

Who should now come upon the promenading student but Sugarman the Shadchan, his hand full of papers, and his blue bandanna trailing from his left coat-tail!

"Ah, you are the very person I was coming to see," he cried gleefully in his corrupt German accent. "What is your sister's address now?"

"Why?" said Salvina distrustfully.

"I have a fine young man for her!"

Salvina's pallid cheek coloured with modesty and resentment. "My sister doesn't need your services."

"Maybe not," said Sugarman, unruffled. "But the young man does. He saw your sister once years ago, before he went to the Cape. Now he is a Takif (rich man) and wants a wife."

"He's not rich enough to buy Kitty." Salvina's romantic soul was outraged, and she spoke with unwonted asperity.

"He is rich enough to buy Kitty all she wants. He is quite in love with her—she can ask for anything."

"Then let him go and tell her so himself. What does he come to you for? He must be a very poor lover."

"Poor! I tell you he is rolling in gold. It's the luckiest thing that could have happened to your family. You will all ride in your carriage. You ought to fall on your knees and bless me. Your sister is not so young any more, at nineteen a girl can't afford to sniff. Believe me there are thousands of girls who would jump at the chance—yes, girls with dowries, too. And your sister hasn't a penny."

"My sister has a heart and a soul," retorted Salvina witheringly, "and she wants a heart and a soul to sympathize with hers, not a money-bag."

"Then, won't you take a ticket for the lotteree?" rejoined Sugarman pleasantly. "Then you get a money-bag of your own."

"No, thank you."

"Not even half a ticket? Only thirty-six shillings! You needn't pay me now. I trust you."

She shook her head.

"But think—I may win you the great prize—a hundred thousand marks."

The sum fascinated Salvina, and for an instant her imagination played with its marvellous potentialities. They could all move to the country, and there among the birds and the flowers she could study all day long, and even try for a degree with Honours. Her father would be saved from the cigar factory, her sister from exile amid strangers, her mother should have a servant, her brother the wife he coveted. All her Spitalfields circle had speculated through Sugarman, not without encouraging hits. She smiled as she remembered the vendor of slippers who had won sixty pounds and was so puffed up that when his wife stopped in the street to speak to a shabby acquaintance, he cried vehemently, "Betsey, Betsey, do learn to behave according to your station."

"You don't believe me?" said Sugarman, misapprehending her smile. "You can read it all for yourself. A hundred thousand marks, so sure my little Nehemiah shall see rejoicings. Look!"

But Salvina waved back the thin rustling papers with their exotic Continental flavour. "Gambling is wicked," she said.

Sugarman was incensed. "Me in a wicked business! Why, I know more Talmud than anybody in London, and can be called up the Law as Morenu! You'll say marrying is wicked, next. But they are both State Institutions. England is the only country in the world without a lotteree."

Salvina wavered, but her instinct was repugnant to money that did not accumulate itself by slow, painful economies, and her multifarious reading had made the word "Speculation" a prism of glittering vice.

"I daresay you think it's not wrong," she said, "and I apologize if I hurt your feelings. But don't you see how you go about unsettling people?"

"Me! Why, I settle them! And if you'd only give me your sister's address—"

His persistency played upon Salvina's delicate conscience; made her feel she must not refuse the poor man everything. Besides, the grand address would choke him off.

"She's at Bedford Square, with the Samuelsons."

"Ah, I know. Two daughters, Lily and Mabel," and Sugarman instead of being impressed nodded his head, as if even the Samuelsons were mortal and marriageable.

"Yes, my sister is their governess and companion. But you'll only waste your time."

"You think so?" he said triumphantly. "Look at this likeness!"

And he drew out the photograph of a coarse-faced middle-aged man, with a jaunty flower in his frock-coat and a prosperous abdomen supporting a heavily trinketed watch-chain. Underneath swaggered the signature, "Yours truly, Moss M. Rosenstein."

Salvina shuddered: "He was wise to send you," she said slyly.

"Is it not so? Ah, and your brother, too, would have done better to come to me instead of falling in love with a girl with a hundred pounds. But I bear your family no grudge, you see. Perhaps it is not too late yet. Tell Lazarus that if he should come to break with the Jonases, there are better fish in the sea—gold fish, too. Good-bye. We shall both dance at your sister's wedding." And he tripped off.

Salvina resumed her Greek, but the grotesque aorists could not hold her attention. She was hungry and worn out, and even when her mother came, it would be some time before her evening meal could be prepared. She felt she must sit down, if only on her doorsteps, but their whiteness was inordinately marred as by many dirty boots—she wondered whose and why—and she had to content herself with leaning against the stucco balustrade. And gradually as the summer twilight faded, the grammar dropped in her hand, and Salvina fell a-dreaming.

What did she dream of, this Board School drudge, whose pasty face was craned curiously forward on sloping shoulders? Was it of the enchanted land of love of which Sugarman had reminded her, but over whose roses he had tramped so grossly? Alas! Sugarman himself had never thought of her as a client for any but the lottery section of his business. Within, she was one glow of eager romance, of honour, of quixotic duty, but no ray of this pierced without to give a sparkle to the eye, a colour to the cheek. No faintest dash of coquetry betrayed the yearning of the soul or gave grace to walk or gesture: her dress was merely a tidy covering. Her exquisite sensibility found bodily expression only as a clumsy shyness.

Poor Salvina!

II

At last the welcome jar and creak of the gate awoke her.

"Why, I thought you knew I had to go to the Borough!" began a fretful voice, forestalling reproach, and a buxom woman resplendent with black satin and much jewellery came up the tiny garden-path.

"It doesn't matter, mother—I haven't been waiting long."

"Well, you know how difficult it is to get a 'bus in this weather—at least if you want to sit outside, and it always makes my head ache frightfully to go inside—I'm not strong and young like you—and such a long way, I had to change at the Bank, and I made sure you'd get something to eat at one of the girls', and go straight to the People's Palace."

Still muttering, Mrs. Brill produced a key, and after some fumbling threw open the door. Both made a step within, then both stopped, aghast.

"It's the wrong house," thought Salvina confusedly, conscious of her power of making such mistakes.

"Kisshuf (witchcraft)!" whispered her mother, terrified into her native idiom. The passage lay before them, entirely bare of all its familiar colour and furniture: the framed engravings depicting the trials of William Lord Russell, in the Old Bailey, and Earl Stafford in Westminster Hall, the flower-pots on the hall table, the proudly purchased hat-rack, the metal umbrella-stand, all gone! And beyond, facing them, lay the parlour, an equally forlorn vacancy striking like a blast of chilly wind through its wide-open door.

"Thieves!" cried Mrs. Brill, reverting from the supernatural and the Yiddish. "Murder! I'm ruined! They've stolen my house!"

"Hush! Hush!" said Salvina, strung to calm by her mother's incoherence. "Let us see first what has really happened."

"Happened! Haven't you got eyes in your head? All the fruit of my years of toil!" And Mrs. Brill wrung her jewelled hands. "Your father would have me call on those Sperlings, though I told him they'd be glad to dance on my tomb. And why didn't Lazarus stay at home?"

"You know he has to be out looking for work."

"And my gilt clock that I trembled even to wind up, and the big vase with the picture on it, and my antimacassars, and my beautiful couch that nobody had ever sat upon! Oh my God, oh my God!"

Leaving her mother moaning out a complete inventory in the passage, Salvina advanced into the violated parlour. It was an aching void. On the bare mantelpiece, just where the gilt clock had announced a perpetual half-past two, gleamed an unstamped letter. She took it up wonderingly. It was in her father's schoolboyish hand, addressed to her mother. She opened it, as usual, for Mrs. Brill did not even know the alphabet, and refused steadily to make its acquaintance, to the ironic humiliation of the Board School teacher.

"You would not let me give you Get," [ran the letter abruptly], "so you have only yourself to blame. I have left the clothes in the bed-rooms, but what is mine is mine. Good-bye.

"MICHAEL BRILL.

"P.S.—Don't try to find me at the factory. I have left."

Salvina steadied herself against the mantelpiece till the room should have finished reeling round. Get! Her father had wanted to put away her mother! Divorce, departure, devastation—what strange things were these, come to wreck a prosperity so slowly built up!

"Quick, Salvina, there goes a policeman!" came her mother's cry.

The room stood still suddenly. "Hush, hush, mother," Salvina said imperiously. "There's no thief!" She ran back into the passage, the letter in her hand.

A fierce flame of intelligence leapt into the woman's face. "Ah, it's your father!" she cried. "I knew it, I knew he'd go after that painted widow, just because she has a little money, a black curse on her bones. Oh! oh! God in heaven! To bring such shame on me, for the sake of a saucy-nosed slut whose sister sold ironmongery in Petticoat Lane—a low lot, one and all, and not fit to wipe my shoes on, even when she was respectable, and this is what you call a father, Salvina! Oh my God, my God!"

Salvina was by this time dazed, yet she had a gleam of consciousness left with which to register this culminating destruction of all her social landmarks. What! That monstrous wickedness of marquises and epauletted officers which hovered vaguely in the shadow-land of novels and plays had tumbled with a bang into real life; had fallen not even into its natural gilded atmosphere, but through the amulet-guarded doors of a respectable Jewish family in the heart of a Hackney Terrace, amid the horsehair couches and deal tables of homely reality. Nay—more sordid than the romantic wickedness of shadowland—it had even removed those couches and tables! And oddly blent with this tossing chaos of new thought in Salvina's romantic brain surged up another thought, no less new and startling. Her father and mother had once loved each other! They, too, had dawned upon each other, fairy prince and fairy princess; had laid in each other's hand that warm touch of trust and readiness to live and die for each other. It was very wonderful, and she almost forgot their hostile relationship in a rapid back-glance upon the years in which they had lived in mutual love before her unsuspecting eyes. Their prosaic bickering selves were transfigured: her vivid imagination threw off the damage of the years, saw her coarse, red-cheeked father and her too plump mother as the idyllic figures on the lamented parlour vase. And when her thought struggled painfully back to the actual moment, it was with a new concrete sense of its tragic intensity.

"O mother, mother!" she cried, as she threw her arms round her. The Greek grammar and the letter fell unregarded to the floor.

The fountain of Mrs. Brill's wrongs leapt higher at the sympathy. "And I could have had half-a-dozen young men! The boils of Egypt be upon him! Time after time I said, 'No,' though the Shadchan bewitched my parents into believing that Michael was an angel without wings."

"But you also thought father an angel," Salvina pleaded.

"Yes; and now he has got wings," said Mrs. Brill savagely.

Salvina's tears began to ooze out. Poor swain and shepherdess on the parlour vase! Was this, then, how idylls ended? "Perhaps he'll come back," she murmured.

The wife snorted viciously. "And my furniture? The beautiful furniture I toiled and scraped for, that he always grumbled at, though I saved it out of the housekeeping money, without its costing him a penny, and no man in London had better meals—hot meat every day and fish for Sabbath, even when plaice were eightpence a pound—and no servant—every scrap of work done with my own two hands! Now he carts everything away as if it were his."

"I suppose it is by law," Salvina said mildly.

"Law! I'll have the law on him."

"Oh, no, mother!" and Salvina shuddered. "Besides, he has left our clothes."

Mrs. Brill's eye lit up. "I see no clothes."

"In our rooms. The letter says so."

"And you still believe what he says?" She began to mount the stairs. "I am sure he packed in my Paisley shawl while he was about it. It is fortunate I wore all my jewellery. And you always say I put on too much!"

Sustained by this unanswerable vindication of her past policy, Mrs. Brill ascended the stairs without further wailing.

Salvina, whose sense of romance never exalted her above the practical, remembered now that her brother Lazarus might come back at any moment clamorously hungry. This pinned her to the concrete moment. How to get him some supper! And her mother, too, must be faint and tired. She ran into the kitchen, and found enough odds and ends left to make a meal, and even a cracked teapot and a few coarse cups not worth carrying away; and, with a sense of Robinson Crusoe adventure, she extracted light, heat, and cheerfulness from the obedient gas branch, which took on the air of a case of precious goods not washed away in the household wreck. When her mother at last came down, cataloguing the wardrobe salvage in picturesque Yiddish, Salvina stopped her curses with hot tea. They both drank, leaning against the kitchen-dresser, which served for a table for the cups.

Salvina's Crusoe excitement increased when her mother asked her where they were to sleep, seeing that even the beds had been spirited away.

"I have five shillings in my purse; I'll go out and buy a cheap mattress. But then there's Lazarus! Oh dear!"

"Lazarus has his own bed. Yes, yes, thank God, we'll be able to borrow his wedding furniture."

"But it's all stored away in the Jonas's attic."

A smart rat-tat at the door denoted the inopportune return of Lazarus himself. Salvina darted upstairs to let him in and break the shock. He was a slimmer and more elegant edition of his father, a year older than Kitty, and taller than Salvina by a jaunty head and shoulders.

"And why isn't the hall lamp alight?" he queried, as her white face showed itself in the dusky door-slit. "It looks so beastly shabby. The only light's in the kitchen; I daresay you and the mater are pigging there again. Why can't you live up to your position?"

The unexpected reproach broke her down. "We have no position any more," she sobbed out. And all the long years of paralyzing economies swept back to her memory, all the painful progress—accelerated by her growing salary—from the Hounsditch apartments to the bow-windows and gas-chandeliers of Hackney!

"What do you mean? What is the matter? Speak, you little fool! Don't cry." He came across the threshold and shook her roughly.

"Father's run away with the furniture and some woman," she explained chokingly.

"The devil!" The smart cane slipped from his fingers and he maintained his cigar in his mouth with difficulty. "Do you mean to say the old man has gone and—the beastly brute! The selfish hypocrite! But how could he get the furniture?"

"He made mother go on a visit to the Borough."

"The old fox! That's your religious chaps. I'll go and give 'em both brimstone. Where are they?"

"I don't know where—but you must not—it is all too horrible. There's nothing even to sleep on. We thought of borrowing your furniture!"

"What! And give the whole thing away to the Jonases—and lose Rhoda, perhaps. Good heavens, Sally. Don't be so beastly selfish. Think of the disgrace, if we can't cover it up."

"The disgrace is for father, not for you."

"Don't be an idiot. Old Jonas looked down on us enough already, and if it hadn't been for Kitty's calling on him in the Samuelsons' carriage, he might never have consented to the engagement."

"Oh, dear!" said Salvina, melted afresh by this new aspect. "My poor Lazarus!" and she gazed dolefully at the handsome youth who had divided with Kitty the good looks of the family. "But still," she added consolingly, "you couldn't have married for a long time, anyhow."

"I don't know so much. I had a very promising interview this afternoon with the manager of Granders Brothers, the big sponge-people."

"But you don't understand travelling in sponge."

"Pooh! Travelling's travelling. There's nothing to understand. Whatever the article is, you just tell lies about it."

"Oh, Lazarus!"

"Don't make eyes—you ain't pretty enough. What do you know of the world, you who live mewed up in a Board School? I daresay you believe all the rot you have to tell the little girls."

Her brother's shot made a wound he had not intended. Salvina was at last reminded of her own relation to the sordid tragedy, of what the other teachers would think, ay, even the little girls, so sharp in all that did not concern school-learning. Would her pupils have any inkling of the cloud on teacher's home? Ah, her brother was right. This disgrace besplashed them all, and she saw herself confusedly as a tainted figure holding forth on honour and duty to rows of white pinafores.

III

Meantime, her mother had toiled up—her jewels glittering curiously in the dusk—and now poured herself out to the fresh auditor in a breathless wail; recapitulated her long years of devotion and the abstracted contents of the house. But Lazarus soon wearied of the inventory of her virtues and furniture.

"What's the use of crying over spilt milk?" he said. "You must get a new jug."

"A new jug! And what about the basin and the coffee-pot and the saucepans and the plates! And my new blue dish with the willow-pattern. Oh, my God!"

"Don't be so stupid."

"She's a little dazed, Lazarus, dear. Have patience with her. Lazarus says it's no use crying and letting the neighbours hear you: we must make the best of a bad job, and cover it up."

"You'll soon cover me up. I won't need my clothes then—only a clean shroud. After twenty years—he wipes his mouth and he goes away! Tear the rent in your garments, children mine, your mother is dead."

"How can any one have patience with her?" cried Lazarus. "One would think it was such a treat for her to live with father. Judging by the rows you've had, mother, you ought to be thankful to be rid of him."

"I am thankful," she retorted hysterically. "Who said I wasn't? A grumbling, grunting pig, who grudged me my horsehair couch because he couldn't sit on it. Well, let him squat on it now with his lady. I don't care. All my enemies will pity me, will they? If they only knew how glad I was!" and she broke into more sobs.

"Come, mother; come downstairs, Lazarus: don't let us stay up in the dark."

"Not me," said Lazarus. "I'm not going down to hear this all over again. Besides, where am I to sit or to sleep? I must go to an hotel." He struck a match to relight his cigar and it flared weirdly upon the tear-smudged female faces. "Got any money, Salvina," he said more gently.

"Only five shillings."

"Well, I daresay I can manage on that. Good-night, mother, don't take on so, it'll be all the same a hundred years hence." He opened the door; then paused with his hand on the knob, and said awkwardly: "I suppose you'll manage to find something to sleep on just for to-night."

"Oh, yes," said Salvina reassuringly; "we'll manage. Don't worry, dear."

"I'll be in the first thing in the morning. We'll have a council of war. Good-night. It is a beastly mean trick," and he went out meditatively.

When he was gone, Salvina remembered that the five shillings were for the mattress. But she further bethought herself that the sum would scarcely have sufficed even for a straw mattress, and that the little gold ring Kitty had given her when she matriculated would fetch more. Her mother's jewellery must be left sacred; the poor creature was smarting enough from the sense of loss. Bidding her sit on the stairs till she returned, she hastened into Mare Street, the great Hackney highway, christened "The Devil's Mile" by the Salvation Army. Early experience had familiarized her with the process of pawning, but now she slipped furtively into the first pawn-shop and did not stay to make a good bargain. She spent on a telegram to the central post-office sixpence of the proceeds, so that she might be able to draw out without delay the few pounds she had laid by for her summer holiday. While she was purchasing the mattress at the garishly illuminated furniture store, the words "Hire System" caught her eye, and seemed a providential solution of the position. She broached negotiations for the furnishing of a bed-room and a kitchen, minus carpet and oilcloth (for these would not fit the cheaper apartments into which they would now have to revert), but she found there were tedious formalities to be gone through, and that her own signature would be invalid, as she was legally a child. However, she was able to secure the porterage of the mattress at once, and, followed by a bending Atlas, she hurried back to her mother—who sat on her stair, moaning—and diverted her from her griefs by teaching her to sign her name, in view of the legal exigencies of the morrow. It was a curious wind-up to her day's teaching. Poor Mrs. Brill's obstinate objection to education had to give way at last under such unexpected conditions, but she insisted on the shortest possible spelling, and so the uncouth "Esther Brills" pencilled at the top of the sheet were exchanged for more flowing "E. Brills" lower down. Even then, the good woman took the thing as a pictorial flourish, or a section of a map, and disdained acquaintance with the constituent letters, so that her progress in learning remained only nominal.

Then the "infant" at law put her mother to bed and lay down beside her on the mattress, both in their clothes for lack of blankets. The mother soon dozed off, but the "child" lay turning from side to side. The pressure of her little tasks had dulled the edge of emotion, but now, in the silence of the night, the whole tragic position came back with all its sordid romanticism, its pathetic meanness; and when at last she slept, its obsession lay heavy upon her dreams, and she sat at her examination desk in the London University, striving horridly to recall the irregularities of Greek verbs, and to set them down with a pen that could never dip up any ink, while the inexorable hands of the clock went round, and her father, in the coveted Bachelor's gown, waited to spirit away her desk and seat as soon as the hour should strike.

IV

The next morning Salvina should have awakened with a sense through all her bones that it was Friday— the last day of the school-week, harbinger of such blessed rest that the mere expectation of it was also a rest. Alas! she woke from the nightmare of sleep to the nightmare of reality, and the week-end meant only time to sound the horror of the new situation.

In one point alone, Friday remained a consolation. Only one day to face her fellow-teachers and her children, and then two days for hiding from the world with her pain, for preparing to face it again; to say nothing of the leisure for practical recuperation of the home.

Lazarus turned up so late that the council of war was of the briefest and held almost on the door-step, for Salvina must be in school by nine. The thought of staying away—even in this crisis—simply did not occur to her.

She arranged that Lazarus was to meet her in the city after morning school, when she would have drawn her savings from the post-office: more than enough for the advance on the furniture, which must be delivered that very afternoon. Lazarus had been for telegraphing at once to Kitty for assistance, but Salvina put her foot down.

"Let us not frighten her—I will go and break it to her on Sunday afternoon. You know she can't spare any money; it is as much as she can do to dress up to the position."

"I do hope the scandal won't spread," said Lazarus gloomily. "It would be a nice thing if she lost the position and fell back on our hands."

"Yes, he has ruined all my children," sobbed Mrs. Brill, breaking out afresh. "But what did he care? Ah, if it wasn't for me, you would have been in the workhouse long ago."

"Well then, go and do your Sabbath marketing or else we'll have to go there now," said Lazarus not unkindly; "the tradespeople will give you credit."

"Rather! They know I never ran away."

"And mind, mother," said Salvina as she snatched up her Greek grammar, "mind the fried fish is as good as usual; we're a long way from the workhouse yet! And if you're not in to-night, Lazarus," she whispered as she ran off, "I'll never forgive you."

"Well, I'm blowed!" said Lazarus, looking after the awkward little figure, flying to catch the 8.21.

"Yes, but I've no frying pan!" Mrs. Brill called after her.

"You'll have it by this afternoon," Salvina called back reassuringly.

The sun was already strong, the train packed, and Salvina stood so jammed in that she could scarcely hold her grammar open, and the irregular verbs danced before her eyes even more than their strange moods and tenses warranted. At the school her thrilling consciousness of her domestic tragedy interposed some strange veil between her and her fellow-teachers, and they seemed to stand away from her, enveloped in another atmosphere. She heard herself teaching—five elevens are fifty-five— and her own self seemed to stand away from her, too. She noted without protest two of the girls pulling each other's hair in some far-off hazy world, and the answering drone of the class—five elevens are fifty-five—seemed like the peaceful buzzing of a gigantic blue-bottle on a drowsy afternoon. It occurred to her suddenly that she was fifty-five years old, and when Miss Rolver, the Christian head-mistress, came into her room, Salvina had an unexpected feeling of advantage in life-experience over this desiccated specimen of femininity, redolent of time-tables, record-parchments, foolscap, and clean blotting-paper. Outside all this scheduled world pulsed a large irregular life of flesh and blood; all the primitive verbs in every language were irregular, it suddenly flashed upon her, and she had an instant of vivifying insight into the Greek language she had unquestioningly accepted as "dead"; saw Grecian men and women breathing their thoughts and passions—even expressing the shape of their throats and lips—through these erratic aorists.

"You look tired, dear," said the head-mistress.

"It's the heat," Salvina murmured.

"Never mind; the summer holidays will soon be here."

It sounded a mockery. Summer holidays would no longer mean Ramsgate, and delicious days of study on sunny cliffs, with the relaxation of novels and poems. These slowly achieved luxuries of the last two years were impossible for this year at least. And this thought of being penned up in London during the dog days oppressed her: she felt choking. Her next sensation was of water sprinkling on her face, and of Miss Rolver's kind anxious voice asking her if she felt better. Instead of replying, Salvina wondered in a clouded way where the school-managers were.

Even her naïve mind had been struck at last by the coincidence that whenever, after a managers' meeting, these omnipotent ladies and gentlemen from a higher world strolled through the school, Miss Rolver happened to be discovered in an interesting attitude. If it was the play-hour, she would be—for this occasion only—in the playground leading the games, surrounded by clamorously affectionate little ones. If it was working-time, she was found as a human island amid a sea of sewing: billows of pinafores and aprons heaved tumultuously around her. Or, with a large air of angelic motherhood, she would be tying up some child's bruised finger. Her greatest invention—so it had appeared to the scrupulous Salvina—was the stray, starved, half-frozen, sweet little kitten, lapping up milk from a saucer before a ruddy blazing fire at the very instant of the great personages' passage. How they had beamed, one and all, at the touching sight.

Hence it was that Salvina's dazed vision now sought vaguely for the school-managers. But in another instant she realized that this present solicitude was not for another but for herself, and that it had nothing of the theatrical. A remorseful pang of conscience added to her pains. She said tremulously that she felt better and was gently chided for over-study and admonished to go home and rest.

"Oh, no, I am all right now," she responded instinctively.

"But I'll take your class," Miss Rolver insisted, and Salvina found herself wandering outside in the free sunshine, with a sense of the forbidden. An acute consciousness of Board School classes droning dutifully all over London made the streets at that hour strange and almost sinful. She went to the post-office and drew out as much of her money as red tape allowed, and while wandering about in Whitechapel waiting for the hour of her rendezvous with Lazarus, she had time to purchase a coarse but white table-cloth, a plush cover embroidered with "Jerusalem" in Hebrew, and a gilt goblet. These were for the Friday-night table.

V

But the Sabbath brought no peace. Though miracles were wrought in that afternoon, and, except that it was laid in the kitchen, the Sabbath table had all its immemorial air, with the consecration cup, the long plaited loaves under the "Jerusalem" cover, and the dish of fried fish that had grown to seem no less religious; yet there could be no glossing over the absence of the gross-paunched paternal figure that had so unctuously presided over the ceremony. His vacant place held all the emptiness of death, and all the fulness of retrospective profanation. How like he was to Moss M. Rosenstein, Salvina thought suddenly. Lazarus had ignored the gilt goblet and the shilling bottle of claret, and was helping himself from the coffee-pot, when his mother cried bitterly: "What! are we to eat like the animals?"

"Oh bother!" Lazarus exclaimed. "You know I hate all these mummeries. I wouldn't say if they really made people good. But you see for yourself—"

"Oh, but you must say Kiddush, Lazarus," said Salvina, half pleadingly, half peremptorily. She fetched the prayer-book and Lazarus, grumbling inarticulately, took the head of the table, and stumbled through the prayer, thanking God for having chosen and sanctified Israel above all nations, and in love and favour given it the holy Sabbath as an inheritance.

But oh! how tamely the words sounded, how void of that melodious devotion thrilling through the joyous roulades of the father. It was a sort of symbol of the mutilated home, and thus Salvina felt it. And she remembered the last ceremony at which her father had presided—that of the Separation when the Sabbath faded into work-day—the ceremony of Division between the Holy and the Profane, and she shivered to think it had indeed marked for the unhappy man the line of demarcation.

"Blessed art thou, O Lord our God, who hallowest the Sabbath," Lazarus was mumbling, and in another instant he was awkwardly distributing the ritual morsels of bread.

But the mother could not swallow hers, for indignant imaginings of the rival Sabbath board. "May her morsel choke her!" she cried, and nearly was choked by her own.

"Oh, mother, do not mention her—neither her nor him.—Never any more," said Salvina. And again the new note of peremptoriness rang in her voice, and her mother stopped suddenly short like a scolded child.

"Will you have plaice or sole, mother?" Salvina went on, her voice changing to a caress.

"I can't eat, Salvina. Don't ask me."

"But you must eat." And Salvina calmly helped her to fish and to coffee and put in the lumps of sugar; and the mother ate and drank with equal calm, as if hypnotized.

All through the meal Salvina's mind kept swinging betwixt the past and the future. Strange odds and ends of scenes came up in which her father figured, and her old and new conceptions of him interplayed bewilderingly. Her sudden vision of him as Moss M. Rosenstein persisted, and could only be laid by concentrating her thoughts on the early days when he used to take herself and Kitty to Victoria Park, carrying her in his arms when she was tired. But it made her cry to see that little tired happy figure cuddling the trusted giant, and she had to jump for refuge into the future.

They must move back to Hounsditch. She must give up the idea of becoming a "Bachelor": the hours of evening study must now be devoted to teaching others. Her University distinction was already great enough to give her an unusual chance of pupils, while her "Yiddish," sucked in with her mother's milk, had become exceptionally good German under study. She might hope for as much as two shillings an hour and thus earn a whole sovereign extra per week.

And over this poor helpless blighted mother, she would watch as over a child. All the maternal instinct in her awoke under the stress of this curiously inverted position. Her remorseful memory summoned a penitential procession of bygone petulances. Never again would she be cross or hasty with this ill-starred heroine. Yes, her mother was become a figure of romance to her, as well as a nursling. This woman, whose prosaic humours she had so often fretted under, was in truth a woman who had lived and loved. She had ceased to be a mere mother; a large being who presided over one's childhood. And this imaginative insight, she noted with surprise, would never have been hers but for her father's desertion: like one who realizes the virtues of a corpse, she had waited till love was slain to perceive its fragrance.

A postman's knock, as the meal was finished, made her heart give a corresponding pit-a-pat, and she turned quite faint. All her nerves seemed to be on the rack, expecting new sensational developments. The letter was for Lazarus.

"Ah, you abomination!" cried his mother, as he tore open the envelope. He did not pause to defend his Sabbath breaking, but cried joyfully: "What did I tell you? Granders Brothers offer me travelling expenses and a commission!"

"Oh, thank God, thank God!" ejaculated his mother, her eyes raised piously. He took up his hat. "Where are you going?" said Mrs. Brill.

"To see Rhoda of course. Don't you think she's as anxious about it as you?"

Salvina's eyes were full of sympathetic tears: "Yes, yes, let him go, mother."

VI

On the Sunday afternoon, feeling much better for the Saturday rest, and scrupulously gloved, shod, and robed in deference to the grandeur of her destination, Salvina boarded an omnibus, and after a tedious journey, involving a walk at the end, she arrived at the West End square in which her sister bloomed as governess and companion in a newly enriched Jewish family. She stood an instant in the porch to compose herself for the tragic task before her and felt in her pocket to be sure she had not lost the little bottle of smelling-salts with which she had considerately armed herself, in anticipation of a failure of Kitty's nerves. Then she knocked timidly at the door, which was opened by a speckless boy in buttons, who also opened up to her imagination endless vistas of aristocratic association. His impressive formality, as of the priest of a shrine, seemed untinged by any remembrance that on her one previous visit she had been made free of the holy of holies. But perhaps it was not the same boy. He was indeed less a boy to her than a row of buttons, and less a row of buttons than a symbol of all the elegances and opulences in which Kitty moved as to the manner born; the elaborate ritual of the toilette, the sacramental shaving of poodles, the mysterious panoramic dinners in which one had to be constantly aware of the appropriate fork.

Salvina had not waited a minute in the imposing hall, ere a radiant belle flew down the stairs—with a vivacity that troubled the sacro-sanct atmosphere—and caught Salvina in her arms.

"Oh, you dear Sally! I am so glad to see you," and a fusillade of kisses accompanied the hug. "Whatever brings you here? Oh, and such a dowdy frock! You needn't flush up so, silly little child; nobody expects you to know how to dress like us ignoramuses, and it doesn't matter to-day, there's no one to see you, for they're all out driving, and I'm lying down with a headache."

"Poor Kitty. But then you ought to be out driving." She was divided between sympathy for the sufferer, and admiration of the finished, fine ladyhood implied in indifference to the chance of a carriage-drive.

"Yes, but I've so many letters to write, and they don't really drive on Sundays, just stop at house after house, and not good houses either. It is such a bore. They've never shaken off the society they had before they made their money."

"Well, but that's rather nice of them."

"Perhaps, but not nice for me. But come upstairs and you shall have some tea."

Salvina mounted the broad staircase with a reverence attuned to her own hushed footfalls, but her task of breaking the news to her sister weighed the heavier upon her for all this subdued magnificence. It seemed almost profane to bring the squalid episodes of Hackney into this atmosphere, appropriate indeed to the sinful romances of marquises and epauletted officers, but wholly out of accord with surreptitious furniture vans. What a blow to poor Kitty the news would be! She dallied weakly, till the tea was brought by a powdered footman. Then she had an ingenious idea for a little shock to lead up to a greater. She would say they were going to move. But as she took off her white glove not to sully it with the tea and cake, Kitty cried: "Why what have you done with my ring?"

Here was an excellent natural opening, but Salvina was taken too much aback to avail herself of it, especially as the artificial opening preoccupied her mind. "Oh, your ring's all right," she said hastily; "I came to tell you we are going to move."

Kitty clapped her hands. "Ah! so you've taken my advice at last! I'm so glad. It wasn't nice for me to stay with you at that dingy hole, even for a day or two a year. Mustn't mother be pleased!"

Salvina bit her lip. Her task was now heavier than ever.

"No, mother isn't pleased. She is crying about it."

"Crying? Disgusting. How she still hankers after Spitalfields and the Lane!"

"She isn't crying for that, but because father won't go with us."

"Oh, I have no patience with father. He hasn't a soul above red herrings and potatoes."

"Oh, yes he has. He has left us."

"What! Left you?" Kitty's pretty eyes opened wide. "Because he won't move to a better house!"

"No, we are moving to a worse house because he has moved to a better."

"What are you talking about? Is it a joke? A riddle? I give it up."

"Father—can't you guess, Kitty?—father has gone away. There is some other woman."

"No?" gasped Kitty. "Ha! ha! ha! ha!" and she shook with long peals of silvery laughter. "Well, of all the funny things! Ha! ha! ha!"

"Funny!" and Salvina looked at her sternly.

"What, don't you see the humour of it? Father turning into the hero of a novelette. Romance and red herrings! Passion and potatoes! Ha! ha! ha!"

"If you had seen the havoc it wrought, you wouldn't have had the heart to laugh."

"Oh well, mother was crying. That I understand. But that's nothing new for her. She'd cry just as much if he were there. The average rainfall is—how many inches?"

Salvina's face was stern and white. "A mother's tears are sacred," she said in low but firm protest.

"Oh, dear me, Sally, I always forget you have no sense of humour. Well, what are you going to do about it?" and her own sense of humour continued to twitch and dimple the corners of her pretty mouth.

"I told you. We cannot afford to keep up the house—we must go back to apartments in Spitalfields."

Instantly Kitty's face grew as serious as Salvina's. "Oh, nonsense!" she said instinctively. The thought of her family returning to the discarded shell of apartments was humiliating; her own personality seemed being dragged back.

"We can't pay the rent. We must give a quarter's notice at once."

"Absurd! You'll only save a few shillings a week. Why can't you let apartments yourselves? At least you would preserve a decent appearance."

"Is it worth while having the responsibility of the rent? There's only mother and I—we shan't need a house."

"But there's Lazarus!"

"He'll have a place of his own. He'll marry before our notice expires."

"That same Jonas girl?"

"Yes."

"Ridiculous. Small tradespeople, and dreadfully common, all the lot. I thought he'd got over his passion for that bold black creature who's been seen licking ice-cream out of a street-glass. To connect us with that family! Men are so selfish. But I still don't see why you can't remain as you are—let your drawing-room, say, furnished."

"But it isn't furnished."

"Not furnished. Why, I've sat on the couch myself."

"Yes," said Salvina, a faint smile tempering her deadly gravity. "You are the only person who has ever done that. But there's no couch now. Father smuggled all the furniture away in a van."

Again Kitty's silver laughter rang out unquenchably.

"And you don't call that funny! Eloped with the chairs! I call it killing."

"Yes, for mother," said Salvina.

"Pooh! She'll outlive all of us. I wish you were as sure of getting the furniture back. She's not a bad mother, as mothers go, but you take her too seriously."

"But, Kitty, consider the disgrace!"

"The disgrace of having a wicked parent! I've endured for years the disgrace of having a poor one—and that's worse. My people—the Samuelsons, I mean—will never even hear of the pater's escapade—gossip keeps strictly to its station. And even if they do, they know already my family's under a cloud, and they have learned to accept me for myself."

"Well, I am glad you don't mind," said Salvina, half-relieved, half-shocked.

"I mind, if it makes you uncomfortable, you dear, silly Sally."

"Oh, don't worry about me. I think I'll go back to mother, now."

"Nonsense, why, we haven't begun to talk yet. Have another cup of tea. No? How's old Miss What's-a-name, your head-mistress? Any more frozen little kittens?"

"She's very kind, really. I'm sorry I told you about the kitten. She let me go home early on Friday."

"Why? To track the van?"

"No; I wasn't very well."

"Poor Sally!" and Kitty hugged her again. "I daresay you were more upset than mother."

Tears came into Salvina's eyes at her sister's affectionateness. "Oh, no; but please don't talk about it any more. Father is dead to us now."

"Then we must speak well of him."

Salvina shuddered. "He is a wicked, heartless man, and mother and I never wish to see his face again."

A cloud darkened Kitty's blonde brow.

"Yes, but she isn't going to marry another man, I hope."

"How can she?" said Salvina. "I wouldn't let her make any public scandal."

"But aren't there funny laws in our religion—Get and things like that—which dispense with the English courts."

"I believe there are—I read about something of the kind in a novel—oh, yes! and father did offer mother Get before he went off, so I suppose he considers his conscience clear."

"Well, I rely upon you, Sally, to see that she doesn't marry or complicate things more. We don't want two wicked parents."

"Of course not. But I am sure she doesn't dream of any new complications. You don't do her justice, Kitty. She's just broken-hearted; a perpetual widow, with worse than her husband's death to lament."

"Yes—her lost furniture."

"Oh, Kitty, do realize what it means."

"I do, my dear. I do realize it—it's too killing. Passion in a Pantechnicon or Elopements economically conducted. By the day or hour. Oh, dear, oh, dear! But do promise me, Salvina, that you won't go back to Spitalfields."

"I must be somewhere near the school, dearest. It will save train-fares."

Kitty pouted. "Well, you know I couldn't drive up to see you any more; Hackney was all but outside the radius—the radius of respectability. I couldn't ask coachman to go to Spitalfields—unless I pretended to be slumming."

"Well, pretend."

"Oh, Salvina! I thought you were so conscientious. No, I'll have to come in a cab. You're quite sure you won't have some more tea? Oh, do, I insist. One piece of sugar?"

"Yes, thank you, dear. By the way, has Sugarman the Shadchan been here?"

"You mean—has he gone?"

"Oh, poor Kitty! It was my fault. I let him know your address. I do hope the horrid man hasn't worried you."

"Sugarman?"

"No—Moss M. Rosenstein."

"How pat you have his name! But why do you call him horrid?"

Salvina stared. "But have you seen his photograph?"

"Oh, you can't go by photographs. He has been here."

"What! Sugarman had the impudence to bring him!"

Kitty flushed slightly. "No, he called alone—this afternoon, just before you."

"What impertinence! A brazen commercial courtship! You wouldn't receive him, of course."

"Oh, well, I thought it would be fun just to look at him," said Kitty uneasily. "A commercial courtship, as you express it, is not unamusing."

"I don't see anything amusing in it—it's an outrage."

"I told you you had no sense of humour. I find it comic to be loved before first sight by a man who has no h's, but only l's, s's, and d's."

"Sugarman says he did see you before loving you—noticed you before he went to the Cape. But you must have been a little girl then."

"He didn't tell me that—that would have been even more romantic. He only said he fell in love with my photograph, as paraded by Sugarman."

"Why, where should Sugarman get—"

"You never know what mother's been up to," interrupted Kitty dryly.

"Much more likely father."

"What's the odds? Do have another piece of cake."

"No, thank you. But what did you say to the man?"

"The same as you. Don't stare so, you stupid dear. I said, No, thank you."

"That I knew. Of course you couldn't possibly marry a bloated creature from the Cape. I meant, in what terms did you put him in his place?"

"Oh, really," said Kitty, laughing, but without her recent merriment. "This is too prejudiced. I can't admit that mere residence in the Cape is a disqualification."

"Oh, yes, it is. Why do they go there? Only to make money. A person whose one idea in life is money can't be a nice person."

"But money isn't his one idea—now his one idea is matrimony. That is a joke. You ought to laugh."

"It makes me cry to think that some nice girl may be driven into marrying him just for his money."

"Poor man! So because of his money he is to be prevented from having a nice wife."

Salvina was taken aback by this obverse view.

"How is he ever to improve?" asked Kitty, pursuing her advantage.

"Yes, that's true," Salvina admitted. "The best thing would be if some nice girl could fall in love with him. But that doesn't make his methods less insulting. I wish all these Shadchans could be slaughtered off."

"What a savage little chit! They often make as good marriages as are made in heaven."

"Don't tease. You know you think as I do."

Salvina took an affectionate leave of her sister, and walked down the soft staircase, confused but cheerful. The boy in buttons let her out. To do so he hurriedly put down the infant of the house who was riding on his shoulders. Such a touch of humanity in a row of buttons gave Salvina a new insight and a suspicion that even the powdered footman who brought the tea might have an emotion behind his gorgeous waistcoat. But the crowds fighting for the omnibuses that fine Sunday afternoon depressed her again. All the seats outside were packed, and it was only after standing a long time on the pavement that she squeezed her way into an inside seat. The stuffiness and jolting made her feel sick and dizzy. By a happy accident her fingers encountered the bottle of smelling-salts in her pocket, and, as she pulled it out eagerly, she remembered it had been intended for Kitty.

VII

Lazarus remained out late that evening, and, as he had forgotten to borrow the key, Salvina was sitting up for him.

She utilized the time in preparing her sewing. She was making a night-dress with dozens and dozens of tiny tucks at the breast, all run by hand, and she was putting into the fine calico an artistic needlework absolutely futile, and with its perpetual "count two, miss two,"—infinitely trying to the eyes, especially by gas-light. The insane competition of the teachers, refining upon a Code in itself stupidly exacting, made the needlework the most distressing of all the tasks of the girl-teachers of that day. Salvina herself, with her morbid conscientiousness and desire to excel, underwent nightmares from the vexatiousness of learning how to cut holes so that they could not possibly be darned, and then darning them. When, at the head-centre, the lady demonstrator, armed with a Brobdingnagian whalebone needle, threaded with a bright red cord, executed herringboned fantasias on a canvas frame resembling a violin stand, it all looked easy enough. But when Salvina herself had to unravel a little piece of stockinette with a real needle and then fill in the hole so as to leave no trace of the crime, she was reduced to hysteria. Even the coloured threads with which she worked were a scant relief to the eye. And all this elaborate fancywork was entirely useless. At home Salvina was always at work, darning and mending; never was there a defter needle. Even the "hedge-tear-down" was neatly and expeditiously repaired, so long as she avoided the scholastic methods. "What's all this madness?" her mother had asked once, when she had tried the orthodox "Swiss darning" on a real article. And Mrs. Brill surveyed in amazement the back of the darn, which looked like Turkish towelling.

To-night Salvina could not long continue her taxing work. Her eyes ached, and she at last resolved to rise early in the morning and proceed with the night-dress then. She turned the gas low, so as to reduce the bill, and it was as if she had turned down her own spirits, for a strange melancholy now took possession of her in the silent fuscous kitchen in the denuded house, and the emptiness of the other rooms seemed to strike a chill upon her senses. There were strange creaks and ghostly noises from all parts. She fixed her thought on the one furnished bed-room now occupied by her mother, as on a symbol of life and recuperation. But the uncanny noises went on; rustlings, and patterings, and Salvina felt that she might shriek and frighten her mother. She had almost resolved to turn up the gas, when the sound of a harmonium came muffled through the wall, and the softened voices of her Christian neighbours sang a Sunday hymn. Salvina ceased to be alone; and tears bathed her cheeks, as the crude melody lilted on. She felt absorbed in some great light and love, which was somehow both a present possession and a beckoning future that awaited her soul, and it was all mysteriously mixed with the blue skies of Victoria Park, in those far-off happy days when she had gone home on her father's shoulder; and with the blue skies of those enchanted sunlit lands of art and beauty, in which she would wander in the glorious future, when she should be making a hundred and fifty a year. Paris, Venice, Athens, Madrid—how the mellifluous syllables thrilled her! One by one, in her annual summer holiday, she and her mother might see them all. Meantime she saw them all in her imagination, bathed in the light that never was on sea or land, and it was not her mother with whom she journeyed but a noble young Bayard, handsome and tender-hearted, who had imperceptibly slipped into her mother's place. Poor Salvina, with all her modesty, never saw herself as others saw her, never lost the dream of a romantic love. Lazarus's rat-tat recalled her to reality.

"I know I'm late," he said, with apologetic defiance, "but it's no pleasure to sit in an empty house. You may like it, but your tastes were always peculiar, and that straw mattress on the floor isn't inviting."

"I am so sorry, dear. But then mother must have the bed."

"Well, it won't last long, thank Heaven. I made the Jonases consent to the marriage before the scandal gets to them."

"So soon!" said Salvina with unconscious social satire.

"Yes, and we'll have our honeymoon travelling for Granders Brothers. She's a good sort, is Rhoda, she doesn't mind gypsying. And that saves us from the expense of completing the furniture." He paused, and added awkwardly, "I'd lend it to you, only that might give us away."

"But we don't need the furniture, dear, and don't you think they ought to know—it is the rest of the world that it doesn't concern."

"They are bound to know after the marriage. We've kept it dark so far, thanks to being in Hackney away from our old acquaintances and to mother's stinginess in not having encouraged new people to drop in. I've told the Jonases father was ill and might have to go away for his health. That'll pave the way to his absence from the wedding. It sounds quite grand. We'll send him to a German Spa."

Salvina did not share her brother's respect for old Jonas, who bored her with trite quotations from English literature or the Hebrew Bible. He was in sooth a pompous ignoramus, acutely conscious of being an intellectual light in an ignorant society; a green shade he wore over his left eye added to his air of dignified distinction. Foreign Jews in especial were his scorn, and he seriously imagined that his own stereotyped phrases uttered with a good English pronunciation gave his conversation an immeasurable superiority over the most original thinking tainted by a German or Yiddish accent. Salvina's timid corrections of his English quotations made him angry and imperilled Lazarus's wooing. The young man was indeed the only member of the family who cultivated relations with the Jonases, though now it would be necessary to exchange perfunctory visits. Lazarus presided over these visits in fear and trembling, glossing over any slips as to the father, who was gone to the seaside for his health. On second thoughts, Lazarus had not ventured on a German Spa.

VIII

Ere the wedding-day arrived, Salvina had to go to the seaside. Clacton-on-Sea was the somewhat plebeian place and the school-fête the occasion. Salvina looked forward to it without much personal pleasure, because of the responsibilities involved, but it was a break in the pupil-teacher's monotonous round of teaching at the school and being taught at the Centres; and in the actual expedition the children's joy was contagious and made Salvina shed secret tears of sympathy. Arrived at the beach of the stony, treeless, popular watering-place, most of the happy little girls were instantly paddling in the surf with yells of delight, while the tamer sort dug sand-pits and erected castles. Salvina, whose office on this occasion was to assist an "assistant teacher," had to keep her eye on a particular contingent. She sat down on the noisy sunlit sands with her back to the sea-wall so as to sweep the field of vision. Her nervous conscientiousness made her count her sheep at frequent intervals, and be worried over missing now this one, now that one. How her heart beat furiously and then almost stopped, when she saw a child wading out too far. No, decidedly it was a trying form of pleasure for the teacher. One bright little girl who had never beheld the sea before picked up a wonderfully smooth white pebble, and bringing it to Salvina asked if it was worth any money. Salvina held it up, extemporizing an object lesson for the benefit of the little bystanders.

"No," she said, "this is not worth any money, because you can get plenty of them without trouble, and even beautiful things are not considered valuable if anybody can have them. This stone was polished without charge by the action of the waves washing against it for millions and millions of years, and if it—"

The sudden blare of a brass band on the other side of the sea-wall made her turn her head, and there, in a brand-new room of a brand-new house on the glaring Promenade, a room radiating blatant prosperity from its stony balcony, she perceived her father, in holiday attire, and by his side a woman, buxom and yellow-haired. A hot wave of blood seemed to flood Salvina up to the eyes. So there he was luxuriating in the sun, rich and careless. All her homely instincts of work and duty rose in burning contempt. And poor Mrs. Brill had to remain cooped at home, drudging and wailing. For a second she felt she would like to throw the stone at him, but her next feeling was pain lest the sight of her should painfully embarrass him; and turning her face swiftly seawards she went on, with scarce a pause perceptible to the little girls, "If it gets worn away some more millions of years, it will be ground down to sand, like all the other stones that were once here," and as she spoke, she began to realize her own words, and a tragic sense of her own insignificance in this eternal wash of space and time seemed to reduce her to a grain of sand, and blow her about the great spaces. But the mood passed away before a fresh upwelling of concrete resentment against the self-pampered pair at the Promenade window. Nevertheless, her feeling of how their seeming satisfaction would be upset at the sight of her, made her carefully minimize the contingency, and the dread of it hovered over the day, adding to the worries over the children. But she vowed that her mother should be revenged; she, too, poor wronged one, should wallow in Promenade luxury in her future holidays; no more should she be housed in back streets without sea-views.

At night, after Mrs. Brill was in bed, Salvina could not resist saying to Lazarus, whose supper she had been keeping hot for him: "How strange! Father is at the seaside."

"The dickens!" He paused, fork in hand. "You saw him at Clacton-on-Sea?"

"Yes, but don't tell mother. So we didn't tell a lie after all. I'm so glad."

"Oh, go to blazes, you and your conscience. Where was he staying?"

"In a house in the very centre of the Promenade; it's simply shocking!"

"Make me some fresh mustard, and don't moralize. Did you have a good time?"

"Not very; a little cripple-girl in my class went paddling, and joking, and dropped her crutch, and it floated away—"

"Bother your little cripple-girls. They always seem to be in your class!"

"Because my class is on the ground floor."

"Ha! ha! ha! Just your luck. By the way," he became grave, "look what a beastly letter from Kitty! Not coming to the wedding. I call it awfully selfish of her."

Kitty wrote her deep regrets, but her people had suddenly determined to go abroad and she could not lose this chance of seeing the world; "the governess's honeymoon," she christened it. Paris, Switzerland, Rome—all the magic places were to be hers—and Salvina, reading the letter, gasped with sympathy and longing.

But the happy traveller was represented at the wedding by a large bronze-looking knight on horseback, which towered in shining green over the insignificant gifts of the Jonas's circle; the utilitarian salad-bowls, and fish-slices, and dessert sets. One other present stood out luridly, but only to Salvina. It was a glossy arm-chair, and on the seat lay a card: "From Rhoda's loving father-in-law." When Salvina first saw this—at a family card-party, the Sunday evening before the wedding—she started and flushed so furiously that Lazarus had to give her a warning nudge, and to whisper: "Only for appearance." At the supper-table old Jonas, who carved and jested with much appreciation of his own skill in both departments, referred facetiously to the absent father, who might, nevertheless, be said to be "in the chair" on that occasion.

Salvina dressed her mother as carefully for the ceremony as though Kitty's fears were being realized and Mrs. Brill was the bride of the occasion; and so debonair a figure emerged from the ordeal that you could recognize Kitty's mother instead of Salvina's. Lazarus had spent his farewell evening of bachelorhood at an hotel, justly complaining that a mirrorless bed-room with a straw mattress was no place for a bridegroom to issue from. Never had bridegroom been so ill-treated, he grumbled; and he shook his fist imaginatively at the father who had despoiled him.

But he joined his mother and sister in the cab; and as it approached the synagogue, he said suddenly: "Don't be shocked—but I rather expect father will be at the Shool (synagogue)."

"What!" and Mrs. Brill appeared like to faint.

"He wouldn't have the cheek," Salvina said reassuringly, as she pulled out the smelling-salts which Kitty had not needed.

"He wouldn't have the cheek not to come," said Lazarus. "I asked him."

"You!" They glared at him in horror.

"Yes; I wasn't going to have things look funny—I hate explanations. The Jonases thought there was something queer the other night, when you both bungled the explanation of the rheumatism, spite all my coaching."

"But where did you find him?" said the mother excitedly.

"At Clacton-on-Sea."

Salvina bit her lip.

"I sent in my card—'Laurence Beryl, of Granders Brothers.' When he saw me, I thought he would have had a fit. I told him if he didn't come up to the wedding and play heavy father, I'd summons him—"

"Summons him!" echoed Mrs. Brill.

"For stealing my old arm-chair. I remembered—ha! ha! ha!—it was I that had bought the easy-chair for myself, when we lived in Spitalfields and had only wooden chairs."

"So he did send that easy-chair!" said Salvina.

"Yes; that was rather clever of him. And don't you think it's clever of me to save appearances?"

"It'll be terrible for mother!" said Salvina hotly. "Didn't you think of that?"

"She won't have to talk to him. He'll only hang round. Nobody will notice."

"It would have been better to tell the truth," cried Salvina, "or even a lie. This is only acting a lie. And it must be as painful for him as for us."

"Serve him right—the old furniture-sneak!"

"It was a mistake," Salvina persisted.

"Hush, hush, Salvina!" said Mrs. Brill. "Don't disturb your brother's festival."

"He has disturbed it himself," said Salvina, bursting into tears. "I wish, mother, we had not come."

"Here, here! This is a pretty wedding," said Lazarus.

"Hush, Salvina, hush!" said Mrs. Brill. "What does it matter to us if a dog creeps into synagogue?"

At this point the cab stopped.

"We're not there!" cried Mrs. Brill.

"No," Lazarus explained; "but we pick up father here. We must appear to arrive together."

Ere the horrified pair could protest, he opened the door, sprang out, and pushed inside a stout, rubicund man with a festal rose in his holiday coat, but a miserable, shamefaced look in his eyes. Lazarus took his seat ere a word could be spoken. The cab rolled on.

"Good-morning, Esther," he muttered. "I offered you Get."

"Silence!" cried Salvina, as if she had been talking to the little girls. "How dare you speak to her?" She held her mother's hand and felt the pulse beating madly.

"You old serpent—" began Mrs. Brill hotly.

"Mother!" pleaded Salvina; "not a word; he doesn't deserve it."

"In Jerusalem I could have two wives," he muttered. But no one replied.

The four human beings sat in painful silence, their knees touching. The culprit shot uneasy, surreptitious glances at his wife, so radiant in jewels and finery and with so Kitty-like a complexion. It was as if he saw her freshly, or as if he were shocked—even startled—by her retaining so much joy of life despite his desertion of her. Fortunately the strange drive only lasted a few minutes. The bridegroom's wedding-party passed into the synagogue through an avenue of sympathetic observers.

Mr. Brill had no part to play in the ceremony. The honours were carried off by Mr. Jonas, who stalked in slowly, with the bride on his arm, and a new green shade over his left eye. The rival father hovered meekly on the outskirts of the marriage-canopy amid a crowd of Jonases. Salvina stationed herself and her mother on the opposite border of the canopy, and throughout bristled, apprehensive, prohibitive, fiery, like a spaniel guarding its mistress against a bull-dog on the pounce. The bull-dog indeed was docile enough; avoiding the spaniel's eye, and trailing a spiritless tail. But the creature revived at the great wedding-feast in the hall of a hundred covers, and under the congratulations and the convivial influences tended to forget he was in disgrace. The bridegroom's parents were placed together, but Salvina changed seats with her mother, and became a buffer between the twain, a non-conducting medium through which the father could not communicate with the mother. With the latter she herself maintained a continuous conversation, and Mr. Brill soon found it more pleasant to forget his troubles in the charms of Mrs. Jonas, his other neighbour.

After the almond-pudding, a succession of speakers ranging from relatives to old friends, and even the officiating minister, gave certificates of character to the bride and the bridegroom, amid the tears of the ladies. Father Jonas made an elaborate speech beginning, "Unaccustomed as I am to public speaking," and interlarded with Hebrew quotations. Father Brill expressed the pleasure it gave him to acknowledge on behalf of himself and his dear wife, the kind things which had been said, and the delight they felt in seeing their son settled in the paths of domestic happiness, especially in connection with a scion of the house of Jonas, of whose virtues much had been said so deservedly that night. Lazarus declared, amid roars of laughter, that on this occasion only he would respond for his dear wife, but he felt sure that for the rest of their lives she would have the last word. Then the tables were cleared away and dancing began, which grew livelier as the dawn grew nearer. But long before that, Salvina had borne her mother away from the hovering bull-dog. Not, however, without a terrible scene in the homeward cab. All the volcanic flames Salvina and etiquette had suppressed during the day shot forth luridly. Burning lava was hurled against her husband, against her son, against Salvina. An impassioned inventory of the lost furniture followed, and the refrain of the whole was that she had been taken to a wedding, when all she wanted was a funeral.

IX

Salvina did not count this break-down against her mother. It was the natural revolt of nerves tried beyond endurance by Lazarus's trick. The whole episode intensified her sense of the romantic situation of her mother, and of the noble courage and dignity with which she confronted it. She wondered whether she herself would have emerged so stanchly from the ordeal of meeting a loved but faithless one, and her protective pity was tempered by a new admiration. Her admiration increased, when, as the secret gradually leaked out, her mother maintained an attitude of defiance against the world's sympathy, refused to hear stigmatizations of her husband, even from old Jonas, reserving the privilege of denunciation for her own mouth and Salvina's ear.

And now began the new life of mother and daughter. With Kitty on the Continent, Lazarus married, and the father blotted out, they had only each other. They moved back to the skirts of the Ghetto, and Mrs. Brill resumed with secret joy her old place among her old cronies. Inwardly, she had fretted at the loss of them, for which the dignity of Hackney had been but a shadowy compensation. But to Salvina she only expressed her outraged pride, the humiliation of it all, and the poor girl, unconscious of how happy her mother really was among the Ghetto gossips, tortured her brain during school-hours with the thought of her mother's lonely misery. And even if Salvina had not been compelled to give private lessons in the evenings to supplement their income, she would in any case have relinquished her Bachelorhood aspirations in order to give her time to her mother. For Mrs. Brill had no resources within herself, so far as Salvina knew. Even the great artificial universe of books and newspapers was closed to her. Salvina resolved to overcome her obstinate reluctance to learn to read, as soon as the pressure of the other private lessons relaxed. Meantime, she lived for her mother and her mother on her.

Oh, the bitterness of those private lessons after the fag of the day; the toiling to distant places on tired feet; the grinding bargains imposed by the well-to-do!

One of these fiends was a beautiful lady, haughty, with fair complexion and frosted hair, and somehow suggested to Salvina a steel engraving. She arranged graciously that Salvina should teach her little girl conversational German at half-a-crown an hour, but when Salvina started on the first lesson in the luxurious sanctum, she found two sweetly dressed sisters; who, she was informed, could not bear to be separated, and might therefore be considered one. The steel engraving herself sat there, as if to superintend, occasionally asking for the elucidation of a point. At the second lesson there were two other little girls, neighbours, the lady informed her, who had thought it would be a good opportunity for them to learn, too. Salvina expressed her pleasure and her gratitude to her patroness. At the third lesson the aunt of the two little girls was also present with a suspicious air of discipleship. When at end of the month, Salvina presented her bill at five shillings an hour, the patroness flew into a towering rage. What did it matter to her how many children partook of the hour? An hour was an hour and a bargain a bargain. Salvina had not the courage or the capital to resist. And this life of ever teaching and never learning went on, week after week, year after year. For when her salary at the school increased, the additional burden of Lazarus and his wife and children fell upon her. For her feckless brother had soon exhausted the patience of Granders Brothers; he had passed shiftlessly from employment to employment, frequently dependent on Salvina and his father-in-law till old Jonas had declared, with all the dignity of his green shade, that his son-in-law—graceless offspring of a graceless sire—must never darken his door-step again.

But the joy Mrs. Brill found in her grandchildren, the filling-out of her life, repaid Salvina amply for all the pinching necessary to subsidize her brother's household. She winced, though, to see her mother drop thoughtlessly into the glossy arm-chair presented by her absentee husband, and therein ensconced dandle Lazarus's children. Salvina was too sensitive to remind her mother, and shrank also from appearing fantastic. But that chair inspired a morbid repugnance, and one day, taking advantage of the fact that the stuffing began to extrude, she bought Lazarus a new and better easy-chair without saying why, and had the satisfaction of noting the relegation of the old one to a bed-room.

Two bright spots of colour dappled those long, monotonous years. One was Kitty; the other was the summer holiday. Kitty's mere letters from the Continent—she wrote twice during the tour—were a source of exhilaration as well as of instruction. She brought nearer all those wonderful places which Salvina still promised herself to behold one day, though year after year she went steadily to Ramsgate. For her mother shrank from sea-voyages and strange places, as much as she loved the familiar beach swarming with Jewish faces and nigger minstrels. Even Salvina's little scheme of enthroning her mother expensively on the parade at Clacton-on-Sea, that mother unconsciously thwarted, though she endured equivalent splendour at Ramsgate at three guineas a week, with much grumbling over her daughter's extravagance.

Once indeed when Salvina had seriously projected Paris in the interest of her French, there had been a quarrel on the subject. There were many quarrels on many subjects, but it was always one quarrel and had always the same groundwork of dialogue on Mrs. Brill's part, whatever the temporal variations.

"A nice daughter! To trample under foot her own flesh and blood, because she thinks I'm dependent on her! Well, well, do your own marketing, you little ignoramus who don't know a skirt steak from a loin chop; you'll soon see if I don't earn my keep. I earned my living before you were born, and I can do so still. I'd rather live in one room than have my blood shed a day longer. I'll send for Kitty—she never stamps on the little mother. She shan't slave her heart out any more among strangers, my poor fatherless Kitty. No, we'll live together, Kitty and I. Lazarus would jump at us—my own dear, handsome Lazarus. I never see him but he tells me how the children are crying day and night for their granny, and why don't I go and live with him? He wouldn't spit upon the mother who suckled him, and even Rhoda has more respect for me than my own real daughter."

Such was the basal theme; the particular variation, when the holiday was concerned, took the shape of religious remonstrance. "And where am I to get kosher food in Paris? In Ramsgate I enjoy myself; there's a kosher butcher, and all the people I know. It's as good as London."

Tears always conquered Salvina. She had an infinite patience with her mother on these occasions, not resenting the basal theme, but regarding it as a mere mechanic explosion of nervous irritation, generated by her lonely life. Sometimes she forgot this and argued, but was always the more sorry afterward. Not that she did not enjoy Ramsgate. Her nature that craved for so much and was content with so little found even Ramsgate a Paradise after a year of the slum-school, to which she always returned looking almost healthy. But this constant absorption in her mother's personality narrowed her almost to the same mental bookless horizon. All the red blood of ambition was sucked away as by a vampire; her energy was sapped and the unchanging rut of school-existence combined to fray away her individuality. She never went into any society; the rare invitation to a social event was always refused with heart-shrinking. Every year made her more shy and ungainly, more bent in on herself, and on the little round of school and home life, which left her indeed too weary in brain and body for aught beside. She sank into the scholastic old maid, unconsciously taking on the very gait and accent of Miss Rolver, into the limitations of whose life she had once had a flash of insight. Yet she was unaware of her decay; her automatic brain was still alive in one corner, where the dreams hived and nested. Paris and Rome and the wonder-places still shone on the horizon, together with the noble young Bayard, handsome and tender-hearted. And twice or thrice a year Kitty would flash upon the scene to remind her that there was truly a world of elegance and adventure. Her mother had begun to worry over the beautiful Kitty's failure to marry; she had imagined that in those gilded regions she would have snapped up a South African millionaire or other ingenuous person. How nearly Kitty had actually come to doing so, even without the spring-board of Bedford Square, Salvina never told her. She had kept both Sugarman and Moss M. Rosenstein from pestering her mother, by telling the Shadchan that Kitty's voice and Kitty's alone weighed with Kitty in such a matter. When the swarthy capitalist returned to the Cape, despairing, Salvina had written to congratulate her sister on her high-mindedness. In the years that followed, she had to endure many a bad quarter of an hour of maternal reproach because Kitty did not marry, but Mrs. Brill's vengeance was unconscious. Kitty herself never heard a word of these complaints; to her the mother was all wreathed smiles, for she never came without bringing a trinket, and every one of these trinkets meant days of happiness. The little lockets and brooches were shown about to all the neighbours and hitched them on to the bright spheres which Kitty adorned. Carriages and footmen, soft carpets and gilded mirrors gleamed in the air. "My Kitty!" rolled under Mrs. Brill's tongue like a honeyed sweet. Kitty's little gifts, flashing splendidly on the everyday dulness, made more impression than all the steady monotonous services of Salvina. For the rest, Salvina conscientiously repaid these gifts in kind on Kitty's birthdays and other high days.

X

When Salvina was twenty-three years old a change came. Lazarus ceased to demand assistance: he was cheery and self-confident, and inclined to chaff Salvina on her prim ways. He removed to a larger house and her easy-chair disappeared before a more elegant. And the apparent brightness of her brother's prospects brightened Salvina's. Her savings increased, and, under the continuous profit of his self-support, she was soon able to meditate changes on her own account. Either she would give up her night-teaching—which had been more and more undermining her system—or she would procure her mother and Kitty a delightful surprise by migrating back to Hackney.

Her mind hesitated between the joyous alternatives, lingering voluptuously now on one, now on the other, but somehow aware that it would ultimately choose the latter, for Kitty on her rare visits never failed to grumble at the lowness of the neighbourhood and the expense of cabs, and Mrs. Brill still yearned to see horses pawing outside her door-step. But an unexpected visit from Kitty, not six weeks after her last, and equally unexpected in place—for it was at Salvina's school—decided the matter suddenly.

It was about half-past twelve, and Salvina, long since a full "assistant teacher," was seated at her desk, correcting the German exercises of a private pupil. Sparsely dotted about the symmetric benches were a few demure criminals undergoing the punishment of being kept in, and the air was still heavy with the breaths and odours of the blissful departed. A severe museum-case, with neatly ticketed specimens, backed Salvina's chair, and around the spacious room hung coloured diagrams of animals and plants. Kitty seemed a specimen from another world as her coquettish Leghorn hat flowering with poppies burst upon the scholastic scene.

"Oh, dear, I thought you'd be alone," she said pettishly.

"Is it anything important? The children don't matter," said Salvina. "You can tell me in German. I do hope nothing is the matter."

"No, nothing so alarming as that," Kitty replied in German. "But I thought I'd find you alone and have a chat."

"I had to stay here with the children. They must be punished."

"Seems more like punishing yourself. But have you lunched, then?"

"No." Salvina flushed slightly.

"No? What's up? A Jewish fast! Ninth day of Ab, fall of Temple, and funny things like that. One always seems to stumble upon them in the East End."

"How you do rattle on, Kitty!" and Salvina smiled. "No, I shall lunch as soon as these children are released."

"But why wait for that?"

Salvina's blush deepened. "Well, one doesn't want to eat a good dinner before hungry girls."

"A good dinner! Why, what in heaven's name do you get? Truffles and plovers' eggs?"

"No, but I get a very good meal sent in from the Cooking Centre opposite, and compared with what these girls get at home, steak and potatoes are the luxuries of Lucullus."

"Oh, I don't believe it. They all look fatter than you. Then this is double punishment for you—extra work and hunger. Do send them away. They get on my nerves. And have your lunch like a sensible being." And without waiting for Salvina's assent: "Go along, girls," she said airily.

The girls hesitated and looked at Salvina, who coloured afresh, but said, "Yes, this lady pleads for you, and I said that if you all promised to—"

"Oh, yes, teacher," they interrupted enthusiastically, and were off.

"Well, what I came to tell you, Sally, is that I'm not sure of my place much longer."

Salvina turned pale, and that much-tried heart of hers thumped like a hammer. She waited in silence for the facts.

"Lily is going to be married."

"Well? All the more reason for Mabel to have a companion."

Kitty shook her head. "It's the beginning of the end. Marriage is a contagious complaint in a family. First one member is taken off, then another. But that's not the worst."

"No?" Poor Salvina held her breath.

"Who do you think is the happy man? You'll never guess."

"How should I? I don't know their circle."

"Yes, you do. I mean, you know him."

Salvina wrinkled her forehead vainly.

"No, you'll never guess after all these years! Moss M. Rosenstein!"

"Is it possible?" Salvina gasped. "Lily Samuelson!"

"Yes—Lily Samuelson!"

"But he must be an old man by now."

"Well, she isn't a chicken. And you thought it was such an outrage of him to ask for me. I suppose having once got inside the door to see me, he had the idea of aspiring higher."

"Oh, don't say higher, Kitty. Richer, that's all—and now, I should say, lower, inasmuch as Lily Samuelson stoops to pick up what you passed by with scorn. And picks him up out of Sugarman's hand, probably."

"Yes, it's all very well, and it's revenge enough in a way to think to myself what I do think to myself, when I see the young couple going on, and Moss is mortally scared of me, as I shoot him a glare, now and again. I shouldn't be surprised if he eggs them on to get rid of me. It would be too bad to be done out of everything."

"Well, we must hope for the best," said Salvina, kissing her. "After all, you can always get another place."

"I'm getting old," Kitty said glumly.

"You old!" and the anæmic little school-mistress looked with laughing admiration at her sister's untarnished radiance. But when Kitty went, and lunch came, Salvina could not eat it.

XI

It was clear, however, that of the alternatives—giving up the night-work or returning to Hackney—the latter was the one favoured by Providence. Kitty might at any moment return to the parental roof, and there must be something, that Kitty would consider a roof, to shelter her.

On Saturday Salvina went house-hunting alone in Hackney, and there—as if further pointed out by Providence—stood their old house "To let!" It had a dilapidated air, as if it had stood empty for many moons and had lost hope. It seemed to her symbolic of her mother's fortunes, and her imagination leapt at the idea of recuperating both. Very soon she had re-rented the house, though from another landlord, and the workmen were in possession, making everything bright and beautiful. Salvina chose wall-papers of the exact pattern of aforetime, and ordered the painting and decorations to repeat the old effects. They were to move in, a few days before the quarter.

Her happy secret shone in her cheeks, and she felt all bright and refreshed, as if she, too, were being painted and cleaned and redecorated. The task of keeping it all from her mother was a great daily strain, and the secret had to overbrim for the edification of Lazarus. Lazarus hailed the change with expressions of unselfish joy, that brought tears into Salvina's eyes. He even went with her to see how the repairs were getting on, chatted with the workmen, disapproved of the landlord's stinginess in not putting down new drain pipes, and made a special call upon that gentleman.

One day on her return from school Salvina found a postcard to the effect that the house was ready for occupation. Salvina was for once glad that she had never yet found time to persuade her mother to learn to read. She went to feast her eyes on the new-old house and came home with the key, which she hid carefully till the Sunday afternoon, when she induced her mother to make an excursion to Victoria Park. The weather was dull, and the old woman needed a deal of coaxing, especially as the coaxing must be so subtle as not to arouse suspicion.

On the way back in the evening from the Park, which, as there was an unexpected band playing popular airs, her mother enjoyed, Salvina led her by the old familiar highways and byways back to the old home, keeping her engrossed in conversation lest it should suddenly befall her to ask why they were going that way. The expedient was even more successful than she had bargained for, Mrs. Brill's sub-consciousness calmly accepting all the old unchanged streets and sights and sounds, while her central consciousness was absorbed by the talk. Her legs trod automatically the dingy Hackney Terrace to which she had so often returned from her Park outing, her hand pushed open mechanically the old garden-gate, and as Salvina, breathlessly wondering if the spell could be kept up till the very last, opened the door with the latch-key, her mother sank wearily, and with a sigh of satisfaction, upon the accustomed hall-chair. In that instant of maternal apathy, the astonishment was wholly Salvina's. That hall-chair on which her mother sat was the very one which had stood there in the bygone happy years; the hat-rack was the one with which her father had "eloped"; on it stood the little flower-pots and on the wall hung the two engravings of the trials of Lord William Russell and Earl Stafford exactly in the same place, and facing her stood the open parlour with all the old furniture and colour. In that uncanny instant Salvina wondered if she had passed through years of hallucination. There was her mother, natural and unconcerned, bonneted and jewelled, exactly as she had come from Camberwell years ago when they had entered the house together. Perhaps they were still at that moment; she knew from her studies as well as from experience that you can dream years of harassing and multiplex experience in a single second. Perhaps there had been no waking hallucination; perhaps the long waiting for her mother to appear with the house-key had made her sleepy, and in that instant of doze she had dreamed all those horrible things— the empty house, her father's flight, his reappearance at her brother's marriage; the long years of evening lessons. Perhaps she was still seventeen, studying the Greek verbs for the Bachelorhood of Arts, perhaps her mother was still a happy wife. Her eyes filled with tears, and she let herself dwell upon the wondrous possibility a second or so longer than she believed in it. For the smell of new paint was too potent; it routed the persuasions of the old furniture. And in another instant it had penetrated through Mrs. Brill's fatigue. She started up, aware of something subtly wrong, ere clearer consciousness dawned.

"Michael!" she shrieked, groping.

"Hush, hush, mother!" said Salvina, with a pain as of swords at her heart. She felt her mother had stumbled—with whatever significance—upon the word of the enigma. "Another trick has been played on us."

"A trick!" Mrs. Brill groped further. "But you brought me. How comes this house here? What has happened?"

"I wanted to surprise you. I have rented the old house, and some one else has put in the old furniture."

"Michael is coming back! You and your father have plotted."

"Oh, mother! How can you accuse me of such a thing!" All the expected joy of the surprise had been changed to anguish, she felt, both for her and for her mother. Oh, what a fatal mistake! "I won't have the furniture, we'll pitch it into the street—we are going to live here together, mammy, you and I, in the old home. We can afford it now."

She laid her cheek to her mother's, but Mrs. Brill broke away petulantly and ran toward the parlour. "And does he think I'll have anything to do with him after all these years!" she cried.

"Dear mother, he doesn't know you if he thinks that!" said Salvina, following her.

"No, indeed! And a chip out of my best vase, just as I thought! And that isn't my chair—he's shoved me in one of a worse set. The horsehair may seem the same, but look at the legs—no carving at all. And where's the extra leaf of the table? Gone, too, I daresay. And my little gilt shovel that used to stand in the fender here, what's become of that? And do you call this a sofa? with the castors all off! Oh, my God, she has ruined all my furniture," and she burst into hysteric tears.

Salvina could do nothing till the torrent had spent itself. But she was busy, thinking. She saw that again her brother and her father had conspired together. Hence Lazarus's officiousness toward the landlord and the workmen—that he might easily get the entry to the house. But perhaps the conspiracy had not the significance her mother put upon it. Perhaps Lazarus was principal, not agent; in the flush of his new prosperity he had really projected a generous act; perhaps he had resolved to put the coping-stone on the surprise Salvina was preparing for her mother, and had hence negotiated with the father for the old things. If so, she felt she had not the right to make her mother refuse them; the rather, she must hasten at once to Lazarus to pour out her appreciation of his thoughtfulness.

"Come along, mother," she said at last, "don't sit there, crying. I think Lazarus must have bought back the things for you. You see, mammy, I wanted to give you a little surprise, and dear Lazarus has given me a little surprise."

"Do you really think it's only Lazarus?" asked Mrs. Brill, and to Salvina's anxious ear there seemed a shade of disappointment in the tone.

"I'm sure it is—father couldn't possibly have the impudence. After all these years, too!"

But when she at last got her mother to Lazarus, that gentleman confessed aggressively that he had been only the agent.

"I don't see why you shouldn't let the poor old man come back," he said. "The other person died a year ago, only nobody liked to tell mother, she was so bristly and snappy."

"Ah," interrupted Mrs. Brill exultantly, "then Heaven has heard my curses. May she burn in the lowest Gehenna. May her body become one yellow flame like her dyed hair."

"Hush!" said Salvina sternly. "God shall judge the dead."

"Oh, of course you always take everybody's part against your mother." And Mrs. Brill burst into tears again and sank into the new easy-chair.

"I do think mother's right," said Lazarus sullenly. "Why do you stand in her way?"

"I?" Salvina was paralyzed.

"Yes, if it wasn't for you—"

"Mother, do you hear what Lazarus is saying? That I keep you from father!"

"Father! A pretty father to you! He waits till she's dead, and then he wants to creep back to us. But let him lie on her grave. He'll swell to bursting before he crosses my door-step."

"There, Lazarus, do you hear?"

"Yes, I hear," he said incredulously. "But does she know what father offers her—every comfort, every luxury? He is rich now."

"Rich?" said Mrs. Brill. "The old swindler!"

"He didn't swindle—he's very sorry for the past now, and awfully kind and generous."

Salvina had a flash of insight. "Ho! So this is why—" She checked herself and looked round the handsome room, and the new easy-chair in which her mother sat became suddenly as hateful as the old.

"Well, suppose it is?" said Lazarus defiantly. "I don't see why we shouldn't share in his luck."

"And where does the luck come from?" Salvina demanded.

"What's that to do with us? From the Stock Exchange, I believe."

"And where did he get the money to gamble with?"

"Oh, they always had money."

Salvina's eyes blazed. The nerveless creature of the school became a fury. "And you'd touch that!"

"Hang it all, he owes us reparation. You, too, Salvina—he is anxious to do everything for you. He says you must chuck up school—it's simply wearing you away. He says he wants to take you abroad—to Paris."

"Oh, and so he thinks he'll get round mother by getting round me, does he? But let him take his furniture away at once, or we'll pitch it into the street. At once, do you hear?"

"He won't mind." Lazarus smiled irritatingly. "He wants to put better furniture in, and his real desire is to move to a big house in Highbury New Park. But I persuaded him to put back the old furniture—I thought it would touch you—a token, you know, that he wanted 'auld lang syne.'"

"Yes, yes, I understood," said Salvina, and then she thought suddenly of Kitty and a burst of hysteric laughter caught her. "Elopements economically conducted," went through her mind. "By the day or hour!" And she imagined the new phrases Kitty would coin. "The Prodigal Father and the Pantechnicon"—"The old Love and the old Furniture," and the wild laughter rang on, till Lazarus was quite disconcerted.

"I don't see where the fun comes in," he said wrathfully. "Father is very sorry, indeed he is. He quite cried to me—on that very chair where mother is sitting. I swear to you he did. And you have the heart to laugh!"

"Would you have me cry, too? No, no; I am glad he is punished."

"Yes—a nice miserable lonely old age he has before him."

"He has plenty of money."

"You're a cold, unfeeling minx! I don't envy the man who marries you, Salvina."

Salvina flushed. "I don't, either—if he were to treat me as mother has been treated."

"Yes, no one has had a life like mine, since the world began," moaned Mrs. Brill, and her waning tears returned in full flood.

"My poor mammy," and Salvina put a handkerchief to the flooded cheeks. "Come home, we have had enough of this."

Mrs. Brill rose obediently.

"Oh, yes, take her home," said Lazarus savagely, "take her to your shabby, stinking lodging, when she might have a house in Highbury New Park and three servants."

"She has a house at Hackney, and I'll give her a servant, too. Come, mother."

Salvina mopped up her mother's remaining tears, and with an inspiration of arrogant independence, she rang for Lazarus's servant and bade her hail a hansom cab.

"If you don't want all Hackney to come and gaze at a furnished road," she said, in parting, "you'll take away that furniture yourself."

Mrs. Brill bowled homeward, half consoled for everything by this charioted magnificence. Some neighbours stood by gossiping as she alighted, and then her unspoken satisfaction was complete.

XII

They moved into the new-old house, after Salvina had carefully ascertained that the furniture had returned to the cloud under which it had so long lived. In her resentment against its reappearance, she spent more than she could afford on the rival furniture that succeeded it, and which she now studied to make unlike it, so that quite without any touch of conscious taste, it became light, elegant, and even artistic in comparison with the old horsehair massiveness.

Then began a very bad year for Salvina, even though the Damocles sword of Kitty's dismissal never fell, and Lily's migration to the Cape with Moss M. Rosenstein left Kitty still in power as companion to Mabel, to judge at least by Kitty's not seeking the parental roof, even as visitor. Mrs. Brill's happiness did not keep pace with the restored grandeurs and Salvina's own spurt of hope died down. She grew wanner than ever, going listlessly to her work and returning limp and fagged out.

"You mew me up here with not a soul to speak to from morning till night," her mother burst forth one day.

Salvina was not sorry to have her mother's silent lachrymosity thus interpreted. But she regretted that her helpless parent had not expressed her satisfaction with gossip when the Ghetto provided it, instead of yearning for higher scenes. She tried again to persuade Mrs. Brill to learn to read by way of mental resource, and Mrs. Brill indeed made some spasmodic efforts to master the alphabet and the vagaries of pronunciation from an infant's primer. But her brain was too set; and she forgot from word to word, and made bold bad guesses, so that even when "a fat cat sat on a mat" she was capable of making a fat cow eat in a mug. She struggled loyally though, except when Salvina's attention relaxed for an instant, and then she would proceed by leaps and bounds, like a cheating child with the teacher's eye off it, getting over five lines in the time she usually took to spell out one, and paradoxically pleased with herself at her rapid progress.

Salvina was in despair. There is no crêche for mothers, or she might have sent Mrs. Brill to one. She bethought herself of at last laying on a servant, as providing the desired combination of grandeur and gossip. To pay for the servant she undertook two hours of extra night-teaching. But the maid-of all-work proved only an exhaustless ground for grumbling. Mrs. Brill had never owned a servant, and the girl's deviation from angelhood of character and unerring perfection of action in every domestic department were a constant disappointment and grief to the new mistress.

"A nice thing you have done for me," she wept to Salvina, having carefully ascertained the servant was out of ear-shot, "to seat a mistress on my head—and for that I must pay her into the bargain."

"Aren't you glad you haven't got three servants?" said Salvina, with a touch of irresistible irony.

"Don't throw up to me that you're saving me from falling on your father. I can be my own bread-winner. I don't want your doll's house furniture that one is scared to touch—like walking among eggshells. I'd rather live in one room and scrub floors than be beholden to anybody. Then I should be my own mistress, and not under a daughter's thumb. If only Kitty would marry, then I could go to her. Why doesn't she marry? It isn't as if she were like you. Is there a prettier girl in the whole congregation? It's because she's got no money, my poor, hardworking little Kitty. Her father would give her a dowry, if he were a man, not a pig."

"Mother!" Salvina was white and trembling. "How can you dream of that?"

"Not for myself. I'd see him rot before I'd take a farthing of his money. But I'm not domineering and spiteful like you. I don't stand in the way of other people benefiting. The money will only go to some other vermin. Kitty may as well have some."

"Lazarus has some. That's enough, and more than enough."

"Lazarus deserves it—he is a better son to me than you are a daughter!" and the tears fell again.

Salvina cast about for what to do. Her mother's nerves were no doubt entirely disorganized by her sufferings and by the shock of Lazarus's trick. Some radical medicine must be applied. But every day Duty took Salvina to school and harassed her there and drove her to private lessons afterward, and left her neither the energy nor the brain for further innovations. And whenever she met Lazarus by accident—for she was too outraged to visit a house practically kept up by dishonourable money, apart from her objection to its perpetually festive atmosphere of solo-whist supper-parties—he would sneer at her high and mighty airs in casting out the furniture. "Oh, we're very grand now, we keep a servant; we have cut our father off with a shilling."

She wished her mother would not go to see Lazarus, but she felt she had not the right to interfere with these visits, though Mrs. Brill returned from them, fretful and restive. Evidently Lazarus must be still insinuating reconciliation.

"Lazarus worries you, mother, I feel sure," she ventured to say once.

"Oh, no, he is a good son. He wants me to live with him."

"What! On her money!"

"It isn't her money—your father made it on the Stock Exchange."

"Who told you so?"

"Didn't you hear Lazarus say so yourself?"

Then a horrible suspicion came to Salvina. "He doesn't set father at you when you go there?" she cried.

Mrs. Brill flushed furiously. "I'd like to see him try it on," she murmured.

Salvina stooped to kiss her. "But he tells you tales of father's riches, I suppose."

"Who wants his riches? If he offered me my own horse and carriage, I wouldn't be seen with him after the disgrace he's put upon me."

"I wish, mother, Lazarus had inherited your sense of honour."

Mrs. Brill was pleased. "There isn't a woman in the world with more pride! Your father made a mistake when he began with me!"

XIII

A horse and carriage did come, one flamboyant afternoon, but it was the Samuelsons', and brought the long-absent Kitty. And Kitty as usual brought a present. This time it was a bracelet, and Mrs. Brill clasped and unclasped it ecstatically, feeling that she had at least one daughter who loved her and did not domineer. Salvina was at school, and Mrs. Brill took Kitty all over the house, enjoying her approval, and accepting all the praise for the lighter and more artistic furniture. She told her of the episode of the return of the old furniture—"And didn't have the decency to put new castors on the sofa she had sprawled on!"

Kitty's laughter was as loud and ringing as Salvina had anticipated; Mrs. Brill coloured under it, as though she were found food for laughter. "What a ridiculous person he is!" Kitty added hastily.

"Yes," said Mrs. Brill with eager pride and relief. "He thought he could coax me back like a dog with a bit of sugar."

"It would be too funny to live with him again." And Kitty's eyes danced.

"Do you think so?" said Mrs. Brill anxiously. And under the sunshine of her daughter's approval she confided to her that he had really turned up twice at Lazarus's, beautifully costumed, with diamonds on his fingers and a white flower in his button-hole, but that she had repulsed him as she would repulse a drunken heathen. He had put his arms round her, but she had shaken him off as one shakes off a black beetle.

Kitty turned away and stuffed her handkerchief into her mouth. She knew there was a tragic side, but the comic aspect affected her more.

"Then you think I was right?" Mrs. Brill wound up.

"Of course," Kitty said soothingly. "What do you want of him?"

"But don't tell Salvina, or she'd eat my head off." And then, the eager upleaping fountain of her mother's egoistic babblings beginning at last to trickle thinly, Kitty found a breathing-space in which to inform her of the great news that throbbed in her own breast.

"Lily Samuelson's dead! Mrs. Rosenstein, you know!"

"Oh, my God!" ejaculated Mrs. Brill, trembling like a leaf. Nothing upset her more than to find that persons within her ken could actually die.

"Yes, we had a cable from the Cape yesterday."

"Hear, O Israel! Let me see—yes, she must have died in child-birth."

"She did—the house is all in hysterics. I couldn't stand it any longer. I ordered the carriage and came here."

"My poor Kitty! That Lily was too old to have a baby. And now he will marry Mabel."

"Oh, no, mother."

"Oh, yes, he will. Mabel will jump at him, you'll see."

"But it isn't legal—you can't marry your deceased wife's sister."

"I know you can't in England—what foolishness! But they'll go to Holland to be married."

"Don't be so absurd, mother."

"Absurd!" Mrs. Brill glared. "You mark my words. They'll be in Holland before the year's out, like Hyam Emanuel's eldest brother-in-law and the red-haired sister of Samuel, the pawnbroker."

"Well, I don't care if they are," said Kitty, yawning.

"Don't care! Why, you'll lose your place. They kept you on for Mabel, but now—"

Kitty cut her short. "Don't worry, mother. I'll be all right. He's not married Mabel yet."

This reminder seemed to come to Mrs. Brill like a revelation, so fast had her imagination worked. She calmed down and Kitty took the opportunity to seek to escape. "Tell Salvina the news," she said. "She'll be specially interested in it. In fact, judging by the last time, she'll be more excited than I am," and she smiled somewhat mysteriously. "Tell her I'm sorry I missed her—I was hoping to find her having a holiday, but apparently I haven't been lucky enough to strike some Jewish fast."

But partly because Mrs. Brill was enraptured by her beautiful daughter, partly to keep the pompous equipage outside her door as long as possible, she detained Kitty so unconscionably that Salvina arrived from school. Kitty flew to embrace her as usual, but arrested herself, shocked.

"Why, Sally!" she cried. "You look like a ghost! What's the matter?"

"Nothing," said Salvina with a wan smile. "Just the excitement of seeing you, I suppose."

Kitty performed the postponed embrace but remained dubious and shaken. Was it that her mind was morbidly filled with funereal images, or was it that her fresh eye had seen what her mother's custom-blinded vision had missed—that there was death in Salvina's face?

This face of death-in-life stirred up unwonted emotions in Kitty and made her refrain apprehensively from speaking again of Lily's death; and some days later, when the first bustle of grief had subsided in Bedford Square, Kitty, still haunted by that grewsome vision, wrote Salvina a letter.

"MY DEAR OLD SALLY—You must really draw in your horns. You were not looking at all well the other day. You are burning the candle at both ends, I am sure. That horrid Board School is killing you. I am going to beg a fortnight's holiday for you, and I am going to take you to Boulogne for a week, and then, when you are all braced up again, we can have the second week at Paris."

"MY DEAREST AND BEST OF SISTERS," [Salvina replied,] "How shocking the news mother has told me of the death of poor Lily! If she did wrong she was speedily punished. But let us hope she really loved him. I am sure that your brooding on her sad fate and your sympathy with the family in this terrible affliction has made you fancy all sorts of things about me, just as mother is morbidly apprehensive of that horrible creature marrying Mabel and thus robbing you of your place. But your sweet letter did me more good than if I had really gone to Paris. How did you know it was the dream of my life? But it cannot be realized just yet, for it would be impossible for me to be spared from school just now. Miss Green is away with diphtheria, and as this is examination time, Miss Rolver has her hands full. Besides, mother would be left alone. Don't worry about me, darling. I always feel like this about this time of year, but the summer holiday is not many weeks off and Ramsgate always sets me up again.

"Your loving sister,
"SALVINA.

"P.S. Mother told me you advised her not to go to Lazarus's any more, and she isn't going. I am so glad, dear. These visits have worried her, as Lazarus is so persistent. I am only sorry I didn't think of enlisting your influence before—it is naturally greater than mine. Good-bye, dear.

"P.P.S. I find I have actually forgotten to thank you for your generous offer. But you know all that is in my heart, don't you, darling?"

All the same Kitty's alarm began to communicate itself to Salvina, especially after repeated if transient premonitions of fainting in her class-room. For what would happen if she really fell ill? She could get sick leave of course for a time; though that would bring her under the eagle eye of the Board Doctor, before which every teacher quailed. He might brutally pronounce her unfit for service. And how if she did break down permanently? Or if she died! Her savings were practically nil; her salary ceased with her breath. Who would support her mother? Kitty of course would nobly take up the burden, but it would be terribly hard on her, especially when Mabel Samuelson should come to marry. Not that she was going to die, of course; she was too used to being sickly. Death was only a shadow, hovering far off.

XIV

What was to be done? An inspiration came to her in the shape of a pamphlet. Life Assurance! Ah, that was it. Scottish Widows' Fund! How peculiarly apposite the title. If her mother could be guaranteed a couple of thousand pounds, Death would lose its sting. Salvina carefully worked out all the arithmetical points involved, and discovered to her surprise that life assurance was a form of gambling. The Company wagered her that she would live to a certain age, and she wagered that she would not. But after a world of trouble in filling up documents and getting endorsers, when she went before the Company's Doctor she was refused. The bet was not good enough. "Heart weak," was the ruthless indictment. "You ought not to teach," the Doctor even told her privately, and amid all her consternation Salvina was afraid lest by some mysterious brotherhood he should communicate with the Board Doctor and rob her of her situation. She began praying to God extemporaneously, in English. That was, for her, an index of impotence. She was at the end of her resources. She could see only a blank wall, and the wall was a great gravestone on which was chiselled: "Hic jacet, Salvina Brill, School Board Teacher, Undergraduate of London University. Unloved and unhappy."

She wept over the inscription, being still romantic. Poor mother, poor Kitty, what a blow her death would be to them! Even Lazarus would be sorry. And in the thought of them she drifted away from the rare mood of self-pity and wondered again how she could get together enough money before she died to secure her mother's future. But no suggestion came even in answer to prayer. Once she thought of the Stock Exchange, but it seemed to her vaguely wicked to conjure with stocks and shares. She had read articles against it. Besides, what did she understand? True, she understood as much as her father.

But who knew whether his money really came from this source? She dismissed the Stock Exchange despairingly.

And meanwhile Mrs. Brill continued peevish and lachrymose, and Salvina found it more and more difficult to hide her own melancholy. One day, as she was leaving the school-premises, Sugarman the Shadchan accosted her. "Do make a beginning," he said winningly. "Only a sixteenth of a ticket. You can't lose."

Sugarman still never thought of her even as a refuge for impecunious bachelors, but with that shameless pertinacity which was the secret of his success, both as British marriage-maker and continental lottery agent, he had never ceased cajoling her toward his other net. He was now destined to a success which surprised even himself. Her scrupulous conscientiousness undermined by her analysis of the Assurance System, Salvina inquired eagerly as to the prizes, and bought three whole tickets at a quarter of the price of one Assurance instalment.

Sugarman made a careful note of the numbers, and so did Salvina. But it was unnecessary in her case. They were printed on her brain, graven on her heart, repeated in her prayers; they hovered luminous across her day-dreams, and if they distracted feverishly her dreams of the night, yet they tinged the school-routine pleasantly and made her mother's fretfulness endurable. They actually improved her health, and as the May sunshine warmed the earth, Salvina felt herself bourgeoning afresh, and she told herself her fears were morbid.

Nevertheless there was one thing she was resolved to complete, in case she were truly doomed, and that was her mother's education in reading, so often begun, so often foiled by her mother's pertinacious subsidence into contented ignorance. Of what use even to assure Mrs. Brill's physical future, if her mind were to be left a pauper, dependent on others? How, without the magic resource of books, could she get through the long years of age, when decrepitude might confine her to the chimney-corner? Already her talk groaned with aches and pains.

Since the servant had been installed, the reading lessons had dropped off and finally been discontinued. Now that Salvina persisted in continuing, she found that her mother's brain had retained nothing. Mrs. Brill had to begin again at the alphabet, and all the old routine of audacious guessing recommenced. Again a fat cow ate in a mug, for though Mrs. Brill had no head at all for corrections, she had a wonderful memory for her own mistakes, and took the whole sentence at a confident jump. It was an old friend.

One evening, in the kitchen to which Mrs. Brill always gravitated when the servant was away, she paused between her misreadings to dilate on the inconsiderateness of the servant in having this day out, though she was paid for the full week, and though the mistress had to stick at home and do all the work. As Salvina seemed to be spiritless this evening, and allowed the domestic to go undefended, this topic was worn out more quickly than usual, but the never failing subject of Mrs. Brill's aches and pains provided more pretexts for dodging the hard words. And meantime in a chair beside hers, poor Salvina, silent as to her own aches and pains, and the faintness which was coming over her, strained her attention to follow in correction on the heels of her mother's reading; but do what she would, she could not keep her eyes continuously on the little primer, and whenever Mrs. Brill became aware that Salvina's attention had relaxed, she scampered along at a breakneck speed, taking trisyllables as unhesitatingly as a hunter a three-barred gate. But every now and again Salvina would struggle back into concentration, and Mrs. Brill would tumble at the first ditch.

At last, Mrs. Brill, to her content, found herself cantering along, unimpeded, for a great stretch. Salvina lay back in her chair, dead.

"The broken dancer only merry danger," read Mrs. Brill, at a joyous gallop. Suddenly the knocker beat a frantic tattoo on the street door. Up jumped Mrs. Brill, in sheer nervousness.

Salvina lay rigid, undisturbed.

"She's fallen asleep," thought her mother, guiltily conscious of having taken advantage of her slumbers. "All the same, she might spare my aged bones the trouble of dragging upstairs." But, being already on her feet, she mounted the stairs, and opened the door on Sugarman's beaming, breathless face.

"Your daughter—Number 75,814," he gasped.

Mrs. Brill, who knew nothing of Salvina's speculations, took some seconds to catch his drift.

"What, what?" she cried, trembling.

"I have won her a hundred thousand marks—the great prize!"

"The great prize!" screamed Mrs. Brill. "Salvina! Salvina! Come up," and not waiting for her reply, and overturning the flower-pots on the hall-table, she flew downstairs, helter-skelter. "Salvina!" she shook her roughly. "Wake up! You have won the great prize!"

But Salvina did not wake up, though she had won the great prize.

XV

One Sunday afternoon nearly five months later a nondescript series of vehicles, erratically and unpunctually succeeding one another, drew up near the mortuary of the Jewish cemetery, but, from the presence of women, it was obvious that something else than a funeral was in progress. In fact, the two four-wheelers, three hansom cabs, several dog-carts, and one open landau suggested rather a picnic amid the tombs. But it was only the ceremony of the setting of Salvina's tombstone, which was attracting all these relatives and well-wishers.

In the landau—which gave ample space for their knees—sat the same quartette that had shared a cab to Lazarus's wedding, except that Salvina was replaced by Kitty. That ever young and beautiful person was the only member of the family who had the air of having fallen in the world, for despite that Salvina's great prize was now added to Mr. Brill's capital (he being the legal heir), he had refused to set up a groom in addition to a carriage. A coachman, he insisted, was all that was necessary. It was the same tone that he had taken about the horsehair sofa, and it helped Mrs. Brill to feel that her husband was unchanged, after all.

Arrived on the ground, the Brills found a gathering of the Jonases, reconciled by death and riches. Others were to arrive, and the party distributed itself about the cemetery with an air of conscious incompleteness. Old Jonas shook hands cordially with Lazarus, and wiped away a tear from under his green shade. A few of Salvina's fellow-teachers had obeyed the notification of the advertisement in the Jewish papers, and were come to pay the last tribute of respect. The men wore black hat-bands, the women crape, which on all the nearer relatives already showed signs of wear. And among all these groups, conversing amiably of this or that in the pleasant October sunshine, the genteel stone-mason insinuated himself, pervading the gathering. His breast was divided between anxiety as to whether the parents would like the tombstone, and uncertainty as to whether they would pay on the spot.

"Have you seen the stone? What do you think of it?" he kept saying to everybody, with a deferential assumption of artistic responsibility; though, as it was a handsome granite stone, the bulk of the chiselling had been done in Aberdeen, for the sake of economy, whilst the stone was green, and his own contribution had been merely the Hebrew lettering. One by one, under the guidance of the artist, the groups wandered toward the tombstone, and a spectator or two admiringly opened negotiations for future contingencies. An old lady who knew the stonemason's sister-in-law strove to make a bargain for her own tombstone, quite forgetting that the money she was saving on it would not be enjoyed by herself.

"What will you charge me?" she asked, with grotesque coquetry. "I think you ought to do it cheaper for me."

And in the House of the Priests the minister in charge of the ceremonial impatiently awaited the late comers, that he might intone the beautiful immemorial Psalms. He had made a close bargain with the cabman, and was anxious not to set him grumbling over the delay; apart from his desire to get back to his pretty wife, who was "at home" that afternoon.

At last the genteel stone-mason found an opportunity of piercing through the throng of friends that surrounded Mr. Brill, and of obsequiously inviting the generous orderer of this especially handsome and profitable tombstone to inspect it. Kitty followed in the wake of her parents. Almost at the tomb, a corpulent man with graying hair, issuing suddenly from an avenue of headstones, accosted her. She frowned.

"You oughtn't to have come," she said.

"Since I belong to the family, Kitty," he remonstrated, playing nervously with his massive watch seals.

"No, you don't," she retorted. Then, relentingly: "I told you, Moss, that I could not give you my formal consent till after my sister's tombstone was set. That is the least respect I can pay her." And she turned away from the somewhat disconcerted Rosenstein, feeling very right-minded and very forgiving toward Salvina for delaying by so many years her marriage with the South African magnate.

Meantime Mr. Brill, in his heavily draped high hat, stood beside the pompous granite memorial, surveying it approvingly. His wife's hand lay tenderly in his own. Underneath their feet lay the wormy dust that had once palpitated with truth and honour, that had kept the conscience of the household.

"That bit of scroll-work," said the stone-mason admiringly, and with an air of having thrown it in at a loss; "you don't often see a bit like that—everybody's been saying so."

"Very fine!" replied Mr. Brill obediently.

"I paid the synagogue bill for you—to save you trouble," added the stone-mason, insinuatingly.

But Mr. Brill was abstractedly studying the stone, and the mason moved off delicately. Mrs. Brill tried to spell out a few of the words, but, as there was no one to reprimand her, admitted her break-down.

"Read it to me, dear heart," she whispered to Mr. Brill.

"I did read it you, my precious one," he said, "when Kitty sent it us. It says:—

"'SALVINA BRILL,
Whom God took suddenly,
On May 29th, 1897,
Aged twenty-five;
Loved and lamented by all
For her perfect goodness.'

Then come the Hebrew letters."

"Poor Salvina!" sighed Mrs. Brill. "She deserves it, though she did spoil our lives for years." He pressed her hand. "I can't tell you how frightened I was of her," she went on. "She almost made me think I ought not to forgive you even on the Day of Atonement. But I don't bear her malice, and I don't grudge her what the stone says."

"No, you mustn't," he said piously. "Besides, everybody knows one never puts the whole truth on tombstones."

VIII

SATAN MEKATRIG

"Suffer not the evil imagination to have dominion over us ... deliver me from the destructive Satan."—Morning Prayer.

Without, the air was hot, heavy and oppressive; squadrons of dark clouds had rolled up rapidly from the rim of the horizon, and threatened each instant to shake heaven and earth with their artillery. But within the little synagogue of the "Congregation of Love and Mercy," though it was crowded to suffocation, not a window was open. The worshippers, arrayed in their Sabbath finery, were too intent on following the quaint monotonous sing-song of the Cantor reading the Law to have much attention left for physical discomfort. They thought of their perspiring brows and their moist undergarments just about as little as they thought of the meaning of the Hebrew words the reader was droning. Though the language was perfectly intelligible to them, yet their consciousness was chiefly and agreeably occupied with its musical accentuation, their piety being so interwoven with these beloved and familiar material elements as hardly to be separable therefrom. Perspiration, too, had come to seem almost an ingredient of piety on great synagogal occasions. Frequent experience had linked the two, as the poor opera-goer associates Patti with crushes. And the present was a great occasion. It was only an ordinary Sabbath afternoon service, but there was a feast of intellectual good things to follow. The great Rav Rotchinsky from Brody was to deliver a sermon; and so the swarthy, eager-eyed, curly-haired, shrewd-visaged cobblers, tailors, cigar-makers, peddlers, and beggars, who made up the congregation, had assembled in their fifties to enjoy the dialectical subtleties, the theological witticisms and the Talmudical anecdotes which the reputation of the Galician Maggid foreshadowed. And not only did they come themselves; many brought their wives, who sat in their wigs and earrings behind a curtain which cut them off from the view of the men. The general ungainliness of their figures and the unattractiveness of their low-browed, high-cheekboned, and heavy-jawed faces would have made this pious precaution appear somewhat superfluous to an outsider. The women, whose section of the large room thus converted into a place of worship was much smaller than the men's, were even more closely packed on their narrow benches. Little wonder, therefore, that just as a member of the congregation was intoning from the central platform the blessing which closes the reading of the Law, a woman disturbed her neighbours by fainting. She was carried out into the open air, though not without a good deal of bustle, which invoked indignant remonstrances in the Jüdisch-Deutsch jargon, of "Hush, little women!" from the male worshippers, unconscious of the cause. The beadle went behind the curtain, and, fearing new disturbances, tried to open the window at the back of the little room, to let in some air from the back-yard on which it abutted. The sash was, however, too inert from a long season of sloth to move even in its own groove, and so the beadle elbowed his way back into the masculine department, and by much tugging at a cord effected a small slit between a dusty skylight and the ceiling, neglecting the grumblings of the men immediately beneath.

Hardly had he done so, when all the heavy shadows that lay in the corners of the synagogue, all the glooms that the storm-clouds cast upon the day, and that the grimy, cobwebbed windows multiplied, were sent flying off by a fierce flash of lightning that bathed in a sea of fire the dingy benches, the smeared walls, the dingily curtained Ark, the serried rows of swarthy faces. Almost on the heels of the lightning came the thunder—that vast, instantaneous crash which denotes that the electric cloud is low.

The service was momentarily interrupted; the congregation was on its feet; and from all parts rose the Hebrew blessing, "Blessed art thou, O Lord, performing the work of the Creation;" followed, as the thunder followed the lightning, by the sonorous "Blessed art thou, O Lord, whose power and might fill the Universe." Then the congregation, led by the great Rav Rotchinsky, to whose venerable thought-lined face, surmounted by its black cap, all eyes had instinctively turned, sat down again, feeling safe. The blessing was intended to mean, and meant no more than, a reverential acknowledgment of the majesty of the Creator revealed in elemental phenomena; but human nature, struggling amid the terrors and awfulness of the Universe, is always below its creed, and scarce one but felt the prayer a talisman. A moment afterward all rose again, as Moshé Grinwitz, wrapped in his Talith, or praying-shawl, prepared to descend from the Al Memor, or central platform, bearing in his arms the Scroll of the Law, which had just been reverentially wrapped in its bandages, and devoutly covered with its embroidered mantle and lovingly decorated with its ornamental bells and pointer.

Now, as Moshé Grinwitz stood on the Al Memor with his sacred burden, another terrible flash of lightning and appalling crash of thunder startled the worshippers. And Moshé's arms were nervously agitated, and a frightful thought came into his head. Suppose he should drop the Holy Scroll! As this dreadful possibility occurred to him he trembled still more. The Sepher Torah is to the Jew at once the most precious and the most sacred of possessions, and in the eyes of the "Congregation of Love and Mercy" their Sepher Torah was, if possible, invested with a still higher preciousness and sanctity, because they had only one. They were too poor to afford luxuries; and so this single Scroll was the very symbol and seal of their brotherhood; in it lay the very possibility of their existence as a congregation. Not that it would be rendered "Pasul," imperfect and invalid, by being dropped; the fall could not erase any of the letters so carefully written on the parchment; but the calamity would be none the less awful and ominous. Every person present would have to abstain for a day from all food and drink, in sign of solemn grief. Moshé felt that if the idea that had flitted across his brain were to be realized, he would never have the courage to look his pious wife in the face after such passive profanity. The congregation, too, which honoured him, and which now waited to press devout kisses on the mantle of the Scroll, on its passage to the Ark—he could not but be degraded in its eyes by so negligent a performance of a duty which was a coveted privilege. All these thoughts, which were instinctively felt, rather than clearly conceived, caused Moshé Grinwitz to clasp the Sacred Scroll, which reached a little above his head, tightly to his breast. Feeling secure from the peril of dropping it, he made a step forward, but the bells jangled weirdly to his ears, and when he came to the two steps which led down from the platform, a horrible foreboding overcame him that he would stumble and fall in the descent. He stepped down one of the steps with morbid care, but lo! the feeling that no power on earth could prevent his falling gained tenfold in intensity. An indefinable presentiment of evil was upon him; the air was charged with some awful and maleficent influence, of which the convulsion of nature seemed a fit harbinger. And now his sensations became more horrible. The conviction of the impending catastrophe changed into a desire to take an active part in it, to have it done with and over. His arms itched to loose their hold of the Sepher Torah. Oh! if he could only dash the thing to the ground, nay, stamp upon it, uttering fearful blasphemies, and shake off this dark cloud that seemed to close round and suffocate him. A last shred of will, of sanity, wrestled with his wild wishes. The perspiration poured in streams down his forehead. It was but a moment since he had taken the Holy Scroll into his arms; but it seemed ages ago.

His foot hovered between the first and second step, when a strange thing happened. Straight through the narrow slit opened in the skylight came a swift white arrow of flame, so dazzling that the awed worshippers closed their eyes; then a long succession of terrific peals shook the room as with demoniac laughter, and when the congregants came to their senses and opened their eyes they saw Moshé Grinwitz sitting dazed upon the steps of the Al Memor, his hands tightly grasping the ends of his praying-shawl, while the Sepher Torah lay in the dust of the floor.

For a moment the shock was such that no one could speak or move. There was an awful, breathless silence, broken only by the mad patter of the rain on the roof and the windows. The floodgates of heaven were opened at last, and through the fatal slit a very cascade of water seemed to descend. Automatically the beadle rushed to the cord and pulled the window to. His action broke the spell, and a dozen men, their swarthy faces darker with concern, rushed to raise up the prostrate Scroll, while a hubbub of broken ejaculations rose from every side.

But ere a hand could reach it, Moshé Grinwitz had darted forward and seized the precious object. "No, no," he cried, in the jargon which was the common language of all present. "What do you want? The mitzvah (good deed) is mine. I alone must carry it." He shouldered it anew.

"Kiss it, at least," cried the great Rav Rotchinsky in a hoarse, shocked whisper.

"Kiss it?" cried Moshé Grinwitz, with a sneering laugh. "What! with my wife in synagogue! Isn't it enough that I embrace it?" Then, without giving his hearers time to grasp the profanity of his words, he went on: "Ah, now I can carry thee easily. I can hold thee, and yet breathe freely. See!" And he held out the Scroll lengthwise, showing the gilded metal chain and the pointer and the bells contorted by the lightning. "I didn't hurt thee; God hurt thee," he said, addressing the Scroll. With a quick jerk of the hand he drew off the mantle and showed the parchment blackened and disfigured.

A groan burst from some; others looked on in dazed silence. The pecuniary loss, added to the manifestation of Divine wrath, overwhelmed them. "Thou hast no soul now to struggle out of my hands," went on Moshé Grinwitz contemptuously. "Look!" he added suddenly: "The lightning has gone back to hell again!" The men nearest him shuddered, and gazed down at the point on the floor toward which he was inclining the extremity of the Scroll. The wood was charred, and a small hole revealed the path the electric current had taken. As they looked in awestruck silence, a loud wailing burst forth from behind the curtain. The ill-omened news of the destruction of the Sepher Torah had reached the women, and their Oriental natures found relief in profuse lamentation. "Smell! smell!" cried Moshé Grinwitz, sniffing the sulphurous air with open delight.

"Woe! woe!" wailed the women. "Woe has befallen us!"

"Be silent, all!" thundered the Maggid, suddenly recovering himself. "Be silent, women! Listen to my words. This is the vengeance of Heaven for the wickedness ye have committed in England. Since ye left your native country ye have forgotten your Judaism. There are men in this synagogue that have shaved the corners of their beard; there are women who have not separated the Sabbath dough. Hear ye! To-morrow shall be a fast day for you all. And you, Moshé Grinwitz, bench gomel—thank the Holy One, blessed be He, for saving your life."

"Not I," said Moshé Grinwitz. "You talk nonsense. If the Holy One, blessed be He, saved my life, it was He that threatened it. My life was in no danger if He hadn't interfered."

To hear blasphemies like this from the hitherto respectable and devout Moshé Grinwitz overwhelmed his hearers. But only for a moment. From a hundred throats there rose the angry cry, "Epikouros! Epikouros!" And mingled with this accusation of graceless scepticism there swelled a gathering tumult of "His is the sin! Cast him out! He is the Jonah! He is the sinner!" The congregants had all risen long ago and menacing faces glared behind menacing faces. Some of more heady temperament were starting from their places. "Moshé Grinwitz," cried the great Rav, his voice dominating the din, "are you mad?"

"Now for the first time am I sane," replied the man, his brow dark with defiance, his tall but usually stooping frame rigid, his narrow chest dilated, his head thrown back so that the somewhat rusty high hat he wore sloped backward half off his skull. It was always a strange, arrestive face, was Moshé Grinwitz's, with its sallow skin, its melancholy dark eyes, its aquiline nose, its hanging side-curls, and its full, fleshy mouth embowered in a forest of black beard and mustache; and now there was an uncanny light about it which made it almost weird. "Now I see that the Socialists and Atheists are right, and that we trouble ourselves and tear out our very gall to read a Torah which the Overseer himself, if there is one, scornfully shrivels up and casts beneath our feet. Know ye what, brethren? Let us all go to the Socialist Club and smoke our cigarettes. Otherwise are you mad!" As he uttered these impious words, another flash of flame lit up the crowded dusk with unearthly light; the building seemed to rock and crash; the fingers of the storm beat heavily upon the windows. From the women's compartment came low wails of fear: "Lord, have mercy! Forgive us for our sins! It is the end of the world!" But from the men's benches there arose an incoherent cry like the growl of a tiger, and from all sides excited figures precipitated themselves upon the blasphemer. But Moshé Grinwitz laughed a wild, maniacal laugh, and whirled the sacred Scroll round and dashed the first comers against one another. But a muscular Lithuanian seized the extremity of the Scroll, and others hung on, and between them they wrested it from his grasp. Still he fought furiously, as if endowed with sinews of steel, and his irritated opponents, their faces bleeding and swollen, closed round him, forgetting that their object was but to expel him, and bent on doing him a mischief. Another moment and it would have fared ill with the man, when a voice, whose tones startled all but Moshé Grinwitz, though they were spoken close to his ear, hissed in Yiddish: "Well, if this is the way the members of the Congregation of Love and Mercy spend their Sabbath, methinks they had done as well to smoke cigarettes at the Socialist Club. What say ye, brethren?" These words, pregnant and deserved enough in themselves, were underlined by an accent of indescribable mockery, not bitter, but as gloating over the enjoyment of their folly. Involuntarily all turned their eyes to the speaker.

Who was he? Where did he spring from, this black-coated, fur-capped, red-haired hunchback with the gigantic marble brow, the cold, keen, steely eyes that drew and enthralled the gazer, the handsome clean-shaven lips contorted with a sneer? None remembered seeing him enter—none had seen him sitting at their side, or near them. He was not of their congregation, nor of their brotherhood, nor of any of their crafts. Yet as they looked at him the exclamations died away on their lips, their menacing hands fell to their sides, and a wave of vague, uneasy remembrance passed over all the men in the synagogue. There was not one that did not seem to know him; there was not one who could have told who he was, or when or where he had seen him before. Even the great Rav Rotchinsky, who had set foot on English soil but a fortnight ago, felt a stir of shadowy recollection within him; and his corrugated brow wrinkled itself still more in the search after definiteness. A deep and sudden silence possessed the synagogue; the very sobs of the unseeing women were checked. Only the sough of the storm, the ceaseless plash of the torrent, went on as before. Without, the busy life of London pulsed, unchecked by the tempest; within, the little synagogue was given over to mystery and nameless awe.

The sneering hunchback took the Holy Scroll from the nerveless hands of the Lithuanian, and waved it as in derision. "Blasted! harmless!" he cried. "The great Name itself mocked by the elements! So this is what ye toil and sweat for—to store up gold that His words may be inscribed finely on choice parchment; and then this is how He laughs at your toil and your self-sacrifice. Listen to Him no more; give not up the seventh day to idleness when your Lord worketh His lightnings thereon. Blind yourselves no longer over old-fashioned pages, dusty and dreary. Rise up against Him and His law, for He is moved with mirth at your mummeries. He and His angels laugh at you—Heaven is merry with your folly. What hath He done for His chosen people for their centuries of anguish and martyrdom? It is for His plaything that He hath chosen you. He hath given you over into the hand of the spoiler; ye are a byword among nations; the followers of the victorious Christ spit in your faces. Here in England your lot is least hard; but even here ye eat your scanty bread with sorrow and travail. Sleep may rarely visit your eyes; your homes are noisome styes; your children perish around you; ye go down in sorrow to the grave. Rouse yourselves, and be free men. Waste your lives neither for God nor man. Or, if you will worship, worship the Christ, whose ministers will pour gold upon you. Eat, drink, and be merry, for to-morrow ye die."

A charmed silence still hung over his auditors. Their resentment, their horror, was dead; a waft of fiery air seemed to blow over their souls, an intoxicating flush of evil thoughts held riot in their hearts. They felt their whole spirit move under the sway of the daring speaker, who now seemed to them merely to put into words thoughts long suppressed in their own hearts, but now rising into active consciousness. Yes, they had been fools: they would free themselves, and quaff the wine of life before the Angel of Death, Azrael, spilled the goblet. Moshé Grinwitz's melancholy eyes blazed with sympathetic ardour.

"Hush, miserable blasphemer!" faltered the great Rav Rotchinsky, who alone could find his tongue. "The guardian of Israel neither slumbereth nor sleepeth." The hunchback wheeled round and cast a chilling glance at the venerable man. Then, smiling, "The maidens of England are beautiful," he said. "They are even fairer than the women of Brody."

The great Rav turned pale, but his eyes shone. He struck out feebly with his arms, as though beating back some tempting vision.

"You and I have spoken together before, Rabbi," said the hunchback. "We shall speak again—about women, wine, and other things. Your beard is long and white, but many days of sunshine are still before you, and the darkness of the grave is afar."

The rabbi tried to mutter a prayer, but his lips only beat tremulously together.

"Profane mocker," he muttered at length, "go to thy work and thy wine and thy pleasure, if thou wouldst desecrate the sacred Sabbath-day; but tempt not others to sin with thee. Begone; and may the Holy One, blessed be He, blast thee with His lightnings."

"The Holy One blasteth only that which is holy," grimly rejoined the dwarfish stranger, exhibiting the Scroll, while a low sound of applause went up from the audience. "Said I not, ye were a sport and a mockery unto Him? Ye assemble in your multitude for prayer, and the vapour of your piety but prepares the air for the passage of His arrows. Ye adorn His Scroll with bells and chains, and the gilded metal but draws His lightnings."

He looked around the room and a cat-like gleam of triumph stole into his wonderful eyes as he noted the effect of his words. He paused, and again for a moment the tense, awful silence reigned, emphasized by the loud but decreasing patter of the rain. This time it was broken in a strange, unexpected fashion.

"Yisgadal, veyiskadash shemé rabbo," rang out a clear, childish voice from the rear of the synagogue. A little orphan child, who had come to repeat the Kaddish, the Hebrew mourners' unquestioning acknowledgment of the Supreme Goodness, had fallen into a sleep, overcome by the heat, and had slept all through the storm. Awakening now amid a universal silence, the poor little fellow instinctively felt that the congregation was waiting for him to pronounce the prayer. Alone of the male worshippers he had neither seen the blaspheming hunchback nor listened to his words.

The hunchback's handsome face was distorted with a scowl; he stamped his broad splay-foot, but hearing no verbal interruption, the child, its eyes piously closed, continued its prayer—

"In the world which He hath created...."

"The rain has ceased, brethren," huskily whispered the hunchback, for his words seemed to stick in his throat. "Come outside and I will tell you how to enjoy this world, for world-to-come there is none." Not a figure stirred. The child's treble went unfalteringly on. The stranger hurried toward the door. Arrived there, he looked back. Moshé Grinwitz alone followed him. He hurled the Scroll at the child's head, but the lad just then took the three backward steps which accompany the conclusion of the prayer. The Scroll dashed itself against the wall; the stranger was gone and with him Moshé Grinwitz. A great wave of trembling passed through the length and breadth of the synagogue; the men drew long breaths, as if some heavy and sulphurous vapour had been dissipated from the atmosphere; the child lifted up with difficulty the battered Scroll, kissed it and handed it to his neighbour, who deposited it reverently in the Ark; a dazzling burst of sunshine flooded the room from above, and transmuted the floating dust into the golden shafts of some celestial structure; the Cantor and the congregation continued the words of the service at the point interrupted, as though all the strange episode had been a dream. They did not speak or wonder among themselves at it; nor did the rabbi allude to it in the marvellous exhortation that succeeded the service, save at its close, when he reminded them that on the morrow they must observe a solemn fast. But ever afterward they shunned Moshé Grinwitz as a leper; for the sight of him recalled his companion in blasphemy, the atheist and socialist propagandist, who had insidiously crept into their midst, after perverting and crazing their fellow as a preliminary; and the thought of the strange hunchback set their blood tingling and their brain surging with wild fancies and audacious thoughts. The tidings of their misfortune induced a few benevolent men to join in purchasing a new Scroll of the Law for them, and before the Feast of Consecration of this precious possession was well over, the once vivid images of that stormy and disgraceful scene were as shadows in the minds of men not unaccustomed to heated synagogal discussions, and not altogether strangers to synagogal affrays.

"She will do him good and not evil all the days of her life."—Prov. xxxi. 12.

As Moshé Grinwitz followed his new-found friend down the narrow windings that led to his own home, his whole being surrendered itself to the new delicious freedom. The burst of sunshine that greeted him almost as soon as he crossed the threshold of the synagogue seemed to him to typify the new life that was to be his. He drew up his gaunt form to his full height, stiffened his curved shoulders, bent by much stooping over his machine, and adjusted his high hat firmly on his head. It was not a restful, placid feeling that now possessed him; rather a busy ferment of ideas, a stirring of nerve currents, an accumulation of energy striving to discharge itself, a mercurial flowing of the blood. The weight of old life-long conceptions, nay, the burden of old learning, of which his store had been vast, was cast off. He did not know what he should do with the new life that tingled in his veins; he only felt alive in every pore.

"Ha! brother!" he shouted to the hunchback, who was hurrying on before. "These fools in the synagogue would do better to come out and enjoy the fine weather."

"They breathe the musty air to offer it up as a sweet incense," responded the dwarf, slackening his steps to allow his companion to come up with him.

Their short walk was diversified by quite a number of incidents. A driver lashed his horse so savagely that the animal bolted; two children walking hand in hand suddenly began to fight; a foreign-looking, richly dressed gentleman, half-drunk, staggered along. Moshé felt it a shame that one wealthy man should wear a heavy gold chain, which would support a poor family for a month; but ere his own temptation had gathered to a head, the poor gentleman was felled by a sudden blow, and a respectably clad figure vanished down an alley with the coveted spoil. Moshé felt glad, and made no attempt to assist the victim, and his attention was immediately attracted by some boys, who commenced to tie a cracker to a cat's tail. Occupied by all these observations, Moshé suddenly noted with a start that they had reached the house in which he lived. His companion had already entered the passage, for the door was always ajar, and Moshé had the impression that it was very kind of his new friend to accept his invitation to visit him. He felt very pleased, and followed him into the passage, but no sooner had he done so than an impalpable cloud of distrust seemed to settle upon him. The house was a tall, old-fashioned and grimy structure, which had been fine, and even stately, a century before, but which now sheltered a dozen families, mainly Jewish. Moshé Grinwitz's one room was situated at the very top, its walls forming part of the roof. Every flight of stairs Moshé went up, his spirit grew darker and darker, as if absorbing the darkness that hung around the cobwebbed, massive balustrades, upon which no direct ray of sunlight ever fell; and by the time he had reached the dusky landing outside his own door the vague uneasiness had changed into a horrible definite conception; a memory had come back upon him which set his heart thumping guiltily and anxiously in his bosom. His wife! His pure, virtuous, God-fearing wife! How was he to make her understand? But immediately a thought came, by which the burden of shame and anxiety was half lifted. His wife was not at home; she would still be in the Synagogue of Love and Mercy, where, mercifully blinded by the curtain, she, perhaps, was still ignorant of the part he had played. He turned suddenly to his companion, and caught the vanishing traces of an ugly scowl wrinkling the high white forehead under the fur cap. The hunchback's hair burnt like fire on the background of the gloom; his eyes flashed lightning.

"Probably my wife is in the synagogue," said Moshé. "If so, she has the key, and we can't get in."

"The key matters little," hissed the hunchback. "But you must first tear down this thing."

Moshé's eyes followed in wonder the direction of his companion's long, white forefinger, and rested on the Mezuzah, where, in a tin case, the holy verses and the Name hung upon the door-post.

"Tear it down?" repeated Moshé.

"Tear it down!" replied the hunchback. "Never will I enter a home where this superstitious gew-gaw is allowed to decorate the door."

Moshé hesitated; the thought of what his wife would say, again welled up strongly within him; all his new impious daring seemed to be melting away. But a mocking glance from the cruel eyes thrilled through him. He put his hand on the Mezuzah, then the unbroken habit of years asserted its sway, and he removed the finger which had lain on the Name and kissed it. Instantly another semi-transformation of his thoughts took place; he longed to take the hunchback by the throat. But it was an impotent longing, for when a low hiss of intense scorn and wrath was breathed from the clenched lips of his companion, he made a violent tug at the firmly fastened Mezuzah. It was half-loosed from the woodwork when, from behind the door, there issued in clear, womanly tones the solemn Hebrew words:—

"Blessed is the man that walketh not in the council of the ungodly, nor standeth in the way of sinners, nor sitteth in the seat of the scornful."

It was Rebecca Grinwitz commencing the Book of Psalms, which she read through every Sabbath afternoon.

A violent shudder agitated Moshé Grinwitz's frame; he paused with his hand on the Mezuzah, struggled with himself awhile, then kissed his finger again, and, turning to defy the scorn of his companion, saw that he had slipped noiselessly downstairs. A sob of intense relief burst from Moshé's lips.

"Rivkoly, Rivkoly!" he cried hysterically, beating at the door; and in another moment he was folded in the quiet haven of his wife's arms.

"Who told thee it was I?" said Rebecca, after a moment of delicious happiness for both. "I told them not to alarm thee, nor to spoil thy enjoyment of the sermon, because I knew thou wouldst be uneasy and be wanting to leave the synagogue if thou knewest I had fainted."

"No one told me thou hadst fainted!" Moshé exclaimed, instantly forgetting his own perturbation.

"And yet thou didst guess it!" said Rebecca, a happy little smile dimpling her pale cheek, "and came away after me." Then, her face clouding, "The Satan Mekatrig has tempted us both away from synagogue," she said, "and even when I commence to say Tehillim (Psalms) at home, he interrupts me by sending me my darling husband."

Moshé kissed her in acknowledgment of the complimentary termination of a sentence begun with unquestionable gloom. "But what made my Rivkoly faint?" he asked, glad, on reflection, that his wife's misconception obviated the necessity of explanations. "They ought to have opened the window at the back of the women's room."

Rebecca shuddered. "God forbid!" she cried. "It wasn't the heat—it was that." Her eyes stared a moment at some unseen vision.

"What?" cried Moshé, catching the contagion of horror.

"He would have come in," she said.

"Who would have come in?" he gasped.

"The Satan Mekatrig," replied his wife. "He was outside, and he glared at me as if I prevented his coming in."

A nervous silence followed. Moshé's heart beat painfully. Then he laughed with ghastly merriment. "Thou didst fall asleep from the heat," he said, "and hadst an evil dream."

"No, no," protested his wife earnestly. "As sure as I stand here, no! I was looking into my Chumosh (Pentateuch), following the reading of the Torah, and all at once I felt something plucking my eyes off my book and turning my head to look through the window immediately behind me. I wondered what Satan Mekatrig was distracting my thoughts from the service. For a long time I resisted, but when the reading ceased for a moment the temptation overcame me and I turned and saw him."

"How looked he?" Moshé asked in a whisper that strove in vain not to be one.

"Do not ask me," Rebecca replied, with another shudder. "A little crooked demon with red hair, and a fur cap, and a white forehead, and baleful eyes, and a cock's talons for toes."

Again Moshé laughed, a strange, hollow laugh. "Little fool!" he said, "I know the man. He is only a brother-Jew—a poor cutter or cigar-maker who laughs at Yiddishkeit (Judaism), because he has no wife like mine to show him the heavenly light. Why, didst thou not see him afterward? But no, thou must have been gone by the time he came inside."

"What I saw was no man," returned Rebecca, looking at him sternly. "No earthly being could have stopped my heart with his glances. It was the Satan Mekatrig himself, who goeth to and fro on the earth, and walketh up and down in it. I must have been having wicked thoughts indeed this Sabbath, thinking of my new dress, for my Sabbath Angel to have deserted me, and to let the Disturber and the Tempter assail me unchecked." The poor, conscience-stricken woman burst into tears.

"My Rivkoly have wicked thoughts!" said Moshé incredulously, as he smoothed her cheek. "If my Rivkoly puts on a new dress in honour of the Sabbath, is not the dear God pleased? Why, where is thy new dress?"

"I have changed it for an old one," she sobbed. "I do not want to see the demon again."

"The Satan Mekatrig has no real existence, I tell thee," said Moshé, irritated. "He only means our own inward thoughts, that distract us in the performance of the precepts; our own inward temptations to go astray after our eyes and after our hearts."

"Moshé!" Rebecca exclaimed in a shocked tone, "have I married an Epikouros after all? My father, the Rav, peace be unto him, always said thou hadst the makings of one—that thou didst ask too many questions."

"Well, whether there is a Satan or not," retorted her husband, "thou couldst not have seen him; for the person thou describest is the man I tell thee of."

"And thou keepest company with such a man," she answered; "a man who scoffs at Yiddishkeit! May the Holy One, blessed be He, forgive thee! Now I know why we have no children, no son to say Kaddish after us." And Rebecca wept bitterly—for the children she did not possess.

Their common cause of grief coming thus unexpectedly into their consciousness softened them toward one another and dispelled the gathering irritation. Both had a melancholy vision of themselves stretched out stiff and stark in their shrouds, with no filial Kaddish breaking in upon and gladdening their ears. O if their souls should be doomed to Purgatory, with no son's prayers to release them! Very soon they were sitting hand in hand, reading together the interrupted Psalms.

And a deep peace fell upon Moshé Grinwitz. So the immortal allegorist, John Bunyan, must have felt when the mad longing to utter blasphemies and obscenities from the pulpit was stifled; and when he felt his soul once more in harmony with the Spirit of Good. So feel all men who have wrestled with a Being in the darkness and prevailed.

They were a curious contrast—the tall, sallow, stooping, black-bearded man, and the small, keen-eyed, plump, pleasant-looking, if not pretty woman, in her dark wig and striped cotton dress, and as they sat, steadily going through the whole collection of Psalms to a strange, melancholy tune, fraught with a haunting and indescribable pathos, the shadows of twilight gathered unnoticed about the attic, which was their all in all of home. The iron bed, the wooden chairs, the gilt-framed Mizrach began to lose their outlines in the dimness. The Psalms were finished at last, and then the husband and wife sat, still hand in hand, talking of their plans for the coming week. For once neither spoke of going to evening service at the Synagogue of Love and Mercy, and when a silver ray of moonlight lay broad across the counterpane, and Rebecca Grinwitz, peering into the quiet sky that overhung the turbid alley, announced that three stars were visible, the devout couple turned their faces to the east and sang the hymns that usher out the Sabbath.

And when the evening prayer was over Rebecca produced from the cupboard the plainly cut goblet of raisin wine, and the metal wine-cup, the green twisted waxlight, and the spice-box, wherewith to perform the beautiful symbolical ceremony of the Havdalah, welcoming in the days of work, the six long days of dreary drudgery, with cheerful resignation to the will of the Maker of all things—of the Sabbath and the Day of Work, the Light and the Shadow, the Good and the Evil, blent into one divine harmony by His inscrutable Wisdom and Love.

Moshé filled the cup with raisin wine, and, holding it with his right hand, chanted a short majestic Hebrew poem, whereof the burden was:—

"Lo! God is my salvation; I will trust, and I will not be afraid. Be with us light and joy, gladness and honour." Then blessing the King of the Universe, who had created the fruit of the Vine, he placed the cup on the table and took up the spices, uttering a blessing over them as he did so. Then having smelled the spice-box, he passed it on to his wife and spread out his hands toward the light of the spiral wax taper, reciting solemnly: "Blessed be Thou, O Lord, our God, King of the Universe, who createst the Light of the Fire." And then looking down at the Shade made by his bent fingers, he took up the wine-cup again, and chanted, with especial fervour, and with a renewed sense of the sanctities and sweet tranquillities of religion: "Blessed be Thou, O Lord our God, King of the Universe, who makest a distinction between the Holy and the non-Holy, between Light and Darkness."

"As for that night, let darkness seize upon it."—Job iii. 6.

It was Kol Nidré night, the commencement of the great White Fast, the Day of Atonement. Throughout the Jewish quarter there was an air of subdued excitement. The synagogues had just emptied themselves and everywhere men and women, yet under the solemn shadow of passionate prayer, were meeting and exchanging the wish that they might weather the fast safely. The night was dark and starless, as if Nature partook of the universal mournfulness.

Solitary, though amidst a crowd, a slight, painfully thin woman shuffled wearily along, her feet clad in the slippers which befitted the occasion, her head bent, her worn cheek furrowed with still-falling tears. They were not the last dribblets of an exhausted emotion, not the meaningless, watery expression of over-excited sensibility. They were real, salt, bitter tears born of an intense sorrow. The long, harassing service, with its untiring demands upon the most exalted and the most poignant emotions, would have been a blessing if it had dulled her capacity for anguish. But it had not. Poor Rebecca Grinwitz was still thinking of her husband.

It was of him she thought, even when the ministers, in their long white cerements, were pouring forth their souls in passionate vocalization, now rising to a wail, now breaking to a sob, now sinking to a dread whisper; it was of him she thought when the weeping worshippers, covered from head to foot in their praying-shawls, rocked to and fro in a frenzy of grief, and battered the gates of Heaven with fiery lyrics; it was of him she thought when she beat her breast with her clenched fist as she made the confession of sin and clamoured for forgiveness. Sins enough she knew she had—but his sin! Ah! God, his sin!

For Moshé had gone from bad to worse. He refused to reënter the synagogue where he had been so roughly handled. His speech became more and more profane. He said no more prayers; wore no more phylacteries. Her peaceful home-life wrecked, her reliance on her husband gone, the poor wife clung to him, still hoping on. At times she did not believe him sane. Gradually rumours of his mad behaviour on the Sabbath on which she had fainted reached her ears, and remembering that his strangeness had begun from the Sunday morning following that delicious afternoon of common Psalm-saying, she was often inclined to put it all down to mental aberration. But then his talk—so clever, if so blasphemous; bristling with little pointed epigrams and maxims such as she had never before heard from him or any one else. He was full of new ideas, too, on politics and the social system and other unpractical topics, picturing endless potentialities of wealth and happiness for the labourer. Meantime his wages had fallen by a third, owing to the loss of his former place, his master having been the president of the Congregation of Love and Mercy. What wonder, therefore, if Moshé Grinwitz intruded upon all his wife's thoughts—devotional or worldly? In a very real sense he had become her Satan Mekatrig.

Up till to-night she had gone on hoping. For when the great White Fast comes round, a mighty wave as of some subtle magnetism passes through the world of Jews. Men and women who have not obeyed one precept of Judaism for a whole year suddenly awake to a remembrance of the faith in which they were born, and hasten to fast and pray, and abase themselves before the Throne of Mercy. The long-drawn, tremulous, stirring notes of the trumpet that ushers in the New Year, seem to rally and gather together the dispersed of Israel from every region of the underworld of unfaith and to mass them beneath the cope of heaven. And to-night surely the newly rooted nightshade of doubt would wither away in her husband's bosom. Surely this one link still held him to the religion of his fathers; and this one link would redeem him and yet save his soul from the everlasting tortures of the damned. But this last hope had been doomed to disappointment. Utterly unmoved by all the olden sanctities of the Days of Judgment that initiate the New Year, the miserable man showed no signs of remorse when the more awful terrors of the Day of Atonement drew near—the last day of grace for the sinner, the day on which the Divine Sentence is sealed irrevocably. And so the wretched woman had gone to the synagogue alone.

Reaching home, she toiled up the black staircase and turned the handle of the door. As she threw open the door she uttered a cry. She saw nothing before her but a gigantic shadow, flickering grotesquely on the sloping walls and the slip of ceiling. It must be her own shadow, for other living occupant of the room she could see none. Where was her husband? Whither had he gone? Why had he recklessly left the door unlocked?

She looked toward the table gleaming weirdly with its white tablecloth; the tall wax Yom Kippur Candle, specially lit on the eve of the solemn fast and intended to burn far on into the next day, had all but guttered away, and the flame was quivering unsteadily under the influence of a draught coming from the carelessly opened window. Rebecca shivered from head to foot; a dread presentiment of evil shook her soul. For years the Candle had burnt steadily, and her life also had been steady and undisturbed. Alas! it needed not the omen of the Yom Kippur Candle to presage woe.

"May the dear God have mercy on me!" she exclaimed, bursting into fresh tears. Hardly had she uttered the words when a monstrous black cat, with baleful green eyes, dashed from under the table, sprang upon the window-sill, and disappeared into the darkness, uttering a melancholy howl. Almost frantic with terror, the poor woman dragged herself to the window and closed it with a bang, but ere the sash had touched the sill, something narrow and white had flashed from the room through the gap, and the reverberations made in the silent garret by the shock of the violently closed window were prolonged in mocking laughter.

"Well thrown, Rav Moshé!" said a grating voice. "Now that you have at last conquered your reverence for a bit of tin and a morsel of parchment, I will honour your mansion with my presence."

Instantly Rebecca felt a wild longing to join in the merriment and to laugh away her fears; but, muttering a potent talismanic verse, she turned and faced her husband and his guest. Instinct had not deceived her—the new-comer was the hunchback of that fatal Sabbath. This time she did not faint.

"A strange hour and occasion to bring a visitor, Moshé," she said sternly, her face growing even more rigid and white as she caught the nicotian and alcoholic reek of the two men's breaths.

"Your good Frau is not over-polite," said the visitor. "But it's Yom Kippur, and so I suppose she feels she must tell the truth."

"I brought him, Rivkoly, to convince thee what a fool thou wast to assert that thou hadst seen—but I mustn't be impolite," he broke off, with a coarse laugh. "There's no call for me to tell the truth because it's Yom Kippur. Down at the Club we celebrated the occasion by something better than truth—a jolly spread! And our good friend here actually stood a bottle of champagne! Champagne, Rivkoly! Think of it! Real, live champagne, like that which fizzes and sparkles on the table of the Lord Mayor. Oh, he's a jolly good fellow! and so said all of us, too. And yet thou sayest he isn't a fellow at all."

A drunken leer overspread his sallow face, and was rendered more ghastly by the flame leaping up from the expiring candle.

"Roshah, sinner!" thundered the woman. Then looking straight into the cruel eyes of the hunchback, her wan face shining with the stress of a great emotion, her meagre form convulsed with fury, "Avaunt, Satan Mekatrig!" she screamed. "Get thee down from my house—get thee down. In God's name, get thee down—to hell."

Even the brazen-faced hunchback trembled before her passion; but he grasped his friend's hot hand in his long, nervous fingers, and seemed to draw courage from the contact.

"If I go, I take your husband!" he hissed, his great eyes blazing in turn. "He will leave me no more. Send me away, if you will."

"Yes, thou must not send my friend away like this," hiccoughed Moshé Grinwitz. "Come, make him welcome, like the good wife thou wast wont to be."

Rebecca uttered a terrible cry, and, cowering down on the ground, rocked herself to and fro.

The drunkard appeared moved. "Get up, Rivkoly," he said, with a tremour in his tones. "To see thee one would think thou wast sitting Shivah over my corpse." He put out his hand as if to raise her up.

"Back!" she screamed, writhing from his grasp. "Touch me not; no longer am I wife of thine."

"Hear you that, man?" said the hunchback eagerly. "You are free. I am here as a witness. Think of it; you are free."

"Yes, I am free," repeated Moshé, with a horrible, joyous exultation on his sickly visage. The gigantic shadow of himself that bent over him, cast by the dying flame of the Yom Kippur Candle, seemed to dance in grim triumph, his long side-curls dangling in the spectral image like barbaric ornaments in the ears of a savage, while the unshapely, fantastic shadow of the hunchback seemed to nod its head in applause. Then, as the flame leaped up in an irregular jet, the distorted shadow of the Tempter intertwined itself in a ghastly embrace with her own. With frozen blood and stifled breath the tortured woman turned away, and, as her eyes fell upon the many-cracked looking-glass which adorned the mantelpiece, she saw, or her overwrought fancy seemed to see—her husband's dead face, wreathed with a slavering serpent in the place of the phylacteries he had ceased to wear, and surrounded by endless perspectives of mocking marble-browed visages, with fiery snakes for hair and live coals for eyes.

She felt her senses slipping away from her grasp, but she struggled wildly against the heavy vapour that seemed to choke her. "Moshé!" she shrieked, in mad, involuntary appeal for help, as she clutched the mantel and closed her eyes to shut out the hideous vision.

"I am no longer thy husband," tauntingly replied the man. "I may not touch thee."

"Hear you that, woman?" came the sardonic voice of the hunchback. "You are free. I am here as a witness."

"I am here as a witness," a thousand mocking voices seemed to hiss in echoed sibilance.

A terrible silence followed. At last she turned her white shrunken face, which the contrast of the jet-black wig rendered weird and death-like, toward the man who had been her husband, and looked long and slowly, yearningly yet reproachfully, into his bloodshot eyes.

Again a great wave of agitation shook the man from head to foot.

"Don't look at me like that, Rivkoly," he almost screamed. "I won't have it. I won't see thee. Curse that candle! Why does it flicker on eternally and not blot thee from my sight?" He puffed violently at the tenacious flame and a pall fell over the room. But the next instant the light leaped up higher than ever.

"Moshé!" Rebecca shrieked in wild dismay. "Dost thou forget it is Kol Nidré night? How canst thou dare to blow out a light? Besides, it is the Yom Kippur Candle—it is our life and happiness for the New Year. If you blow it out, I swear, by my soul and the great Name, that you shall never look upon my face again."

"It is because I do not wish to see thy face that I will blow it out," he replied, laughing hysterically.

"No, no!" she pleaded. "I will go away rather. It is nearly dead of itself; let it die."

"No! It takes too long dying; 'tis like thy father, the Rav, who had the corpse-watchers so long in attendance that one died himself," said Moshé Grinwitz with horrible laughter. "I will kill it!" And bending down low over the broad socket of the candlestick, so that his head loomed gigantic on the ceiling, he silenced forever the restless tongue of fire.

Immediately a thick blackness, as of the grave, settled upon the chamber. Hollow echoes of the blasphemer's laughter rang and resounded on every side. Myriads of dreadful faces shaped themselves out of the gloom, and mowed and gibbered at the woman. At the window, the green, baleful eyes of the black cat glared with phosphorescent light. A wreath of fiery serpents twisted themselves in fiendish contortions, shedding lurid radiance upon the cruel marble brow they garlanded. An unspeakable Eeriness, an unnameable Unholiness, floated with far-sweeping, rustling pinions through the Darkness.

With stifling throat that strove in vain to shriek, the woman dashed out through the well-known door, fled wildly down the stairs, pursued at every step by the sardonic merriment, met at every corner by the gibbering shapes—fled on, dashing through the heavy, ever-open street door into the fresher air of the night—on, instinctively on, through the almost deserted streets and alleys, where only the vile gin-houses gleamed with life—on, without pause or rest, till she fell exhausted upon the dusty door-step of the Synagogue of Love and Mercy.

"All Israel have a portion in the world to come."—Ethics of the Fathers.

The aged keeper of the synagogue rushed out at the noise.

"Save me! For God's sake, save me, Reb Yitzchok!" cried the fallen figure. "Save me from the Satan Mekatrig! I have no home—no husband—any more! Take me in!"

"Take you in?" said Reb Yitzchok pityingly, for he dimly guessed something of her story. "Where can I take you in? You know my wife and I are allowed but one tiny room here."

"Take me in!" repeated the woman. "I will pass the night in the synagogue. I must pray for my husband's soul, for he has no son to pray for him. Let me come in! Save me from the Satan Mekatrig!"

"You would certainly meet many a Satan Mekatrig in the streets during the night," said the old man musingly. "But have you no friends to go to?"

"None—none—but God! Let me in that I may go to Him. Give me shelter, and He will have mercy on you when the great Tekiah sounds to-morrow night!"

Without another word Reb Yitzchok went into his room, returned with the key, and threw open the door of the women's synagogue, revealing a dazzling flood of light from the numerous candles, big and little, which had been left burning in their sconces. The low curtain that served as a partition had been half rolled back by devoted husbands who had come to inquire after their wives at the end of the service, and the synagogue looked unusually large and bright, though it was hot and close, with lingering odours of breaths, and snuff, and tallow, and smelling-salts.

With a sob of infinite thankfulness Rebecca dropped upon a wooden bench.

"Would you like a blanket?" said the old man.

"No, no, God bless you!" she replied. "I must watch and weep, not sleep. For the Scroll of Judgment is written and the Book of Life is all but closed."

With a pitying sigh the old man turned and left her alone for the night in the Synagogue of Love and Mercy.

For a few moments Rebecca sat, prayerless, her soul full of a strange peace. Then she found herself counting the chimes as they rolled out sonorously from a neighbouring steeple: One, Two, Three, Four, Five, Six, Seven, Eight, Nine, Ten, Eleven, TWELVE!

Starting up suddenly when the last stroke ceased to vibrate on the air, Rebecca Grinwitz found, to her surprise, that a merciful sleep must have overtaken her eyelids, that hours must have passed since midnight had struck, and that the great Day of Atonement must have dawned. Both compartments of the synagogue were full of the restless stir of a praying multitude. With a sense of something vaguely strange, she bent her eyes downward on her neighbour's Machzor. The woman immediately pushed the prayer-book more toward Rebecca, with a wonderful smile of love and tenderness, which seemed to go right through Rebecca's heart, though she could not clearly remember ever having seen her neighbour before. Nor, wonderingly stealing a first glance around, could she help feeling that the entire congregation was somewhat strange and unfamiliar, though she could not quite think why or how. The male worshippers, too, why did they all wear the shroud-like garments, usually confined on this solemn occasion to the ministers and a few extra-devout personages? And had not some transformation come over the synagogue? Was it only the haze before her tear-worn eyes or did dim perspectives of worshippers stretch away boundlessly on all sides of the clearly seen area, which still retained the form of the room she knew so well?

But the curious undercurrent of undefined wonder lasted but a moment. In another instant she was reconciled to the scene. All was familiar and expected; once more she was taking part in divine service with no sorrowful thoughts of her husband coming to distract her, her whole soul bathing in and absorbing the Peace of God which passeth all understanding. Then suddenly she felt a stir of recollection coming over her, and a stream of love warming her heart, and looking up at her neighbour's face she saw with joyous content that it was that of her mother.

The service went on, mother and daughter following it in the book they had in common. After several hours, during which the huge, far-spreading congregation alternated with the Cantor in intoning the beautiful poems of the liturgy of the day, the white curtain with its mystic cabalistic insignia was rolled back from the Ark of the Covenant and two Scrolls were withdrawn therefrom. Rebecca noted with joy that the Ark was filled with Scrolls big and little, in rich mantles, and that those taken out were swathed in satin beautifully embroidered, and that the ornaments and the musically tinkling bells were of pure gold.

Then some of the worshippers were called up in turn to the Al Memor to be present at the reading of a section of the Law. They were all well known to Rebecca. First came Moses ben Amram. He walked humbly up to the Al Memor with bowed head, his long Talith enveloping him from crown to foot. Rebecca saw his face well, for though it was covered with a thick veil, it shone luminously through its draping.

"Bless ye the Lord, who is blessed," said Moses ben Amram, the words seeming all the sweeter from his lips for the slight stammering with which they were uttered.

"Blessed be the Lord, who is blessed to all eternity and beyond," responded the endless congregation, in a low murmur that seemed to be taken up and vibrated away and away into the infinite distances for ever and ever.

"Blessed be the Lord, who is blessed to all eternity and beyond," echoed the melodious voice. Then, in words that seemed to roll and fill the great gulfs of space with a choral music of sacred joy, Moses continued, "Blessed be Thou, O Lord, our God, the King of the Universe, who hath chosen us from all peoples, and given unto us His Law. Blessed art Thou, O Lord, who givest the Law."

After him came Aaron ben Amram, whose white beard reached to his knees. Abraham ben Terah, Isaac ben Abraham, and Jacob ben Isaac—all venerable figures, with faces which Rebecca felt were radiant with infinite tenderness and compassion for such poor helpless children as herself—were also called up, and after the Patriarchs, Elijah the Prophet. Lastly came a white-haired, stooping figure, whose gait and whose every gesture told Rebecca that it was her father. How glad she felt to see him thus honoured! As she listened to his quavering tones the dusty tombstones of dead years seemed rolled away, and all their simple joys and griefs to live again, not quite as of yore, but transfigured by some solemn pathos.

When the reading of the Law was at an end, David ben Jesse, a royal-looking graybeard, held up the Scroll to the four corners of space, and it was rolled up by his son Solomon, the Preacher; the carrying of it to the Ark being given to Rabbi Akiba, whose features wore a strange, ecstatic look, as though ennobled by suffering. The vast multitude rose with a great rustling, the sound whereof reached afar, and sang a hymn of rejoicing, so that the whole universe was filled with melody. Rebecca alone could not sing. For the first time she missed her husband, Moshé. Why was he not here, like all the other friends of her life, whose beloved faces surrounded her on every side and made a sweet atmosphere of security for her soul? What was he doing outside of this mighty assembly? Why was he not there to have the sacred duty of carrying the Scroll entrusted to him? She felt the tears pouring down her cheeks. She was ready to sink to the earth with sudden lassitude. "Mother! dear mother!" she cried, "I feel so faint."

"You must have some air, my child, my Rivkoly," said the mother, the dearly remembered voice falling for the first time with ineffable sweetness on Rebecca's ears. And she put out her hand, and lo! it grew longer and longer, till it reached up to the skylight, and then suddenly the whole roof vanished and the free air of heaven blew in like celestial balm upon Rebecca's hot forehead. Yet she noted with wonder that the holy candles burnt on steadily, unfluttered by the refreshing breeze. And then, lo! the starless heavens above her opened out in indescribable Glory. The Dark budded into ineffable Beauty; a supernally pure, luminous Splendour, transcendently dazzling, filled the infinite depths of the Firmament with melodious coruscations of Infinite Love made visible, and white-winged hosts of radiant Cherubim sang "Holy, holy, holy is the Lord of Hosts, the whole earth is full of His Glory." And all the vast congregation fell upon their faces and cried "Holy, holy, holy is the Lord of Hosts, the whole earth is full of His Glory." And Moses ben Amram arose, and he lifted his hands toward the Splendour and he cried, "Lord, Lord God, merciful and gracious, long-suffering and full of kindness and truth. Lo, Thou sealest the seals before the twilight. Seal Thy People, I pray Thee, in the Book of Life, though Thou blot me out. Forgive them, and pardon their transgressions for the sake of the merits of the Patriarchs and for the sake of the merits of the Martyrs, who have shed their blood like water and offered their flesh to the flames for the Sanctification of the Name. Forgive them, and blot out their transgressions."

And all the congregation said "Amen."

Then a surging wave of hope rose within Rebecca's breast, and it lifted her to her feet and stretched out her arms toward the Splendour. And she said: "Lord God, forgive Thou my husband, for he is in the hand of the Tempter. Save him from the power of the Evil One by Thine outstretched arm and Thy mighty hand. Save him and pardon him, Lord, in Thine infinite mercy." Then a strange, dread, anxious silence fell upon the vast spaces of the Firmament, till from the heart of the Celestial Splendour there fell a Word that floated through the Universe like the sweet blended strains of all sweet instruments, a Word that mingled all the harmonies of winds and waters and mortal and angelic voices into one divine cadence—Salachti.

And with the sweet Word of Forgiveness lingering musically in her charmed ears, and the sweet assurance at her heart that she, the poor, miserable tailor's wife, despised and trodden under foot by the rich and by the heathen around, could lean upon the breast of an Almighty Father, who had prepared for her immortal glories and raptures amid all her loved ones in a world where He would wipe the tears from off all eyes, Rebecca Grinwitz awoke to find the bright morning sunshine streaming in upon her and the fresh morning air blowing in upon her fevered brow from the skylight which Reb Yitzchok had just opened.

"Surely He shall deliver thee from the snare of the fowler."—Psalm xci. 3.

A shroud of newly fallen snow enveloped the dead earth, over which the dull, murky sky looked drearily down. Within his fireless garret, which was almost empty of furniture, Moshé Grinwitz lay, wasted away to a shadow. His beard was unkempt, his cheek-bones were almost fleshless, his feverish eyes large and staring, his side-curls tangled and untended. There did not seem enough strength left in the frame to resist a babe; yet, when he coughed, the whole skeleton was agitated as though with galvanic energy.

"Will he never come back?" he murmured uneasily.

"Fear not; so far as lies in my power, I shall be with you always," replied the voice of the hunchback as he entered the room. "But, alas! I have little comfort to bring you. One pawnbroker after another refused to advance anything on my waistcoat, and at last I sold it right out for a few pence. See; here is some milk. It is warm."

Moshé tried to clutch the jug, but fell back, helpless. A shade of anxiety passed over his companion's face. "Have I miscalculated?" he muttered. He held the jug to the sick man's lips, supporting his head with the other. Moshé drank, then fell back, and pressed his friend's hand gratefully.

"Poor Moshé," said the hunchback. "What a shame I tossed into the gutter the gold my father left me seven months ago! How could I foresee you would be struck down with this long sickness?"

"No, no, don't regret it," quavered Moshé, his white face lighting up. "We had jolly old times, jolly old times, while the money lasted. Oh, you've been a good friend to me—a good friend. If I had never known you, I should have passed away into nothingness, without ever having known the mad joys of wine and riot. I have had wild, voluptuous moments of revelry and mirth. No power in heaven or hell can take away the past. And then the sweet freedom of doing as you will, thinking as you will, flying with wings unclogged by superstition—to you I owe it all! And since I have been ill you have watched over me like—like a woman."

His words died away in a sob, and then there was silence, except when his cough sounded strange and hollow in the bare room. Presently he went on:—

"How unjust Rivkoly was to you! She once said"—here the speaker laughed a little melancholy laugh— "that you were the Satan Mekatrig in person."

"Poor afflicted woman!" said his friend, with pitying scorn. "In this nineteenth century, when among the wise the belief in the gods has died out, there are yet fools alive who believe in the devil. But she could only have meant it metaphorically."

The sick man shook his head. "She said the evil influence—of course, it seemed evil to her—you wielded over her thoughts, and I suppose mine, too, was more than human—was supernatural."

"Oh, I don't say I'm not more strong-minded than most people. Of course I am, or I should be howling hymns at the present moment. But why does a soldier catch fire under the eye of his captain? What magnetism enables one man to bewitch a nation? Why does one friend's unspoken thought find unuttered echo in another's? Go to Science, study Mesmerism, Hypnotism, Thought-Transference, and you will learn all about Me and my influence."

"Yes, Rivkoly never had any idea of anything outside her prayer-book. Rivkoly—"

"Mention not her name to me," interrupted the hunchback harshly. "A woman who deserts her husband—"

"She swore to go if I blew out the Yom Kippur light. And I did."

"A woman who goes out of her wits because her husband gets into his!" sneered the other. "Doubtless her superstitious fancy conjured up all sorts of sights in the dark. Ho! ho! ho!" and he laughed a ghastly laugh. "Happily she will never come back. She's evidently able to get along without you. Probably she has another husband more to her pious taste."

Moshé raised himself convulsively. "Don't say that again!" he screamed. "My Rivkoly!" Then a violent cough shook him and his white lips were reddened with blood.

The cold eyes of the hunchback glittered strangely as he saw the blood. "At any rate," he said, more gently, "she cannot break the mighty oath she sware. She will never come back."

"No, she will never come back," the sick man groaned hopelessly. "But it was cruel of me to drive her away. Would to G—"

The hunchback hastily put his hand on the speaker's mouth, and tenderly wiped away the blood. "When I am better," said Moshé, with sudden resolution, "I will seek her out: perhaps she is starving."

"As you will. You know she can always earn her bread and water at the cap-making. But you are your own master. When you are rid of this sickness—which will be soon—you shall go and seek her out and bring her to abide with you." The words rang sardonically through the chamber.

"How good you are!" Moshé murmured, as he sank back relieved.

The hunchback leaned over the bed till his gigantic brow almost touched the sick man's, till his wonderful eyes lay almost on his. "And yet you will not let me hasten on your recovery in the way I proposed to you."

"No, no," Moshé said, trembling all over. "What matters if I lie here a week more or less?"

"Lie here!" hissed his friend. "In a week you will lie rotting."

A wild cry broke from the blood-bespattered lips! "I am not dying! I am not dying! You said just now I should be better soon."

"So you will; so you will. But only if we have money. Our last farthing, our last means of raising a farthing, is gone. Without proper food, without a spark of fire, how can you hold out a week in this bitter weather? No, unless you would pass from the light and the gladness of life to the gloom and the shadow of the tomb, you must be instantly baptized."

"Shmad myself! Never!" said the sick man, the very word conjuring up an intolerable loathing, deeper than reason; and then another violent fit of coughing shook him.

"See how this freezing atmosphere tells on you. You must take Christian gold, I tell you. Thus only shall I be able to get you fire—to get you fire," repeated the hunchback with horrible emphasis. "You call yourself a disbeliever. If so, what matters? Why should you die for a miserable prejudice? But you are no true infidel. So long as you shrink from professing any religion under the sun, you still possess a religion. Your unfaith is but foam-drift on the deep sea of faith; but lip-babble while your heart is still infected with superstition. Come, bid me fetch the priest with his crucifix and holy water. Let us fool him to the top of his bent. Rouse yourself; be a man and live."

"No, no, brother! I will be a man and die."

"Fool!" hissed the hunchback. "It fits not one who has lived for months by Christian gold to be so nice."

"You lie!" Moshé gasped.

"The seven months that you and I have known each other, it is Christian gold that has warmed you and fed you and rejoiced you, and that, melted down, has flowed in your veins as wine. Whence, then, took I the money for our riotings?"

"From your father, you said."

"Yes, from my spiritual father," was the grim reply. "No, having that belief, which you still lack, in the hollowness and mockery of all save pleasure, I became a Christian. For a time they paid me well, but as soon as I had been put on the annual report I had served my purpose and the supplies fell off. I could be converted again in another town or country, but I dare not leave you. But you are a new man, and should I drag you into the fold they will reward us both well. Instead of subsisting on dry bread and milk you will fare on champagne and turtle-soup once more."

Moshé sat up and gazed wildly one long second at the Tempter. He looked at his own fleshless arms, and shuddered. He felt the icy hand of Death upon him. He knew himself a young man still. Must he go down into the eternal darkness, and be folded in the freezing clasp of the King of Terrors, while the warm bosom of Life offered itself to his embrace? No; give him Life, Life, Life, polluted and stained with hypocrisy, but still Life, delicious Life.

The steely eyes of the hunchback watched the contest anxiously. Suddenly a change came over the wildly working face—it fell back chill and rigid on the pillow, the eyes closed. The room seemed to fill with an impalpable, brooding Vapour, as if a thick fog were falling outside. The watcher caught madly at his friend's wrist and sought to detect a pulsation. His eyes glowed with horrible exultant relief.

"Not yet, not yet, Brother Azrael," he said mockingly, as if addressing the impalpable Vapour; "Thou who art wholly woven of Eyes, canst Thou not see that it is not yet time to throw the fatal pellet into his throat? Back, back!"

The Vapour thickened. The minutes passed. The hunchback peered expectant at the corpse-like face on the dingy pillow. At last the eyes opened, but in them shone a strange, rapt expression.

"Thank God, Rivkoly!" the dying lips muttered. "I knew thou wouldst come."

As he spoke there was a frantic beating at the door. The hunchback's face was convulsed.

"Hasten, hasten, Brother Azrael!" he cried.

The Vapour lightened a little. Moshé Grinwitz seemed to rally. His face glowed with eagerness.

"Open the door! open the door!" he cried. "It's Rivkoly—my Rivkoly!"

The vain battering at the door grew fiercer, but none noted it in the house. Since the shadow of the hunchback had first fallen within that thickly crowded human nest, the doves had become hawks, the hawks vultures. All was discord and bickering.

"Lie still," said the hunchback; "'tis but your fevered imagination. Drink."

He put the jug to the dying man's lips, but it was dashed violently from his hand and shattered into a hundred pieces.

"Give me nothing bought with Christian money!" gasped Moshé hoarsely, his breath rattling painfully in his throat. "Never will I knowingly gain by the denial of the Unity of God."

"Then die like a dog!" roared the hunchback. "Hasten, Brother Azrael!"

The Vapour folded itself thickly about the room. The rickety door was shaken frantically, as by a great gale.

"Moshé! Moshé!" shrieked a voice. "Let me in—me—thy Rivkoly! In God's name, let me in! I bring thee a precious gift. Or art thou dead, dead, dead? My God, why didst Thou not cause me to know he was ill before!"

"Your husband is dying," said the hunchback. "When he is dead, you shall look upon his face. But he may not look upon your face again. You have sworn it."

"Devil!" cried the fierce voice of the woman. "I swore it on Kol Nidré night, when I had just asked the Almighty to absolve me from all rash oaths. Let me in, I tell you."

"I will not have a sacred oath treated thus lightly," said the hunchback savagely. "I will keep your soul from sin."

"Cursed be thou to eternity of eternities!" replied the woman. "Pray, Moshé, pray for thy soul. Pray, for thou art dying."

"Hear, O Israel, the Lord our God, the Lord is one," rose the sonorous Hebrew.

"Hear, O Israel, the Lord our God, the Lord is one," wailed the woman. The very Vapour seemed to cling round and prolong the vibrations of the sacred words. Only the hunchback was silent. The mocking words died on his lips, and as the woman, with one last mighty blow, dashed in through the flying door, he seemed to glide past her and melt into the darkness of the staircase.

Rivkoly heeded not his contorted, malignant visage, crowned with its serpentine wreath of fiery hair; she flew straight through the heavy Vapour, stooped and kissed the livid mouth, read in a moment the decree of Death in the eyes, and then put something small and warm into her husband's fast chilling arms.

"Take it, Moshé," she cried, "and comfort thy soul in death. 'Tis thy child, for God has at last sent us a son. Yom Kippur night—now six long months ago—I had a dream that God would forgive thee, and I was glad. But when I thought to go home to thee in the evening, I learnt that thou hadst been feasting all that dread Day of Atonement with the Satan Mekatrig; and my heart fell, for I knew that my dream was but the vain longing of my breast, and that through thine own misguided soul thou couldst never be saved from the eternal vengeance. Then I went away, far from here, and toiled and lived hard and lone; and I believed not in my dream. But I prayed and prayed for thy soul, and lo! very soon I was answered; for I knew we should have a child. And then I entreated that it should be a son, to pray for thee, and perhaps win thee back to God, and to say the Kaddish after thee when thou shouldst come to die, though I knew not that thy death was at hand; and a few weeks back the Almighty was gracious and merciful to me, and I had my wish."

She ceased, her wan face radiant. The Shadow of Death could not chill her sublime faith, her simple, trustful hope. The husband was clasping the feebly whimpering babe to his frozen breast, and showering passionate kisses on its unconscious form.

"Rivkoly!" he whispered, as the tears rolled down his cheeks, "how pale and thin thou art grown! O God, my sin has been heavy!"

"No, no," she cried, her loving hand in his. "It was the Satan Mekatrig that led thee astray. I am well and strong. I will work for our child, and train it up to pray for thee and to love thee. I have named it Jacob, for it shall wrestle with the Recording Angel and shall prevail."

The hue of death deepened on Moshé Grinwitz's face, but it was overspread by a divine calm.

"Ah, the good old times we had at the Cheder in Poland," he said. "The rabbi was sometimes cross, but we children were always in good spirits; and when the Rejoicing of the Law came round it was such fun carrying the candles stuck in hollowed apples, and gnawing at your candlestick as you walked. I always loved Simchath Torah, Rivkoly. How long is it to the Rejoicing?"

"It will soon be here again, now Passover is over," she said, pressing his hand.

"Is Pesach over?" he said mournfully. "I don't remember giving Seder. Why didst thou not remind me, Rivkoly? It was so wrong of thee. Thou knowest how I loved the sight of the table—the angels always seemed to hover about it. Chad Gadyah! Chad Gadyah!" he commenced to sing in a cracked, hoarse whisper. The child burst into a wail. "Hush, hush, Yaankely," said the mother, taking it to her breast.

"A—a—ah!" A wild scream rose from Moshé Grinwitz's lips. "My Kaddish! Take not away my Kaddish!" He sat up, with clammy, ghastly brow, and glared with sightless eyes, his arms groping. A thin stream of blood oozed from his mouth.

"Hear, O Israel!" screamed the woman, as she put her hand to his mouth to stanch the blood.

He beat her back wildly. "Not thee! I want not thee! My Kaddish!" came the mad, hoarse whisper. "I have blasphemed God! Give me my Kaddish! give me my Kaddish!"

She put the child into his arms, and he clutched it in his dying frenzy. As he felt its feeble form, the old divine peace came over his face. The babe's cries were hushed in fear. The mother was dumb and stony. And silently the Vapour crawled in sluggish folds through the heavy air.

But in a moment the silence was broken by a deep, stertorous rattle. Moshé Grinwitz's head fell back; his arms relaxed their hold of his child, which was caught with a wild cry to its mother's bosom. And the dark Vapour lifted, and showed the three figures to the baleful, agonized eyes of the hunchback at the open door.

IX

DIARY OF A MESHUMAD

Tchemnovosk, Saturday (midnight).—So! The first words have been written. For the first time in my life I have commenced a diary. Will it prove the solace I have heard it is? Shall I find these now cold, blank pages growing more and more familiar, till I shall turn to them as to a sympathetic friend; till this little book shall become that loved and trusted confidant for whom my lonely soul longs? Instead of either Black or White Clergy, this record in black and white shall be my father confessor. Our village pope, to whom I have so often confessed everything but the truth, would be indeed shocked, if he could gossip with this, his new-created brother. What a heap of roubles it would take to tranquillize him! Ah, God! Ach, God of Israel! how is it possible that a man who has known the tenderest human ties should be so friendless, so solitary in his closing years, that not even in memory can he commune with a fellow-soul? Verily, the old curse has wrought itself out, that penalty of apostasy which came to my mind the other day after nearly forty years of forgetfulness, that curse which has filled my spirit with shuddering awe, and driven me to seek daily communion through thee, little book, even with my own self of yesterday— "And that soul shall be cut off from among its people." Yea, and from all others, too! For so many days and years Caterina was my constant companion; I loved her as my own soul. Yet was she but a sun that dazzled my eyes so that I could not gaze upon my own soul; but a veil between me and my dead youth. The sun has sunk forever below the horizon; the veil is rent. No phantom from the other world hovers to remind me of our happiness. Those years, with all their raptures and successes, are a dull blank. It is the years of boyhood and youth which resurge in my consciousness; their tints are vivid, their tones are clear.

Why is this? Is it Caterina's death? Is it old age? Is it returning to these village scenes after half a lifetime spent in towns? Is it the sight of the izbas, and their torpid, tow-haired, sheepskin-clad inhabitants, and the great slushy cabbage gardens, that has rekindled the ashen past into colours of flame? And yet, except our vodka-seller, there isn't a Jew in the place. However it be, Caterina's face is filmy, phantasmal, compared with my mother's. And mother died forty years ago; the grass of two short years grows over my wife's grave. And Paul? He is living—he kissed me but a few moments back. Yet his face is far-away—elusive. The hues of life are on my father's—poor, ignorant, narrow-minded, warm-hearted father, whose heart I broke. Happily I have not to bear the remembrance of his dying look, but can picture him as I saw him in those miserable, happy days. My father's kiss is warm upon the lips which my son's has just left cold. Poor St. Paul, living up there with your ideals and your theories like a dove in a balloon! And yet, golubtchik, how I love you, my handsome, gifted boy, fighting the battle of life so pluckily and well! Ah! it is hard fighting when one is hampered by a conscience. Is it your fault that the cold iron bar of a secret lies between our souls; that a bar my own hands have forged, and which I have not the courage or the strength to break, keeps you from my inmost heart, and makes us strangers? No; you are the best of sons, and love me truly. But if your eyes were purged, and you could see the ugly, hateful thing, and through and beyond it, into my ugly, hateful soul! Ah, no! That must never be. Your affection, your reverential affection, is the only sacred and precious thing yet left to me on earth. If I lost that, if my spirit were cut off even from the semblance of human sympathy, then might the grave close over my body, as it would have already closed over my soul. And yet should I have the courage to die? Yes; for then Paul would know; Paul would obey my wishes and see me buried among my people. Paul would hire mourners (God! hired mourners, when I have a son!) to say the Kaddish. Paul would do his duty, though his heart broke. Terrible, ominous words! Break my son's heart as I did my father's! The saints—voi! I mean God—forfend! And for opposite reasons. Ach, it is a strange world. Is religion, then, a curse, eternally dividing man from man? No, I will not think these blasphemous thoughts. My poor, brave Paul!

To-morrow will be a hard day.

Sunday Night.—I have just read over my last entry. How cold, how tame the words seem, compared with the tempest with which I am shaken. And yet it is a relief to have uttered them; to have given vent to my passion and pain. Already this scrawl of mine has become sacred to me; already this study in which I write has become a sanctuary to which my soul turns with longing. All day long my diary was in my thoughts. All my turbulent emotions were softened by the knowledge that I should come here and survey them with calm; by the hope that the tranquil reflectiveness which writing induces would lead me into some haven of rest. And first let me confess that I am glad Paul goes back to St. Petersburg on Tuesday. It is a comfort to have him here for a few days, and yet, oh, how I dread to meet his clear gaze! How irksome this close contact, with the rough rubs it gives to all my sore places! How I abhorred myself to-day as I went through the ghastly mimicries of prayer, and crossing myself, and genuflexion, in our little church. How I hate the sight of its sky-blue dome and its gilt minarets! When the pope brought me the Gospel to kiss, fiery shame coursed through my veins. And then when I saw the look of humble reverence on Paul's face as he pressed his lips to the silver-bound volume, my blood was frozen to ice. Strange, dead memories seemed to float about the incense-laden air; shadowy scenes; old, far-away cadences. And when the deacon walked past me with his bougie, there seemed to flash upon me some childish recollection of a joyous candle-bearing procession, whereat my eyes grew filled with sudden tears. The marble altar, the silver candlesticks, the glittering jewelled scene faded into mist. And then the choir sang, and under the music I grew calm again. After all, religions were made for men. And this one was just fitted for the simple muzhiks who dotted the benches with their stupid, good natured figures. They must have their gold-bedecked gods in painting and image; and their saints in gold brocade to kneel before at all hours to solace themselves with visions of a brocaded Paradise.

And yet what had I to do with these childish superstitions?—I whose race preached the great doctrine of the Unity to a world sunk in vice and superstition; whose childish lips were taught to utter the Shemang as soon as they could form the syllables; who know that the Christian creed is a monstrous delusion! To think that I have lent the sanction of my manhood to these grotesque beliefs. Grotesque, say I? when to Paul they are the essence of all lofty feeling and aspiration! And yet I know that he is blind, or sees things with that strange perversion of vision of which I have heard him accuse the Jews—my brethren. He believes what he has been taught. And who taught him? Bozhe moi! was it not I who have brought him up in these degrading beliefs, which he imagines I share? God! is this my punishment, that he is faithful to the creed taught him by a father who was faithless to his own? And yet there were excuses enough for me, Thou knowest. Why did these forms and ceremonies, which now loom beautiful to me through a mist of tears, seem hideous chains on the free limbs of childhood? Was it my father's fault or my own that the stereotyped routine of the day; that the being dragged out of bed in the gray dawn to go to synagogue, or to intone in monotonous sing-song the weary casuistries of the rabbis; that the endless precepts or prohibitions, made me conceive religion as the most hateful of tyrannies? Through the cloud of forty years I can but dimly recall the violence of the repulsion with which things Jewish inspired me—of how it galled me to feel that I was one of that detested race, that I was that mockery and byword, a Zhit; that, with little sympathy with my people, I was yet destined to partake of its burdens and its disabilities. Bitter as my soul is within me to-day, I can yet understand, can yet half excuse, that fatal mistake of ignorant and ambitious youth.

It were easy for me now to acknowledge myself a Jew, even with the risk of Siberia before me. I am rich, I have some of the education for which I longed, above all, I have lived. Ah, how differently the world, with its hopes and its fears, and its praise and censure, looks to the youth who is climbing slowly up the hill, and the man who is swiftly descending to the valley! But the knowledge of the vanity of all things comes too late; this, too, is vanity. Enough that I sacrificed the sincerity and reality of life for unrealities, which then seemed to me the only things worth having. There was none to counsel, and none to listen. I fled my home; I was baptized into the Church. At once all that hampered me was washed away. Before me stretched the free, open road of culture and well-being. I was no longer the slave of wanton laws, the laughing-stock of every Muscovite infant, liable to be kicked and cuffed and spat at by every true Russian. What mattered a lip-profession of Christianity, when I cared as little for Judaism as for it? I never looked back; my prior life faded quickly from my memory. Alone I fought the battle of life—alone, unaided by man or hope in God. A few lucky speculations on the Bourse, starting from the risking of the few kopecks amassed by tuition, rescued me from the need of pursuing my law-studies. I fell in love and married. Caterina, your lovely face came effectively between me and what vague visions of my past, what dim uneasiness of remorse, yet haunted me. You never knew—your family never knew—that I was not a Slav to the backbone. The new life lay fold on fold over the old; the primitive writing of the palimpsest was so thickly written over, that no thought of what I had once been troubled me during all those years of wedded life, made happier by your birth and growth, my Paul, my darling Paul; no voice came from those forgotten shores, save once, when—who knows through what impalpable medium?—I learnt or divined my father's death, and all the air was filled with hollow echoes of reproach. During those years I avoided contact with Jews as much as I could; when it was inevitable, I made the contact brief. The thought of the men, of their gabardines and their pious ringlets, of their studious dronings and their devout quiverings and wailings, of the women with their coarse figures and their unsightly wigs; the remembrance of their vulgar dialect, and their shuffling ways, and their accommodating morality, filled me with repulsion. As if to justify myself to myself, my mind conceived of them only in their meanest and tawdriest aspects. The black points alone caught my eye, and linked themselves into a perfect-seeming picture.

Da, I have been a good Russian, a good Christian. I have not stirred my little finger to help the Jews in their many and grievous afflictions. They were nothing to me. Over the vodka and the champagne I have joined in the laugh against them, without even feeling I was of them. Why, then, these strange sympathies that agitate me now; these feelings, shadowy, but strong and resistless as the shadow of death? Am I sane, or is this but incipient madness? Am I sinking into a literal second childhood, in which all the terrors and the sanctities that once froze or stirred my soul have come to possess me once more? Am I dying? I have heard that the scene of half a century ago may be more vivid to dying eyes than the chamber of death itself. Has Caterina's death left a blank which these primitive beloved memories rush in to fill up? Was it the light of her face that blinded me to the dear homely faces of my father and mother? If I had not met her, how would things have been? Should I have repented earlier of my hollow existence? Was it the genuineness of her faith in her heathen creed that made me acquiesce in its daily profession and its dominance in our household life? And are the old currents flowing so strongly now, only because they were so long artificially dammed up? Of what avail to ask myself these questions? I asked them yesterday and I shall be no wiser to-morrow. No man can analyze his own emotions, least of all I, unskilled to sound the depths of my soul, content if the surface be unruffled. Perhaps, after all, it is Paul who is the cause of the troubling of the waters, which yet I am glad have not been left in their putrid stagnation. For since Caterina's clay-cold form was laid in the Moscow churchyard, and Paul and I have been brought the nearer together for the void, my son has opened my eyes to my baseness. The light that radiates from his own terrible nobleness has shown me how black and polluted a soul is mine. My whole life has been shuffled through under false colours. Even if I shared few of the Jew's beliefs, it should have been my duty—and my proud duty—to proclaim myself of the race. If, as I fondly believed, I was superior to my people, then it behoved me to allow that superiority to be counted to their credit and to the honour of the Jewish flag. My poor brethren, sore indeed has been your travail, and your cry of pain pierces the centuries. Perhaps—who knows?—I could have helped a little if I had been faithful, as faithful as Paul will be to his own ideals. Ah, if Paul had been a Jew—! My God! is Paul a Jew? Have I upon my shoulders the guilt of this loss to Judaism, too?

Analyze myself, reproach myself, doubt my own sanity how I may, one thing is clear. From the bottom of my heart I long, I yearn, I burn to return to the religion of my childhood. I long to say and to sing the Hebrew words that come scantily and with effort to my lips. I long to join my brethren at prayer, to sit with them in the synagogue, in the study, at the table; to join them in their worship and at their meals; to share with them their joys and sorrows, their wrongs and their inner delights. Laugh at myself how I will, I long to bind my arm and brow with the phylacteries of old and to wrap myself in my fringed shawl, and to abase myself in the dust before the God of Israel; nay, to don the greasy gabardine at which I have mocked, and to let my hair grow even as theirs. As yet this is all but a troubled aspiration, but it is irresistible and must work itself out in deeds. It cannot be argued with. The wind bloweth as it listeth; who shall say why I am tempest-tossed?

Monday Night.—Paul has retired to rest to rise early to-morrow for the journey to Moscow. For something has happened to alter his plans, and he goes thither instead of to the capital. He is sleeping the sleep of the young, the hopeful, and the joyous. Ach, that what gives him joy should be to me—; but let me write down all. This morning at breakfast Paul received a letter, which he read with a cry of astonishment and joy. "Look, little father, look," he exclaimed, handing it to me. I read, trying to disguise my own feelings and to sympathize with his gladness. It was a letter from a firm of well-known publishers in Moscow, offering to publish a work on the Greek Church, the MS. of which he had submitted to them.

"Nu vot, batiushka," said he, "I will tell you that this book donnera à penser to the theologians of the bastard forms of Christianity."

The ribald remark that rose to my lips did not pass them. "But why did you not tell me of this before?" I asked instead, endeavouring to infuse a note of reproach into my indifference.

"Ah, father, I did not want you to distress yourself. I knew your affection for me was so great that you might want to stint yourself, and put yourself to trouble to help me to pay the expenses of publication myself. You would have shared my disappointments. I wanted you to share my triumph—as now. It is two years that I have been trying to get it published. I wrote it in the year before mother, whose soul is with the saints, left us. But, eka! I am recompensed at last." And his pale face beamed and his dark eyes flashed with excitement.

Yes, Paul was right. As Paul always is. Brought up, I think wisely, to believe in my comparative poverty, he has become manlier for not having a crutch to lean upon. Was it not enough that he was devoid from the start of the dull, dead weight of Judaism which clogged my own early years? Up to the present, though, he has not done so well as I. Russian provincial journalism scatters few luxuries to its votaries. Paul is so stupidly contented with everything that he is not likely to write anything to make a sensation. He has not invented gunpowder.

Paul's voice broke in curiously on my reflections. "It ought to make some sensation. I have collected a whole series of new arguments, partly textual, partly historical, to show the absolute want of locus standi of any other than the Orthodox Church."

"Indeed," I murmured, "and what is the Orthodox Church?" Paul stared at me.

"I mean," I added hastily, "your conception of the Orthodox Church."

"My conception?" said Paul. "I suppose you mean how do I defend the conception which is embodied in our ceremonies and ritual?" And before I could stop him, he had given me a summary of his arguments under which I would not have kept awake if I had not been thinking of other things. My poor boy! So this wire-drawn stuff about the Sacrament and the Lord's Supper is what has cost you toilsome days and sleepless nights, while to me the thought that I had embraced one variety of Christianity rather than another had never before occurred. All forms were the same to me, from Catholicism to Calvinism; the baptismal water had glided from my back as from a duck's. True, I have lived with all the conventional surroundings of my Christian fellow-countrymen, as I have lived with the language of Russia on my lips, and subservient to Russian customs and manners. But all the while I was neither a Russian nor a Christian. I was a Jew.

Every now and again I roused myself to laudatory assent to one of Paul's arguments when I divined by his tone that it was due. But when he wound up with a panegyric on "our glorious Russian State," and "our little father, the Czar, God's Vicegerent on earth, who alone of European monarchs incarnates and unites in his person Church and State, so that loyalty and piety are one," I could not refrain from pointing out that it was a pure fluke that Russia was "orthodox" at all.

"Suppose," said I, "Wladimir, when he made his famous choice between the Creeds of the world, had picked Judaism? It all turned on a single man's whim."

"Father," Paul cried in a pained tone, "do not be blasphemous. Wladimir was divinely inspired to dower his country with the true faith. Just therein lay the wisdom of Providence in achieving such great results through the medium of an individual. It is impossible that God should have permitted him to incline his ear to the infidel Israelite, who has survived to be at once a link with the past and a living proof of the sterility of the soul that refuses the living waters. The millions of holy Russia perpetuating the stubborn heresy of the Jews—adopting an unfaith as a faith! The very thought makes the blood run cold. Nay, then would every Russian deserve to be sunk in squalor, dishonesty, and rapacity, even as every Jew."

"Not every Jew, Paul," I remonstrated.

"No, not perhaps every Jew in squalor," he assented, with a sarcastic laugh; "for too many of the knaves have feathered their nests very comfortably. Even the Raskolnik is more tolerable. And many of them are not even Jews. The Russian Press is infested with these fellows, who take the bread out of the mouths of honest Christians, and will even write the leaders in the religious papers. Believe me, little father, these Jewish scribblers who have planted their flagstaffs everywhere have cost me many a heartache, many a disappointment."

I could not help thinking this sentiment somewhat unworthy of my Paul, though it threw a flood of light on the struggle, whose details he had never troubled me with. I began to doubt my wisdom in sending so unpractical a youth out into the battle of life, to hew his way as best he might. But how was I to foresee that he would become a writing man, that he would be tripped up at every turn by some clever Hebrew, and that his aversion from the race would be intensified?

"But surely," I said, after a moment of silence, "our Slavic journalists are not all Christians, either."

"They are not," he admitted sadly. "The Universities have much to answer for. Instead of rigidly excluding every vicious book that unsettles the great social and religious ideals of which God designed Russia to be the exponent, the works of Spencer and Taine, and Karl Marx and Tourguénieff, and every literary Antichrist, are allowed to poison faith in the sap. The censor only bars the superficially anti-Russian books. But there will come a reaction. A reaction," he added solemnly, "to which this work of mine may, by the grace of God, be permitted to contribute."

I could have laughed at my son if I had not felt so inclined to weep. Paul's pietism irritated me for the first time. Was it that my reaction against my past had become stronger than ever, was it that Paul had never exposed his own narrowness so completely before? I know not. I only know I felt quite angry with him. "And how do you know there will ever be a reaction?" I asked.

"Christ never leaves himself without a witness long," he answered sententiously. "And already there are symptoms enough that the creed of the materialist does not satisfy the soul. Look at our Tolstoï, who is coming back to Christianity after ranging at will through the gaudy pleasure-grounds of science and life; it is true his Christianity is cast after his own formula, and that he has still much intellectual pride to conquer, but he is on the right road to the fountain of life. But, little father, you are unlike yourself this morning," he went on, putting his hand to my hot forehead. "You are not well." He kissed me. "Let me give you another cup of tea," he said, and turned on the tap of the samovar with an air that disposed of the subject.

I sipped at my cup to please him, remarking in the interval between two sips as indifferently as I could, "But what makes you so bitter against the Jews?"

"And what makes you so suddenly their champion?" he retorted.

"When have I championed them?" I asked, backing.

"Your pardon," he said. "Of course I should have understood you are only putting in a word for them for argument's sake. But I confess I have no patience with any one who has any patience with these bloodsuckers of the State. Every true Russian must abhor them. They despise the true faith, and are indifferent to our ideals. They sneak out of the conscription. They live for themselves, and regard us as their natural prey. Our peasantry are corrupted by their brandy-shops, squeezed by their money-lenders, and roused to discontent by the insidious utterances of their peddlers, d——d wandering Jews, who hate the Government and the Tschinn and everything Russian. When did a Jew invest his money in Russian industries? They are a filthy, treacherous, swindling set. Believe me, batiushka, pity is wasted upon them."

"Pity is never spent upon them," I retorted. "They are what the Russians—what we Russians—have made them. Who has pent them into their foul cellars and reeking dens? They work with their brains, and you—we—abuse them for not working with their hands. They work with their hands, and the Czar issues a ukase that they are to be driven off the soil they have tilled. It is Æsop's fable of the wolf and the lamb."

"In which the wolf is the Jew," said Paul coolly. "The Jew can always be trusted to take care of himself. His cunning is devilish. Till his heart is regenerate, the Jew remains the Ishmael of the modern world, his hand against every man's, every man's against his."

"'Love thy neighbour as thyself,'" I quoted bitterly.

"Even so," said Paul. "The Jew must be cut off, even as the Christian must pluck out his own eye if it offendeth him. Christ came among us to bring not peace but a sword. If the Kingdom of Christ is delayed by these vermin, they must be poisoned off for the sake of Russia and humanity at large."

"Vermin, indeed!" I cried hotly, for I could no longer restrain myself. "And what know you of these vermin of whom you speak with such assurance? What know you of their inner lives, of their sanctified homes, of their patient sufferings? Have you penetrated to their hearths and seen the beautiful naïveté of their lives, their simple faith in God's protection, though it may well seem illusion, their unselfish domesticity, their sublime scorn of temptation, their fidelity to the faith of their ancestors, their touching celebrations of fast and festival, their stanchness to one another, their humble living and their high respect for things intellectual, their unflinching toil from morn till eve for a few kopecks of gain, their heroic endurance of every form of torment, vilification, contempt—?" I felt myself bursting into tears and broke from the breakfast table.

Paul followed me to my room in amazement. In the midst of all my tempest of emotion I was no less amazed at my own indiscretion.

"What is the matter with you?" he said, clasping his arm around my neck. "Why make yourself so hot over this accursed race, for whom, from some strange whim or spirit of perverseness, you stand up to-day for the first time in my recollection?"

"It is true; why indeed?" I murmured, striving to master myself. After all, the picture I had drawn was as ideal in its beauty as Paul's in its ugliness. "Nu, I only wanted you to remember that they were human beings."

"Ach, there is the pity of it," persisted Paul; "that human beings should fall so low. And who has been telling you of all these angelic qualities you roll so glibly off your tongue?"

"No one," I answered.

"Then you have invented them. Ha! ha! ha!" And Paul went off into a fit of good-humoured laughter. That laughter was a sword between his life and mine, but I let a responsive smile play across my features, and Paul went to his own room in higher spirits than ever.

We met again at dinner, and again at our early supper, but Paul was too full of his book, and I of my own thoughts to permit of a renewal of the dispute. Even a saint, I perceive, has his touch of egotism, and behind all Paul's talk of Russia's ideals, of the misconceptions of their fatherland's function by feather-brained Nihilists and Democrats possessed of that devil, the modern spirit, there danced, I am convinced, a glorified vision of St. Paul floating down the vistas of the future, with a nimbus of Russian ideals around his head. If he has only put them as eloquently into his book as he talks of them he will at least be read.

But I have bred a bigot.

And the more bigoted he is, the more my heart faints within me for the simple, sublime faith of my people. Behind all the tangled network of ceremony and ritual, the larger mind of the man who has lived and loved sees the outlines of a creed grand in its simplicity, sublime in its persistence. The spirit has clothed itself on with flesh, as it must do for human eyes to gaze on it and live with it; and if, in addition, it has swaddled itself with fold on fold of garment, even so the music has not gone out of its voice, nor the love out of its eyes.

As soon as Paul is gone to-morrow, I must plan out my future life. His book will doubtless launch him on the road to fame and fortune. But what remains for me? To live on as I am doing would be intolerable. To do nothing for my people, either with voice or purse, to live alone in this sleepy hamlet, cut off from all human fellowship, alienated from everything that makes my neighbours' lives endurable—better death than such a death-in-life. And yet is it possible that I can get into touch again with my youth, that after a sort of Rip Van Winkle sleep, I can take up again and retwine the severed strands? How shall my people receive again a viper into its bosom? Well, come what may, there must be an end to this. Even at this moment reproachful voices haunt my ear; and in another moment, when I put down my pen to go to my sleepless bed, I shall take care to light my bed-room candle before extinguishing my lamp, for the momentary darkness would be filled with impalpable solemnity bordering on horror. Flashes and echoes from the ghostly world of my youth, the faces of my dead parents, strange fragments of sound and speech, the sough of the wind in the trees of the "House of the Living," the far-away voice of the Chazan singing some melancholy tune full of heart-break and weirdness, the little crowded Cheder where the rabbi intoned the monotonous lesson, the whizz of the stone little Ivanovitch flung at my forehead because I had "killed Christ"—. No, my nerves are not strong enough to bear these visions and voices.

All my life long I see now I have been reserved and solitary. Never has any one been admitted to my heart of hearts—not even Caterina. But now I must unburden my soul to some one ere I die. And to another living soul. For this dead sheet of paper will not, I perceive, do after all.

Saturday Night.—Nearly a week has passed since I wrote the above words, and I am driven to your pages again. I would have come to you last night, but suddenly I recollected that it was the Sabbath. I have kept the Sabbath. I have prayed a few broken fragments of prayer, recovered almost miraculously from the deeps of memory. I have rested from every toil. I stayed myself from stirring up the fire, though it was cold and I was shivering. And a new peace has come to me.

I have heard from Paul; he has completed the negotiations with the Moscow booksellers. The book is to have every chance. Of course, in a way I wish it success. It cannot do much harm, and I am proud of Paul, after all. What a rabbi he would have made! It seems these publishers are also the owners of a paper, and Paul is to have some work on it, which will give him enough to live upon. So he will stay in Moscow for a few months and see his book through the press. He fears the distance is too great for him to come to and fro, as he would have done had he been at the capital. Though I know I shall long for his presence sometimes in my strange reactions, yet on the whole I feel relieved. To-morrow without Paul will be an easier day. I shall not go to church, though honest old Clara Petroffskovna may stare and cross herself in holy horror, and spoil the borsch. As for the neighbours—let the startchina and the starostas and the retired major from Courland, and even the bibulous Prince Shoubinoff, gossip as they will. I cannot remain here now for more than a few weeks. Besides, I can be unwell. No, on second thoughts, I shall not be unwell. I have had enough of shuffling and deceit.

Sunday.—A day of horrible ennui and despair. I tried to read the Old Testament, of course in Russian, for Hebrew books I have none, and it is doubtful whether I could read them if I had. But the black cloud remained. It chokes me as I write. My limbs are as lead, my head aches. And yet I know the ailment is not of the body.

Monday.—The depression persists. I made a little expedition into the country. I rowed up the stream in a duscehubka. I tried to forget everything but the colours of the forest and the sparkle of the waters. The air was less cold than it has been for the last few days, but the russet of the pine-leaves spoke to me only of melancholy and decay. The sun set in blood behind the hills. Once I heard the howl of the wolves, but they were far away.

Monday.—So. Just a week. Nicholas Alexandrovitch says I must not write yet, but I must fill up the record, even if in a few lines. It is strange how every habit—even diary-keeping—enslaves you, till you think only of your neglected task. Ah, well! if I have been ill, I have been lucky in my period, for those frightful storms would have kept me indoors. Nicholas Alexandrovitch says it was a mild attack of influenza. God preserve me from a severe one! And yet would it not be better if it had carried me off altogether? But that is a cowardly thought. I must face the future bravely, for my own hands have forged my fate. How the writing trembles and contorts itself! I must remember Nicholas's caution. He is a frank, good-hearted fellow, is our village doctor, and I have had two or three talks with him from between the bedclothes. I don't think friend Nicholas is a very devout Christian, by the by; for he said one or two things which I should have taken seriously, had I been what he thinks I am; but which had an audacious, ironical sound to my sympathetic, sceptical ears. How funny was that story about the Archimandrite of Czernovitch!

Thursday Afternoon.—My haste to be out of bed precipitated me back again into it. But the actual pain has been small. I have grown very friendly with Nicholas Alexandrovitch, and he has promised to spend the evening with me. I am better now in body, though still troubled in mind. Paul's silence has brought a new anxiety. He has not written for twelve days. What can be the matter with him? I suppose he is overworking himself. And now to hunt up my best cigarettes for Monsieur le médecin. Strange that illness should perhaps have brought me a friend. Nothing, alas! can bring me a confidant.

11 p.m.—Astounding discovery! Nicholas Alexandrovitch is a Jew! I don't know how it was, but suddenly something was said; we looked at each other, and then a sort of light flashed across our faces; we read the mutual secret in each other's eyes; a magnetic impulse linked our hands together in a friendly clasp, and we felt that we were brothers. And yet Nicholas is a whole world apart from me in feeling and conviction. How strange and mysterious is this latent brotherhood which binds our race together through all differences of rank, country, and even faith! For Nicholas is an agnostic of agnostics; he is even further removed from sympathy with my new-found faith than the ordinary Christian, and yet my sympathy with him is not only warmer than, but different in kind from, that which I feel toward any Christian, even Caterina's brother. I have told him all. Yes, little book, him also have I told all. And he sneers at me. But there lurks more fraternity in his sneer than in a Christian's applause. We are knit below the surface like two ocean rocks, whose isolated crests rise above the waters. Nicholas laughs at there being any Judaism to survive, or anything in Judaism worth surviving. He declares that the chosen people have been chosen for the plaything of the fates, fed with illusions and windy conceit, and rewarded for their fidelity with torture and persecution. He pities them, as he would pity a dog that wanders round its master's grave, and will not eat for grief. In fact, save for this pity, he is even as I was until these new emotions rent me. He is outwardly a Christian, because he could not live comfortably otherwise, but he has nothing but contempt for the poor peasants whose fever-wrung brows he touches with a woman's hand. He looks upon them only as a superior variety of cattle, and upon the well-to-do people here as animals with all the vices of the muzhiks, and none of their virtues. For my Judaic cravings he has a good-natured mockery, and tells me I was but sickening for this influenza. He says all my symptoms are physical, not spiritual; that the loss of Caterina depressed me, that this depression drove me into solitude, and that this solitude in its turn reacted on my depression. He thinks that religion is a secretion of morbid minds, and that my Judaism will vanish again with the last traces of my influenza. And, indeed, there is much force in what he says, and much truth in his diagnosis and analysis of my condition. He advises me to take plenty of outdoor exercise, and to go back again to one of the great towns. To go back to Judaism, to ally one's self with an outcast race and a dying religion is, he thinks, an act of folly only paralleled by its inutility. The world will outgrow all these forms and prejudices in time is his confident assurance, as he puffs tranquilly at his cigarette and sips his Chartreuse. He points out, what is true enough, that I am not alone in my dissent from the religion I profess; for, as he epigrammatically puts it, the greatest Raskolniks[2] are the Orthodox. The religious statistics of the Procurator of the State Synod are, indeed, a poor index to the facts. Well, there is comfort in being damned in company. I do not agree with him on any other point, but he has done me good. The black cloud is partially lifted—perhaps the trouble was only physical, after all. I feel brighter and calmer than for months past. Anyhow, if I am to become a Jew again, I can think it out quietly. Even if I could bear Paul's contempt, there would always be, as Nicholas points out, great peril for me in renouncing the Orthodox faith. True, it would be easy enough to bribe the priest and the authorities, and to continue to receive my eucharistical certificate. But where is the sacrifice in that? It is hypocrisy exchanged for hypocrisy. And then what would become of Paul's prospects if it were known his father

was a Zhit? But I cannot think of all this now. Paul's silence is beginning to fill me with a frightful uneasiness. A presentiment of evil weighs upon me. My dear dove, my dusha Paul!

Friday Afternoon.—Still no letter from Paul. Can anything have happened? I have written to him, briefly informing him that I have been unwell. I shall ride to Zlotow and telegraph, if I do not hear in a day or two.

Saturday Morning.—All petty and stupid thoughts of my own spiritual condition are swallowed up in the thought of Paul. Ever selfish, I have allowed him to dwell alone in a far-off city, exposed to all the vicissitudes of life. Perhaps he is ill, perhaps he is half-starved on his journalistic pittance.

Saturday Night.—A cruel disappointment! A letter came, but it was only from my man of business, advising investment in some South American loan. Have given him carte blanche. Of what use is my money to me? Even Paul couldn't spend it now, with the training I have given him. He is only fitted for the cowl. He may yet join the Black Clergy. Why does he not write, my poor St. Paul?

Sunday.—Obedient to the insistent clamour of the bells, I accompanied Nicholas Alexandrovitch to church, and mechanically asked help of the Virgin at the street corner. For I have gone back into my old indifference, as Nicholas predicted. I have given the necessary orders. The paracladnoi is ready. To-morrow I go to Zlotow; thence I take the train for Moscow. He will not tell me the truth if I wire.... The weather is bitterly cold, and the stoves here are so small.... I am shivering again, but a glass of vodka will put me right.... A knock.... Clara Petroffskovna has run to the door. Who can it be? Paul?

Monday Afternoon.—No, it was not Paul. Only Nicholas Alexandrovitch. He had heard in the village that I was making preparations for a journey, and came to inquire about it, and to reproach me for not telling him. He looked relieved when I told him it was only to Moscow to look after Paul. I fancy he thought I had had a fit of remorse for my morning's devotions, and was off to seek readmission into the fold. Except our innkeeper, there is not a Jew in this truly God-forsaken place. Of course, I don't reckon myself—or the doctor. I wonder if our pope is a Jew! I laugh—but who knows? Anyhow I am here, wrapped in my thickest fur cloak, while it is Nicholas who is on the road to Moscow. He spoke truly in saying I was too weak yet to undertake the journey—that springless paracladnoi alone is enough to knock a healthy man up; though whether he was equally veracious in professing to have business to transact in Moscow, I cannot say. Da, he is a good fellow, is my brother Nicholas. To-morrow I shall know if anything has happened to my son, to my only child.

Tuesday Night.—Thank God! A wire from Nicholas. "Have seen Paul. No cause for uneasiness. Will write." Blessings on you, my friend, for the trouble you have taken for me. I feel much better already. Paul has, I suppose, been throwing himself heart and soul into this new journalistic work, and has forgotten his loving father. After all, it is only a fortnight, though it has seemed months. Anyhow, he will write. I shall hear from him in a day or two now. But a sudden thought. "Will write." Who will write? Paul or Nicholas? Oh, Paul; Paul without doubt. Nicholas has told him of my anxiety. Yes. To-morrow night or the next morning I shall have a letter from Paul. All is well.

If I were to tell Paul the truth, I wonder what he would say! I am afraid I shall never know.

Thursday Noon.—A letter from Nicholas. I cannot do better than place it here.

"MY DEAR DEMETRIUS—I hope you got my telegram and are at ease again. I had a lively journey up here, travelling in company with a Government employé, who is very proud of his country, and of the Stanislaus cross round his neck. Such a pompous ass I have never met; he beats even our friend, Prince Shoubinoff, in his Sunday clothes, with the barina on his arm. As you may imagine, I drew him out like a telescope. I have many a droll story for you when I return. To come to Paul. I made it my business at once to call upon the publishers—it is one of the largest firms here—and from them I learnt that your son was still at the same address, in the Kitai-Gorod, as that given in the first and only letter you have had from him. I did not care about going there direct, for I thought it best that he should be unaware of my presence, in case there should be anything which it would be advisable for me to find out for your information. However, by haunting the neighbourhood of the offices of his newspaper, I caught sight of him within a couple of hours. He has a somewhat over-wrought expression in his countenance, and does not look particularly well. I fancy he is exciting himself about the production of his book. He has not seen me yet, nor shall I let him see me till I ascertain that he is not in any trouble. It is only his silence to you that makes me fancy something may be the matter; otherwise I should unhesitatingly put down his pallor and intensity of expression to over-work and, perhaps, religious fervour. He went straight to the Petrovski Cathedral on leaving the offices. I am here for a few days longer, and will write again. It is frightfully cold. The thermometer is at freezing point. I sit in my shuba and shiver. Au revoir.

"NICHOLAS ALEXANDROVITCH."

There is something not quite satisfying about this letter. It looks as if there was more beneath the surface. Paul is evidently looking ill or ecstatic, or both. But, at any rate, my main anxiety is allayed. I can wait with more composure for Nicholas's second letter. But why does not the boy write himself? He must have got the letter telling him I had been unwell. And yet not a word of sympathy! I don't half like Nicholas's idea of playing the spy, though, as if my son is not to be trusted. What can he suspect? But Nicholas Alexandrovitch dearly loves to invent a mystery for the sake of ferreting it out. These scientific men are so sharp that they often cut themselves.

Friday Afternoon.—At last Paul has written.

"MY DARLING PAPASHA—I am surprised you should be anxious about me. I am quite comfortable here, and have now conquered all the difficulties that beset me at the first. How came you to allow yourself to be unwell? I hope Nicholas Alexandrovitch is taking care of you. By the by, I almost thought I saw him here this morning on the bridge, looking over into the reka, but there was a church procession, and I had hurried past the man before the thought struck me, and the odds were so much against its being our zemski-doktor, that I would not trouble to turn back. I have already corrected the proofs of several sheets of my book. It will be dedicated, by special permission, to Archbishop Varenkin. My articles in the Courier are attracting considerable attention. I have left orders for the publishers to send you my last, which will appear to-morrow. May the holy Mother and the saints watch over you.

—Your devoted son, PAUL.

"P.S.—I am making more money than I want, and I shall be glad to send you some, if you have any wants unsupplied."

My darling boy! How could I ever have felt myself alienated from you? I will come to you and live with you and share your triumphs. No miserable scruples shall divide our lives any more. The past is ineradicable; the future is its inevitable fruit. So be it. My spiritual yearnings and wrestlings were but the outcome of a morbid physical condition. Nicholas was right. And now to read my son's article, which I have here, marked with a blue border. Why should I, with my superficial ponderings, be right and he wrong?

Saturday Night.—I have a vague remembrance that three stars marked the close of the Sabbath. And here in the frosty sky I see a whole host scintillating in the immeasurable depths. The Sabbath is over and once more I drag myself to my writing desk to pour out the anguish of a tortured spirit. All day I have sat as in a dumb trance gazing out beyond the izbas and the cabbage fields toward the eternal hills. How beautiful and peaceful everything is! God, wilt Thou not impart to me the secret of peace?

Little did I divine what awaited my eyes when they rested fondly on the first sentence of Paul's article. Voi, it was a pronouncement on the Jewish question, venomous, scathing, mordant, terrific. It was an indictment of the race, lit up with all the glow of moral indignation; cruel and slanderous, yet noble and righteous in its tone and ideals; base as hell, yet pure as heaven; breathing a savagery as of Torquemada, and a saintliness as of Tolstoï. Paul in every line, my own noble, bigoted, wrong-headed Paul. As I read it, my whole frame trembled. A corresponding passion and indignation stirred my blood to fever-heat. All my slumbering Jewish instincts woke again to fresh life; and I knew myself for the weak, miserable wretch that I am. To think that a son of mine should thus vilify his own race. What can I do? Bozhe moi, what can I do? How can I stop this horrible, unnatural thing? I dare not open Paul's eyes to what he is doing. And yet it is my duty.... It is my duty. By that token I know I shall not do it. Heaven have pity on me!

Tuesday.—Heaven have pity on Paul! Here is Nicholas's promised letter.

"DEAR DEMETRIUS—I have strange news for you. It is quite providential (I use the word without prejudice, as the lawyers say) that I came here. But all is well now, so you may read what follows without alarm. Last Thursday morning, during my purposeful wanderings within Paul's usual circuit, I came face to face with our young gentleman. His eyes stared straight at me without seeing me. His face was ghastly white, and the lines were rigid as if with some stern determination. His lips were moving, but I could not catch his mutterings. He held a sealed letter in his hand. I saw the superscription. It was addressed to you. Instantly the dread came to my mind that he was about to commit suicide, and that this was his farewell to you. I followed him. He posted the letter at the post-office, turned back, threaded his way like a somnambulist across the bridge, without, however, approaching the parapet, walked mechanically onward to his own apartments, put the latch-key into the house-door, and then fell back in a dead faint—into my arms. I took him upstairs, explained what had happened, put him to bed, and—I write this from the bedside. For the crisis is over now; the brain fever has abated, and he has now nothing to do but to get well, though he will be longer about it than a young fellow of his age has a right to be. His body is emaciated with fasts and vigils and penances. I curse religion when I look at him. As if the struggle for life were not hard enough without humanity being hampered by these miserable superstitions. But you will be wanting to know what is the matter. Well, batiushka, what should be the matter but the old, old matter? La femme is, strange to relate, a fine specimen of our own race of lovely women, my dear Demetrius. She is a Jewess of the most orthodox family in Moscow, and therein lies the crux of the situation. (I am not playing upon words, but the phrase is doubly significant here.) Of course Paul has not the slightest idea I know all this; but of course I have had it from his hot lips all the same. As far as I have been able to piece his broken utterances together, they have had some stolen love passages, each followed by swift remorse on both sides, and—another furtive love passage. Paul has been comparing himself to St. Anthony, and even to Jesus, when Satan, ce chef admirable, spread a first-class dinner in the wilderness. But the poor lad must have suffered much behind all his heroics. And what his final resolution to give her up cost him is pretty evident. I suppose he must have told you of it in that letter. Isn't it the oddest thing in the world? Rachel Jacobvina is the girl's name, and her people keep a clothes' store round the corner, and her father is the Parnass (you will remember what that means) of his synagogue. She is a sweet little thing; and Paul evidently has a taste for other belles than belles-lettres. From what you told me of him I fully expected this sort of thing. The poor fellow is looking at me now from among his iced bandages with a piteous air of resignation to the will of Nicholas Alexandrovitch in bringing him back to this world of trouble when he already felt his wings sprouting. Poor Paul! He little dreams what I am writing; but he will get over this, and marry some fair, blue-eyed Circassian with corresponding tastes in fasting, and an enthusiastic longing for the Kingdom of God, when the year shall be a perpetual Lent. In his failure to realize history, he thinks it a crime to adore a Jewish virgin, though he spends half his time in adoring the Madonna. How shocked he would be if I pointed this out! People who look through ecclesiastical spectacles so rarely realize that the Holy Family was a Jewish one. But my pen is running away with me, and our patient looks thirsty. Proshchaï.

"NICHOLAS."

"P.S.—There is not the slightest danger of a relapse unless the image of this diabolical girl comes before him again. And I keep his attention distracted. Besides, he had finally conquered his passion. This illness was at once the seal and the witness of his unchangeable resolve. I have heard him repeat the terms of the letter of farewell he sent her. It was final."

So this was the meaning of your silence; this the tragedy that lay behind your simple sentence, "I have now conquered all the difficulties which beset me at the first." This was the motive that guided your hand to write those bitter lines about our race, so that you might henceforth cut yourself off from the possibility of allying yourself with it even in thought. I understand all now, my poor high-mettled boy. How you must have suffered! How your pride must have rebelled at the idea that you might have to make such a confession to me—little knowing I should have hailed it with delight. That temptation should have assailed you, too, at such a period—when you were publishing your great work on the ideals of Holy Russia! Mysterious, indeed, are the ways of Providence. And yet why may not all be well after all, and Heaven grant me such grace as I would willingly sacrifice my life to deserve? It is impossible that my son's passion can be utterly dead. Such fires are only covered up. I will go to him and tell him all. The news that he is a Jew will revolutionize him. His love will flame up afresh and take on the guise and glamour of duty. Love, posing as logic, will whisper in his ear that no bars of early training can avail to keep him from the race to which he belongs by blood and by his father's faith. In this girl's eyes he will read God's message of command, and I, God's message of Peace and Reconciliation. The tears are in my eyes; I can hardly see to write. The happiness I foresee is too great. Blessings on your sweet face, Rachel Jacobvina, my own darling daughter that is to be. To you is allotted the blessed task of solving a fearful problem, of rescuing and reuniting two human lives. Yes, Heaven is indeed merciful. To-morrow I start for Moscow.

Thursday.—How can I write it? No, there is no pity in Heaven. The sky smiles in steely blankness. The air cuts like a knife. Paul is well, or as well as a convalescent can be. He must have had a heart of ice. But it is fortunate he had, seeing what the icy fates have wrought. I arrived at Moscow, and hurried in a droshky across the well-known bridge to Paul's lodgings. A ghastly procession stopped me. Some burlaks were bearing the corpse of a young girl who had thrown herself into the ice-laden river. A clammy foreboding gathered at my heart, but ere I had time to say a word, an old, caftan-clad man, with agonized eyes and a white, streaming beard, dashed up, pulled off the face-cloth, revealing a strange, weird loveliness, uttered a scream which yet rings in my ears, threw himself passionately on the body, rose up again, murmured something solemnly and resignedly in Hebrew, rent his garments, readjusted the face-cloth, and followed weeping in the rear. And from lip to lip, that for once forgot to curl in scorn, flew the murmur: "Rachel Jacobvina."

Saturday Night.—I slouched into the synagogue this morning, the cynosure of suspicious eyes. I nearly uncovered my head in forgetfulness. Somebody offered me a Talith, which I wrapped round myself with marked awkwardness. The service moved me beyond measure. I have neither the pen nor the will to describe my sensations. I was a youth again. The intervening decades faded away. Rachel's father said the Kaddish. The peace of God has touched my soul. Paul is asleep. I have made Nicholas take his much-needed rest. I am reading the Hebrew Psalms. The language comes back to me bit by bit.

Monday.—Paul is sitting up reading—proofs. I have been to condole with Rachel's father, as he sat mourning upon the ground. I explained that I was a stranger in the town, and had heard of the accident. I have given five hundred roubles to the synagogue. The whole congregation is buzzing with the generosity of the rich Jewish farmer from the country. Fortunately there is no danger of Paul hearing anything of my doings. He is a prisoner; and Nicholas and myself keep watch over him by turns.

Tuesday.—I have just come from a meeting of the Palestine Colonization Society. Heavens, what ideals burn in these breasts supposed to throb only with cupidity and cunning! Their souls still turn to the Orient, as the needle turns to the pole. And how the better-off among them pity their weaker brethren! With what enthusiasm they plot and plan to get them beyond the frontier into freer countries, but chiefly into the centre of all Jewish aspiration, the Holy Land! How they wept when I doubled their finances at a stroke. My poor, much-wronged brethren!

Odessa, Monday.—It is almost a year since I closed this book, and now, after a period of peace, I am driven to it again. Paul has made an irruption into my tranquil household. For eleven months now I have lived in this little two-storied house overlooking the roadstead, with Isaac and the ekonomka for my sole companions. So long as I could pour my troubles into the ear of the venerable old rabbi (who was starving for material sustenance when I took him, as I was for spiritual), so long I had no need of you, my old confidant. But this visit of Paul has reopened all my sores. I have smuggled the rabbi out of the way; but even if he were here, he could not understand the terrible situation. The God of Israel alone knows what I feel at having to deny Him, at having to hide my faith from my own son. He must not stay. The New Year is nigh, with its feasts and fasts. Moreover, surrounded as one is by spies, Paul's presence here may lead to discoveries that I am not what the authorities imagine. Perhaps it would have been better if I had gone back to the village. But no. There was that church-going. A village is so small. In this great and bustling seaport I am lost, or comparatively so. A few roubles in the ecclesiastical palm, and complete oblivion settles on me.

To-night I shall know to what I owe this sudden visit. Paul is radiant. He plays with his untold news like a child with a new toy. He drops all sorts of mysterious hints. He frisks around me like a fond spaniel. But he reserves his tit-bit for to-night, when the tramp of the sailors and the perambulating peasantry shall have died away, and we shall be seated cosily in my study, smoking our cigarettes, and looking out toward the quiet lights of the shipping. Of course it is good news—Heaven help me, I fear Paul's good news. Good news that Paul has come all the way from St. Petersburg to tell me, which only his own lips may tell me, must, if past omens speak truly, be terrible. God grant I may survive the telling.

What a coward I am! Have I not long since made up my mind that Paul must go his way and I mine? What difference, then, can his news make to me? He will never know now that I am a Zhit unless he hears it from my dying lips as I utter the declaration of the Unity. I made up my mind to that when I came here. Paul threatens to make his mark as a writer on theological subjects. To tell him the truth would only sadden him and do him no good; while to reveal my own Judaism to the world would but serve to damage him and injure his prospects. This may seem but a cover for my cowardice, for my fear of State reprisals; but it is true for all that. Bozhe moi, is it not punishment enough not to be able to join my brethren in their worship? I must remain here, where I am unknown, practising my religion unostentatiously and in secret. The sense of being in a Jewish city satisfies my soul. We are here more than a fourth of the population. House-rent and fuel are very dear, but we thrive and prosper, thanks to God. I give to our poor, through Isaac, but they hardly want my help. I rejoice in the handsome synagogues, though I dare not enter them. Yes, I am best here. Why be upset by my boy's visit? Paul will tell me his news, I shall congratulate him, he will go back to the capital, and all will be as before.

Monday Midnight.—No, all can never be as before. One last step remained to divide our lives to all eternity. Voi, Paul has taken it.

All came off as arranged. We sat together at my window. It was a glorious night, and a faint, fresh wind blew in from the sea. The lights in the harbour twinkled, the stars glistened in the sky. But as Paul told me his good news, the whole horizon was one great flame before my eyes. He began by recapitulating, though with fuller details than was possible by letter, what I knew pretty well already; the story of the great success of his book, which had been reviewed in all the theological magazines of Europe, and had gone through four editions in the year, and been translated into German and Italian; the story of how he had been encouraged to come to St. Petersburg, and how he had prospered on the press there. And then came the grand news—he was offered the editorship of the Novoe Vremia, the great St. Petersburg paper!

In an instant I realized all it meant, and in my horror I almost fainted. Paul would direct this famous Government and anti-Semitic organ, Paul would pen day after day those envenomed leaders, goading on the mob to turn and rend their Jewish fellow-citizens, denying them the rights of human beings. Paul would direct the flood of sarcasm and misrepresentation poured forth day after day upon my inoffensive brethren. The old anguish with which I had read that article a year ago returned to me; but not the old tempest of wrath. By sheer force of will I kept myself calm. A great issue was at stake, and I nerved myself for the contest.

"Paul," said I, "you are a lucky fellow." I kissed him on the brow with icy lips. He saw my great emotion, but felt it was but natural.

"Da," said he, "I am a lucky fellow. It is a great thing. Few men have had such an opportunity at twenty-five."

"Nutchozh? And how do you propose to utilize it?" I asked.

"Och, I must conduct the paper on the same general lines," he said; "of course, with improvements."

"Amongst the latter the omission of the anti-Semitic bias, I hope."

He stared at me. "Certainly not. The proprietors make its continuance on the same general lines a condition. They are very good. They even guard me against possible prosecutions by paying a handsome salary to a man of straw. Ish-lui, it is a fine berth that I've got."

Should I tell him the thing was impossible—that he was a Jew? No; time for that when all other means had failed. "Och, you have accepted it?" I said.

"Of course I have, father. Why should I give them time to change their minds?"

"I should have thought you would have consulted me first."

"Nu, uzh, I have never consulted you yet about accepting work," he said in a wondering, disappointed tone.

"Nuka, but this puts you finally into a career, does it not?"

"Certainly. That is why I accepted it, and I thought you would be glad."

"That is why you should have refused it. But I am glad all the same."

"I do not understand you, father."

"Nuka, golubtchik, listen," I said in my most endearing tone, drawing my arm round his neck. "Your struggles for existence were but struggles for the sake of the struggle. You are not as other young men. You have succeeded; and the moment you win the prize is the moment for retiring gracefully, leaving it in the hands of him who needs it. Your fight was but a game I allowed you to play. You are rich."

"Rich?"

"Rich! Nearly all my life I have been a wealthy man. I own land in every part of Russia; I hold shares in all the most successful companies. I have kept this knowledge from you so that you might enjoy your riches more when you knew the truth."

"Rich?" He repeated the word again in a dazed tone. "Ach, why did I not know this before?"

"You had not succeeded. You had not had your experience, my son, my dearest Paul. But now your work is over, or rather your true work begins. Freed from the detestable routine of a newspaper office, you shall write your books and work out your ideas at leisure, and relieved from all material considerations."

"Da, it would have been a beautiful ideal—once," he said; then added fiercely: "Rich? And I did not know it."

"But you were the happier for your ignorance."

"No, father. The struggle is too terrible. Often have I sat and wept. Ish-lui, time after time my book—destined as it was to success—came back to me from the publishers. And I could have produced it myself all along!"

Pangs of remorse agitated me. Had my plan been, indeed, a failure? "But you have the pride of unhelped success."

"And the bitter memories. And once—" He paused.

"Once?" I said.

"Once I loved a girl. She is dead now, so it doesn't matter. There were many and complicated obstacles to our union. With money they would have been overcome."

"Poor boy!" I said wonderingly, for I knew nothing of this apparently new love episode. "Forgive me, my son, if I have acted mistakenly. Anyhow, from this moment your happiness is my sole care."

"No," he said, with sudden determination. "It is too late now. You meant it for the best, papasha. But I do not want the money now. I have money of my own—and glory. Why should I give up what my own hands have won?"

"Because I ask it of you, Paul; because I ask you to allow me to make reparation for the mischief I have done."

"The truest reparation will be to let things go unrepaired," he said, with a touch of sarcasm. "I shall be happier as editor of this paper. What finer medium for my ideas than a great newspaper? What more potent lever to my hand for raising Holy Russia to a yet higher plane? No, father. Let bygones be bygones. Give my share of your wealth to a society for helping struggling talent. I struggle no longer. Leave me to go on in the path my pen has carved out."

I fell at his feet and begged him to let me have my way, but some obstinate demon seemed to have taken possession of his breast. I opened my desk and showered bank-notes upon him. He spurned them, and one flew out into the night. Neither of us put out a hand to arrest its flight.

I saw that nothing but the truth had any chance to alter his resolve. But I played one more card before resorting to this dangerous weapon.

"Listen, my own dearest Paul," I burst out. "If money will not tempt you, let a father's petition persuade you. Learn, then, that I dread your taking this position because you will perpetually have to attack the Jews—"

"As they deserve," he put in.

"Be it so. But I—I have a kindness for this oppressed race."

He looked at me in silence, as if awaiting further explanation. I gave it, blurting out the shameful lie with ill-concealed confusion.

"Once upon a time I—I loved a Jewess. I could not marry her, of course. But ever since that time I have had a soft place in my heart for her unhappy race."

A look of surprise flashed into Paul's eyes. Then his face grew tender. He took my hand in his.

"Father, we have a common sorrow," he said. "The girl I spoke of was a Jewess."

"How?" I exclaimed, surprised in my turn. It was the same affair, then.

"Yes, she was a Jewess. But I taught her the truth. Christ was revealed to her prisoned soul. She would have fled with me if we had had the means, and if I had been able to support her in some other country. But she did not dare be baptized and stay in Moscow or anywhere near. She said her father would have killed her. The only alternative was for me to embrace Judaism. Impossible as you may think it, father, and I confess it to my eternal shame, at the very period I was correcting the proofs of my book, I was wrestling with a temptation to embrace this Satanic heresy. But I conquered the temptation. It was easy to conquer. To renounce the faith which was my blessed birthright would, as you know, have cost me dear. Selfishness warred for once on the side of salvation. Rachel wished to fly with me. I knew she would have been poor and unhappy. I refused to take advantage of her girlish impetuousness. I heard afterward that she had drowned herself." The tears rained down his cheeks.

"We had arranged to wait till I could save a stock of money. Voi, the delay undid us. One day Rachel's father called on me. He had got wind of our secret. He fell at my feet and tore his hair, and wept and conjured me not to darken his home and his life. A Jewess could only wed a Jew, he said. If I had only been born a Jew all would have been well. But his Rachel had, perhaps, talked of becoming a Christian. Did I not know that was impossible? As well expect the sheep to howl like the wolf. Blood was thicker than baptismal water. Her heart would always cleave to her own religion. And was my love so blind as not to see that even if she spoke of Christianity it was only to please me? that she only kissed the crucifix that I might kiss her, and knelt to the Virgin that I might kneel to her? At home, he swore it with fearful oaths, she was always bitterly sarcastic at the expense of the true faith. I believed him. My God, I believed him! For at times I had feared it myself. I would be no party to such carnal blasphemy, and charged him with a note of farewell. When he went I felt as if I had escaped from a terrible temptation. I fell on my knees and thanked the saints."

"But why did you not tell me this at the time?" I cried in intolerable anguish.

"Nu; to what end? It would only have worried you. I did not know you were rich."

"And at this time you offered to send me money!" I said, with sudden recollection.

"Since I had not enough, you might as well have some of it. Anyhow, father, you see all this has made no difference to me. I shall never marry now, of course; but it hasn't altered the opinion I have always had of the Jews—rather corroborated it. Rachel told me enough of the superstitious slavery amid which she was forced to live. I have no doubt now that her father lied. But for his pigheaded tribalism, Rachel would have been alive to-day. So why your love for a Jewish girl should make you tender to the race I do not see, dearest father. There are always exceptions to everything—Rachel was one; the woman you loved was another. And now it is very late; I think I will go to bed."

He kissed me and went out at the door. Then he came back and put his head inside again. A sweet, sad, winning smile lit up his pale, thoughtful face.

"I will put you on the free list of the Novoe Vremia, father," he said. "Good-night, papasha."

What could I say? What could I do? I called up a smile to my trembling lips.

"Good-night, Paul," I said.

I shall never tell him now.

Tuesday, 3 a.m.—I reopen these pages to note an ironic climax to this bitter day. Through the excitement of Paul's coming I had not read my letters. After sitting here in a numb trance for hours, I suddenly bethought me of them. One is from my business man, informing me that he has just sold the South American stock, respecting which I gave him carte blanche. I go to bed richer by five thousand roubles.

Odessa, Wednesday Night.—Six months have passed. I am on the free list of the Novoe Vremia. Almost every day brings me a fresh stab as I read. But I am a "constant reader." It is my penance, and I bear it as such. After a long silence, I have just had a letter from Nicholas Alexandrovitch, and I reopen my diary to note it. He is about to marry a prosperous widow, and is going over to Catholicism. He writes he is very happy. Lucky, soulless being. He does not know he will be a richer man when I die. Happily, I am ready, though it were to-day. My peace is made, I hope, with God and man, though Paul knows nothing even now. He could not fail to learn it, though, if he came to Odessa again. I have bribed the spies and the clergy heavily. Thanks to their silence, I am one of the most prominent Jews of the town, and nobody dreams of connecting me with the trenchant editor of the Novoe Vremia. I see now that I could have acted so all along, if I had not been such a coward. But I keep Paul away. It is my last cowardice. In a postscript Nicholas writes that Paul's articles are causing a great sensation in the remotest parts of Russia. Alas, I know it. Are there not anti-Jewish riots in all parts, encouraged by cruel Government measures? Do not the local newspapers everywhere reproduce Paul's printed firebrands? Have I not the pleasure of coming across them again in our own Odessa papers, in the Wiertnik and the Listok? I should not wonder if we had an outbreak here. There was a little affray yesterday in the pereouloks of the Jewish quarter, though we are quiet enough down this way.... Great God! What is that noise I hear?... Yes! it is! it is! "Down with the Zhits! Down with the Zhits!" There is red on the horizon. Bozhe moi! It is flame! Voi! They are pillaging the Jewish quarter. The sun sinks in blood, as on that unhappy day among the village hills.... Ach! Paul, Paul! Why did I not stop your murderous pen?... But if not you, another would have written.... No, that is no excuse.... Forgive me, O God, I have been weak. Ever weak and cowardly from the day I first deserted Thee, even unto this day.... I am not worthy of my blood, of my race.... They are coming this way. It goes through me like a knife. "Down with the Zhits! Down with the Zhits!" And now I see them. They are mad, drunk with the vodka they have stolen from the Jewish inns. Great God! They have knives and guns. And their leader is flourishing a newspaper and shouting out something from it. There are soldiers among them, and sailors, native and foreign, and mad muzhiks. Where are the police?... The mob is passing under my window. God pity me, it is Paul's words they are shouting.... They have passed. No one thinks of me. Thank God, I am safe. I am safe from these demons. What a narrow escape!... Ah, God, they have captured Rabbi Isaac and are dragging him along by his white beard toward the barracks. My place is by his side. I will rouse my brethren. We are not a few. We will turn on these dogs and rend them. Proshchaï, my loved diary. Farewell! I go to proclaim the Unity.

FOOTNOTES:
[1] In order to preserve the local colour, the Translator has occasionally left a word or phrase of the MS. in the original Russian.
[2] Dissenters.

X

"Cast off among the dead, like the slain that lie in the grave. Whom Thou rememberest no more, and they are cut off from Thy hand. Thou hast laid me in the lowest pit, in dark places, in the deeps. Thy wrath lieth hard upon me and Thou hast afflicted me with all Thy waves. Thou hast put mine acquaintance far from me; Thou hast made me an abomination unto them; I am shut up and I cannot come forth. Mine eye wasteth away by reason of affliction. I have called daily upon Thee, O Lord, I have spread forth my hands unto Thee."—Eighty-eighth Psalm.

There was a restless air about the Refuge. In a few minutes the friends of the patients would be admitted. The Incurables would hear the latest gossip of the Ghetto, for the world was still very much with these abortive lives, avid of sensations, Jewish to the end. It was an unpretentious institution—two corner houses knocked together—near the east lung of London; supported mainly by the poor at a penny a week, and scarcely recognized by the rich; so that paraplegia and vertigo and rachitis and a dozen other hopeless diseases knocked hopelessly at its narrow portals. But it was a model institution all the same, and the patients lacked for nothing except freedom from pain. There was even a miniature synagogue for their spiritual needs, with the women's compartment religiously railed off from the men's, as if these grotesque ruins of sex might still distract each other's devotions.

Yet the Rabbis knew human nature. The sprightly, hydrocephalous, paralytic Leah had had the chair she inhabited carried down into the men's sitting-room to beguile the moments, and was smiling fascinatingly upon the deaf blind man, who had the Braille Bible at his fingers' ends, and read on as stolidly as St. Anthony. Mad Mo had strolled vacuously into the ladies' ward, and, indifferent to the pretty white-aproned Christian nurses, was loitering by the side of a weird, hatchet-faced cripple with a stiletto-shaped nose supporting big spectacles. Like most of the patients she was up and dressed; only a few of the white pallets ranged along the walls were occupied.

"Leah says she'd be quite happy if she could walk like you," said Mad Mo in complimentary tones. "She always says Milly walks so beautiful. She says you can walk the whole length of the garden." Milly, huddled in her chair, smiled miserably.

"You're crying again, Rebecca," protested a dark-eyed, bright-faced dwarf in excellent English, as she touched her friend's withered hand. "You are in the blues again. Why, that page is all blistered."

"No—I feel so nice," said the sad-eyed Russian in her quaint musical accent. "You sall not tink I cry because I am not happy. Ven I read sad tings—like my life—den only I am happy."

The dwarf gave a short laugh that made her pendent earrings oscillate. "I thought you were brooding over your love affairs," she said.

"Me!" cried Rebecca. "I lost too young my leg to be in love. No, it is Psalm eighty-eight dat I brood over. 'I am afflicted and ready to die from my yout' up.' Yes, I vas only a girl ven I had to go to Königsberg to find a doctor to cut off my leg. 'Lover and friend hast dou put far from me, and mine acquaintance into darkness!'"

Her face shone ecstatic.

"Hush!" whispered the dwarf, with a warning nudge and a slight nod in the direction of a neighbouring waterbed on which a pale, rigid, middle-aged woman lay, with shut sleepless eyes.

"Se cannot understand Englis'," said the Russian girl proudly.

"Don't be so sure, look how the nurses here have picked up Yiddish!"

Rebecca shook her head incredulously. "Sarah is a Polis' woman," she said. "For years dey are in England and dey learn noting."

"Ick bin krank! Krank! Krank!" suddenly moaned a shrivelled Polish grandmother—an advanced centenarian—as if to corroborate the girl's contention. She was squatting monkey-like on her bed, every now and again murmuring her querulous burden of sickness, and jabbering at the nurses to shut all the windows. Fresh air she objected to as vehemently as if it were butter or some other heterodox dainty.

Hard upon her crooning came bloodcurdling screams from the room above, sounds that reminded the visitor he was not in a "Barnum" show, that the monstrosities were genuine. Pretty Sister Margaret—not yet indurated—thrilled with pity, as before her inner vision rose the ashen perspiring face of the palsied sufferer, who sat quivering all the long day in an easy-chair, her swollen jelly-like hands resting on cotton-wool pads, an air-pillow between her knees, her whole frame racked at frequent intervals by fierce spasms of pain, her only diversion faint blurred reflections of episodes of the street in the glass of a framed picture; yet morbidly suspicious of slow poison in her drink, and cursed with an incurable vitality.

Meantime Sarah lay silent, bitter thoughts moving beneath her white, impassive face like salt tides below a frozen surface. It was a strong, stern face, telling of a present of pain, and faintly hinting at a past of prettiness. She seemed alone in the populated ward, and indeed the world was bare for her. Most of her life had been spent in the Warsaw Ghetto, where she was married at sixteen, nineteen years before. Her only surviving son—a youth whom the English atmosphere had not improved—had sailed away to trade with the Kaffirs. And her husband had not been to see her for a fortnight!

When the visitors began to arrive, her torpor vanished. She eagerly raised the half of her that was not paralyzed, partially sitting up. But gradually expectation died out of her large gray eyes. There was a buzz of talk in the room—the hydrocephalous girl was the gay centre of a group; the Polish grandmother who cursed her grandchildren when they didn't come and when they did, was denouncing their neglect of her to their faces; everybody had somebody to kiss or quarrel with. One or two acquaintances approached the bed-ridden wife, too, but she would speak no word, too proud to ask after her husband, and wincing under the significant glances occasionally cast in her direction. By and by she had the red screen placed round her bed, which gave her artificial walls and a quasi-privacy. Her husband would know where to look for her—

"Woe is me!" wailed her centenarian country-woman, rocking to and fro. "What sin have I committed to get such grandchildren? You only come to see if the old grandmother isn't dead yet. So sick! So sick! So sick!"

Twilight filled the wards. The white beds looked ghostly in the darkness. The last visitor departed. Sarah's husband had not yet come.

"He is not well, Mrs. Kretznow," Sister Margaret ventured to say in her best Yiddish. "Or he is busy working. Work is not so slack any more." Alone in the institution she shared Sarah's ignorance of the Kretznow scandal. Talk of it died before her youth and sweetness.

"He would have written," said Sarah sternly. "He is awearied of me. I have lain here a year. Job's curse is on me."

"Shall I to him"—Sister Margaret paused to excogitate the Yiddish word—"write?"

"No! He hears me knocking at his heart."

They had flashes of strange savage poetry, these crude yet complex souls. Sister Margaret, who was still liable to be startled, murmured feebly, "But—"

"Leave me in peace!" with a cry like that of a wounded animal.

The matron gently touched the novice's arm and drew her away. "I will write to him," she whispered.

Night fell, but sleep fell only for some. Sarah Kretznow tossed in a hell of loneliness. Ah, surely her husband had not forgotten her—surely she would not lie thus till death—that far-off death her strong religious instinct would forbid her hastening! She had gone into the Refuge to save him the constant sight of her helplessness and the cost of her keep. Was she now to be cut off forever from the sight of his strength?

The next day he came—by special invitation. His face was sallow, rimmed with swarthy hair; his under lip was sensuous. He hung his head, half veiling the shifty eyes.

Sister Margaret ran to tell his wife. Sarah's face sparkled.

"Put up the screen!" she murmured, and in its shelter drew her husband's head to her bosom and pressed her lips to his hair.

But he, surprised into indiscretion, murmured: "I thought thou wast dying."

A beautiful light came into the gray eyes.

"Thy heart told thee right, Herzel, my life. I was dying—for a sight of thee."

"But the matron wrote to me pressingly," he blurted out. He felt her breast heave convulsively under his face; with her hands she thrust him away.

"God's fool that I am—I should have known; to-day is not visiting day. They have compassion on me—they see my sorrows—it is public talk."

His pulse seemed to stop. "They have talked to thee of me," he faltered.

"I did not ask their pity. But they saw how I suffered—one cannot hide one's heart."

"They have no right to talk," he muttered in sulky trepidation.

"They have every right," she rejoined sharply. "If thou hadst come to see me even once—why hast thou not?"

"I—I—have been travelling in the country with cheap jewellery. The tailoring is so slack."

"Look me in the eyes! Law of Moses? No, it is a lie. God shall forgive thee. Why hast thou not come?"

"I have told thee."

"Tell that to the Sabbath Fire-Woman! Why hast thou not come? Is it so very much to spare me an hour or two a week? If I could go out like some of the patients, I would come to thee. But I have tired thee out utterly—"

"No, no, Sarah," he murmured uneasily.

"Then why—?"

He was covered with shame and confusion. His face was turned away. "I did not like to come," he said desperately.

"Why not?" Crimson patches came and went on her white cheeks; her heart beat madly.

"Surely thou canst understand!"

"Understand what? I speak of green and thou answerest of blue!"

"I answer as thou askest."

"Thou answerest not at all."

"No answer is also an answer," he snarled, driven to bay. "Thou understandest well enough. Thyself saidst it was public talk."

"Ah—h—h!" in a stifled shriek of despair. Her intuition divined everything. The shadowy, sinister suggestions she had so long beat back by force of will took form and substance. Her head fell back on the pillow, the eyes closed.

He stayed on, bending awkwardly over her.

"So sick! So sick! So sick!" moaned the wizened grandmother.

"Thou sayest they have compassion on thee in their talk," he murmured at last, half deprecatingly, half resentfully; "have they none on me?"

Her silence chilled him. "But thou hast compassion, Sarah," he urged. "Thou understandest."

Presently she reopened her eyes.

"Thou art not gone?" she murmured.

"No—thou seest I am not tired of thee, Sarah, my life! Only—"

"Wilt thou wash my skin, and not make me wet?" she interrupted bitterly. "Go home. Go home to her!"

"I will not go home."

"Then go under like Korah."

He shuffled out. That night her lonely hell was made lonelier by the opening of a peep-hole into Paradise—a paradise of Adam and Eve and forbidden fruit. For days she preserved a stony silence toward the sympathy of the inmates. Of what avail words against the flames of jealousy in which she writhed?

He lingered about the passage on the next visiting day, vaguely remorseful, but she would not see him. So he went away, vaguely indignant, and his new housemate comforted him, and he came no more.

When you lie on your back all day and all night you have time to think, especially if you do not sleep. A situation presents itself in many lights from dawn to dusk and from dusk to dawn. One such light flashed on the paradise, and showed it to her as but the portico of purgatory. Her husband would be damned in the next world, even as she was in this. His soul would be cut off from among its people.

On this thought she brooded till it loomed horribly in her darkness. And at last she dictated a letter to the matron, asking Herzel to come and see her.

He obeyed, and stood shame-faced at her side, fidgeting with his peaked cap. Her hard face softened momentarily at the sight of him, her bosom heaved, suppressed sobs swelled her throat.

"Thou hast sent for me?" he murmured.

"Yes—perhaps thou didst again imagine I was on my death-bed!" she replied, with bitter irony.

"It is not so, Sarah. I would have come of myself—only thou wouldst not see my face."

"I have seen it for twenty years—it is another's turn now."

He was silent.

"It is true all the same—I am on my death-bed."

He started. A pang shot through his breast. He darted an agitated glance at her face.

"Is it not so? In this bed I shall die. But God knows how many years I shall lie in it."

Her calm gave him an uncanny shudder.

"And till the Holy One, blessed be He, takes me, thou wilt live a daily sinner."

"I am not to blame. God has stricken me. I am a young man."

"Thou art to blame!" Her eyes flashed fire. "Blasphemer! Life is sweet to thee—yet perchance thou wilt die before me."

His face grew livid. "I am a young man," he repeated tremulously.

"Dost thou forget what Rabbi Eliezer said? 'Repent one day before thy death'—that is to-day, for who knows?"

"What wouldst thou have me do?"

"Give up—"

"No, no," he interrupted. "It is useless. I cannot. I am so lonely."

"Give up," she repeated inexorably, "thy wife."

"What sayest thou? My wife! But she is not my wife. Thou art my wife."

"Even so. Give me up. Give me Get (divorce)."

His breath failed, his heart thumped at the suggestion.

"Give thee Get!" he whispered.

"Yes. Why didst thou not send me a bill of divorcement when I left thy home for this?"

He averted his face. "I thought of it," he stammered. "And then—"

"And then?" He seemed to see a sardonic glitter in the gray eyes.

"I—I was afraid."

"Afraid!" She laughed in grim mirthlessness. "Afraid of a bed-ridden woman!"

"I was afraid it would make thee unhappy." The sardonic gleam melted into softness, then became more terrible than before.

"And so thou hast made me happy instead!"

"Stab me not more than I merit. I did not think people would be cruel enough to tell thee."

"Thine own lips told me."

"Nay—by my soul," he cried, startled.

"Thine eyes told me, then."

"I feared so," he said, turning them away. "When she came into my house, I—I dared not go to see thee—that was why I did not come, though I always meant to, Sarah, my life. I feared to look thee in the eyes. I foresaw they would read the secret in mine—so I was afraid."

"Afraid!" she repeated bitterly. "Afraid I would scratch them out! Nay, they are good eyes. Have they not seen my heart? For twenty years they have been my light.... Those eyes and mine have seen our children die."

Spasmodic sobs came thickly now. Swallowing them down, she said, "And she—did she not ask thee to give me Get?"

"Nay, she was willing to go without. She said thou wast as one dead—look not thus at me. It is the will of God. It was for thy sake, too, Sarah, that she did not become my wife by law. She, too, would have spared thee the knowledge of her."

"Yes; ye have both tender hearts! She is a mother in Israel, and thou art a spark of our father Abraham."

"Thou dost not believe what I say?"

"I can disbelieve it, and still remain a Jewess."

Then, satire boiling over into passion, she cried vehemently, "We are threshing empty ears. Thinkest thou I am not aware of the Judgments—I, the granddaughter of Reb Shloumi (the memory of the righteous for a blessing)? Thinkest thou I am ignorant thou couldst not obtain a Get against me—me who have borne thee children, who have wrought no evil? I speak not of the Beth-Din, for in this impious country they are loath to follow the Judgments, and from the English Beth-Din thou wouldst find it impossible to obtain the Get in any case, even though thou didst not marry me in this country, nor according to its laws. I speak of our own Rabbonim—thou knowest even the Maggid would not give thee Get merely because thy wife is bed-ridden. That—that is what thou wast afraid of."

"But if thou art willing—" he replied eagerly, ignoring her scornful scepticism.

His readiness to accept the sacrifice was salt upon her wounds.

"Thou deservest I should let thee burn in the lowest Gehenna," she cried.

"The Almighty is more merciful than thou," he answered. "It is He that hath ordained it is not good for man to live alone. And yet men shun me—people talk—and she—she may leave me to my loneliness again." His voice faltered with self-pity. "Here thou hast friends, nurses, visitors. I—I have nothing. True, thou didst bear me children, but they withered as by the evil eye. My only son is across the ocean; he hath no love for me or thee."

The recital of their common griefs softened her toward him.

"Go!" she whispered. "Go and send me the Get. Go to the Maggid, he knew my grandfather. He is the man to arrange it for thee with his friends. Tell him it is my wish."

"God shall reward thee. How can I thank thee for giving thy consent?"

"What else have I to give thee, my Herzel, I who eat the bread of strangers? Truly says the Proverb, 'When one begs of a beggar the Herr God laughs!'"

"I will send thee the Get as soon as possible."

"Thou art right, I am a thorn in thine eye. Pluck me out quickly."

"Thou wilt not refuse the Get, when it comes?" he replied apprehensively.

"Is it not a wife's duty to submit?" she asked with grim irony. "Nay, have no fear. Thou shalt have no difficulty in serving the Get upon me. I will not throw it in the messenger's face.... And thou wilt marry her?"

"Assuredly. People will no longer talk. And she must needs bide with me. It is my one desire."

"It is mine likewise. Thou must atone and save thy soul."

He lingered uncertainly.

"And thy dowry?" he said at last. "Thou wilt not make claim for compensation?"

"Be easy—I scarce know where my Cesubah (marriage certificate) is. What need have I of money? As thou sayest, I have all I want. I do not even desire to purchase a grave—lying already so long in a charity-grave. The bitterness is over."

He shivered. "Thou art very good to me," he said. "Good-bye."

He stooped down—she drew the bedclothes frenziedly over her face.

"Kiss me not!"

"Good-bye, then," he stammered. "God be good to thee!" He moved away.

"Herzel!" She had uncovered her face with a despairing cry. He slouched back toward her, perturbed, dreading she would retract.

"Do not send it—bring it thyself. Let me take it from thy hand."

A lump rose in his throat. "I will bring it," he said brokenly.

The long days of pain grew longer—the summer was coming, harbingered by sunny days that flooded the wards with golden mockery. The evening Herzel brought the Get, Sarah could have read every word on the parchment plainly, if her eyes had not been blinded by tears.

She put out her hand toward her husband, groping for the document he bore. He placed it in her burning palm. The fingers closed automatically upon it, then relaxed, and the paper fluttered to the floor. But Sarah was no longer a wife.

Herzel was glad to hide his burning face by stooping for the fallen bill of divorcement. He was long picking it up. When his eyes met hers again, she had propped herself up in her bed. Two big round tears trickled down her cheeks, but she received the parchment calmly and thrust it into her bosom.

"Let it lie there," she said stonily, "there where thy head hath lain. Blessed be the true Judge."

"Thou art not angry with me, Sarah?"

"Why should I be angry? She was right—I am but a dead woman. Only no one may say Kaddish for me, no one may pray for the repose of my soul. I am not angry, Herzel. A wife should light the Sabbath candles, and throw in the fire the morsel of dough. But thy home was desolate, there was none to do these things. Here I have all I need. Now thou wilt be happy, too."

"Thou hast been a good wife, Sarah," he murmured, touched.

"Recall not the past; we are strangers now," she said, with recurrent harshness.

"But I may come and see thee—sometimes." He had stirrings of remorse as the moment of final parting came.

"Wouldst thou reopen my wounds?"

"Farewell, then."

He put out his hand timidly; she seized it and held it passionately.

"Yes, yes, Herzel! Do not leave me! Come and see me here—as a friend, an acquaintance, a man I used to know. The others are thoughtless—they forget me—I shall lie here—perhaps the Angel of Death will forget me, too." Her grasp tightened till it hurt him acutely.

"Yes, I will come—I will come often," he said, with a sob of physical pain.

Her clasp loosened, she dropped his hand.

"But not till thou art married," she said.

"Be it so."

"Of course thou must have a 'still wedding.' The English synagogue will not marry thee."

"The Maggid will marry me."

"Thou wilt show me her Cesubah when thou comest next?"

"Yes—I will contrive to get it from her."

A week passed—he brought the marriage certificate.

Outwardly she was calm. She glanced through it. "God be thanked," she said, and handed it back. They chatted of indifferent things, of the doings of the neighbours. When he was going, she said, "Thou wilt come again?"

"Yes, I will come again."

"Thou art so good to spend thy time on me thus. But thy wife—will she not be jealous?"

He stared, bewildered by her strange, eerie moments.

"Jealous of thee?" he murmured.

She took it in its contemptuous sense and her white lips twitched. But she only said, "Is she aware thou hast come here?"

He shrugged his shoulders. "Do I know? I have not told her."

"Tell her."

"As thou wishest."

There was a pause. Presently the woman spoke.

"Wilt thou not bring her to see me? Then she will know that thou hast no love left for me—"

He flinched as at a stab. After a painful moment he said: "Art thou in earnest?"

"I am no marriage-jester. Bring her to me—will she not come to see an invalid? It is a mitzvah (good deed) to visit the sick. It will wipe out her trespass."

"She shall come."

She came. Sarah stared at her for an instant with poignant curiosity, then her eyelids drooped to shut out the dazzle of her youth and freshness. Herzel's wife moved awkwardly and sheepishly. But she was beautiful—a buxom, comely country girl from a Russian village, with a swelling bust and a cheek rosy with health and confusion.

Sarah's breast was racked by a thousand needles. But she found breath at last.

"God bless—thee, Mrs.—Kretznow," she said gaspingly.

She took the girl's hand.

"How good thou art to come and see a sick creature."

"My husband willed it," the new wife said in deprecation. She had a simple, stupid air that did not seem wholly due to the constraint of the strange situation.

"Thou wast right to obey. Be good to him, my child. For three years he waited on me, when I lay helpless. He has suffered much. Be good to him!"

With an impulsive movement she drew the girl's head down to her and kissed her on the lips. Then with an anguished cry of "Leave me for to-day," she jerked the blanket over her face and burst into tears. She heard the couple move hesitatingly away. The girl's beauty shone on her through the opaque coverings.

"O God!" she wailed. "God of Abraham, Isaac, and Jacob, let me die now. For the merits of the Patriarchs take me soon, take me soon."

Her vain passionate prayer, muffled by the bedclothes, was wholly drowned by ear-piercing shrieks from the ward above—screams of agony mingled with half-articulate accusations of attempted poisoning— the familiar paroxysm of the palsied woman who clung to life.

The thrill passed again through Sister Margaret. She uplifted her sweet humid eyes.

"Ah, Christ!" she whispered. "If I could die for her!"

XI

THE SABBATH-BREAKER

The moment came near for the Polish centenarian grandmother to die. From the doctor's statement it appeared she had only a bad quarter of an hour to live. Her attack had been sudden, and the grandchildren she loved to scold could not be present.

She had already battled through the great wave of pain, and was drifting beyond the boundaries of her earthly Refuge. The nurses, forgetting the trouble her querulousness and her overweening dietary scruples had cost them, hung over the bed on which the shrivelled entity lay. They did not know she was living again through the one great episode of her life.

Nearly forty years back, when (though already hard upon seventy and a widow) a Polish village was all her horizon, she received a letter. It arrived on the eve of Sabbath on a day of rainy summer. It was from her little boy—her only boy—who kept a country inn seven-and-thirty miles away, and had a family. She opened the letter with feverish anxiety. Her son—her Kaddish—was the apple of her eye. The old woman eagerly perused the Hebrew script, from right to left. Then weakness overcame her and she nearly fell.

Embedded casually enough in the four pages was a passage that stood out for her in letters of blood. "I am not feeling very well lately; the weather is so oppressive and the nights are misty. But it is nothing serious; my digestion is a little out of order, that's all." There were roubles for her in the letter, but she let them fall to the floor unheeded. Panic fear, travelling quicker than the tardy post of those days, had brought rumour of a sudden outbreak of cholera in her son's district. Already alarm for her boy had surged about her heart all day; the letter confirmed her worst apprehensions. Even if the first touch of the cholera-fiend was not actually on him when he wrote, still he was by his own confession in that condition in which the disease takes easiest grip. By this time he was on a bed of sickness—nay, perhaps on his death-bed, if not dead. Even in those days the little grandmother had lived beyond the common span; she had seen many people die, and knew that the Angel of Death does not always go about his work leisurely. In an epidemic his hands are too full to enable him to devote much attention to each case. Maternal instinct tugged at her heart-strings, drawing her toward her boy. The end of the letter seemed impregnated with special omen—"Come and see me soon, dear little mother. I shall be unable to get to see you for some time." Yes, she must go at once—who knew but that it would be the last time she would look upon his face?

But then came a terrible thought to give her pause. The Sabbath was just "in"—a moment ago. Driving, riding, or any manner of journeying was prohibited during the next twenty-four hours. Frantically she reviewed the situation. Religion permitted the violation of the Sabbath on one condition—if life was to be saved. By no stretch of logic could she delude herself into the belief her son's recovery hinged upon her presence—nay, analyzing the case with the cruel remorselessness of a scrupulous conscience, she saw his very illness was only a plausible hypothesis. No; to go to him now were beyond question to profane the Sabbath.

And yet beneath all the reasoning, her conviction that he was sick unto death, her resolve to set out at once, never wavered. After an agonizing struggle she compromised. She could not go by cart—that would be to make others work into the bargain, and would moreover involve a financial transaction. She must walk! Sinful as it was to transgress the limit of two thousand yards beyond her village—the distance fixed by Rabbinical law—there was no help for it. And of all the forms of travelling, walking was surely the least sinful. The Holy One, blessed be He, would know she did not mean to work; perhaps in His mercy He would make allowance for an old woman who had never profaned His rest-day before.

And so, that very evening, having made a hasty meal, and lodged the precious letter in her bosom, the little grandmother girded up her loins to walk the seven-and-thirty miles. No staff took she with her, for to carry such came under the Talmudical definition of work. Neither could she carry an umbrella, though it was a season of rain. Mile after mile she strode briskly on, toward that pallid face that lay so far beyond the horizon, and yet ever shone before her eyes like a guiding star. "I am coming, my lamb," she muttered. "The little mother is on the way."

It was a muggy night. The sky, flushed with a weird, hectic glamour, seemed to hang over the earth like a pall. The trees that lined the roadway were shrouded in a draggling vapour. At midnight the mist blotted out the stars. But the little grandmother knew the road ran straight. All night she walked through the forest, fearless as Una, meeting neither man nor beast, though the wolf and the bear haunted its recesses, and snakes lurked in the bushes. But only the innocent squirrels darted across her path. The morning found her spent, and almost lame. But she walked on. Almost half the journey was yet to do.

She had nothing to eat with her; food, too, was an illegal burden, nor could she buy any on the holy day. She said her Sabbath morning prayer walking, hoping God would forgive the disrespect. The recital gave her partial oblivion of her pains. As she passed through a village the dreadful rumour of cholera was confirmed; it gave wings to her feet for ten minutes, then bodily weakness was stronger than everything else, and she had to lean against the hedges on the outskirts of the village. It was nearly noon. A passing beggar gave her a piece of bread. Fortunately it was unbuttered, so she could eat it with only minor qualms lest it had touched any unclean thing. She resumed her journey, but the rest had only made her feet move more painfully and reluctantly. She would have liked to bathe them in a brook, but that, too, was forbidden. She took the letter from her bosom and reperused it, and whipped up her flagging strength with a cry of "Courage, my lamb! the little mother is on the way." Then the leaden clouds melted into sharp lines of rain, which beat into her face, refreshing her for the first few moments, but soon wetting her to the skin, making her sopped garments a heavier burden, and reducing the pathway to mud, that clogged still further her feeble footsteps. In the teeth of the wind and the driving shower she limped on. A fresh anxiety consumed her now—would she have strength to hold out? Every moment her pace lessened, she was moving like a snail. And the slower she went the more vivid grew her prescience of what awaited her at the journey's end. Would she even hear his dying word? Perhaps—terrible thought!—she would only be in time to look upon his dead face! Mayhap that was how God would punish her for her desecration of the holy day. "Take heart, my lamb!" she wailed. "Do not die yet. The little mother comes."

The rain stopped. The sun came out, hot and fierce, and dried her hands and face, then made them stream again with perspiration. Every inch won was torture now, but the brave feet toiled on. Bruised and swollen and crippled, they toiled on. There was a dying voice—very far off yet, alas!—that called to her, and as she dragged herself along, she replied: "I am coming, my lamb. Take heart! the little mother is on the way. Courage! I shall look upon thy face, I shall find thee alive."

Once a wagoner observed her plight and offered her a lift, but she shook her head steadfastly. The endless afternoon wore on—she crawled along the forest-way, stumbling every now and then from sheer faintness, and tearing her hands and face in the brambles of the roadside. At last the cruel sun waned, and reeking mists rose from the forest pools. And still the long miles stretched away, and still she plodded on, torpid from over-exhaustion, scarcely conscious, and taking each step only because she had taken the preceding. From time to time her lips mumbled: "Take heart, my lamb! I am coming." The Sabbath was "out" ere, broken and bleeding, and all but swooning, the little grandmother crawled up to her son's inn, on the border of the forest. Her heart was cold with fatal foreboding. There was none of the usual Saturday night litter of Polish peasantry about the door. The sound of many voices weirdly intoning a Hebrew hymn floated out into the night. A man in a caftan opened the door, and mechanically raised his forefinger to bid her enter without noise. The little grandmother saw into the room behind. Her daughter-in-law and her grandchildren were seated on the floor—the seat of mourners.

"Blessed be the true Judge!" she said, and rent the skirt of her dress. "When did he die?"

"Yesterday. We had to bury him hastily ere the Sabbath came in."

The little, grandmother lifted up her quavering voice, and joined the hymn, "I will sing a new song unto Thee, O God; upon a harp of ten strings will I sing praises unto Thee."

The nurses could not understand what sudden inflow of strength and impulse raised the mummified figure into a sitting posture. The little grandmother thrust a shrivelled claw into her peaked, shrunken bosom, and drew out a paper, crumpled and yellow as herself, covered with strange crabbed hieroglyphics, whose hue had long since faded. She held it close to her bleared eyes—a beautiful light came into them, and illumined the million-puckered face. The lips moved faintly; "I am coming, my lamb," she mumbled. "Courage! The little mother is on the way. I shall look on thy face. I shall find thee alive."

Israel Zangwill – A Short Biography

Israel Zangwill was born in London on 21st January 1864, to a family of Jewish immigrants from the Russian Empire. His father, Moses, was from modern-day Latvia, and his mother, Ellen Hannah Marks Zangwill, from modern-day Poland.

Zangwill was initially educated in Plymouth and Bristol. At age 9 he was enrolled into the Jews' Free School in Spitalfields in east London. The school was for the children of Jewish immigrants and added to its teaching, of both secular and religious matters, with supplies of clothing, food, and health care. Zangwill excelled here. He began to teach part-time at the school and eventually full time. Whilst teaching he also studied with the University of London and by 1884 had earned his BA with triple honours in philosophy, history, and the sciences.

He had already co-written a tale entitled 'The Premier and the Painter' when he resigned as a teacher owing to differences with the managers of the school. Zangwill now turned to journalism for his new career path, initiating Ariel, The London Puck, as well as working in various capacities for the London press.

His writing earned him the sobriquet "the Dickens of the Ghetto" primarily based on his much lauded novel 'Children of the Ghetto: A Study of a Peculiar People' in 1892 and its glimpse of the poverty-stricken life in London's Jewish quarter.

As a writer he was keen to reflect on his political and social outlooks. His simulation of Yiddish sentence structure in English aroused great interest. His mystery work, 'The Big Bow Mystery' (1892) was the first locked room mystery novel. Social satire flowed with 'The King of Schnorrers' (1894). A follow up to 'Children of the Ghetto' was 'Ghetto Tragedies' in 1894 and 'Dreamers of the Ghetto' in 1898 which included essays on famous Jews such as Baruch Spinoza, Heinrich Heine and Ferdinand Lassalle.

Zangwill was also involved with narrowly focused Jewish issues as an assimilationist, an early Zionist, and later a territorialist. In the early 1890s he had joined the Lovers of Zion movement in England. A few years later, in 1897, he took part in the "pilgrimage" of English Jews to Palestine. That same year he also joined Theodor Herzl (considered the father of modern political Zionism) in founding the World Zionist Organization and would take part in the first seven Zionist congresses. Zangwill was much admired as an orator and spoke movingly and eloquently on the issues he was passionate on.

In 1901 he had written that "Palestine is a country without a people; the Jews are a people without a country". On Herzl's visits to London, they worked closely together. In a debate at the Article Club in November 1901 however Zangwill was still mis-using the facts: "Palestine has but a small population of Arabs and fellahin and wandering, lawless, blackmailing Bedouin tribes." And made a direct plea to "restore the country without a people to the people without a country. For we have something to give as well as to get. We can sweep away the blackmailer—be he Pasha or Bedouin—we can make the wilderness blossom as the rose, and build up in the heart of the world a civilisation that may be a mediator and interpreter between the East and the West."

In 1902, Zangwill wrote that Palestine "remains at this moment an almost uninhabited, forsaken and ruined Turkish territory". But from this point on Zangwill began to see things differently which would, in 1905, result in his breakaway from Zionism.

Zangwill quit the established philosophy of Zionism when his plan for a homeland in Uganda was rejected and instead founded his own organisation; the Jewish Territorialist Organization. Its stated goal was to create a Jewish homeland in whatever territory in the world could be found for them. At that point in time suggestions were as varied as Canada, Australia, Mesopotamia, Argentina, Uganda and Cyrenaica.

Amongst the challenges in his life he found time to write poetry. He had translated a medieval Jewish poet in 1903 and his own volume 'Blind Children' in 1908 shows his promise in this new endeavour.

In 1908, Zangwill told a London court that he had been naive when he made his 1901 speech and had since recognised that the Arab population was twice that of the United States.

Zangwill was a supporter of both feminism and pacifism, but his greatest effect was as a writer who gained a wide audience with the idea of combining ethnicities into a single, American nation. The hero of 'The Melting Pot', proclaims: "America is God's Crucible, the great Melting-Pot where all the races of Europe are melting and reforming... Germans and Frenchmen, Irishmen and Englishmen, Jews and Russians – into the Crucible with you all! God is making the American."'

'The Melting Pot' made Zangwill's name as an admired playwright. The title itself was popularised as the phrase to use to describe American absorption of immigrants when it ran in the United States.

When the play opened in Washington D.C. on 5th October 1909, former President Theodore Roosevelt leaned over the edge of his box and shouted, "That's a great play, Mr. Zangwill, that's a great play." In a later letter in 1912 Roosevelt went further "That particular play I shall always count among the very strong and real influences upon my thought and my life."

'The Melting Pot' shone a spotlight on America's growth through the input of its new waves of immigrants. Zangwill was writing as "a Jew who no longer wanted to be a Jew. His real hope was for a world in which the entire lexicon of racial and religious difference is thrown away."

According to Ze'ev Jabotinsky, Zangwill told him in 1916 that, "If you wish to give a country to a people without a country, it is utter foolishness to allow it to be the country of two peoples. This can only cause trouble. The Jews will suffer and so will their neighbours. One of the two: a different place must be found either for the Jews or for their neighbours".

In 1917 he wrote "'Give the country without a people,' magnanimously pleaded Lord Shaftesbury, 'to the people without a country.' Alas, it was a misleading mistake. The country holds 600,000 Arabs."

With the end of World War I, and a more clearly defined idea of a Jewish settlement in Palestine, Zangwill once more returned to the Zionist effort and made efforts on behalf of the Balfour Declaration, proclaiming the right of a Jewish homeland in Palestine

In 1921 Zangwill wrote "If Lord Shaftesbury was literally inexact in describing Palestine as a country without a people, he was essentially correct, for there is no Arab people living in intimate fusion with the country, utilizing its resources and stamping it with a characteristic impress: there is at best an Arab encampment, the break-up of which would throw upon the Jews the actual manual labor of regeneration and prevent them from exploiting the fellahin, whose numbers and lower wages are moreover a considerable obstacle to the proposed immigration from Poland and other suffering centers".

Despite his advocacy on Jewish matters he would be disappointed to know that despite Israel now being established the quarrels of the Middle East continue to divide.

Israel Zangwill died on 1st August 1926 in Midhurst, West Sussex.

Israel Zangwill – A Concise Bibliography

The Bachelors' Club (1891)
The Old Maid's Club (1892)
Children of the Ghetto: A Study of a Peculiar People (1892)
Grandchildren of the Ghetto (1892)
The Big Bow Mystery (1892)
Merely Mary Ann (1893)
The King of Schnorrers (1894)
The Master (1895) (based on the life of George Wylie Hutchinson)
Without Prejudices (1896)
Dreamers of the Ghetto (1898)
Ghetto Tragedies, (1899)
"The Return to Palestine", New Liberal Review, (Dec. 1901)
Children of the Ghetto (1902)
"Providence, Palestine and the Rothschilds", The Speaker, vol. 4, no. 125 (22 February 1902)
Selected Religious Poems (1903) Translation of the Jewish Medieval Poet Solomon in Cabirol.
The Grey Wig: Stories and Novelettes (1903)
The Serio-Comic Governess (1904)
Merely Mary Ann (1904)
Ghetto Comedies, (1907)
Blind Children (1908) Poetry
The Melting Pot (1909)
Italian Fantasies (1910) Travel
Chosen Peoples, (1919)
The War For The World (1916)
The Principle of Nationalities (1917)
Chosen Peoples (1918)
Hands Off Russia: Speech by Mr. Israel Zangwill at the Albert Hall, February 8th, 1919. London: Workers' Socialist Federation, n.d. (1919)
The Voice of Jerusalem. (1921)

Filmography

Children of the Ghetto (1915, based on the play Children of the Ghetto)
The Melting Pot (1915, based on the play The Melting Pot)
Merely Mary Ann (1916, based on the play Merely Mary Ann)
The Moment Before (1916, based on the play The Moment of Death)
Mary Ann (1918, based on the play Merely Mary Ann)
Nurse Marjorie (1920, based on the play Nurse Marjorie)
Merely Mary Ann (1920, based on the play Merely Mary Ann)
The Bachelor's Club (1921, based on the novel We Moderns)
We Moderns (1925, based on the play We Moderns)
Too Much Money (1926, based on the play Too Much Money)
Perfect Crime (1928, based on the novel The Big Bow Mystery)
Merely Mary Ann (1931, based on the play Merely Mary Ann)
The Crime Doctor (1934, based on the novel The Big Bow Mystery)
The Verdict (1946, based on the novel The Big Bow Mystery)

www.ingramcontent.com/pod-product-compliance
Lightning Source LLC
Chambersburg PA
CBHW070502260626
47161CB00004B/1415